THE BRIDESMAID PACT

Julia Williams grew up in North London, one of eight children. She has herself been married to the same (very patient) man for twenty years and they have four children. Their wedding was a memorable affair, categorised mainly by all their friends drinking lots of fine wine.

A wedding wouldn't be a wedding without its stressful moments and there were plenty of those *en route*. Julia vividly remembers the arguments between her own bridesmaids about which colour to wear (they went for gold in the end). Two months before the wedding, the owner of the hotel where the reception was to be held ran away with the cook. Fortunately, the solution to have a marquee in the back garden proved to be a much better result. Thanks to the bride and groom leaving it rather late to order their wedding rings, they nearly had to get married without. Luckily, a local jeweller stepped in, and lent them a pair, memorably saying to Julia, 'you can't go up the aisle naked my dear.'

But none of that mattered in the end. The day itself was perfect and quite possibly the best party Julia has ever been to, although a discreet veil should probably be drawn over the Scottish country dancing.

As to married life, Julia would recommend it highly, but suggests that to keep sane both parties need tolerance, kindness and a huge dollop of humour.

To find out more about Julia go to her website at www.juliawilliamsauthor.com or visit her blog at www.maniacmum.blogspot.com.

By the same author:

Pastures New
Strictly Love
Last Christmas

JULIA WILLIAMS

The Bridesmaid Pact

matters, and Emma Lothian and Michael Ware for generously sharing their experience of IVF, and my brother Fr
John Moffatt SJ for insights into modern day Catholicism.
Any mistakes on these and other matters, are purely my
own.

AVON

AVON

A division of HarperCollins*Publishers*
77–85 Fulham Palace Road,
London W6 8JB

www.harpercollins.co.uk

A Paperback Original 2010
1

Copyright © Julia Williams 2010

Julia Williams asserts the moral right to
be identified as the author of this work

A catalogue record for this book is
available from the British Library

ISBN-13: 978-1-84756-087-2

Set in Minion by Palimpsest Book Production Limited,
Grangemouth, Stirlingshire

Printed and bound in Great Britain by
Clays Ltd, St Ives plc

Mixed Sources
Product group from well-managed
forests and other controlled sources
www.fsc.org Cert no. SW-COC-001806
© 1996 Forest Stewardship Council

FSC is a non-profit international organisation established to promote
the responsible management of the world's forests. Products carrying
the FSC label are independently certified to assure consumers that they
come from forests that are managed to meet the social, economic
and ecological needs of present and future generations.

Find out more about HarperCollins and the environment at
www.harpercollins.co.uk/green

For Karen, who was so bright and beautiful

As usual, I am going to be all diva-actress like and thank lots of people for the help they gave me with this book. And really this time there are a ridiculous number to thank, starting first with my wonderful agent, Dot Lumley and the incomparably supportive team at Avon who patiently put up with the many delays in the author's delivery schedule, and who were extremely understanding during a rather tricky time. A special thank you to my outgoing editor, Maxine Hitchcock, whose idea this was, and my new editor Kate Bradley, who's made the transition so smooth, and to the usual crew of Keshini Naidoo, Sammia Rafique and Caroline Ridding who are always so enthusiastic on my behalf.

And in their fiftieth anniversary year, I'd like to say a big hurrah for the Romantic Novelists' Association, without whom I wouldn't be doing what I am today.

I'd also like to thank: Sarah Iles, for help on pres

I wrote this book during a particularly rocky patch in my life, so huge thanks go to my family for their support. I couldn't have done it without you guys.

Most of all, this is a book about friendship. During my life I've been really lucky with my friends and I'd like to extend huge thanks to the many friends who have been there for me whether in times past, or present. To that end I'd like to give a big shout out to: Deirdre Ridley, Geraldine Ormonde, and my twin Virginia Moffatt – the original Fab Four, and to Sarah McWilliams, the Fab Fifth, for all those fun times at Pizza Hut; Liz Flach, whom I've known for far more years than I care to remember; and Pete Graham for being there over many many years. Also waving across the continent to Caroline Deighton, Jane Evans and Patrick O'Hare who shared some special years in Liverpool, and Ann Farrar who made me laugh all the way through my English studies.

The friends I have today have made the time spent at home rearing children, profitable and productive ones, so with that in mind, I'd like to say big thanks to: Kate Chinn, Tracey Clark, Jane Hunnable, Sarah Iles, Lisa Lacourarie, Jackie O' Neill for letting me mouth off about the trials of domesticity on a regular basis, and to my lovely friend Dawn Pearce for always being there, and never saying no when I ask.

Finally, this is also a book about weddings as suggested by my lovely outgoing editor Maxine Hitchcock, who during the course of this book, got married herself, so was fantastically helpful in reminding me what fun it all was. I'd like to say thanks also to Karen Howard and Helen Gard who shared my wedding year, and gave me the inspiration for Doris, and for Liz Lamb for suggesting

I put her in a book and Sue and Dave Howard for their support.

I've recently celebrated 20 years of marriage myself. And my husband was and remains my best friend, so thanks to you too, Dave. For all of it, even the times that *haven't* been fun . . .

Prologue

Sarah

It was Doris's idea of course. Back then, everything tended to emanate from Doris. Beautiful, dappy, gorgeous Doris, with her brown ringlets, blue eyes, infectious giggle, and cute American accent. She was the glue that bound us all together. Like Sid the sloth in *Ice Age*, Dorrie was the sticky stuff that kept us together. Without Doris we were nothing. And even then we knew it.

'It's on, it's on,' she said, proudly brandishing the control of her parents' state of the art Beta Max video machine. Though of course we didn't say state of the art then. Nor did we realize that Doris's parents, ahead of the trends as ever, had invested in a bit of technology that was going to be obsolete in a few short years. At eight years old, we were still marvelling at the idea of being able to watch our favourite TV moment of the year, again and again. And I was still pinching myself that I had been allowed to enter the inner sanctum of Dorrie's vast mansion. Ever since she'd arrived at our school from America, like some exotic creature from another planet, Dorrie had fascinated me. I had longed to be welcomed into her life and now here I was.

'Go straight to the kiss,' Caz demanded, her dark eyes

1

bright and concentrated, her hands thrust into her pointy chin, while her dark scrappy hair flopped over her face. She was always the most impatient one.

'No, we have to watch it *all*,' Beth was most emphatic on that point. Her serious, pale little face peeped up between two dark plaits. 'I didn't get to see it because my mum and dad are anti-royalsomething.'

'Royalist,' interjected Doris.

'They don't like the Queen,' said Beth. 'So I wasn't allowed to watch any of it.'

Silently we were all amazed at this. All term we'd talked about nothing but the wedding, about what she'd wear and who the bridesmaids would be. We'd even had a day off school to watch it – Doris's mum and dad had taken her up to London and they'd camped outside St Paul's Cathedral and seen her go into the church and *everything* – and poor Beth hadn't seen any of it.

'Lucky Mom and Dad videoed it then, isn't it?' said Doris. 'Now *sssshhh*.'

We all settled down on the beanbags and cushions, stifling giggles as we passed popcorn to one another in the room that Doris's American professor dad called the den. Doris's house was like nothing the rest of us had ever seen. We all lived in the suburban centre of Northfields, near our school, whereas Doris lived on the more countrified and posher side of town. Her parents had money but believed in state education, and as our school had the best reputation in the area, they'd sent her there.

You had to walk down a gravelly drive before you arrived at a massive house with ornate pillars, and a vast oak front door. The lounge was so big it could have fitted the whole of the downstairs of my house in, and the dining room had a table that seated twenty. And Doris's dad had his own games room in the basement as well as a study, from where he would absentmindedly emerge from time to time to ask us how we were doing. Upstairs were five or six bedrooms and en suite bathrooms for *every* bedroom. Imagine that. Even Doris had one.

For me who shared a tiny suburban three-bedroomed semi with my parents and two much older brothers, it seemed like a fairy palace. I still couldn't believe I was here. Doris was the most popular girl in the class. I had been thrilled when she chose me to be part of her gang. Being Doris, she'd generously allowed me to bring my best mate, Caz, along too and, together with Beth, the four of us were developing into firm friends.

It would have been easy to hate her, with her ringletted beauty, her film star mother, clever professor father, and her amazing house, but somehow, it was impossible to dislike Doris. She was kind and generous and funny, and hid her cleverness (inherited from her father) under a carefully cultivated dizzy blondeness – except of course, she wasn't blonde. I was the blonde one and frequently felt at a disadvantage to the other three who always seemed to be quicker and cleverer than I was.

The posh voice of the commentator was describing the guests as they arrived and pointing out Prince Charles waiting with Prince Andrew for Diana to arrive. We all oohed and aahed as the carriages pulled up bearing the Queen and Prince Philip.

'I *have* to have that dress when I'm a bridesmaid next year for my Auntie Sophie in Switzerland.' Doris paused the tape so we could ogle the bridesmaids, who to our eight-year-old minds just looked perfect in their ivory white dresses, with puffy sleeves, full-out skirts and pale gold sashes. The little ones had flowers in their hair, and I longed for a pair of pretty white shoes just like theirs. After some critical discussion, we all agreed that Doris was much prettier than India Hicks (our favourite brides-maid), and would suit the dress better. It never even occurred to me to think about any of *us* wearing the dress.

'Why is it always you?' Caz burst out furiously. Her untidy black hair tumbled over her dark eyes, and two bright points of red flamed her cheeks, her attitude spiky and pugnacious, as ever. 'Why can't the rest of us get to wear that dress? Just because you're rich and we're not!'

'That's not fair!' Doris leapt up and shouted. 'Don't I always let you have my stuff and invite you over?'

'So you can feel good,' spat back Caz, eyes blazing, ready as ever to take on the world. 'I know you only have me here because you feel sorry for me.'

'That's not true,' said Beth, timidly. Ever the peacemaker, she could never bear any of us fighting. 'Caz, I think you should say sorry.'

As Caz's best friend, I felt duty bound to take her part, though I didn't think she was being fair either. As the pret-tiest, richest one of us, and the only one who was going to *actually* be a bridesmaid, I felt that Doris was quite within her rights to lay first claim to India Hicks's dress. I might have felt jealous of someone else, but I couldn't feel jealous of Doris, who generously shared all that she had with us. I had only just become accepted into her circle and I was loath to do anything to get me ejected from it. But Caz and I had been friends from the first day of St Philomena's primary school, when something about her uncared-for

4

appearance tapped into my innate need to look after people. I had to stick up for her.

'Doris, you do usually take charge,' I said reluctantly. Like Beth, I always hated confrontation. And a part of me seethed that just as I'd got to being accepted by Doris, here was Caz trying to muck it up for me again. As she always did. I loved Caz to bits, but why did she have to be so angry all the time?

'Do I?' Doris looked stricken, her blue eyes filling with tears, and I felt even worse. 'Gee, I don't mean to. I'm really sorry, Caz, I didn't mean to upset you.'

Seeing her lower lip begin to quiver, and tears dangerously start to wobble down her cheeks, Caz softened uncharacteristically. Perhaps even hard as nails Caz couldn't resist Doris's charm.

'It's OK,' she said sulkily. 'I didn't mean to upset you either.'

Relieved that everything had gone back to normal, Doris ran to the huge kitchen and produced ice creams for us all as we settled down to watch Diana finally emerge from her carriage, arranging the voluminous train as it blew in the wind, to more oohs and aahs and squeals from the four of us. She stood up to go up the steps of St Paul's Cathedral and we squealed some more, as the dress was revealed in all its puffed-sleeve, huge-skirted glory.

'That dress,' I breathed, 'is the most beautiful thing I've ever seen.'

'She's just like a fairy princess,' said Beth.

'It's so romantic,' I said. 'I hope my wedding day is like that.'

'I'm going to have that dress when I get married,' announced Doris solemnly.

'I think she looks like a marshmallow,' said Caz, who didn't have a romantic bone in her body.

'How can you say that?' I cried. 'This is just like a fairytale wedding.'

'I don't believe in fairytales,' growled Caz. 'There aren't any happy endings in real life.'

We all threw our ice cream wrappers at her, and settled down in blissful silence to watch as Charles Windsor took Diana Spencer to be his lawful wedded wife.

'To have and to hold, for richer for poorer, in sickness and in health, till death do us part,' we chanted in unison.

'That's so cute,' said Doris. 'I want to marry a prince when I grow up.'

'Me too,' said Beth earnestly, fiddling with her plaits. 'I *believe* in happy endings. I'm going to grow up, get married and have *lots* of children, so there.'

Caz snorted, so we sat on her. By now we were getting bored of the video, so Doris fast forwarded to the kiss, which we watched over and over again, ecstatically imagining what it would feel like to have a boy kiss you on the lips like that. I thought it must feel very rubbery.

'We should make a promise,' Doris said suddenly. She was like that. Full of odd ideas that seemed to come from nowhere.

'What, like some kind of pact?' said Beth.

'What's a pact?' I said.

'Like a really, really important promise,' said Beth. 'That's what you mean, isn't it, Dorrie?'

'Sure do,' said Dorrie. 'We should promise to be friends forever and make a pact that we will be bridesmaids at each other's weddings.'

'I'm never going to get married,' declared Caz firmly.

'You can still be a bridesmaid though,' said Doris. She was impossible to resist, so even Caz was persuaded to stand in a circle with us. We all raised our hands together and held them up so they touched.

'We solemnly declare,' intoned Doris, 'that we four will be friends forever.'

We looked at each other and giggled before reciting after her, 'And we promise that when we get married we will only have our three friends as bridesmaids. And we promise that we will be bridesmaids for our friends.'

'From this day forth, forever and ever, shall this vow be binding,' said Doris. And then she made us cut a lock off our hair, and bind them together. She put the locks of hair, two dark, one light brown, and one fair together with a signed written copy of the words we'd solemnly declared in her special jewellery box.

'There,' she said, with satisfaction. 'Now we've taken an oath and we can never ever break it.'

Part One

To Have and to Hold

Caz

'Have you heard the news?' Dorrie came bursting into the champagne bar at Kettner's, where Sarah and I were tucking into a bottle of champagne to celebrate her engagement. I was glad to see Dorrie. The tension between Sarah and me these days was nigh on unbearable. I thought she was making a terrible mistake, but when I said as much she accused me of jealousy. I couldn't fault her on that, I was jealous that Steve had chosen her not me, but I still thought she'd regret marrying him.

As it was Christmas, the bar was heaving with partying office workers, and it took Dorrie a while to reach our table. Sarah was on an early shift and had got here first, while the photo shoot I'd been working on had descended into a pre Christmas bash, so I had escaped before I got too plastered and decided Charlie was the thing I needed in my life right now. I had enough complications as it was, I didn't need to bring him into the equation.

'Ooh, champagne, lovely,' said Dorrie, squeezing herself into a spot in the corner. 'Lucky I'm skinny isn't it?' She took off her faux fur black coat, to reveal a polka dot black and white vintage dress, which she'd matched with bright red boots.

11

With her Rachel from *Friends* haircut and her fabulous figure, it was no wonder that nearly every man in the room turned to look at her. But as usual Dorrie was oblivious to her effect on people. She really had no idea how much people adored her, which was part of her ongoing charm. She soon had Sarah and me in stitches, and any latent resentment festering between us was temporarily forgotten.

'No Beth yet?' Dorrie asked.

I shrugged my shoulders. 'I did ask her but she's been so low since Andy the bastard dumped her, I'm not sure she'll make it.'

'Oh, that's a shame,' said Dorrie. 'We should make it our next project to get Beth a man.'

'What do you mean, our next project?' said Sarah suspiciously – Dorrie had a habit of involving us in her schemes to make the whole world happy – flicking back her short fair hair. She always said she wore her hair short because it made work easier, but I rather suspected she'd gone for a Meg Ryan look because Steve fancied the pants off her in *When Harry Met Sally*. Which was just one of many reasons I thought Sarah was making a big mistake.

'Doh,' said Dorrie. 'The Bridesmaid Pact, remember? You're the first one to get married, so we all have to be your bridesmaids.'

'Don't I get any say in the matter?' laughed Sarah.

'Nope,' said Dorrie.

'You said you had some news?' I said.

'Oh, yes,' said Dorrie. 'Haven't you heard? It's all over the papers. Charles and Di are getting divorced. Can you believe it? It's so sad.'

'Er, yes,' I said. 'There's the small matter of his infidelity, her infidelity and all that three people in a marriage stuff.

I'm surprised after that *Panorama* interview the Queen didn't march Di off to the Tower. All that doe-eyed blinking. They're as bad as each other.'

'Yeah well, you'd know all about that, wouldn't you?' Sarah muttered bitchily.

'Meaning?' I said.

'Meaning I feel sorry for Di,' said Sarah. She smiled at me sweetly, but there were daggers in her eyes.

I was about to retort that some men just couldn't keep it in their trousers, when Beth pitched up. She looked wan and too thin, as she was wont to do. Her black hair was greasy, and she wore a frumpy grey coat that looked as if it belonged to her mother. My heart sank. She was in such a bad way. I longed to give her a makeover, but I'd tried that once before, and she'd pushed me away.

'Hi,' she said, shyly. Even after all this time, Beth was still timid with us. I longed for her to come out of her shell a bit more. It was unlike me to care about someone the way I did about Beth, but something about her vulnerability touched me. Maybe it was my way of feeling superior. People mostly felt sorry for me. It was nice to feel sorry for someone else for a change.

'Congrats, Sarah. When's the big day?' Beth had taken off her coat to reveal a dull blouse with big lapels and a ghastly bow, and a dark skirt, which hung limply from her skinny frame. Damn, it was difficult to sit there and not suggest ways of improving the way she looked, but I didn't want to hurt her feelings. A haircut would be a good start. She'd look good in a bob, I thought, though probably not the longish one I sported, which I'd modelled on Uma Thurman's in *Pulp Fiction*. She needed to cut those lanky locks into a shortish bob that framed her pretty oval face.

'Thanks, Beth,' said Sarah. 'We haven't fixed a date yet, but we're probably going for September '97.'

'Why not next year?' I said. 'What's the delay? Surely you want to get on with it, just in case he changes his mind.'

'Caz!' Beth looked at me shocked. 'That was a bit mean.'

'Sorry,' I mumbled, 'bit uncalled for.'

Sarah didn't say anything, and glossed over my bitchy comment with, 'I just want everything to be perfect.'

'Did you see the news?' said Beth.

'About Charles and Di?' said Dorrie. 'I know. Isn't it awful?'

'Oh come on,' I laughed. 'Dorrie, how can you take it so seriously? Two people we don't know and are never likely to meet are getting divorced. People do it all the time.'

'I know,' said Dorrie, 'but it was such a fairytale. And now it's gone wrong.'

'It is really sad,' said Beth.

'Fairytales, schmairytales,' I snorted. 'There's no such thing as a happy ending.'

'Blimey, that's cynical,' said Sarah. 'Even for you.'

'Yeah, well,' I said, 'I haven't had the luck some of you've had.'

I was overtaken with a sudden feeling of bitterness, and I got up to go to the loo, just to get away for five minutes. In the safety of the toilets, I stared long and hard at myself in the mirror, before leaning back against the cold tiles. I thought about Sarah and Steve and the things I'd promised never to think about again. Why did I always make such a mess of things? And now I was ruining my best friend's special night.

'Pull yourself together, girl,' I admonished myself in the mirror, reapplying my bright red lipstick as a means of boosting my confidence. Face fixed, I went back to meet the world head on.

When I got back, a slightly geekish-looking bloke was sitting in my place. He was tall and gangly and wore dark specs, and was mooning over Dorrie, who seemed to be mooning back.

'Aren't you going to introduce me to your friend?' I said, squeezing back into the tiny space the guy had left.

'Oh yes, sorry. Caz, meet Darren. He's a microbiologist and works in the next lab to mine.'

Dorrie might look like a film star, but she's actually super bright and has a fantastically clever job in some kind of medical research that I wouldn't pretend to understand.

'Pleased to meet you,' said Darren.

I went to shake his hand, and he pulled it away.

'Sorry, too many germs,' he said. 'Do you know the average person never washes their hands after using the toilet?'

'Well I do,' I snapped. 'Why don't you carry antibacterial spray around with you and have done with it?'

'I do,' said Darren. 'You never know what anyone else has been touching.'

I burst out laughing. 'Dorrie, your friend is priceless. I shall call him Yakult Man.'

Darren blushed.

'Don't mind Caz,' said Dorrie, 'she's not like other folk.' She touched his arm lightly, and he didn't pull away.

They sat staring at each other for a bit till Sarah, Beth and I felt quite awkward.

Eventually, Darren got up.

'Best be off,' he mumbled. 'Places to go and all that. Have a great Christmas. Nice meeting you all.'

He walked away, back to his mates who were at the bar, looking the worse for wear.

'Is he for real?' I marvelled. 'You've kept him quiet.'

'There's nothing to keep quiet about,' protested Doris. 'He's a work colleague is all.'

'Oh, is he?' I nudged Doris. Yakult Man hadn't made it to the bar. He had turned round and was striding purposefully back.

'You see, the thing is . . . well . . .' he said.

'Well?' said Dorrie.

'Well, I was wondering, if you're not too busy . . . I'm sure a gorgeous girl like you has got plenty of dates, but if you hadn't . . .'

'I haven't,' said Doris with a grin.

'Well. If you haven't . . . Did you say you hadn't?'

'Sure did.'

'Oh. That's OK then. It's all settled. Great.'

He smiled a dopey smile and walked away again.

'Er, what's settled?' she called after him. He stopped and turned around, grinning at her.

'You, me. A date. Next week. I'll ring you.' He continued walking away, backwards this time, until he bumped into a couple of drunks who spilled beer all over him. Our last sight was of him rushing to the toilet, no doubt to get rid of all the millions of germs that had just been dumped unceremoniously on top of him.

'Dorrie Bradley, how do you do it?' said Sarah, clapping her hands over her mouth and giggling her head off. 'That's the nuttiest proposition I've ever heard.'

'Me too,' I said.

'I wish someone would do that to me,' sighed Beth.

'Your turn will come,' said Sarah. 'Look at me.'

Yes, look at you, I thought silently, but kept my mouth shut for once. This was Sarah's night.

16

'To Sarah and Steve,' said Dorrie, raising a glass. 'Long life and happiness.'

'Sarah and Steve,' we all echoed.

'And here's to the Bridesmaid Pact,' continued Dorrie. 'I can't wait to fulfil it.'

'One four all and all four one,' we chorused the mantra of our childhood, before downing our drinks in one. I put my glass down and sat back and looked at Sarah. For someone who was celebrating the happiest event of her life, she looked remarkably pensive. I hoped I hadn't done that to her.

'I hope you and Steve are really happy,' I said with a smile I didn't feel.

'Do you? Really?' Sarah said, searchingly.

'Yes, I do,' I said. 'Sorry I've been a bit of a cow about it. Just jealous that your happy-ever-after's come along I guess. I hope you'll be very, very happy.'

I took a sip of my champagne, and looked away. At the time, I really thought I meant it.

Chapter One

Caz

Now

I turned the invitation over and over in my hands, despite the feeling of nausea rising up from the pit of my stomach and the sheer panic that seeing that handwriting for the first time in what – over four years? – had engendered in me. You had to hand it to Dorrie, she certainly knew how to break the ice. Only she could have sent me an invitation to her hen weekend on Mickey Mouse notepaper.

Dorrie and Daz are finally tying the knot, it read and I snorted with laughter. Trust Doris to make her forthcoming nuptials sound like some kids' TV programme. I was glad she was finally getting hitched to Yakult Man. About time too. They were made for each other. I had been surprised when Mum had sneered disapprovingly that my Goody Two-Shoes friend had had a baby out of wedlock, because it seemed so unlikely. Dorrie was always capable of surprises though, so maybe she'd relaxed about doing things the right way round since we last spoke. I had no clue as to what was going on in her private life, apart from the news I gleaned from Mum. I was no longer part of the inner circle. No one confided in me any more. My fault of course.

I looked at the invitation again. *You are invited*, it said, *to Dorrie's extra special hen weekend at Euro Disney. Fri 27-Sun 29 March. Fab Four members only. One four all and all four one.* Trust Doris to remember that stupid tag line we'd had as kids. At the bottom, Doris had scrawled in her unforgettably untidy handwriting (amazing how someone as beautifully presented as Doris could have such terrible writing, but then, that was Doris all over, a mass of impossible contradictions), *Please come. It won't be the same without you.*

Doris. How could her parents have been so unkind as to give her that name? She always claimed it was because her mum was a fan of Doris Day, but it seemed like for once in her impeccably toned and manicured life, Doris's mum had made a major faux pas. Not that Doris seemed to mind. She'd inherited the happy-go-lucky nature of her screen namesake, and took *que sera, sera* as her motto. And because she was just so bloody wonderful and fabulous, no one ever seemed to even tease her about her name. Now if it had been me . . .

I turned the invitation over in my hands. Should I go? It seemed to me that Doris was offering me another chance. Typical of her generosity that. And I didn't deserve it. I felt my stomach twist with guilt and shame as I remembered how I'd treated her last time we'd met.

'Hey Caz.' Dorrie had turned up on my doorstep unexpectedly one day five years previously, just before Beth's wedding.

'Hi,' I said. I was conscious that I looked unkempt, my normally short, slicked-back black hair – styled on Trinity from *The Matrix* – a tangled mess, whereas Dorrie, as ever, was done up to the nines, immaculate in a flowery vintage dress, black suede boots and a fabulous leather jacket.

'Are you OK? You look a bit rough.' Instantly Dorrie thought about me. I should have been more gracious, but I'd had a rough night in A & E with Mum. None of the girls ever knew about the humiliation of those trips to casualty, and I was too ashamed to tell them.

'I'm fine,' I said sharply, and saw Dorrie flinch.

'Can I come in?'

'I suppose,' I said, but I didn't really want her there, I wanted to curl up and hide from the world.

'I just wanted to see if there's a way we can sort all this out,' Dorrie said as she followed me into the lounge. I knew I should be offering her a drink, but I'd never felt less hospitable.

'All what out?' It came out belligerently. I knew what was coming and moreover I knew Dorrie was right. I had caused a rift in the Fab Four and it was up to me to put it right.

'Oh Caz, this business with you and Beth and her wedding,' said Dorrie. 'Can't you make up with her? She really does want you to be her bridesmaid.'

'So why isn't *she* here asking me?' I demanded.

'She doesn't know I'm here,' admitted Dorrie. 'Look, I'm sure I don't know who's right and who's wrong here—'

'Too right you don't,' I said. 'Just leave it, Dorrie, you don't have a clue what you're talking about.'

'Please don't be like that,' Dorrie said. 'I know I can't properly understand—'

'You have no idea,' I said. 'It's all right for you, with your perfect life and perfect family.'

'If you must know, that's not true,' said Dorrie. 'I've got problems you know nothing about.'

21

'What, Little Miss Perfect has a problem? What could possibly go wrong for you?' I knew I was being unfair, and my guilt and anger were misdirected, but as usual my mouth engaged before my brain had – the words were out before I could stop them.

Dorrie looked as if I had smacked her. 'Sarah was right,' she said. 'She told me you wouldn't listen.'

'So you've cooked this up with Sarah?' I said. 'I might have known. I know you mean well, Dorrie, but I think you'd better go.'

'I wouldn't stay another minute,' said Dorrie. She picked up her huge Gucci handbag, and got up and left the room. When she got to the door, she said sadly, 'You're not the only one with troubles you know.'

I didn't stop to ask her what she meant and let her go. It was only much later that I found out how ill her dad was. I'd always loved Dorrie's dad, who'd been so kind to me growing up. I tried to make amends, but Dorrie never returned my calls. I've felt guilty ever since. But now it seemed like Dorrie had forgiven me.

But what of the others? Could Beth and Sarah ever forgive me for what I'd done to them? We grew up in a culture that taught us that redemption is always possible. But I liked to think I lived in the real world and was realistic enough to know that it didn't happen as often as our teachers told us. Besides. You need to earn redemption. To gain forgiveness, you need to be truly, truly sorry. And even now there's a self-destructive bit of me which isn't sure that I am . . .

The plane touched down at Charles de Gaulle airport and I took a deep breath. Well, here I was. Finally. It had taken all my courage to come – I'd been tempted by a job in

Greece where a famous model was attempting a comeback shoot for M&S. It would have been a great job. Glamorous. In the sun all day, and time in the evenings for some unwinding and Greek dancing in the local tavernas. But Charlie persuaded me to go to France. Charlie was my favourite photographer on the circuit. Down-to-earth and easy-going, he had the most amazing ability to tease the best out of the subjects he shot. Working with Charlie was always a breeze. And he was fun to socialize with too. Not since that mad moment in Las Vegas that we'd ever been anything other than friends, mind. He was firmly hitched to his live-in girlfriend and, attractive as I found him, I wasn't about to go upsetting any apple carts. I'd learnt my lesson too well last time.

I emerged blinking from the airport into the pale March Paris sunshine. I always loved coming to Paris, but it was the café culture, museums and walks along the Seine which were the usual attraction for me. Without Dorrie's invite, I doubt I'd ever have visited Disneyland Paris, but here I was on a train out of Gare du Nord, bound for Mickey Mouseville. Doris was the only person who could have ever persuaded me to come. And I still wasn't sure I was doing the right thing.

The shuttle service to Marne la Vallée proved surprisingly quick, and I had barely time to get my head together and think what on earth I was going to say to everyone when suddenly there I was being deposited in front of Woody's Cowboy Ranch. *Toy Story* being Dorrie's favourite Disney film, she'd insisted we stay here. Despite my nerves I couldn't help but smile as Woody greeted me at the door. I could just imagine how delighted Dorrie must have been when she arrived.

My smile was only temporary though. My heart plunged to my boots as I made my way to the reception desk. Suddenly I was eight years old again, being invited for the first time to Dorrie's mansion. It had felt like such a privilege, and yet in the self-destructive way I have, I'd pretty much blown the chance of making the most of the opportunities being friends with Dorrie and the others had afforded me. I didn't even know if they'd want to see me again, let alone forgive me. Knowing Dorrie, I bet she hadn't told them I was coming.

I checked in at the desk, my nerves making a mash of my schoolgirl French. The unsmiling receptionist responded in perfect English with a look of such sneery disdain and I wanted the ground to swallow me up whole. Giving up on any attempt to speak her language, I said, 'I'm meeting friends; a Doris Bradley?'

'Ah oui, Mademoiselle Bradley is next door to you. I will let her know you have arrived.'

I took my bags and made my way to the third floor, shaking like a leaf. Suppose I ended up ruining Dorrie's big weekend? This had been a dreadful mistake. I was wrong to come.

I found my room, next to Dorrie's. I swallowed hard. Should I dump my bags, freshen up and then go and say hi? Or should I bite the bullet and go straight for it?

The door to room 327 flung wide open, and there in the flesh for the first time in five years stood Dorrie. Larger than life, as ever. Welcoming me in a massive hug. I felt my worries disappear instantly. Dorrie had a way of doing that. It was her special talent.

'Caz! You came! I'm so pleased. Come right in.' I'd forgotten how overpowering she could be. She propelled me into the middle of a massive room. I had a moment to take in the double bed, the cowboy-hat-shaped lampshades, the bridles and saddles decorating the walls, and the huge horseshoe over the bed, before I realized she wasn't alone. Lounging on the bed, sipping champagne, were two faces I hadn't seen in a very, very long time. They both looked up at me and registered their shock.

'You never said *she* was coming.' Sarah shot me a look of such venom, I was quite taken aback. God, did she really hate me that much still?

'It wouldn't have been the same without her,' said Dorrie firmly.

'Lock up your husbands,' said Sarah. 'Sorry Doz, I know you mean well, but I'm not spending any more time with her than I have to.' She got up and stormed out of the room, pushing past me with evident hatred.

I knew I shouldn't have come.

Chapter Two

Beth

I was so shocked when Caz walked through the door. Doris had been yacking on all morning about having a wonderful surprise for Sarah and me, but neither of us had imagined it would be Caz. I suppose we should have known. It was Dorrie who'd instigated the Bridesmaid Pact way back when, so I suppose it would be just like her to assume we'd all come together for her wedding, even though none of us had managed to do it for each other's. Of course, Caz had made a monumental cock-up with her wedding. By her own admission, copious amounts of vodka, and the sheer dizzying excitement of being in Vegas had led her to get carried away. By the time we found out she was married, it was already over, so there was no chance we could get to be bridesmaids for her. Dorrie was the closest I've seen to furious when she found out.

'But what about the Bridesmaid Pact?' she'd wailed.

'What about it?' Caz had laughed. 'C'me on, you didn't seriously expect us to fulfil that daft promise did you?'

But, of course, Dorrie did. When it was Sarah's turn, she talked about nothing else. We were all lined up to be bridesmaids. It had all been sorted for months. But then, Caz did whatever she did – to this day Sarah's none too sure, but Steve swore whatever happened had been at Caz's instigation. And that was that. Caz dropped out of being a bridesmaid but then turned up in the evening anyway, nearly ruining Sarah's day, and Sarah's never, ever forgiven her.

My wedding was next, and I was all for having the Fab Four together on my special day. I didn't need Dorrie to persuade me, and I'd hoped that Sarah and Caz could make up enough for that to happen. Sarah was prepared to put aside their differences for my sake, but then Caz had to go and open her big mouth at my hen night, we argued and I said I didn't want her to be my bridesmaid any more. She didn't even come to the wedding, and thanks to Sarah suffering from terrible morning sickness, half the time it felt as though Dorrie was my only bridesmaid. It wasn't what either of us had planned. Thanks to Caz's erratic behaviour at my hen night, I was terrified about my secret coming out on my wedding day. I couldn't bear it if Matthew had found out. Now I wonder if I was right. I wish sometimes I had told him. Particularly now. Secrets are corrosive, they never do you any good.

I'd had enough of Caz by then. So selfish. So poisonous. So untrustworthy. Wherever she goes she leaves a trail of carnage behind her. One day it will come and bite her on the bum and she'll be sorry.

I thought after that we'd never see her again. The Fab Four shrank down to the Terrific Trio. It was good, but not the way things had been. And though I'd never admit it to the others, there were times when I missed Caz. She was so wild and daring and different – all the things I'd longed to be. And despite her later betrayal, she had been there for me when I needed her. Besides Caz added sparkle to my life, a sparkle I thought had gone forever. Until now. Typical that Dorrie would insist on her coming. There was a time

28

when Dorrie hadn't been able to forgive Caz, but it simply wasn't in her nature to bear grudges.

Caz stood looking awkward in the middle of the room.

'I knew this was a bad idea,' she said, barely looking at me. 'I shouldn't have come. I'm sorry, I'm going to ruin your weekend.'

'*You* are going nowhere,' said Doris firmly. 'I invited you because I wanted you here. I know we've all had our differences' – that's putting it mildly, but Doris is the queen of positive spin – 'a lot of water's gone under the bridge. But this is *my* hen weekend and I want you here. Life's too short to fall out with people. I think it's time we all moved on. So there. Beth, you don't mind do you?'

'I—' What could I say? Doris was right. She usually was. Perhaps it was time to forgive and forget. Caz had undoubtedly hurt me, what she'd done to me was inconsiderate and thoughtless, I'd been holding on to my anger about it for a long time. But like my secret, that anger was corrosive and doing me no good. Seeing Caz in the flesh made me realize how much I missed her.

'Beth, I'm really sorry,' said Caz. 'I know it was a long time ago, but those things I said at your hen night . . . I'd had too much to drink and behaved really, really badly. I'm so ashamed of myself. I didn't mean to cause you, of all people, so much grief. I've never had a chance to tell you before how sorry I was.'

Because I'd never let her, I realized with a jolt.

'I can't say I wasn't upset,' I said, slowly, 'because I was. But I think Dorrie's right. A lot of water has gone under the bridge. I can't promise to forget, but I will try and forgive.'

'I know I don't deserve that,' said Caz, and I could see tears sparkling in her eyes. With that I melted completely.

29

I could barely remember seeing Caz cry. I realized what a big thing it was for her to have walked into the room in the first place, let alone apologize.

'It's history,' I said, 'forget about it.'

We hugged awkwardly and Doris poured her a glass of champagne. Caz sat down on the edge of the bed and we embarked on a serious catch-up.

'How's your family?' Caz asked.

'Oh fine,' I said. 'Parents are older, but still going strong. They moved, you know, out of London, to be by the sea. But then they decided it was too dull for them there and moved back. So now Mum organizes the new parish priest, Father Miserecordie, and Dad sends her mad by building things in the garage, and they're happy as Larry.' I stopped, wondering if I should ask about Caz's mum who had never been happy in her life, but Caz did it for me.

'Mum is sadly still with us,' she said. 'I barely see her. Thank goodness.'

'You can't mean that,' I protested. 'Surely she's not that bad.'

'You don't know the half of it,' said Caz in a tone that brooked no further questions. She looked slightly hesitant and said to Doris, 'I was really sorry to hear about your dad. What happened?'

'You don't know?' Dorrie's face creased in pain. I couldn't begin to imagine what she'd been through. She always kept her cards closely to her chest, but from the little I'd gleaned it had been tough.

'No,' said Caz. 'I mean, I heard he died and I was really sorry, but Mum didn't know any of the details.'

'He had MS,' said Doris. 'It was a progressive type and acted really fast. It was really terrible. He was in a wheelchair being fed by a tube at the end.'

30

Caz looked horrified. I think of all of us she'd loved Dorrie's dad the most. Perhaps not having one of her own, she was more appreciative of him than Sarah and I were.

'I'm so sorry,' said Caz. 'I should have been there for you.'

'You were probably too busy on a drinking spree,' said Doris in an uncharacteristically spiteful manner.

'Ouch,' said Caz, flinching. 'I probably deserved that.'

There was an uncomfortable pause, then Doris said, 'No, no you didn't. I'm the one who should be sorry. That was uncalled for. What happened to Dad was so bloody rotten and unfair, it makes me angry is all.'

'I'm not surprised,' said Caz. 'Your dad was wonderful. What a terrible thing to happen to him.'

Another pause, when we were uncomfortably aware that Doris, cheerful, happy-go-lucky Doris, was blinking away tears.

'This will never bloody do,' she said, pulling herself together. 'This is a hen weekend, not a misery fest. We're here to party. Time to go and do some screaming.'

In our teens, screaming as a result of Doris forcing us onto some god-awful fairground ride was a common occurrence. I'd hated it then and hated it now.

'Do we have to?' I groaned.

'Yup,' said Dorrie. 'That's the deal this weekend. You all have to come on at least one ride where you get to scream.'

'What about Sarah?' said Caz. 'She clearly doesn't want me here. I don't want to ruin things.'

'Leave Sarah to me,' said Doris firmly. 'No one, but no one, is going to spoil my weekend.'

'OK, here's the thing,' said Dorrie as we queued up to go into Euro Disney. 'This is *my* weekend and I want things my way. So Sarah, Caz, I know you have your differences, and I know this isn't easy for you. But, it's really important to me that you're both here, particularly now,' she paused, then added, 'with the wedding and everything. So can we call a truce for the next forty-eight hours? You can go back to hating each other afterwards.'

Sarah looked mutinous but didn't say anything. Like the rest of us, she found it impossible to resist Dorrie, but her resentment of Caz was so deep rooted, she was obviously prepared to make an exception.

'Look, Dorrie,' said Caz looking uncomfortable, 'it clearly isn't OK for Sarah for me to be here. I should go back to the hotel—'

'When did you turn all mealy mouthed, Caz?' snapped Sarah. 'I think I preferred you bitchy.'

'I can do bitchy if you want me to,' Caz snapped right back. 'I am trying, you know.'

Dorrie tried again. 'Come on girls, we're in Euro Disney. Play nice. For me?'

Sarah still looked sulky, but said, 'Anything for you, Dorrie, you know that.'

'Me too,' said Caz, looking relieved.

'Great,' said Dorrie, brightening up. 'Now let's go party.'

As we came through the entrance, we were greeted by a band playing incessantly cheerful music, and the sight of Mickey and Goofy glad-handing people.

'Perfect,' said Dorrie, clapping her hands. 'This is just perfect.'

It was impossible not to get swept up in her enthusiasm. Soon we found ourselves in Frontierland, trying to work out which was the least scary ride. Sarah and I hated rides, while Caz and Dorrie loved them.

'Well that one doesn't look too bad,' Caz pointed at Big Thunder Mountain which seemed to consist of carriages whizzing in and out of tunnels and didn't appear that dangerous.

Half an hour later we were all screaming. Big Thunder Mountain was apparently 'fairly thrilling' according to the scare guide on the map we'd been given as we entered the park. I must be getting old or something, but I started yelling for dear life, the minute the rollercoaster cranked us up to the top and we could see darkness beckoning us below. Within seconds we were plunging down and sideways through endless dark tunnels and Sarah and I were screeching our heads off. How could anyone think this was fun? Behind us I could hear Caz turning the air blue, but Doris was just laughing aloud. I don't know how she does that. She never appears to be fazed by anything.

'Don't – make – me – go – on – anything – else,' Sarah panted out between breaths as we got off. 'That was truly horrible.'

'What, not even the teacups?' Doris was laughing at all of us. Even Caz looked white. But she took pity on us long enough to let us go and buy ourselves candyfloss, and permitted us to wander about weighing up the other rides before we went on them.

'I think we should go on Space Mountain next,' said Doris as we found our way into the space adventure area.

'No, no and no,' I said, staring up in horror as we watched a rocket being cranked up the side of a huge tower.

'I think I might be sick if I went on that,' said Sarah faintly.

'I'm game if you are,' Caz said, grinning at Dorrie, never one to miss out on a dare. She and Sarah had barely spoken to each other all afternoon, leaving Dorrie and me to gamely plug in the gaps, but at least they weren't out and out fighting.

'Oh, I'm game,' said Dorrie. 'You know me. Are you sure you two don't want to go?'

'Absolutely,' we said in unison.

We waved them off to the massive queue and took ourselves off to a Buzz Lightyear ride which consisted of zapping lots of aliens, at which I was rubbish but Sarah proved rather good.

'How come you got so many?' I said in surprise. 'I didn't have you taped as a computer games nerd.'

'It's amazing what you pick up from five-year-olds,' said Sarah. She has two boys the oldest of whom is obsessed with PlayStation. 'It also helps that I was imagining all the aliens with Caz's face on them.'

'Sarah,' I protested weakly. 'Is that fair?'

'The nerve of her!' Sarah suddenly said. 'I can understand why Dorrie asked her. We all know how kind and – well, some might say stupidly forgiving – she is, but Caz didn't have to say yes did she? She must have known it would be awkward.'

'More for her than us, maybe,' I said.

'Oh come on, Beth, you know what she did to me,' said Sarah. 'You might be prepared to forgive and forget, but I don't find it that easy.'

'I know, I know,' I said. 'And I can't say I was all that keen to see her. But can't you make an effort? At least for Doris's sake. It obviously means a lot to her. Can't you at least try?'

'I'll think about it,' said Sarah, in a noncommittal manner, but I noticed when Doris and Caz came back, both looking slightly pale it has to be said, that she made an effort to at least speak to Caz and even shared one or two jokes with her. I grinned encouragingly at Dorrie. Who knows, maybe her madcap reunion scheme might actually work. Stranger things have been known to happen.

34

Chapter Three

Sarah

Had I known what Doris's 'treat' for us was going to be, I'm not sure I'd have gone on her hen weekend. Bless Doris, with her understanding boyfriend who'd do anything for her and dippy but wonderful mum who babysits at the drop of a hat, she can never quite get that life for other people is slightly more complicated. All she has to do is flutter her eyelashes at Daz and he's putty in her hands, so arranging a weekend away without the baby isn't the major undertaking it is for me. Besides, she doesn't have school runs to factor in. Having persuaded Steve that he owed me big time was an undertaking in itself. I didn't directly want to broach the subject of why he owes me, because I couldn't face the lies and self-justifications. Better let him fret a bit about what I knew or didn't know rather than having a full-blown and ultimately meaningless confrontation about it. We'd been there too many times and I just didn't have the energy to do it again.

So Steve agreed to 'babysit' his own children for the weekend. For all his other faults, Stephen is a good dad, when he can be persuaded to take time away from his precious office and pay any attention to the kids. I can't take that away from him, and he hadn't griped as much as I thought he would about me having a girlie weekend with my best friends. Or rather, my best friends barring one.

I knew I hadn't behaved well when Dorrie opened the door and produced Caz. Beth was right. What happened was a long time ago, and maybe I should forgive and forget. But just seeing her again had churned up all my jealous hateful feelings and the white-hot anger that I had carried with me for years. Caz was supposed to be my best friend and she had betrayed me in the worst way imaginable. And although with hindsight and a much better knowledge of my husband's behaviour, I could see her side of the story, it still didn't take anything away from what she'd done. Whatever way you cut it, Caz had broken my trust and I wasn't sure if I could ever forgive her for that. Just seeing her again had been like reopening an old wound. A knife twisted in my stomach as I wondered, yet again, whether Steve had found her more sexy than me, whether he'd ever thought about whether he made the right choice. I know I did.

But this wasn't my weekend to spoil, and I love Dorrie too much to want to ruin things for her. So when Beth and I met them, fresh from their trip up Space Mountain, I took a deep breath and said as casually as I could, 'So, how's it going then?'

Caz looked at me a little cautiously. I couldn't blame her, seeing as I had snapped her head off earlier.

'Er, OK,' she said. 'Still travelling the world, tarting up ungrateful models.'

'Sounds a lot more fun than the school run and the washing,' I said. Honestly, trying to make out her life was somehow dull and mundane, she had no idea how the real world operated. There were days when I'd give anything to be young, free and single again.

'Well it's not all it's cracked up to be,' Caz said. 'There are times when I live out of a suitcase, and generally speaking I see nothing of the country but a series of nameless hotels. It's not that exciting.'

'More exciting than my life,' I said.

'But you've got the kids, and Steve—' she said, then wavered a little.

'Oh yes, Steve,' I said sweetly. 'Yes, I *have* got him, haven't I?'

An awkwardness hung between us, and Dorrie and Beth who'd been looking on nervously from the sidelines, both jumped in with 'Let's get some candyfloss' (Beth) and, 'I don't care how old you are, we are all going to go and have our photo taken with Goofy, *right now*' (Dorrie).

Dorrie grabbed my arm and Beth grabbed Caz's and they manhandled us over to where a queue of children was patiently waiting to have their picture taken with Goofy. We were the only adults in the queue.

'Dorrie, do we have to do this?' Caz groaned. 'I feel like such a dork.'

'Me too,' I said, and momentarily forgetting my animosity to Caz in the face of such mortification, I grinned at her. I'd forgotten this, how Caz and I always used to stand together against Dorrie's battier ideas.

'Yes, we absolutely do,' said Dorrie in mock serious tones. 'This is *my* weekend and you will do things *my* way. That is all.'

Beth giggled, 'Dorrie, everyone else having their photo taken is about two foot tall. We'll look ridiculous.'

37

'I don't care,' said Dorrie. 'We are having a picture with Goofy and that is that.'

So ten minutes later, we all stood posing like idiots next to Goofy. Dorrie of course had thrust her arm through his, but I refused point blank to let him put his arm round me. It was bad enough to be standing next to an adult dressed up as a cartoon character without having to be hugged by him. To make matters worse, Dorrie wanted thousands of pictures with him, 'For posterity,' she said. 'I may never do this again.'

'We certainly won't,' Caz muttered, and I couldn't help grinning.

'Isn't this fun?' Dorrie beamed as she got us to all link arms and stand in front of Goofy for a final photo. Caz and I studiously stood on either end as far apart as we could get.

'Good, can we go now?' I said as we broke up after the last shot. A huge crowd of toddlers was building up, this was getting more embarrassing by the minute.

'Oh look, look,' Dorrie waved madly, 'it's Mickey! Coo-ee, come and have your photo with us, Mickey.'

So we all stood in line again, this time having no choice but to link arms with Mickey and Goofy. I produced a series of contorted smiles as the endless torture went on.

'Honestly, Dorrie, I'm going to kill you for this,' I said.

'But just think of the great photos we're going to have,' said Dorrie, beaming brightly. I have never known anyone be so positive as Dorrie – no wonder she loved all things Disney.

Finally the marathon photo session came to an end, and the poor beleaguered minder was able to hand back Dorrie's camera.

'Right, can we go now?' hissed Caz. 'I've had as much of this as I can take.'

Unfortunately, Goofy didn't seem to think so and insisted that not only was hugging required, but kissing too.

'Dear god,' I said laughing hysterically as we finally made our way to the candyfloss stall. 'I can't believe I have just been snogged by a cartoon character.'

'I told you it would be fun,' said Dorrie, with self-satisfaction. 'I so love it when I'm right.'

'Oh, do shut up,' we said. Suddenly it felt like old times. I glanced at Caz, wondering if she felt the same. Could we possibly reclaim our past after all?

'So, are we still having fun?' Dorrie had gathered us all, like the mother hen she was, and insisted we wait out a spring shower in a café crowded with families: small children darted here and there, toddlers screamed and were pacified with soothers and bottles. I had a pang of longing for my own family, at home without me. I knew the boys would love Euro Disney. I had a sudden fantasy of Steve and me finally sorting out our problems and coming here for a family celebration. Then dismissed it. That was never going to happen.

The café staff were evidently overrun, as the place was overflowing with plastic cups and plates which hadn't been cleared away. I was beginning to get a headache, not helped by the endlessly cheery music. I'd only been here a day and already I was fed up with the place, longing to have a hot drink out of a proper mug, rather than a Styrofoam cup. And really, if I were being honest, I wanted to be at home with the children.

'Yes, Auntie Dorrie,' grinned Caz. 'Honestly, we're not

your children, and we're not Darren. You can talk to us like normal human beings, you know.'

'Sorry,' Dorrie looked shamefaced. 'I don't mean to go on, but you know how much I love everything Disney and I just want everyone to have a good time.'

'It's great,' I assured her, lying through my teeth. The only other people apart from Dorrie who could have dragged me here were the children – I felt the familiar tug of my heart, the boys would have had a blast here. I'd have to promise them I'd take them to make up for leaving them behind for the weekend.

'Good,' beamed Doris. She was always happier when other people were happy. 'So what do you all want to do tonight?'

'Any chance we can escape into Paris?' Caz said hopefully. 'I know some great cafés in Montmartre.'

'Caz, even you must know that's not an option,' laughed Beth. 'I'm sure Dorrie is just being polite. What do *you* want to do tonight, Dorrie? After all, this is your weekend.'

'Well, there's a Wild West show in Disney Village,' said Dorrie.

Caz groaned. 'You are so not going to make us go to that, are you?' she said. 'It's bound to be full of screaming five-year-olds.'

'And what's wrong with five-year-olds?' I snapped, my longing to see the children leaving me slightly oversensitive. Beth shushed me, clearly not wanting to get in a row, but Caz just rolled her eyes.

'We'll go to the later version,' said Dorrie, 'and I promise there'll be drink. And Sarah, no more texting.'

'Sorry,' I said. I'd been surreptitiously texting Steve on and off all day to see how he was getting on. This was the first time I'd ever been away from the kids for any length of time and I was missing them badly. I wasn't, oddly enough, missing Steve. It was peculiarly restful not having to think about Steve, or us, or what I was going to do about the monumental mess my life was in.

'So it's agreed, then?' said Doris. 'Buffalo Bill's Wild West Show and then we can probably still have time to see the fireworks before the evening ends.'

A couple of hours later we were all sitting in hysterics around a barbecue as we watched a spectacular show. It started with two cowboys in a mock brawl, which was so convincing we nearly moved tables as they came crashing towards us. They moved on then to have fun with a bucking bronco, and on discovering it was Dorrie's hen weekend, they insisted she had a go, much to her delight. The show wrapped up with songs from *Annie Get Your Gun* and *Oklahoma!*. It wasn't what I'd have chosen to see, and despite my slight thawing earlier on, I'd still have preferred to have spent the evening without Caz, but I had had enough beer to begin to relax and enjoy myself.

At least Doris had let us give up our Minnie Mouse ears in favour of cowgirl hats. Caz had flirted with the bar staff enough to blag some extra drinks and the mood was mellow. The main thing was that Doris was having a great time. She had been uncharacteristically tense of late, and Beth and I had been worrying that she'd been holding out on us over something, but listening to her launch into some outrageous tale involving Darren, a condom and an embarrassing encounter with Darren's mum, I felt she was relaxing into her old self once more.

'So how are things?' Caz had sidled round to my side of

41

the table, while Doris and Beth were indulging in a giggling conversation with a French actor who called himself Rodeo Bill.

'Fine,' I said, thinking, *If only you knew.* There was a time when Caz knew everything that was going on in my head. Despite what she'd done to me, part of me still missed her friendship terribly.

'Is that fine, as in "Everything's great" fine, or fine as in "Shut up and leave me alone" fine?'

Damn Caz. She always could see right through me.

I picked away at a beer mat, unwanted tears suddenly springing to my eyes.

'Everything's fine, honestly,' I said. 'Not that it's any of your business.'

'No, no of course not.' Caz looked sad when she said this. 'You know, Sarah, if I could turn the clock back—'

'Well you can't,' I said. 'What's done is done.'

'And will I ever be forgiven?' she asked in a small voice.

'I don't know, Caz,' I said. 'How would you feel if you were in my shoes?'

'Point taken,' Caz said. 'I'm sorry. I shouldn't have said anything.'

She looked so forlorn I nearly took pity on her and told her the true state of my marriage, but somehow I couldn't. That would mean acknowledging how wrong I'd been to trust him and not her.

'No, you shouldn't have,' I said harshly.

'I'm sorry,' Caz said again. 'Truly I am.'

'Let's forget it, shall we?' I said. 'Come on, this is Dorrie's night. We shouldn't spoil it for her.'

'Fine by me,' said Caz. She turned to Doris and Beth. 'Is it time for fireworks yet?'

'Lordy, is that the time?' Dorrie said, giggling. Dorrie didn't tend to do really drunk, but I was glad she was having a good time. She got up slightly giddily, and stumbled against the chair. She must have tripped over her feet because suddenly she was lying on her back on the floor looking up at us.

'I didn't realize you'd had that much to drink,' I said laughing. 'Honestly, Dorrie, what are you like?'

Dorrie didn't say anything for a minute, then laughed and said, 'I must have had more than I realized. Come on, pull me up.'

I leant over and helped her to her feet. There was a fleeting moment when I had the slightest of feelings that she wasn't happy about something. But it was gone in an instant. Dorrie was on her feet and demanding to be taken to fireworks.

'Then it's back to my room to polish off the vodka I bought on the way,' she said.

'Fireworks then vodka, it is,' I said, linking arms with her. Beth joined her on the other side, and then I was aware that Caz was hovering next to me. I still hadn't forgiven her, but not to grab her arm seemed really churlish.

The four of us walked arm in arm back towards the park. Well we would have walked, but of course Dorrie insisted we dance and sing 'We're Off to See the Wizard'. I wondered if she really believed in the pot of gold at the end of the rainbow. Knowing Dorrie, she probably did.

'Isn't this great?' Dorrie smiled at us and squeezed my arm. 'The Fab Four finally back together. This has been the perfect hen weekend.'

The Fab Four might have been together temporarily, but

I couldn't see it lasting. I had no plans to see Caz again, whatever Dorrie might have thought. Too much water had gone under the bridge. Caz might be sorry, but for me, it was too late.

Chapter Four

Doris

'Welcome to Disney's Fantallusion!' the audio recording boomed out as we stood in the chilly March night air waiting for the fireworks. We'd missed the start of the parade, but were just in time to see the brightly lit floats carrying all the Disney characters from Jasmine and Aladdin to Belle and the Beast into the Central Plaza and up towards the Town Square. Jasmine and Aladdin's carpet actually flew, and Belle and the Beast did a majestic waltz. It was glitzy and tacky and I didn't care one bit. I was like a pig in clover.

This was why I'd come, for the delicious feeling of it being night and the place being brightly lit and all my favourite Disney characters dancing on great big fuck-off platforms. It reminded me of when Dad took me to Florida every year, and made me feel like a kid again: warm, safe and secure. There was something about the memory of those trips that made me yearn for a more innocent time, when I really did believe in a happy-ever-after. As usual, when I thought about Dad, and remembered the way he used to squeeze my hand, and say, 'Look, kiddo, is that the best or what?' whenever a particularly big rocket went off,

I got a lump in my throat. I still missed him so badly, I could almost hear his voice in my head. I hadn't wanted him to die, but neither had I wanted him to live the way he had been living.

The place was buzzing with families, huddling together for warmth. There were masses of excited children rushing around in the dark, small children trustfully holding their parents' hands, just like I had on that long-ago childhood trip. Mind you, judging by the wails of some of the younger ones, they were ready for their beds. I felt a pang and thought about Woody, my eight-month-old. Tonight was the first night I hadn't put him to bed since he was born, and I missed his baby smell, and his chubby cheeks and the way he cooed when I poured water over his head in the bath. I loved the way he clapped his hands and played peek-a-boo under the blankets. Woody had brought joy back into my life, during a time when I thought I'd never feel happy again. When he was bigger, I'd have to come back with him and Darren. If I were still able to of course. I shoved the thought from my mind. I'd promised myself no negativity this weekend. None. Whatsoever. It wasn't allowed.

'Fantallusion?' Beth rolled her eyes. 'What kind of word is that?'

'Does it matter?' I said. 'Isn't this fun?'

'No!' the other three said in unison. 'We only came because you wanted to.'

'You have to admit, Do, it is incredibly tacky,' said Caz.

'Says the girl who got married in a Las Vegas wedding chapel,' I retorted. 'Nothing wrong with a bit of tack. You lot ought to know me well enough by now. Talking of which, why aren't you all wearing your flashing Minnie Mouse ears?'

'If this wasn't your weekend, I think I might have to kill you,' said Caz, but she put on her ears anyway. And afterwards, even Caz had to admit we'd been treated to the most fabulous firework display any of us had ever seen.

When it was over, we slowly made our way back through the crowds to our hotel. It had been a good call to be staying so close to the park; apart from the obvious pleasure of staying in a *Toy Story*-themed bedroom, I was grateful not to have to walk too far. I tired so easily these days. Darren hadn't wanted me to come, of course, but I had laughed off his concerns. Nothing, but nothing was going to ruin my hen weekend with the girls.

'I hadn't realized you were that pissed,' Caz laughed at me as I stumbled and fell for the second time, as we reached the entrance of the park.

'Must be out of practice,' I said. 'I've had nine months off, remember. And I don't go out that much any more.'

If only I were pissed. If only things were that simple.

We got back to my room, raided the minibar and were soon all sprawled out on the massive double bed having a general gossip session. I hadn't laughed so much in ages. It did me so much good to be with the Fab Four. It always had done. Ever since we first met and I called us by that name.

I'd just moved to Northfields. Mum had got a job on a soap in London, while Dad was able to take up a research post at a London university, and it was convenient for town. They both wanted me to go to school in the UK, because Mum didn't want me growing up with an American accent and Dad preferred the academic rigour of the English education system. They could have afforded to send me private, but it went against their principles and they wanted me to go to a Catholic school, which is how I ended up at St Philomena's primary school, sitting next to Beth McCarthy, who wore dark plaits, had the biggest brown eyes I'd ever seen, and who barely ever said anything, just sat there chewing her pen. It didn't matter to me though, like I was always telling her, I could talk enough for the both of us.

Beth, Sarah and I went to Brownies together, so soon I found myself playing with them on a regular basis. Blonde-haired, blue-eyed Sarah was easy and confident, in a way that Beth wasn't, and I liked her instantly. But I was always conscious of another scraggy-looking dark-haired girl with the palest face and dark circles round her eyes, hovering angrily on the fringes, refusing our offers to play and yet never quite being able to tear herself away. That was Caz. She'd known Sarah forever and was jealous of me to begin with, I think. But I made her laugh, and over time she realized I really was no threat. I just wanted to be friends with everyone. Still do.

'So, how are the wedding plans going?'

'Great,' I said, in reply to Caz, who had asked the question casually, from the edge of the bed, even now acting like the outsider. My heart ached for her. I wish she could give up on some of that stubborn pride and realize that none of us hated her, not even Sarah. Not really. In fact it was Sarah's confession to me about the way things were between her and Steve which had made me determined to have Caz here. I've always thought it stupid for two women to allow a man to come between their friendship. Particularly when it's a worthless one like Steve.

'Are you keeping up the Disney theme?' Caz said – she was the only one who wasn't privy to all my plans.

'What do you think?' Sarah grinned. I shot her a grateful

48

look, I knew how hard this was for her and she was at least trying. 'She's going for the whole Cinderella-getting-married thing. If it were up to Doris she'd even have a pumpkin carriage.'

'Believe you me, I tried,' I said. 'It's the only thing you can't apparently buy on eBay.'

'So what are your bridesmaids going to be wearing then?' Caz asked.

There was an awkward pause and no one said anything.

'What? What have I said?' asked Caz.

Beth looked at me and blushed and then lowered her eyes again.

'I'm not having bridesmaids,' I said.

'What?' Caz looked at me in disbelief. 'But . . . but . . . Bridesmaids. Getting married. The Bridesmaid Pact. I mean that's *your* thing. I know the rest of us have cocked it up, but I just assumed you wouldn't.'

'Speak for yourself,' said Sarah cattily. 'The rest of us didn't cock it up. Besides, if Doris has any sense she'd never invite you to be her bridesmaid. You only bring trouble.'

'Oh that's right, rub it in,' said Caz. 'Isn't it possible that a person can change?'

'You tell me?' The hostility that had been bubbling under the surface all evening suddenly burst out into the open, to my utter dismay. I'd so hoped Caz and Sarah could sort things out. As ever, I was too optimistic. Darren's always telling me my chief failing is that I look for the best in people and situations. Maybe some hurts can never heal.

'Girls, girls,' I said clapping my hands, and trying to lighten the mood, 'that's exactly why I can't have any brides-maids. I don't want it to be pistols at dawn at the altar.

49

If I can't have all of you, I don't want any of you. So there are going to be no bridesmaids at my wedding. End of.'

Caz opened her mouth and shut it again, rendered for once in her life speechless.

'Don't all gawp at me,' I said. 'You should be grateful. You should have seen the dresses I was planning to make you wear.'

Caz

Billy Idol was screaming out it was a nice day for a white wedding, which seemed appropriate in a bar in Las Vegas. I couldn't resist the craving for the next drink, though I knew I needed it like a hole in the head.

'Oi, Charlie boy, gezza 'nother drink.' I was aware vaguely in some dim dark recess in my brain that I'd probably had enough and I was definitely slurring my words. The sensible thing would be to go to bed right now. Call it a day with these very nice and fun-loving work colleagues with whom I'd spent the last couple of days bonding in Las Vegas on the first solo photo shoot of my career as a make-up artist. But my sensible head never won over my drunken one.

'What are you on again?' Charlie looked in about as good shape as I was. He had wandered up to the bar. He turned to look at me as he said this, and leaned rather nonchalantly against the bar. He missed, narrowly avoiding smashing his chin before righting himself.

'Vodka and coke,' I said, giggling hysterically. Our companions, Charlie's boss Finn, and Sal, the PA to the spoilt model whose photos we'd all been involved in taking for the past couple of days, were nuzzling up to each other

51

in one of the deep-red heart-shaped sofas that littered the bar. It had not been a very well kept secret that they were shagging the pants off each other, despite Finn's heavily pregnant wife at home. I wasn't quite sure how I felt about that. I was no angel, it's true, but shagging someone who was hitched with a baby on the way seemed like a complication too far to me. I wondered if he was worth it. Then, looking at his rugged, wrinkled face, I decided he wasn't. Finn must be nearly twenty years older than Sal. What on earth did she see in him?

Now Charlie on the other hand . . . Over the last couple of days I'd decided he was a bit of all right. Tall, dark, conventionally good-looking with a fetching quiff that fell over his eye that he brushed off in a movement that I found at once attractive and endearing, Charlie was rather lovely. And might be just the thing to take my mind off the humiliation of Steve's rejection.

I'd always known Steve would go for Sarah in the end, despite all his flirting. They always did. Her pretty girl-next-door good looks always won them over, even if they were initially attracted to my wildness. My spiky aggressiveness was in the main too much for most of the men I encountered. Far too toxic, as I'd been told on more than one occasion. They enjoyed the shag, but they never hung around long enough to keep their spare PJs in my cupboard.

When we'd met him out drinking in Soho, it was obvious that a cityboy slicker like him would go for Sarah, the safe bet, rather than her more wild and unpredictable friend. Not that it stopped him flirting with me, mind, and making lewd suggestions about what he'd like to do with me when Sarah wasn't around. I'd bet a million dollars he never said anything to her like that. I should have been a better friend to Sarah. I should have warned her what he was like. But annoying prick as he was, Steve also happened to be one of the most gorgeous guys I'd ever met. Talk about love god. And I really did like him, and couldn't help the stab of jealousy when he chose Sarah. So after that, when we were all out together, I never stopped his surreptitious flirting with me, reasoning that it couldn't do any harm. He made me feel so good about myself, and I, despite all my chippiness and bravado, needed a morale boost from time to time. Not that I'd ever admit it to anyone, of course.

So when he finally moved things up a notch, when I bumped into him while clubbing without Sarah, I didn't even think about her. And after we'd danced and snogged and gyrated our way round the dance floor, I thought we'd inevitably end up back at my flat. I didn't think I cared, but the feeling of rejection when he left me so coldly, so humiliatingly on the dance floor was one I was unprepared for. I hated the feelings of churned-up misery he'd stirred up in me. It made me furious to feel so weak. But after all he and Sarah were engaged, what did I expect? And I was left alone. Bruised, sore, guilty, furious with myself for still hankering after him. And not a little jealous.

Yes, I could do with Charlie to lighten things up. He'd been so understanding, and he seemed to like me . . .

'What time is it?' I jerked awake, and suddenly realized I'd dozed off on Charlie's shoulder. There was no sign of the other two. Presumably they'd gone off to consummate their passion. Well, good luck to them.

'Three a.m.,' said Charlie. 'But hey, the night's still young. We're in Vegas don't forget. Ever played blackjack?'

'No,' I said. 'But there's a first time for everything.'

53

So suddenly we found ourselves running through the hotel's casino, like a pair of school kids. There were roulette wheels and card tables, in the plushest of surroundings. It was such an outrageous, extravagant kind of place, like being in a James Bond movie. I felt right at home. I could be anything I wanted here.

We found a table where a game of blackjack was just starting, and soon we were betting money we couldn't afford on a game I barely understood. I was drinking vodka like it was going out of fashion, but here, in this atmosphere, I felt alive in a way I never had, and carried away on a feeling of indulgent recklessness. Charlie was lovely too, really attentive in a way none of the guys I'd ever been with had ever been before. I was enjoying the sensation so much, I let my guard down. And it felt great.

'Hey, look over there,' I nudged Charlie. 'There's a wedding couple.'

'So?' said Charlie, who was looking at his hand trying to work out if he was going to make twenty-one or have to go bust. His last five dollars were riding on it. I'd had to give up a couple of hands before, as I'd run out of money.

'Isn't it cute?' I said, suddenly fascinated with this couple. They seemed to represent something I never thought I'd have. 'I bet there's a little chapel next door where you can get hitched, just like that.'

'There is, honey,' a Texan blonde with a pink rodeo hat and tasselled pink denim jacket next to me, drawled. 'It's called Love Me Tender, and they've got an Elvis impersonator who'll marry you for a few dollars.'

'What a hoot,' I said. I nudged Charlie. 'We should do it.'

'Don't be daft,' said Charlie.

'Come on, where's your sense of adventure?' I said.

'I think marriage should be a bit more serious than that,' said Charlie.

'Oh, don't be so boring,' I said. 'Think what fun we've had tonight. I like you, you like me, we're made for each other. We should get married tonight and go home and make a little Las Vegas baby.'

I didn't know what I was saying. I hated babies. I certainly didn't want one now. But somehow, I felt certain of one thing. Charlie and I had connected tonight, in a way I'd never connected with anyone. We *should* be together.

'You're mad,' said Charlie. He gave me a quizzical look, as if weighing something up. 'Did you mean all that?'

'Course I did,' I said. 'I think you're gorgeous.'

'You're not so bad yourself,' said Charlie, 'but it's hardly a basis for getting married.'

'Haven't you ever heard of love at first sight?' I said teasingly.

'Why, is that what you think's happening?'

'Don't you?' I said. Charlie didn't reply. 'I know. If you win this game, then we get married?'

'All right, if I win, I promise to marry you,' said Charlie, 'which is absolutely fine, because I'm not going to win.'

One by one everyone stuck except Charlie. The tension was mounting. He had eighteen in his hand; the croupier asked him what he was going to do.

'Twist,' said Charlie. I held my breath as he turned over his hand.

'Oh my god,' I said. He'd turned over the three of clubs. Twenty-one.

'I won,' said Charlie in a dazed voice. 'I've just won over two hundred dollars.'

He turned to me and hugged me tight.

'Waahahaay!' he said. 'The night is young.'

'Go on,' I said with more bravado than I was feeling. 'Now you have to do it. A deal's a deal.'

I honestly thought he'd say no. Charlie was a sweetheart, but I didn't think he was as reckless as me, but as he counted off his winnings, he seemed to suddenly shift up a gear.

'Well why the hell not?' he said. 'You only live once, and we are in Vegas.'

'Great,' I said, and grabbed his arm and dragged him off with me. I tried to ignore the shadow of doubt which was telling me I was only doing this to spite Steve. Which is how just an hour later, we found ourselves in front of the Love Me Tender chapel, giggling. The door was heart shaped and the outside of the chapel was a sickly pink which reminded me of the terrible blancmanges Auntie Nora used to make when I was little and Mum was having one of her funny 'turns'. We'd come armed with our marriage licence, which, bizarrely, in Las Vegas you could buy at any time of the night or day over the weekend, and the sun was just rising above the city, which seemed just as busy now as it had done when we'd embarked on our drinking spree all those hours earlier.

I had a moment of panic then. This wasn't how I'd planned my wedding day. I'd always pretended I didn't want to get married, but now I was here, I could admit to myself I wanted the real deal, not this ghastly parody with a boy I barely knew. I thought of Doris with a pang. She'd be furious with me for not fulfilling her silly pact.

'Come on then,' Charlie grabbed my hand, and pulled me through the door. We were met by an Elvis impersonator who was apparently the official who was going to marry us. It also transpired that he was going to give me away. So

I walked down the aisle to the tender strains of 'Love Me Do' and then in a few easily spoken words we were hitched. It felt surreal.

'Let's go and see the sunrise,' said Charlie impulsively. Finding out from Elvis that the best spot for this was out of town, we took a cab out to the desert, and sat holding hands as we watched a deep, pink sunrise in a pale, turquoise sky. The rising sun cast long shadows across the desert, which glowed pink and orange as the day slowly dawned. The morning air was slightly chilly, and Charlie popped his jacket over my shoulders – in my impulsiveness, I'd come without one. Instinctively, I leant my head against his shoulder, it felt natural and right in a way I'd never felt before. It was the perfect end to a bizarre and weird evening. Charlie kissed me gently on the lips and then said, 'Happy Wedding Day, Mrs Cosgrove. Come on, let's go home.'

We got back to the hotel, and then shyly, I followed him up to his room. It was strange. We'd been behaving so recklessly all evening, and now I felt like a fool. I could legitimately sleep with the guy and suddenly, now I was here, it felt all wrong. In the end, we just stumbled into the room, and collapsed cuddling on the bed from exhaustion and overconsumption of alcohol.

I woke at midday. The sun was streaming through the window, and Charlie was still snoring next to me. *Charlie.* I sat bolt upright and looked down at him, the events from the previous night flooding back with sudden and vivid clarity. Oh my god. I'd got married to a guy I barely knew. What on earth had I been thinking? How could I have been so stupid?

I sat on the edge of the bed looking at him sleeping so

peacefully. He truly was lovely to look at. And he was a really nice guy. But I barely knew him. And he wasn't Steve. How the hell was I going to get out of this? We couldn't really be married could we? The only thing I could think to do was to blag my way out of it.

'Good morning Mrs Cosgrove,' Charlie's voice cut into my thoughts.

'Oh my god,' my voice was pure fake Hollywood. 'I can't believe we acted so crazy last night.'

'I thought it was rather fun actually,' said Charlie.

'But come on,' I said. 'Getting married was a bit way out, wasn't it?'

'It doesn't have to be, does it?' Charlie took my hand.

I felt lousy then. Maybe he actually liked me. I'd led him on atrociously. All my pent-up feelings of bitterness against Steve had led me here; this wasn't fair on him. Best to brazen it out and pretend I couldn't see the way he really felt.

'Well it was an adventure, that's for sure,' I laughed. 'Not many people can say they came to Las Vegas and got married and divorced in a day, can they?'

'You want to get divorced?' Charlie said, angrily. 'Make your bloody mind up.'

'Well don't you?' I said.

'I don't know,' said Charlie. 'I know it was a bit wild, but we could try and give it a go, couldn't we?'

'I don't think so,' I said, trying not to look at him.

'What about us being meant for each other?' said Charlie. 'You were the one who seemed to think it was such a good idea last night.'

'That was the drink talking,' I said, trying to joke my way out of things.

'Gee, thanks,' said Charlie.

'Sorry, I didn't mean it like that. But come on,' I said. 'Us staying married would be terrible. We hardly know each other. It's never going to work.'

'You really think so?' said Charlie.

'I do,' I said. 'I'm sorry, I was really drunk last night, and things got out of hand. Believe me, I'm really bad news for you, you'll be grateful to me in the end.'

I couldn't look at him. I felt so guilty, and he looked so forlorn I couldn't believe he was taking it so seriously. I'd had him taped last night as being as wild as I was. Surely he could see this was just a prank that had gone badly wrong?

'You mean it, don't you?'

'Yes I do. Us staying married is a really, really bad idea,' I said.

'The worst,' said Charlie tonelessly.

'So that's it,' I said brightly. 'If it's that easy to get married here, I bet it's a cinch to get divorced.'

I didn't look at him when I said this. I pretended it was all OK. But not for the first time, I felt really lousy. The nicest bloke I'd met in ages, and I'd stuffed it up big time.

Chapter Five

Beth

'Nervous?' Matt held my hand as we sat in the waiting room, on a warm spring day in the middle of April, at the fertility clinic we'd been referred to by our GP, Dr McGrath. My hand felt clammy and sweaty, and my heart was thumping like a railway train. I knew it was my fault we hadn't conceived. Matt's tests had come back all clear, and mine were inconclusive. I couldn't help the nagging feeling that it was my body telling me it was my fault that we couldn't have babies.

Luckily, I'd explained the situation to Dr McGrath. She'd been very understanding, and said that I still might have a chance, and I shouldn't beat myself up about it. But I *knew*. I was being punished for what I'd done, all those years ago. And Matt didn't know. I'd never told him, because when we met it didn't seem important, and now I didn't know how to.

'Mr and Mrs Davies?' A smiling nurse ushered us into the consultant's office.

I sat in silent terror waiting for him to tell us that I had destroyed our chances, thanks to a careless moment with someone unworthy to tie Matt's shoelace. In my panic I zoned out what he was saying, concentrating on the lines in the floor, trying to ignore the pounding in my head which was saying over and over again, *This is when you get found out, this is when you get found out.* I felt sick and hot and dizzy, I wanted so much to be somewhere else.

'Beth, are you OK?' Matt's voice seemed to be coming from a long way away.

'Fine,' I said, and blinked. 'It's a bit hot in here. Sorry, what were you saying?'

'I was just explaining that looking at your test results, I think you two have a really good chance of getting pregnant if we go down the IVF route,' said Mr O'Brian, an avuncular kind of man who seemed to be almost as desperate as we were for us to conceive.

'You do?' I let out the breath I didn't know I'd been holding. Was it that easy? No mention *at all* of my previous gynaecological history and how it might impact on my chances? Just an explanation that I'd need to take fertility drugs, and then come back and have some eggs taken? I thanked the stars for Dr McGrath's discretion.

'Of course, it might not work,' he added. 'You do have to be prepared for that.'

'Of course,' we agreed, but hope is such a bloody awful little emotion, I knew we were both thinking the same thing. *It's not hopeless. We're not hopeless. We* can *still do this.* And for the first time I allowed myself an extra little thought: *Maybe my past doesn't matter after all.*

'Coffee to celebrate?' Matt said to me as we left the hospital. We were both so excited we were practically flying. I was too dizzy to hear all the facts and figures, but the consultant felt we had a better chance than most of conceiving – everything was in good working order according to him. We just needed a little help.

'I shouldn't be drinking coffee now, should I?' I said. 'But I'll have a juice with you.'

We found our way to a little coffee bar on the High Street and sat back, enjoying the feelings of elation washing over us. We'd had so much disappointment over the last few years, and even though I knew the road ahead was going to be tough, and there were no guarantees, I wanted to enjoy this feeling. It had been a long time since I'd felt this hopeful about anything.

'To us,' said Matt, raising his cup of coffee against my orange juice.

'To us,' I said, 'and to Foetus.'

We hardly dared to talk about the possibility of a real baby any more.

Matt leant over, and gently touched my stomach.

'To Foetus,' he said. 'You know, I've got a really good feeling about this.'

I arrived at my desk a couple of hours later. I'd booked the morning off, claiming the dentist. I hadn't told anyone at work about Plan Foetus as we'd taken to calling it. Hell, I hadn't even told Doris and Sarah, though I'm sure they'd both guessed. They'd seen how broody I was when they were both pregnant. I couldn't help but feel a stab of jealousy, particularly when Sarah had had her second baby. Although I knew she'd had problems with sickness and things, she made it look so easy. Sarah seemed to be able to conceive at the drop of a hat, it didn't seem fair. I couldn't bear to let Sarah know how jealous I was, so I pretended to be nonchalant about having children. I'd been making out for ages that my career came first.

To be honest, that was true for a while. When I first met

Matt, babies didn't come into the picture. We were just so happy to be together, and I kept pinching myself that after kissing all those toads, I'd finally found my handsome prince. I didn't want to spoil it with the patter of tiny feet. I assumed, you see, that Matt would be like all the other guys, and run at the first mention of babies. And having finally lost weight after years of dieting, I wasn't too keen to put it all back on again. There was always the nagging doubt that Matt would only fancy me slim. I should have known better of course: he was the one who brought the subject of babies up, and when I mentioned my weight, he just laughed me to scorn and said he'd love me however fat I got.

Today, for the first time in a long time, I felt the same dizzying intoxication that I'd felt when we'd started to plan our family. A crack of light was shining in the dark – it wasn't much, but it was something to hold on to.

'You seem very happy today,' Mel our receptionist said as I sailed jauntily past her, whistling. I never ever whistle.

'Well, spring is in the air, and all that jazz,' I said, which is uncharacteristically chatty of me. Usually I barely say anything to Mel or anyone else at work unless I have to. It's the only way I can keep a tight lid on the things threatening to explode out of my head.

I breezed to my desk and sat down and started ploughing through my invoice tray. I love my work in credit control. It's not to everyone's taste, but I enjoy the balancing act of chasing down debtors and holding off creditors, thereby ensuring that no one ever owes us money, but we invariably owe other people money.

I was so engrossed in my work, I tuned out the sound of my mobile ringing in my handbag for a minute. I don't often get personal phone calls at work. Matt's generally the only person to ring me during the day.

I rooted around in my bag and eventually found the phone, which had inevitably wormed its way to the bottom of my bag. As I picked it up, the phone went dead. Typical. I flicked onto missed calls. It wasn't a number I recognized. I rang it back.

'Hi,' I said tentatively, 'I think you just called me?'

'Beth?' I was shocked to hear Caz's voice. I hadn't seen her since Doris's hen weekend, over a fortnight earlier. I didn't even know she had my number. 'I hope you don't mind, I cadged your number off Doris.'

Caz sounded different. Uncertain. Awkward. Most un-Cazlike.

'Only, I was wondering – if you'd – well, would you mind meeting up for a drink sometime?'

I was stunned. OK, we'd had a nice time when we were away, but still. I hadn't spent any time alone with Caz for at least five years. Why would she suddenly want to talk to me now?

'Look, I'll understand if you say no,' Caz continued. 'It's just that it was so nice meeting you again in Paris. I'd like to catch up properly if you'd like.'

She sounded so tentative and unsure, something crumbled inside me. I had a sudden flashback to the way she was at primary school, just when we'd all started to be friends. Caz was always angry and spoiling for a fight, but we grew to realize that that aggression hid a vulnerability that wasn't on public display. But now she'd been defensive with us all for so long, I'd forgotten how vulnerable she was underneath.

I took a deep breath.

'Of course, that would be great,' I said. 'When are you free?'

'This feels . . . odd,' Caz said as she faced me over a glass of spritzer in a bar in Soho. Caz always went drinking in Soho, I remembered. I never did. If I drank anywhere it was in a pub round the corner from work in Camden High Street before taking the Northern Line home. I rarely ventured into the West End these days.

'You're not drinking?' Caz said, glancing significantly at my orange juice.

'I always leave my car at the station,' I fibbed. There was never anywhere to park at the station, but I was relying on Caz's ignorance about life in the suburbs for her not to have guessed that. I was hazarding a guess that Caz still lived as close to town as she could. She always was a bright-lights, big-city kind of girl, unlike stay-at-home small-town me. Last I'd heard, she had a flat Islington way, which always seemed glamorous to me.

'So, how are things?' Caz said. 'I mean, I know we chatted that weekend, but it wasn't like we did much one to one stuff. Tell me about yourself.'

'Not much to tell,' I said. 'I like my job. Matt and I are happy. We live a quiet life. You know me. Never one for a wild time.'

'Matt well?'

'He's great.' I felt myself relax as I got onto my favourite topic, the general wonderfulness of my gorgeous husband, and my extraordinary luck in catching him. 'I don't know what I'd do without him. He's kind and he's witty and he's caring' – and he's never once made me feel bad about not getting pregnant – 'I don't know what I'd do without him.

66

He's my best friend and husband and lover all rolled into one.' I paused. 'Sorry, I do go on about him. Pathetic really. But I still feel like a love-struck teenager.'

'No, I think it's great,' said Caz. 'I've made such a mess with all that stuff. I'm glad one of us has had a happy ending.'

'Two of us,' I said. 'You couldn't get more loved up than Daz and Dorrie.'

'I'm so glad,' said Caz. 'I can't think why it's taken them so long to get hitched. I'd have had Dorrie down for becoming Mrs Maitland years ago.'

'She hasn't said much about it, but I think it was because of her dad,' I said. 'She always wanted him to walk her down the aisle, and when he couldn't, I don't think she could bear it. Then when he died she went into a bit of a decline really. She seemed very low and her mum is worse. We were all really worried about her for a while. I think the only thing that pulled her out of it has been Woody.'

'I feel so bad about Dorrie's dad,' said Caz. 'I wish I'd known how bad it was. It's not just my relationships with men that I've cocked up. I've made a mess of everything.'

She looked incredibly sad and I felt an unusual feeling of pity for her. I can't remember ever feeling that about Caz before: frustration, fury, anger, yes. Pity? No. Caz wasn't someone you pitied.

'It's never too late to make amends,' I said, leaning over and touching her hand. 'I mean, we've met up, and Dorrie did invite you to her hen weekend. You know what she's like. I'm sure she doesn't hold it against you.'

'That's another reason I called, actually,' said Caz. 'I had an ulterior motive. I felt terrible hearing Doris say she didn't want any bridesmaids. Things didn't work out the way we planned when we were kids, and I'm sure she'd still love them to.'

'Knowing Doris, I'm sure you're right,' I agreed. I had felt Doris had been pretty sad about the bridesmaid thing from the minute she'd announced her engagement.

'So, how do you fancy trying to sort it out?' Caz leaned forward, eyes shining. 'I mean, I know there's the slight difficulty of Sarah to contend with – I mean she hates me, right?'

'Well,' I said, 'hate's a pretty strong word, but yup, you could say you're not her favourite person.'

'But, how about we try to sort out our differences enough for us to give Doris the wedding she deserves?'

'What do you mean?' I said.

'Eighteen years ago we made a vow. And we've failed dismally to keep it so far,' said Caz. 'So I think for Doris's sake, it's time we actually fulfilled the Bridesmaid Pact.'

Chapter Six

Sarah

'Good day at work?' Steve wandered in to the kitchen where I was wrestling with the grill pan which had mysteriously got so filthy it had burst into flames when I'd grilled sausages for the boys' tea. William had been so terrified it had taken me about half an hour to calm him down, while his older brother Sam had laughed him to scorn. Sam was a budding pyromaniac and I was slightly concerned he might have picked up a tip or two. William was watching TV in the den – it made me smile to think that as an adult I had managed to gain a den, when, thanks to Dorrie, I craved one so much as a child; ironic how little happiness it now gave me – and Sam was struggling with homework involving him writing sentences about going to the park.

'So-so,' said Steve. He gave me a perfunctory peck on the cheek. It was an action quite without affection, but he always kissed me when he came in the door. He smelt of booze. Great. He'd obviously been having another 'business' lunch. Lord knows what business they actually did at those lunches. It never ceased to amaze me how Steve kept down his job as a financial advisor. But he was a smooth operator, and even in these dicey financial times, he always seemed to come up smelling of roses.

'What's for tea?' he asked, going to the fridge and opening a can of beer.

'Sorry, I haven't got there yet,' I said. I'd barely sat down since picking the kids up from school. We'd rushed straight to the swimming pool after school, then I'd called in on Steve's mum who'd been in her usual panic about unpaid bills. When Steve's dad was alive he'd dealt with all the paperwork, and even though he'd been dead for five years now, Maggie still couldn't get to grips with it. While I was there she'd let slip something that had un-settled me rather.

'Did you have a nice time when you were away, dear?' she said, once I'd established that she didn't need to write a cheque for her council tax as she paid it by direct debit, and her gas wasn't going to get cut off because she was a week late paying her bill. I hadn't seen Maggie since before going to Euro Disney three weeks earlier, as Steve and I had booked a week in Center Parcs with the kids over the Easter holidays. I wondered afterwards why we'd gone. The boys had had a great time, but Steve barely spoke to me for the whole time we were away.

'Yes it was great, thanks,' I said. 'And Steve did a brilliant job with the kids. I couldn't believe how tidy the house was when I got back.'

'Well, they weren't there that much of course,' said Maggie. 'They came to me for their tea on Saturday, and of course, they were out all day on Sunday.'

'Oh?' I said. Odd. The kids hadn't said anything about going out for the day, nor about having tea at Maggie's. 'That's nice, guys. Did Daddy take you on a treat?'

'We went to the zoo and I had an ice cream and saw a gorilla,' said William proudly.

'Shhh!' Sam furiously dug William in the ribs. 'You know you weren't supposed to say anything about that.'

'Why not?' My heart lurched suddenly. Why was Steve keeping secrets from me, and getting the kids to lie?

'We met Daddy's friend and he said you wouldn't like it,' said William.

'I bet he did,' I said grimly. This was it, the moment that I'd been dreading for months. I'd suspected Steve was cheating on me again, but he'd laughed at my suspicions. Now I knew he was definitely up to something fishy. But getting the kids to lie to me. That was below the belt, even for Steve.

'Oh dear,' Maggie flapped about looking uncomfortable. 'Have I said something I shouldn't?'

Maggie had many faults, not least her inability to manage her domestic affairs without our help, but she was pretty astute about her son. I'd never told her Steve had cheated on me, but from things she'd said over the years, I was pretty sure she knew.

'No, of course not, Maggie,' I smoothed things over, my speciality that. 'Steve must have forgotten to mention it.'

And now, here I was, watching my errant husband fill himself up on beer, and wondering how on earth I was going to mention the elephant in the room. Because I was sick of his lies, and his promises to do better, and his insistence that if he strayed it was somehow my fault. I'd stuck with him for so long because of the kids, but now he was making them deceive me. I'd been a doormat long enough. Time to stand up for myself.

'You didn't mention you'd taken the kids to the zoo,'

71

I said casually, once the boys were in bed, and Steve was flopped out in front of the football.

'So?' Steve lied so flippantly and easily. 'I forgot. It's not a crime.'

'No-o,' I said, 'I just thought you might have mentioned it.'

'Well, I didn't,' Steve sounded bored. God, had he always been so bored of me?

'Who was your friend?' I knew my voice had come out reedy and tinny, but I couldn't help myself. I hated the way Steve made me sound like a nagging wife. It was so bloody demeaning.

'I knew you'd be like this,' said Steve, turning on the offensive. A typical tactic to try and make me appear in the wrong. I wasn't standing for it this time. I was going to have it out with him, whatever the consequences.

'Like what?' Trying to keep my voice calm and level. Trying not to rise to his bait.

'Accusatory. Jealous. Idiotically accusing me of stuff.'

'I haven't actually accused you of anything,' I said, in what I felt to be a perfectly reasonable manner. 'Should I have?'

'How could you say that?' He had the cheek to sound hurt. As if he'd done nothing wrong.

'Well, let me see. There was Stacey in accounts, and Dannii from sales, and Petra from export. Not to mention what did or didn't go on with my best friend. Why on earth should I imagine in any shape or form you are at all trustworthy?'

'Why rake up old stuff?' said Steve. 'You know I love you, babe.'

'Do I? Do I really?' I said. This is the way it always went, but I was tired, tired of always being second best, and tired of his lies.

'I know I don't show it enough,' Steve said, taking my hand, 'but seriously you're the only one that matters to me.'

'So who did you go to the zoo with?' I said. I didn't want to look in his eyes. I didn't want him to seduce me with his weasel words. 'Come on, I want to know.'

'It was Kirsty,' he muttered.

'Kirsty, as in your secretary Kirsty?' That figured. She was a buxom blonde, Steve's normal type (Caz was clearly some kind of wild aberration). I'd had her taped as a potential rival when I met her at the Christmas party.

'When she heard you were away, she offered to help,' said Steve. 'You should be grateful. She was great with the kids.'

'I bet,' I said dryly. 'So why the big secret?'

'Because I knew you'd react like this,' said Steve. He snuggled up to me and I felt my body weakly respond. 'I know I've been a bad boy in the past, but that really is behind me. I don't want to do anything to jeopardize us. I don't want to hurt you.'

He looked at me with those big, puppy pleading eyes. He was so damned plausible. So difficult to resist. I almost believed him. *Almost.* I just couldn't rid myself of the lingering doubt that he was lying to me, again. I just couldn't trust him.

'If you say so,' I said, and responded stiffly to his embrace. I had no proof that he was cheating. Just a gut feeling. And it didn't feel good.

'So you let him get away with it again?' I was round at Dorrie's, having our weekly coffee together. It was a habit I'd got into since Dorrie had stopped work. She'd gone back to her job doing something fantastically clever in biochemistry for her obligatory three months but then decided to stay at home with Woody. Of course, Dorrie being very sociable, she found being at home incredibly isolating, and for a while had seemed quite low, so Beth and I had made it our mission to try and keep her cheerful. Somehow the world didn't seem right when Doris was down in the dumps.

'I suppose so,' I said. 'I wanted to really have it out with him, but I can't prove anything. Besides, there's a bit of me that just doesn't want to know.'

'Coward,' said Dorrie. 'You know you're too good for him.'

'That's what Joe always says,' I said. Steve's younger brother, Joe, was a frequent visitor to our house, often stepping in to help out with the boys, when Steve was on one of his many business trips away. Of late he'd even been taking them to football for me on a Saturday. I didn't know what I'd do without his steady, unwavering support.

Dorrie looked at me slightly askance, eyes narrowed.

'Do you ever wonder if you married the wrong brother?'

'No! No! That's ridiculous,' I said. 'I mean, I like Joe. He's always been really good to me. But he's Steve's brother. I couldn't even begin to think about it. It wouldn't be right.'

'Hmm,' said Dorrie, clearly not believing me, and of course, being right not to. I'd always been fond of Joe, and he was a great help, the kids absolutely loved him. There were times, it's true, when I'd idly wondered how it would have been if I'd married Joe and not Steve. I was pretty sure Joe wouldn't have cheated on me. I shook my head. This was ridiculous. Joe was my brother-in-law. And I was in love with Steve.

'Right, what do you want me to help you with today?' I changed the subject. Another reason for our weekly meets

74

was to help Doris plan the wedding. Her mum was away with the fairies more often than not these days, and not much help. I rather suspected her of being depressed, but Dorrie had never talked about it, and it wasn't my business. For some reason, though she was open about everything else, Dorrie kept a tight lid on what was happening in her family. When her dad was still alive she barely mentioned the problems he was having, and yet it must have been incredibly tough.

'I've just found these great little bags for party favours on Freecycle,' said Doris. She and Darren could probably have afforded to make a big splash, but Dorrie reckoned they needed the money for more important things, namely Woody and any siblings he might have. So she'd set her heart on having a stylish wedding at as little cost as possible. Well, if you can call a Disney theme stylish, I suppose. The way she was going, she was making Posh and Becks' wedding look positively restrained.

'Do you mean these?' I fell about laughing as I picked up a box full of little net pink and blue bags with a draw-string on them. They had stars and the letter D embroidered on them.

'What's wrong with them?' said Doris. 'I think they're cute.'

'Nothing,' I said. She really meant it, bless her. 'Did you decide on the shoes in the end?'

Last week Doris had put in two bids on eBay for satin court shoes. One pair was in baby blue, which would match the Cinderella-style blue wedding dress which she'd got second hand from a fancy-dress shop, the other was a more traditional cream to match the other Cinderella dress which she'd got on eBay. She hadn't decided yet which colour to go for on the day. I preferred the cream, but I knew Doris was determined to get the blue.

'Come upstairs and I'll show you,' Doris said, 'but we'll have to be quiet as Woody's still having his nap.'

She led me into her spare room, which had a big notice on saying: DAZ KEEP OUT! *Important wedding stuff not to be seen before the big day.* The room was jammed from floor to ceiling with wedding paraphernalia.

'My god, how much stuff have you got?' I gasped.

'Ever since I put that ad on Freecycle, people keep sending me things,' said Dorrie. 'Now where did I put them?' She rooted around in a corner of the room. There was so much junk in there, I couldn't believe she could ever find anything.

'Ah, here they are!' She waved a pair of shoes triumphantly under my nose.

'So you went with the blue ones, then?' I said. 'I knew you would.'

'Sorry, I know you liked the cream,' Dorrie said, 'but I just couldn't resist them. Just look at these fabulous bows. Aren't they pretty?'

'They're very you,' I said diplomatically. If anyone could carry those shoes off, it would be Doris.

'I might still get the cream anyway,' said Doris. 'I'm torn between that lovely white dress with the pink roses, and the blue dress.'

'White would be more traditional,' I said.

'I know,' said Dorrie. 'I'm greedy, I guess. I love them both.' She looked round the room. 'I really must sort some of this stuff out, it's getting a bit bonkers in here. I just don't have the energy.'

'Well you do have a very young baby,' I pointed out.

'Tell me about it,' said Dorrie, rubbing her eyes. 'Woody's

molars kept me up most of the night. I just feel so tired all the time though. Is that normal?'

'With a small person in your life?' I laughed. 'Absolutely. Is there anything you want me to do?' I peered at her closely. Dorrie did look tired, as if she'd lost her sparkle somehow. The combination of motherhood and wedding stress must be getting to her.

Doris looked at the room again, and then said, 'Naah. I don't even know where to begin. Let's go and have a cup of tea instead. I've made muffins.'

Amazingly, despite her ability to always produce cake at the drop of a hat, Doris never seems to put on any weight. I envied her that.

'You still off the sugar?' Dorrie asked as she poured the water out of the kettle.

'As part of my calorie-controlled diet,' I said solemnly. 'Of course muffins don't count—'

Doris gave a sudden scream as she dropped the kettle. 'Oh my god, I am such a damned klutz sometimes,' she said, rushing to the cold tap and shoving her hand underneath it.

'Is it a bad burn?' I rushed over to have a look at it. Once a nurse, always a nurse, even if I haven't been near a patient since Sam was born.

'No, it's fine.' Doris showed me a slight pinkish tinge on her arm. 'Luckily most of it went on the floor.'

'Well, no harm done,' I said. 'It's usually Beth who's the clumsy one.'

'I must be catching it off her,' said Doris. 'I'm all fingers and thumbs today.'

As she said this I noticed her hand was shaking, and she looked a little tearful.

'Dorrie, are you OK?' I said.

'Yes, fine,' said Dorrie. 'I'm just overtired is all. Now come on, let's tuck into those muffins and then you can help me decide about place settings.'

'So long as you don't give us all paper plates with Cinderella on them,' I said. Doris looked a little shamefaced. 'You haven't?'

'Well, they were half price in Wilkinson's,' she said. 'I couldn't resist. But that's not the only option, we could have Beauty and the Beast ones instead.'

'You are totally off your trolley,' I said laughing, looking at my friend with affection. But I couldn't help wondering if underneath her laughter, she was hiding something from me.

Chapter Seven

Doris

I heard Darren's key in the door with relief. It was the Friday after I'd seen Sarah, and I'd had a really hard day with Woody, who'd started throwing up in the night and pretty much carried on the whole day. In between clearing up vomit, I'd spent most of the day with him clinging to my shoulder like a limpet. Woody wasn't normally clingy and it was horrible seeing his smiley face so miserable and wan. It was the first time since he'd been born that he'd been ill, and I didn't know what to do. If Mum were only a bit more with it, I could have got her advice, but when I expressed concern that Woody wasn't getting enough fluids, she just said vaguely, 'Oh, all babies get sick. But they bounce back. He'll be better tomorrow, you'll see.'

By mid-afternoon when it was apparent that Woody wasn't able to tolerate any food or drink at all, I rang Sarah, who calmly prescribed small sips of water, and Dioralyte, but suggested taking him to the doctor if it got any worse. I knew she was right, but ever since Dad got ill I'd had a pathological hatred of the medical profession. I wouldn't take him unless I absolutely had to. Luckily, Woody, clearly exhausted by his day's activities, took that moment to decide to crash out. At least if he was sleeping he wasn't being sick, so we cuddled up on the sofa together and I watched crap TV and waited for Darren to get in. I was shattered. I couldn't believe that one little person could create so much work and worry. I couldn't bear the thought of anything hurting him, and I hated seeing him so ill.

'Hi,' said Darren as he came through the door, as ever having performed his daily ritual of hand washing (to get rid of all those nasty germs from travelling by tube, you understand). 'How is he?' I'd been keeping Darren posted as to Woody's condition, and he'd managed to sneak away from work early. Like me, Darren had melted the minute that Woody had come into his life, and we were both like a pair of pathetically anxious clucking hens around him.

'He seems OK at the moment,' I said. 'He's been asleep for ages though and he feels a bit hot.'

'When did you last give him Calpol?' said Darren.

'Just before he went to sleep,' I said. 'I'm not sure how effective it's been, he's thrown up nearly every dose I've given him today.'

Woody stirred in my arms, and gave a slight moan, before wriggling awake. He looked blearily up at his dad.

'Here, let me take him,' said Darren, picking up our son and holding him close.

'I think you'll want this,' I said, proffering a muslin.

Too late, Woody had chucked up all over Darren's back.

'Oh shit, shit,' said Darren. 'He's contaminated me.'

'Darren, he's probably contaminated me,' I said laughing. 'I've been clearing this up most of the day. Just wait there and I'll sort you both out.'

Five minutes later, having persuaded Darren that it really wasn't going to be necessary to burn his jacket, and cleaned both of them up, I took a decision. Woody was no better. Much as I hated it, I was going to have to take him to see the doctor.

The waiting room was crowded. It was nearly the end of surgery hours and there were still plenty of people to see. The doctor's receptionist had squeezed us in as a favour and I felt slightly stupid that I hadn't taken Woody before. He lay pale and listless in my arms. He clearly wasn't well. I should have done something sooner.

When Woody's name was finally called, I felt a mixture of anxiety and relief. Maybe the doctor would take one look at him and say there was nothing to worry about. Darren squeezed my hand as we went in.

'He'll be OK,' he said.

'Hi,' said Dr Linley, as we sat down. 'What seems to be the problem?'

'Woody keeps being sick,' I explained, 'he can't keep anything down, and now he's gone all listless and floppy.'

'Right, and this has been going on how long?' she said, as she proceeded to examine him.

'Since last night,' I said. 'I just thought it was a bug and he'd get over it. But it seems to be getting worse.'

Right on cue, Woody threw up again. Poor little mite, it wasn't even as if he had much to throw up.

Darren was, as usual, prepared with antibacterial spray, wipes and plastic gloves and went into clean-up mode, while the doctor was explaining that Woody might need to go into hospital to have some fluids.

Hospital? My baby in hospital? That had simply never occurred to me. The last time I'd been in our local hospital had been to see Dad all connected up to drips and wires.

I'd vowed I never wanted to set foot in there again, which is why I had elected to have Woody at home.

'Oh,' was all I could manage to say, feeling helpless, while Darren took charge and asked all the right questions, like how serious was it, and how long did she think he'd stay there. It was as if I was cocooned in a great bubble of silence, I could barely register what the doctor was saying, while Darren picked Woody out of my arms, and motioned me to get up.

'I'll ring ahead for you,' I heard, as if in a dream, and she pressed an envelope into my hand, and said, 'Take this with you.'

I felt dizzy and sick. I still couldn't take it in. My baby was going to hospital.

'Are you all right, Doris?' Dr Linley asked. 'No falls, recently?'

'No, I'm fine,' I said, 'just thinking about Woody for now.'

'Right, of course,' she said. 'Was everything OK with Mr Mason?'

Darren shot me a look, but I shushed him. 'Fine,' I said, not about to admit that I hadn't made the follow-up appointment yet.

'Great,' said Dr Linley. She tickled Woody's chin. 'Don't you worry about this little one, he'll be right as rain in no time.'

The journey to St Mary's seemed endless. I'd done this journey so many times to go and see Dad, but I'd forgotten how long it took. We were lucky to have a satellite hospital of one of the major London hospitals so close by. Everyone said so. The treatment there was second to none, but all I could associate with it was heartache, and loss. I so didn't want to take my baby there.

I was pleasantly surprised by the speed with which we got through the triage system and into the paediatric clinic, where a friendly nurse was waiting with toys and a cot to lie Woody down in. It was a far cry from the noisy chaos of A & E that I remembered from the numerous trips in with Dad. Woody was quickly assessed and a drip was set up. No one seemed to be too fussed or worried about him, so I started to breathe again. Darren too, I think. Though he'd gone into full Darren-taking-charge mode, I knew he was covering up how anxious he was feeling. Woody, clearly exhausted by his day, dropped off to sleep, while we waited for a bed to come available on the children's ward.

Once the jolly nurse was sure he'd settled down, she disappeared to deal with the numerous other small patients streaming through the doors.

'I do hope their hygiene procedures are properly in place,' said Darren. 'I'd hate Woody coming out of here with something worse.'

'Don't be daft,' I said. 'Didn't you see all those anti-bacterial hand spray things all over the place? Everyone's so excited about MRSA these days, I'm sure he'll be perfectly fine.' And I was. Once I'd got here, I'd relaxed, Woody was going to be looked after and get better. It wasn't like with Dad. The friendly nurse had explained that Woody was just dehydrated. By morning he would be right as rain.

Darren got up and wandered around the room. He's never very good at sitting still and hospitals make him as nervous as they do me. We'd seen too much of them in the last few years.

'Why didn't you tell Dr Linley the truth?' he said. 'You still haven't booked that appointment with Mr Mason, have you?'

'I will,' I said. 'I promise, I will. But not now. There's just so much to do for the wedding. I'll think about it after then.'

'But Dorrie, you heard what he said the first time,' said Darren, 'they need to monitor you.'

'And what will that do?' I said. 'It's not going to stop the inevitable, is it?'

'Dorrie, nothing is inevitable,' said Darren. 'And we can get through anything together, you know that.'

He came over and put his arms around me, and I put my head on his shoulder. I badly wanted to believe that and I know he *did* believe that, but I just couldn't.

'Look, Darren . . .' I took a deep breath. I knew what I was going to say was going to hurt him, but it had to be said. 'You don't have to go through with this, you know.'

'With what?' Darren looked puzzled. Oh his sweet, sweet dimness, couldn't he see what I was trying to say?

'With the wedding,' I said. 'We don't know what's going to happen, do we? You don't know what you're taking on. It might be better if we didn't commit ourselves . . .'

My voice trailed away. I'd been dreaming of my wedding since I was a little girl, and from the minute I'd met Darren, I'd known he was the one, and yet here I was giving him a Get Out of Jail Free card.

'Doris Bradley, you are a daft cow sometimes,' said Darren, kissing the top of my head. 'I'm already committed, can't you see that? Besides, I don't want Woody being a little bastard *all* his life.' (I'd been so dismayed when I'd found out that despite my best laid plans, my longed for baby was coming before my even more longed for wedding. Darren had teased me ever since about him being our little bastard.)

'Are you really sure?' I said, staring into his beautiful blue eyes for reassurance.

'Really,' said Darren.

'But we don't know what's going to happen,' I said.

'Yeah, well, it's like the guy says at the end of *Blade Runner*,' said Darren. 'None of us know how much time they've got, do they? Come on, enjoy the moment, and let the future take care of itself.'

The jolly nurse returned at that moment to let us know there was a bed available upstairs, and the next hour or so was a blur of getting Woody settled in and checked over. Darren went home to get us some things. Stupidly, I hadn't thought as far as the fact that one of us would need to stay the night. By the time he'd come back, Woody was gurgling happily in his cot.

'He's looking better already, isn't he?' Darren said, giving Woody a tickle under the chin.

'Much,' I said. 'It's such a relief.'

We sat quietly in the semi-darkness watching our son settle down to sleep, sitting close and still, sharing the easing of worry. I held Darren's hand and leant against his shoulder. I just wished my own gnawing anxiety would ebb away so easily.

Chapter Eight

Caz

'So how did it go then?' Charlie was setting up his equipment when I arrived at the top floor of a warehouse near London Bridge. It belonged to a famous architect who let it out for photo shoots and boasted great views of the river, as well as a bright lofty space, making it a favourite location for most of the people we tended to work with. No one else had arrived yet. I always liked to get there before the client, to give myself time to chat to Charlie or whoever the photographer was, to see what they had in mind so I could make up the punters accordingly.

It was the first time I'd seen Charlie properly since before Dorrie's hen weekend. I'd texted him to say it had been fine, but hadn't spoken to him in any depth. Nadia, his girlfriend, kept him on a tight rein, and I had a feeling she didn't like me. I can't say I can blame her. I'd probably be wary of me too, and I'm sure my reputation has preceded me. She couldn't know that I'd changed, or wanted to change, at any rate. Besides, Charlie was safe from me. He was like my big brother and agony uncle rolled into one – and we had the heterosexual equivalent of a fag-hag relationship. Nothing more than that.

'It was OK,' I said. 'Do you want some coffee?'

The architect was never much in evidence when he was letting his flat out, but he always supplied coffee for us, which was pretty decent.

'That'd be great,' said Charlie. 'You look dreadful. Heavy session was it?'

I pulled a face. I knew I looked a fright. Just as well I had got in early, I could spend some time repairing the cracks. No one wants to be made up by someone who looks ugly as sin.

'I didn't get much sleep,' I said.

Charlie gave me a quick sympathetic look, but he knows better than to probe. It was true. I had had a bad night. But it wasn't through drink.

Mum had rung for the first time in a long time. Pissed, of course. She hadn't been aggressive though, which was new. But she *had* been whiny, miserable and self-pitying.

'Caroline, when are you going to come and see me?' she'd whined. 'You never see me any more.'

This was true; my ludicrously expensive therapist had suggested I take a back seat, and not rush round to deal with every calamity. 'You aren't responsible for your mother's actions,' she kept telling me, and I was trying to believe her, but it was so hard to change the habit of a lifetime.

'Mum, have you been drinking?' I said wearily.

'Only a small one,' she said with that defensive tone which meant she'd probably drunk a whole bottle of vodka. 'You never let me have any fun, do you?'

'Mum,' I said, speaking slowly as if to a small child, 'I've told you, I'll come and see you when you've stopped drinking.' This too was the advice of my therapist who said we'd become co-dependent.

'But Caroline, I've got no one else but you,' she said. *Whose fault is that?* I wanted to say, but couldn't face the self-pitying response that would follow.

'I'm going now, Mum,' I said, knowing it was best to be cold, otherwise I'd be round there like a shot, as I had been so many, many times before, never doing any good, never changing anything.

'Caroline, I'm scared,' said Mum. Her voice sounded small and childlike. I just couldn't take it any more and cut the connection. I left the phone off the hook, turned my mobile off and went to bed. Let her ring me if she wanted to.

Then, of course, I'd spent the whole night fretting and wondering whether I should have gone round or done something, even though I know whatever I do won't make any difference. Mum pushed her own self-destruct button long ago. I can't be responsible for that, or her. I'd ring her later to check that she hadn't done anything stupid and leave it at that.

'So go on, then,' Charlie said, stirring his coffee. 'Give me the lowdown. Did Sarah speak to you?'

I pulled a face as I sipped my drink.

'She wasn't at all happy to see me,' I said, 'but at least it wasn't pistols at dawn.'

'See, I told you,' said Charlie. 'I knew you should have gone.'

'Thank you, Charlie the oracle,' I said. 'No, it was fine. Doris was great. Beth's prepared to put up with me. Sarah will probably never forgive me as long as I live, but hey, two out of three ain't bad.'

'You never know,' said Charlie, 'she might come round eventually. Never say die and all that.'

'I doubt it,' I said. 'Sarah's stubborn as hell, and she has every right to hate me. But so long as I'm seeing Doris and Beth again, I think I can live.'

'Hmmphh,' Charlie snorted. He knows me far too well and was the only person I'd ever confided in about how much I missed my old friends. Everyone else I knew thought I was a hard nut who existed in an isolated bubble. But then that was an image I'd gone to great lengths to perfect. I shouldn't have listened to Simon & Garfunkel so much when I was young. A rock mightn't feel any pain, but it doesn't feel much joy either.

Footsteps on the stairs proclaimed the arrival of Gemma, the PR girl, and soon we were caught up in a whirl of activity, as I got everything ready for the model to arrive. Chloe Andrews was fashionably late of course, which meant I had less time to get her ready and Charlie had less time to shoot, but we'd worked together long enough, and I was familiar enough with the stylist, Kerry, for things to go reasonably smoothly, but it was pretty full on for the best part of the day. It got to five thirty and I realized I hadn't rung Mum. I was going to ring her on the way out but then Charlie and Kerry prevailed on me to come to the pub with them, and I thought, it's Friday, why the hell not? When Charlie went home to Nadia, Kerry and I made a bit of a session of it.

It was gone midnight when I stumbled in. The answer-phone was flashing. There were several messages on it, with an increasing level of panic in them.

'If you get this, it's your Auntie Nora. Your mum's had a turn and she's in hospital.' Oh shit.

'Caroline, where are you? I've left at least three messages on your mobile. Ring me now.' Beep.

'Auntie Nora again. Best you ring the hospital direct.' Beep.

90

'When you get this, come straight away.'

Shit, shit, shit. I knew I should have rung Mum. I knew I should have gone to see her. Guilt and anger collided in a vicious gut-twisting punch in my stomach. My heart was pounding, and my head was thumping, I felt so bloody angry that Mum could do this to me again, and yet at the same time make me feel like I was somehow responsible.

I rang the number of the ward that Auntie Nora had given me. A softly spoken nurse answered the phone.

'Yes, Mrs Riley is here. You're her daughter? We've been trying to get hold of you.'

'I'm sorry,' I said tersely. 'I've only just got the messages. How is my mother?'

I was expecting her to say 'raving' or 'wasting our time' or any of the usual responses I got when Mum ended up in hospital, as she did periodically.

'I'm afraid your mother is very poorly,' was the response. 'I think it's best that you come right away.'

My heart went into freefall. When Auntie Nora's husband, Paddy, had gone into hospital when I was eighteen, they kept saying he was 'poorly'. He was dead in three days. What if 'poorly' was nurse code for 'on death row'? But Mum couldn't *die*. That was ridiculous. She had spent the best part of my life lurching from crisis to crisis of her own making, but somehow she always pulled through. The thought of her not being here at all was too weird to contemplate.

All the way to the hospital, I kept telling myself I was imagining things. It was late, I'd had a busy day, I was feeling guilty for not having taken Mum more seriously the night before, everything was going to be fine.

Everything is going to be fine. That had been the mantra

of my childhood, to get through the days and the weeks and the years till I could grow up and escape her. I didn't believe it then and I didn't believe it now. After all, despite my best efforts I'd never managed to escape her entirely.

I sat staring out of the cab window as the dark streets of London fled away from me. I had thought to escape my home and the little family I had by living a bright, shining life in the city, and yet, here I was again, coming back to the place I knew best. Eventually the taxi driver deposited me outside A & E at St Mary's, the hospital I'd been to so many times before. I went in and went hesitantly to the desk. I knew the form. I'd done this often enough, but I always felt ill at ease – as if the fact that Mum was here, again, somehow pronounced badly on me as a daughter. Maybe if I were a better daughter . . .

'I believe . . . I think my mother's here – Mrs Patricia Riley?' I said.

The woman consulted her notes.

'Yes, let's see. She was brought in with a head trauma. They've stabilized her and she's been transferred to ICU.'

She gave me directions and I wandered through the vast labyrinth of the hospital in a daze. It was mainly empty and silent, and I walked down echoing corridors which looked suited more to a horror film than anything else. I kept expecting Jack Nicholson to leap out and tell me 'Daddy's home' any minute.

Eventually I found my way to the right place. Auntie Nora was hovering outside. She looked furious.

'Where have you been?' she hissed. 'I've been ringing you all evening.'

'I'm sorry,' I said. 'I was out and had my phone switched off. What the hell happened?'

'Your mother had one of her little "episodes",' said Auntie Nora. One of the things I hate most about my family is the way no one will ever talk straight about Mum's problems.

'You mean she was drunk,' I said baldly.

'Don't talk about your mother like that,' said Auntie Nora, 'it's disrespectful.'

I could have argued with her, but I was too tired and frantic.

'So what happened?'

'It seems she had a fall,' said Auntie Nora.

'She didn't ring you, then?' I said.

A flash of something – guilt? – whipped across Auntie Nora's face.

'No, unfortunately, she didn't. I went to see her this afternoon, and couldn't get in. I rang and there was no answer, so I called an ambulance. They broke into her house and found her at the bottom of the stairs.'

Oh god. How long had she been lying there? I should have gone round. I *should* have gone round.

'Can I see her?' I said.

'The doctors were with her a minute ago,' said Auntie Nora. 'We'd better wait and see what they say.'

We sat waiting for interminable minutes while the second hand passed slowly on the clock, and we drank indifferent coffee from Styrofoam cups. I thought with a pang how only that morning I'd been laughing over coffee with Charlie. Had Mum already been lying there and I hadn't known? Would it have made any difference to her if I had done?

Eventually a crumpled-looking doctor came out. He looked about fifteen, but I guess he must have been a registrar or something because the nurses all seemed to be showing him due deference.

'Are you Mrs Riley's family?' he asked.

'I'm her daughter and this is her sister,' I said. 'How is she?'

'It's not looking good, I'm afraid,' the doctor said. 'She's sustained a nasty head injury, and we suspect trauma to the brain. She's still unconscious, but even if she does come round, the likelihood is that she'll be brain damaged. I think you have to prepare yourself for the worst.'

I was stunned. I couldn't take it in. Mum was only sixty-two. She couldn't possibly be about to die on me.

'Can we see her now?' I asked.

'I think it's better if you take it one at a time,' he said. 'She shouldn't be disturbed.'

'I'll go and get us another coffee,' said Auntie Nora in a rare and uncharacteristic moment of thoughtfulness. She patted me on the arm and left me to my own devices. In anyone else, I might have detected a snivel, but Auntie Nora wasn't the snivelling kind.

I went into the side room where Mum lay wired up to machines. A livid purple and yellow bruise spread from her forehead down her face. She looked like she'd been beaten up.

'Oh, Mum,' I said, any feelings of anger and guilt dissipating instantly into pity and regret. Even now my relationship with her was so bloody complicated. I wanted to hate her, and somehow seeing her lying there, so pitifully pathetic, I couldn't. I sat down beside her and took her hand.

'Hang on in there,' I said. 'You have to get better. We need you to get better.'

Somewhere deep inside of me a little flame of hope had insisted on burning brightly. Maybe this would be the incident that persuaded Mum to stop drinking – if she got through it of course. I suppressed the thought that the time she'd set fire to her flat, the times she'd hit me, the time she broke her leg while on a bender, none of those things had ever done the trick, because I so wanted to believe it was going to be different.

'I'm sorry, Mum,' I said. 'I should have been there last night. I know I've let you down. But you have to believe me, I wanted to be a good daughter to you.'

Mum stirred suddenly and opened her eyes and stared at me in a slightly unfocused way.

'Caroline?' she said. 'Is that you?'

'I'm here, Mum.' I gripped her hand tightly and squeezed it hard, tears pricking my eyes. 'You've had a nasty fall, but everything's going to be fine, you'll see.'

She mumbled something that sounded like 'ruined everything' but I couldn't be sure.

She shut her eyes again, as if the effort had been too much for her.

'Don't say that,' I said, the tears spilling over now. 'Please don't say that.'

She opened her eyes briefly to give me a look filled with such hatred that I felt quite shaken.

'Mum,' I said urgently, 'say something, please.'

I don't know what I wanted, approval perhaps? But I didn't get it. Mum didn't say anything more and gradually her breathing slowed, till it was barely discernible. Suddenly a beeping from one of the monitors caused the staff to spring into action. Within sections a crash team were in the room, and I was being ushered out. No one seemed to be shouting or rushing, they all moved in an unhurried but focused manner, and I found myself outside the room in moments. It was all over in a few brutal seconds. I was shocked at the speed of it. Auntie Nora returned with her cups of coffee to find me leaning against a wall crying as I had never cried before. My mother had died hating me. Now I really was alone in the world.

Caz

Summer 1997

It seemed appropriate that for weeks the news had been full of Diana and Dodi's affair on the Med. The fairytale had ended, the image of fairytale princesses was getting daily more tarnished and since my spectacular error of judgement in Las Vegas, I'd sworn off men. Charlie had been remarkably forgiving about the whole thing and we'd somehow managed to stay friends. I knew for me the promise of a happy-ever-after wasn't coming anytime soon.

And then, there he was, in a bar in Soho. I hadn't seen Steve on his own for months. He was, after all, just about to get married to my best friend. But once again, there was that connection, and unlike last time, he didn't attempt to brush away my advances.

I knew even as I sat down next to him that I was doing the wrong thing. But a combination of anger at him for not choosing me – let him see what he was missing! – and a sort of self-hatred which has always been my fatal flaw, led me not to care. Besides. He was here with me. Not with her. I knew it was wrong to want him as much as I did. But I had wanted him from the first time we met. And he didn't want me. They never did. I was the one they chose

97

for a quick shag, Sarah was the one they chose for the long term. And this time, he'd really made it clear he was playing the long game. This time, I'd lost him for good.

Except. Here he was, nearly married, in a bar with me. Playing footsie under the table, looking at me with lascivious eyes, accidentally touching my hand when there was no need.

I could lie and say I was so drunk I didn't know what I was doing. I could pretend that it 'just happened' like they always say in the problem pages. But it wouldn't be true. These things don't 'just happen'. You have to lose control of the bit of you that's screaming that this is so *so* wrong, you have to let go of your moral compass and go on a journey into a morass of grubby decisions that you'll later regret. You have to choose all that. It doesn't *just happen*.

Even at the moment I let him into my flat, I could have ended it then, after the coffee, before we'd gone too far. But I was drunk on power and lust and the feeling I'd won for once. Besides, I wanted to know what he was like, this golden boy, whom I'd adored for so long.

And once we'd kissed and cuddled and got down and dirty, there was a point, a moment when I could have said no, this is wrong, we mustn't go any further, but I didn't. I was carried on a wave of passion into a world where there were no commitments, and I didn't betray the people I loved, and the man I was with loved me for myself, not for the undoubted quick bit of fun I undoubtedly was.

It was only in the morning, when I woke up, and saw him already dressed, already distancing himself from me, that I felt ashamed. I didn't know how I was ever going to face her again. I didn't know how I was ever going to face myself. I felt wrong and dirty and so very, very bad. A sudden vision of my mother, in her worst vengeful mode, swam before my eyes. 'You're a dirty little hoor,' she hissed in my ear. 'I always knew you'd turn out no good.' I turned my face to the wall and wept.

Part Two

For Better, for Worse

Sarah

Summer 1997

'Where is she?' I stood in my bridal finery in the changing room of Wedding Belles bridal shop, while Jeanette, the snooty manager who made me feel about five years old, tacked and adjusted my dress for its final fitting. Beth and Dorrie were ready to try on their bridesmaids' dresses but there was no sign of Caz. She was over an hour late and there was no answer from her flat. Even her newly acquired mobile phone appeared to be switched off.

I was beginning to get really fed up with Caz. She could barely bring herself to show any interest in my wedding, apart from teasing me about becoming domesticated and boring. I knew weddings weren't her thing, but I was hurt by her lack of interest. And she never had a good word to say about Steve. I wished she could get off my back and just be happy for me. Now it appeared she couldn't even be bothered to turn up on time for my fitting.

'You're going to look fabulous, girl,' beamed Dorrie, as usual bringing a positive note to the proceedings. And I have to admit, looking at myself in the mirror, I really liked what I saw. The dress was a classically elegant off the shoulder number, with a trimmed-in waist and flowing gown. The diamante beading, which Jeanette had lovingly sewn into the bodice, sparkled and shimmered when I walked and the satin skirt with its lace trimming just looked and felt fabulous. My tiara, my 'something borrowed' from my grandmother, allegedly had real pearls (I thought they were more likely fake myself but they looked the part), and my veil too had the same diamante beading.

'That is very nearly right,' said Jeanette, loosening some material around my waistline, 'though I'm not usually letting out dresses at this stage.'

I wanted to thump her. I had tried desperately hard to lose weight prior to the wedding, but a combination of long shifts and too much overtime to help save money had led me into bad eating habits. I had a month to shift the excess that I'd put on. I didn't think I was going to manage it. Steve's attitude didn't help either, he'd made me painfully aware that I was carrying a little too much weight and it was making me feel insecure. Steve was so gorgeous he could have anyone, and though he'd chosen me, there was always a small part of me that doubted that choice, and wondered if he'd stay the distance.

'Do you think I look too fat?' I said in panic, when Jeanette left the room to fetch more pins. My stomach suddenly appeared to me to look as if I was four months gone.

'Don't be daft,' said Dorrie. 'Ignore her. You look womanly, curvaceous, sexy. Steve's not going to know what's hit him.'

'Are you sure?' I said. I was still a size twelve, just, but as I was more used to being size ten, I felt like a heffalump.

'Absolutely,' said Beth, as usual being quietly observant in the corner. 'You look great.'

'Thanks girls,' I said. I couldn't put my finger on why

I felt so wobbly and uncertain. But Caz's non-appearance had unnerved me, and I hadn't spoken to Steve since yesterday lunchtime. I'd wanted to have a quiet night in with him the previous night, but he'd muttered something about having a pre stag with some of his work colleagues and stayed out in town. If I knew Steve, he'd be fit for nothing till after lunch and even less likely to show any interest in wedding plans. We'd booked to go and see the caterers at the hotel this afternoon to go over the menu and Steve was meant to be organizing the printing of the order of service, but didn't seem to have even started on that.

My stomach shrank into a familiar ball of anxiety. Maybe he was having second thoughts? Perhaps Steve didn't really want to get married after all. Was it right to feel this insecure about the man I was marrying? I know most brides get cold feet, but the way things were going at the moment, mine were like blocks of ice. The only thing I was sure of was that I loved Steve and I wanted to marry him. He said he loved me, but he'd been cagey and elusive of late and it was making me feel agitated.

'You really think so?' I said, biting my lip and trying not to let either of my friends see the way I was feeling.

'We really do,' said Beth.

'You've not got last-minute jitters, have you?' said Dorrie, poking me in the arm.

'I have a bit,' I said.

'That's only natural,' said Beth. 'I'm sure it happens to everyone.' She looked a little wistful. Despite making a bit more effort with her appearance, Beth still hadn't met her Mr Right, and since Andy the bastard, there was an air of victimhood about her that left men wary. I longed to tell her to lighten up but Beth could be so sensitive I didn't want to upset her.

'It won't happen to me,' declared Dorrie. 'I know I've met the man of my dreams already. And I won't have any doubts about marrying him ever.'

'Has Yakult Man asked you yet?' I said. Dorrie had been seeing Darren for the last six months and seemed blissfully happy.

'Not exactly,' said Dorrie, 'but we're made for each other. It's only a matter of time.'

Bless her. How can anyone be that blindly romantic and idealistic? But Dorrie wouldn't be Dorrie if she wasn't.

Jeanette came back to finish tacking and re-tacking, before finally declaring herself satisfied. Then she turned to me and said, 'If your other bridesmaid isn't here, we really had better get on with the fitting, I have another appointment at twelve.'

'I'll try Caz again,' said Dorrie, diplomatically, as I went to get out of my dress. I was furious.

Still finding no answer, I resigned myself to letting the other two get changed and letting Caz go shift for herself.

I'd chosen halterneck dresses of deep-red silk for my brides-maids. It complemented their dark hair, and all three were going to look stunning. Dorrie's current Sarah Jessica Parker-style hair was going to look lovely pulled up away from her face with a few curls dangling down, and now Beth had cut her hair into a neater style, I felt there was something I could do to make her look glamorous on the day. Caz's sharp features were perfectly framed by a Linda Evangelista-type bob, and while I longed for her to have a softer look, she did look great in the dress on the previous time she'd tried it on.

Eventually we were done.

'God I'm starving,' declared Dorrie. 'Pizza Hut anyone?'

Our teens had been dominated by visits to the Pizza Hut on the High Street, which was just a couple of doors down from Wedding Belles.

'Oh, go on then,' I said. 'I still have a soft spot for their salad bar.'

We were making our way up the High Street towards Pizza Hut, when I saw her: Caz was running towards us in a blind panic.

'Sarah,' she said, when she reached us, 'I'm really sorry.'

'Rough night was it?' Dorrie whistled. 'Who's the lucky man?'

Caz looked truly dreadful. Her face was pale and her dark circled eyes looked as if they might have been crying. She had obviously thrown on any old clothes that had come to hand, and hadn't even done her make-up.

'No one,' said Caz, but she didn't catch my eye when she said it. 'Just too much to drink. Sorry, Sarah, I didn't mean to miss the fitting but I only just woke up.'

'Well you're here now,' I said, with a sigh. 'Come on and have a pizza with us.'

'No, I don't think that's a good idea.' Caz looked really uncomfortable. 'I'm not feeling that great, and well, the thing is, I've got something to tell you . . .'

Suddenly my heart turned to ice. I thought back to last night when I'd tried to ring Steve late at night and there was no answer from his flat. Surely she couldn't have been – she wouldn't have, would she?

'Oh?' I tried to keep my voice calm and natural. I was being ridiculous. I knew Caz had liked Steve before I got together with him, but nothing was going on between them. I'd have known.

'It's just . . . sorry, Sarah. You know weddings aren't my thing. I just don't think I can be your bridesmaid after all.'

This was so unexpected, I nearly laughed with relief. But then I felt angry again. How dare she let me down like this at nearly the last moment?

'What the fuck?' I said. 'You can't just do this to me. What about the dress? It's already paid for.'

'I'll pay for the sodding dress,' said Caz. 'I promise I will. I'm sorry, I just can't do it.'

With that she turned round and strode away, leaving the three of us open-mouthed standing on the street.

Chapter Nine

Sarah

I'd just come in from taking the kids to their Saturday morning football lessons. Our tiny hall seemed to be full of fighting children – amazing that two small boys can take up so much space – dropping bags on the floor, causing the usual chaos. They were hungry, and tired. So was I. I'd not been sleeping much recently and today, ringing Steve, who was out at a corporate works do and getting Kirsty smarming at me down the phone had sent my self-esteem plummeting. I'd lost my appetite at lunchtime, but now I felt bizarrely hungry. Steve and I had been skirting around the issue of Kirsty for days now. We had to deal with it eventually. But was I ready to go that far?

The phone rang and Sam picked it up.

'Hello Auntie Beth,' he said. 'I've just swum fifty metres. And William is a poo head.'

'Auntie Beth doesn't need to hear that,' I said laughing. 'Come on, hand it over, scamp.'

'I'm hungry,' wailed William.

'Tea in five minutes,' I promised, taking the phone from Sam. 'Hi, madhouse here, what can I do for you, Beth?'

'Sorry, is this a bad moment?' Beth sounded anxious and strained.

'It's always a bad moment,' I said. *Particularly now*, I thought, but added, 'What's up?'

'I just thought you ought to know,' said Beth.

'Know what?' I was only half paying attention as I yanked William away from the piece of wallpaper he was peeling off.

'Dorrie just rang,' said Beth. 'She spent last night in hospital with Woody—'

'Oh no,' I said. 'Is Woody OK?'

'I think he is now,' said Beth, 'some kind of vomiting bug, but the point is she met Caz there. The thing is, Caz's mum died last night. They think it was heart failure, but . . .'

'We always said the drink would kill her,' I said bluntly. 'Well if you ask me, I'm surprised she lasted this long.'

'Don't be like that,' said Beth. 'I know she was difficult, but she was Caz's mum.'

Caz's mum. She had to be the most vicious spiteful woman on the planet. I once had the misfortune to spend a summer working with her in Marks & Spencer's. No one was immune from her bitter tongue, not even her daughter's best friend. Mind you. I heard how she spoke to Caz, so maybe that was no great surprise. Mum always said it was because Caz's dad had left her with a baby, but then Dad would snort and say he wasn't surprised he left, so who knows, maybe she was always a bitter old bag.

What I did know was that Caz had had the most miserable of upbringings. Though she didn't talk about it much, it was clear as we grew older that her mum drank too much and took it out on her daughter. No wonder Caz was always on the offensive. Of all of us, she found Dorrie's house the most comforting. It must have seemed like a haven from her real life. I had a sudden flashback to the angry, desperate little girl I'd first befriended in reception. Somehow I knew underneath that hard exterior there was a softer Caz just longing for the opportunity to be loved, and to love back. I had a sudden pang of longing for the friendship we'd had and lost. I knew Caz didn't get on with her mum but apart from an aunt, she didn't have any other family. Caz had never bothered to look for her dad, reckoning that if he'd wanted anything to do with her, he'd have come looking by now.

'Yes, sorry,' I said. 'Poor Caz. Have you spoken to her?'

'I sent her a text,' said Beth. 'I didn't know what to say. It's been so long since we've really seen her, I don't know if she even cared that much about her mum.'

'I think what Caz feels about her mum is far more complicated than any of us can understand,' I said. I took a deep breath. Because Caz had no family to speak of, she often said we were better than family. 'Do you think she'd speak to me?'

'I don't know,' said Beth, 'but I think she might. She seemed pretty sorry about everything when we met.'

'When did you meet Caz?' I was surprised. Beth hadn't mentioned seeing her.

'A couple of weeks ago,' said Beth. 'Just after we went to Euro Disney. I just felt I'd like to make things up with her. I can understand you wouldn't feel like that.'

I thought about Steve, who was probably going to ring again tonight saying he was going to be working late, when no doubt he'd be with Kirsty. If it hadn't been Caz, it would have been someone else. For the first time I wondered if it had really all been her fault.

'Well, maybe I won't ever make things up with her,' I said, 'but I feel I should at least acknowledge what's happened.'

'I'm hungry!' William came tugging my legs.

'Damn, have to go,' I said. 'Can you text me Caz's number?'

'Sure thing,' said Beth.

I put the phone down and took William into the kitchen. No time to think about Caz now. Children needed feeding, and I needed to not let them see how exasperated I was with their dad when he did ring to say he was staying longer at work.

It was nine o'clock before I eventually sat down with a glass of wine. Apart from Joe, who had called in at teatime, to let me know he'd got tickets to take the boys to see Arsenal, I had barely seen another adult all day. I hated the feeling of emptiness and loneliness that came over me at this time of the evening. I shouldn't feel so lacking in companion-ship, but I was. Steve hadn't even bothered to ring, just texted to say he'd be late, presumably the corporate do had spread into a drinking session in town. Part of me was relieved. If he wasn't here, we couldn't talk about anything. I knew I was being an ostrich about things, but even though I could feel the inevitable coming – somehow this business with Kirsty seemed much more serious than anyone else that Steve had been involved with – I didn't want to face up to the reality. Diving into domestic chores in all their mind-numbingly boring comfort, was as good a way as any to avoid thinking about things.

I flopped in the sofa and switched on the TV. There was nothing much on, so I turned the TV off and went to the table in the hall where I'd scribbled down Caz's number on a notepad. I wasn't sure she'd want to hear from me. I wasn't even sure I wanted to ring her. But I thought about my parents, fortunately still hale and hearty in their early seventies, and my two lovely brothers, who didn't live nearby but were in regular contact. None of them difficult, all of them loving. I couldn't conceive the kind of life Caz had led with her mum, but I did know that however much Caz might claim to hate her, she had always longed for things to be different. And it was for that reason, and for the memory of the friendship we'd once had, that I picked up the phone.

My hand was shaking as I dialled her number. She might be really angry and think I was interfering. Perhaps I *was* interfering – maybe it was too late for us.

'Hello,' Caz answered the phone. She sounded hesitant and a bit subdued, not at all like her normal confident self.

'Caz, it's me, Sarah,' I said. 'I'm sorry if I've rung at a bad time, but Beth told me what happened with your mum, and I just wanted to say how sorry I am.'

There was an agonising pause – oh my god, was Caz actually crying?

'Caz, are you OK? I'm sorry, I probably shouldn't have rung,' I said.

'No, no, you're fine,' Caz said, sniffing. 'It's just all been a bit of a shock, and well, I've never been good at dealing with kindness. And I know I don't deserve it from you.'

That wasn't the reaction I was expecting at all. I didn't know what to say. 'Is there anything I can do?' I finally said.

'Get me away from Auntie Nora,' said Caz, a little of the old feistiness returning. 'She's driving me demented. Thinks I can't do anything. And there's so much to do.'

'Could you hook up for coffee on Monday? I can be free when Sam's at school and Will's at nursery.' Actually I was free most days. There was housework to do, certainly, but Steve insisted we had a cleaner, as he thought it demeaning for me to do it. He also thought it demeaning for me to go back to work, so most of the time I felt in this kind of useless limbo, of feeling I should be a lady who lunches, when that is so not me. How was it that I had been persuaded to quit nursing, a job I loved, so readily? Not for the first time, it occurred to me that I had let Steve control far too much of my life.

'I'm not sure I can do Monday during the day,' said Caz. 'We have to go to the funeral parlour and I need to sort out the flowers, but I could get away in the evening. Any chance you could meet me in a pub somewhere?'

I took a deep breath. Steve was always difficult when it came to me having evenings out with the girls at the best of times, I could imagine what he'd say when he discovered I was seeing Caz for the evening. I looked at the clock, nearly 9.30 and no sign of him. Bugger Steve. I'd get a babysitter if necessary. And if he didn't like it, tough.

'Yes, that would be great,' I said. 'When and where?'

Caz, it transpired, was staying with her Auntie Nora, who lived in a flat above an electrical shop on the High Street, while they sorted out funeral arrangements. Like Dorrie, I'd come back to live in Northfields after I got pregnant. Steve had bitched about it being away from London, but agreed with me that his city flat wasn't the best place to bring up a child. Luckily he'd had a huge bonus that year, and we were able to retain both the flat, which Steve rented out to various colleagues, as well as put down a deposit on our new house, which was round the corner from my parents, fifteen minutes from the High Street.

So it was a short walk to meet Caz in the Green Man, another of the haunts of our youth, though it was a far cry from the days when we'd snuck in there and tried to get served at the bar. I'd suggested to Beth she join us too, just in case it got awkward, but she mumbled something about feeling under the weather, so I left it. I wondered if she was pregnant. She'd never said anything about babies, but the look in her eye sometimes when she looked at Dorrie with Woody made me rather think she'd like one.

'Couldn't face staying at Mum's,' Caz explained, when we finally met up. 'It's where she – well, anyway. Wussy of me I know, but then I figured Auntie N probably needs the company, even if we do drive each other insane.'

'What happened?' I said. It was weird sitting here with Caz. It wasn't as though the past was erased, but in the light of her mum's death, I was certainly gaining a new perspective on it.

'She – well, oh god, this is so awful.' Caz's bottom lip trembled, and her eyes filled with tears. 'It's all my fault, you see.'

'What, all your fault that she's spent the last thirty years drinking herself into a coma? Yeah, right,' I said. 'Come on Caz, can't you see? She chose her lifestyle, you didn't do that to her.'

'But I did,' said Caz. 'She rang me the other night. I knew she was pissed, and so I ignored her. I've been going over it again and again since. If only I'd gone round, maybe she wouldn't have fallen, and maybe she'd still be here.'

'And maybe the moon is made of cheese,' I said. 'Come on, how many times have you rushed round there in the middle of the night for a false alarm? She chose to live like that. You didn't make her.'

'It's not just that,' said Caz, 'I . . . god, I don't know even how to say this. But the last words she said. Do you know what they were?'

'What?'

'She told me I'd ruined her life. Can you imagine your mum saying that to you?'

'Oh, Caz.' Instinctively I gave her a hug. Whatever she'd done to me, she didn't deserve this. 'Are you sure that's what she said? Maybe you misheard her.'

'Well, she did mumble it,' said Caz, 'so I can't be sure, but I can be sure of the look in her eye. She hated me. My own mother hated me.'

'I'm sure she didn't,' I said. 'For heaven's sake, your mum was an alcoholic, and very mixed up and twisted. It was an evil thing to say and do to you. But then she always was a bit of a witch.'

Caz smiled a little through her tears. 'She was, wasn't she?'

'Do you remember the time we came round to yours after school, and she came home from work and threw us all out and made Beth cry?' I said. 'Other mums never did that. Yours was . . . well, whatever her problems were, they weren't of your making.'

'Do you really think so?' said Caz, shivering. 'I can't get the look of hatred out of my mind.'

'Yes, I do,' I said. 'Come on, let's drown our sorrows and try and forget all about her.'

'So what sorrows are you trying to drown?' Caz asked as I came back from the bar. I noticed she'd been to the loos to sort herself out. She came back immaculately made up, the mask back on. You had to hand it to Caz, she was a control freak extraordinaire.

I made a face. I couldn't quite bring myself to tell Caz

116

what was going on at home. 'Oh, nothing much,' I said. 'Just fed up with domesticity. The children are great, they really are, but sometimes I really miss working.'

'Well you've only yourself to blame,' said Caz. 'That's why I've always steered clear of settling down. Babies seem like far too much hard work for me.'

There was an awkward pause, neither of us wanting to go into the reasons for Caz's lack of domesticity.

'Can't you go back to work?' said Caz. 'That might make you feel better.'

'I have thought about it,' I admitted. 'But it's not that easy finding a part-time job which fits in with the kids. Besides, I've lost my nerve a bit.'

'You?' Caz looked incredulous. 'But you were always the together one, why on earth have you lost your nerve?'

'It's called staying at home with small children,' I said. 'It tends to make you forget your normal skills set. I'm not sure I'd be any good at my job now. It's been six years, suppose I can't hack it?'

'You'll never know till you try,' said Caz. 'What does Steve think?'

Another frisson. The first time his name had been mentioned.

'I haven't told him yet,' I said (not that he'd probably care if I did).

'Oh,' said Caz. 'Sarah, everything is all right, isn't it?'

'Yes, fine,' I said. 'Everything's just fine, why wouldn't it be?'

'No reason,' said Caz. 'I just hope you're happy.'

I resisted the urge to retort that it was none of her business whether I was happy or not, and sipped my drink, before lying, 'Of course I'm happy. I've got two wonderful

117

children, a lovely house and a gorgeous husband. I'm sure most people would envy me.'

'Good,' said Caz, 'I'm glad.'

The conversation turned to other matters and I breathed a sigh of relief. I was only just admitting to myself what a catastrophic mistake my marriage had been. Caz was the last person I wanted to know the truth. Because then I'd have to face up to the fact that she had been right all along.

Chapter Ten

Beth

'Mrs Davies, you can come through now,' a kind-looking nurse ushered me into a room, with a single bed and a curtain round it. She handed me a gown and told me to get undressed. I swallowed nervously. I wasn't sure I was ready for this. Even after being poked about as much as I had been in the last two years, I still had a prudish hatred of anything happening in that region. I blamed my mother, a wonderful woman in many ways, but so devout she had insisted tampons were the work of the devil. Matt had really wanted to come with me today, but I wanted to come alone. I couldn't bear the thought of him near me when something so private and sensitive was going on. I sensed his puzzlement, but memories of before kept flooding through me and though I knew this would be different, I just wanted to do this on my own.

Once changed, I lay on the bed, feeling slightly sick. I'd been taking hormonal injections since the weekend – Sarah had rung to ask me to go for a drink with her and Caz, but I'd said no, not wanting to jinx things – and this was it, the moment when it had been decided that my eggs were mature enough to collect. But the procedure itself wasn't pleasant. Even though I was going to be under sedation, the thought of having a needle shoved up inside me was not a pleasant one. Matt had insisted he at least came to collect me and as I lay there waiting nervously for the doctor to come in, I realized that I did want him there after all, but now it was too late.

The doctor smiled and inserted a cannula into my hand before injecting me with a sedative. It made me feel woozy and comfortable and for the first time since I'd come into the room I felt relaxed and easy. I started gabbling to the nurse who smiled at me and took my hand.

'Do you think it will work?' I said. 'It has to work, we have to have a baby.'

The nurse smiled reassuringly. 'I'm sure everything will be just fine.'

I tried not to wince as the doctor inserted the needle inside me. I had a sudden flashback to another room like this, a long time ago, when I had felt alone and unloved, and panic surged through me. Suppose this all went wrong? My mother would say that IVF wasn't natural. Maybe I would never get my baby.

'Breathe deeply, in and out,' the nurse said, squeezing my hand. She could see the distress in my eyes, and hear the panic in my voice, as I asked over and over again if it would be all right.

'Everything will be fine,' she kept saying, 'you'll see.'

But afterwards when it was over, and I sat waiting for Matt to pick me up, I felt numb and bruised. I had a pain in my stomach similar to period pain, and felt like I was going to throw up. Matt came and found me, looking shell shocked and dazed. He took me in his arms and held me tight.

'Is it worth it?' I said as I lay against him. 'Do you think it's worth it?'

'I'm sure it is,' he said, kissing the top of my head. 'Come on, you knew it was going to be tough. You'll feel different when Foetus gets going, you know you will.'

I sat in the car going home in a daze. I wanted him to be right. I wanted this all to be worth the effort, but the dark poisonous side of my soul wouldn't stop sneaking up behind me and telling me that I didn't deserve a baby. And I shivered, wondering how we would cope if the IVF didn't work.

'Beth? Why are you at home? They said at work you were ill. Is everything all right?' Dorrie was on the phone all bubbling, cheerful concern. It was amazing how even her phone presence seemed to fill the room. Dearly as I loved Doris, I always felt diminished in her presence. I was shy anyway, but Doris always made me feel shyer.

'No, I'm fine,' I said, 'just a bad cold.' I sniffed a bit, hoping that she wouldn't find me out for the phony I was. But luckily being Dorrie, she was on to the next thing.

'Oh that's a shame,' she said. 'I was heading into town with Woody to look for an outfit to go away in. I was wondering if you'd like to meet up with me.'

'Sorry, Dorrie,' I said, 'not today. I really do feel lousy.' Which was perfectly true. I felt bruised and battered, and emotionally I had taken a pummelling. Though they had my eggs, which had been unromantically entwined with Matt's sperm in a Petri dish, I was nowhere near convinced this was going to work. We had one chance to get a freebie on the NHS. One chance. That was it. The financial consequences of it not working were too hideous to contemplate. 'Is Sarah about?'

'No, I think she's busy,' said Doris, 'and I can hardly ask Caz at the moment.'

'Have you heard from her?' I felt guilty. I'd sent her a text it was true, but I'd been so caught up in my own stuff, I hadn't followed it up.

'I spoke to her this morning,' said Dorrie. 'Apparently she and Sarah went out for a drink.'

'I know,' I said. 'Sarah asked me to come too. but I couldn't make it. I was pretty stunned I can tell you. How did it go?'

'Sarah said they had a nice time. Well. Maybe not a nice time, given the circumstances, but apparently they're talking again.'

'Wonders will never cease,' I said. That was the last thing I'd expected. I really thought Sarah and Caz were destined never to make up. 'Do we know when the funeral is yet?'

'Next Wednesday,' said Dorrie. 'You going then?'

'Of course.' It had been my first thought when Caz had rung me to tell me about her mum. Even though we'd been distant for so long, I figured she could do with a friend. 'One four all and all four one and all that.' I shoved aside the thought that if my eggs were fertilized properly, Foetus might be taking precedence. I'd cross that bridge when I came to it.

'Good,' said Doris. 'I said I'd go too. Maybe even Sarah will come now.'

'I hope so,' I said. 'Whatever's happened in the past, Caz had a lousy time with her mum and I think she could use her friends right now.'

'Perhaps I'll leave my shopping till after the funeral,' said Doris. 'It seems a bit superficial to be going now.'

'I don't think you should think like that,' I said. 'Just because Caz's mum died, it doesn't mean your wedding has to stop. It's not as if any of us liked her.'

I certainly hadn't. I still shuddered at the memory of her shouting at us all when we went round once after school. She was so wild and angry, and *drunk* at four in the afternoon. So different from my quiet, calm household. I'd always had a soft spot for Caz after that, which I suppose is why I always forgave her in the end.

'True,' said Dorrie. 'It's not the same going on my own though. I know . . .' I could almost hear the wheels of her excited thoughts turning, '. . . let's all go shopping together. When things have calmed down for Caz I mean. Wouldn't that be great?'

'That's a brilliant idea,' I said, wondering if Caz really would think so, and whether I could think up an excuse not to go if I needed more bed rest.

'Great,' said Doris. 'I'll wait till after the funeral and let the others know. It'll be just like old times, you'll see.'

Three days later, I was back at the hospital. This time, Matt had insisted on accompanying me and I had let him. I was too nervous to do this alone. Besides, it was his baby, it didn't seem right to keep him out of things. Like having sex without him or something.

'You OK?' Matt squeezed my hand as we sat in the waiting room, which was filled with other hopeful couples like us. We had a twenty-five per cent chance of the IVF working, which meant that the majority of the people sitting here would be disappointed.

'Think so,' I said. I felt sick, and hollow inside. Suppose it didn't work? Suppose I got pregnant and then lost the baby? This might be one of our few chances to have a family of our own. It felt huge. And yet, for the first time the possibility that Foetus might actually turn into a proper baby seemed real. After today I could actually be pregnant. In nine months' time, I might be a mother. It was such a responsibility. I swallowed hard.

'Are we doing the right thing?' I said. 'Maybe we're not cut out to be parents. That's why we haven't got pregnant yet. Perhaps this is nature's way of telling us it's not for us.'

'Shh,' Matt put his finger to my lips. 'That's your nutty mother talking. I refuse to allow you to entertain ideas like that, so stop it right now.'

'OK,' I said. I sat back and tried to concentrate on the magazine I was reading until we were called in to see the consultant.

'Right,' he said, shaking both our hands, 'do you want to see your babies?'

'Um . . . Matt?' I said, slightly stunned. 'Babies? We only wanted the one.'

'We fertilized twelve of your eggs, and three of them didn't take,' the consultant explained, 'but you can have a look at the ones that have survived through the microscope if you like.'

Matt squeezed my hand. 'I think that would be great, don't you, Beth?'

I wasn't quite sure I wanted to, but allowed myself to be persuaded. We peered curiously down the microscope at the contents of a Petri dish. I don't know what I expected to see. The shape of a baby perhaps? Even though I knew that was ridiculous, I was absurdly disappointed to see a group of four or five cells overlaid on each other – the doctor said there were actually eight but we couldn't see them all. The important thing was that they were dividing, and thus able to be put back inside me.

Matt was more excited than I was. 'Wow,' he kept saying, 'there's Foetus. Isn't it fantastic?' He grinned at me and squeezed my hand. 'I just can't get over seeing our baby at the beginning like this, it's such a privilege.'

I knew what he meant, but I was feeling cautious too. Foetus becoming a reality relied on those cells multiplying inside me, it seemed an absurdly hopeful project to me. So much could still go wrong.

'Right, shall we get started then?' said the consultant.

I swallowed hard. It was now or never. Once the cells were injected into me, we'd have a nerve-racking two-week wait to find out if I was pregnant or not. Suddenly I wasn't sure I could cope with the stress of it all. But Matt steadied me, smiling encouragement as I was sedated once more, my feet hoiked up in stirrups (why is everything relating to having babies so utterly, utterly humiliating?), feeling naked and exposed while the doctor inserted the eggs.

It was awkward and embarrassing – even more so because Matt was there – and a little uncomfortable, but it was over much quicker than I'd thought.

'Right, that's it.' The doctor took off his plastic gloves with an energetic ping. 'That's you done. Baby or babies Davies now in place. It's up to them now. Make sure you rest and don't do anything stressful or energetic for the next couple of weeks. We'll give you a pregnancy test and you can let us know the result in a fortnight.'

'Does that mean she shouldn't be going to any funerals?' said Matt pointedly.

He'd been really anxious about it ever since he'd heard that I was determined to go.

'I wouldn't advise you to do anything stressful,' said the doctor, 'but so long as you're careful it should be OK. Take it as easy as you can. Your babies need all the help they can get.'

I looked at Matt and he looked at me. I could see the same mixture of anxiety and hope in his eyes as I knew were in mine. Foetus actually existed inside me. And there was nothing either of us could do to make it a reality. Like the doctor said, it was up to Foetus now.

Chapter Eleven

Caz

I sat in the front row of the church staring resolutely ahead. Despite Auntie Nora's disapproval, I'd opted not to follow the coffin as family custom dictated. I knew most of the family wouldn't turn up. Mum had managed to alienate nearly all of her many siblings by one means or another. It took some doing to stop the Riley clan from attending a family funeral, but Mum had pulled it off.

I heard a kerfuffle at the back of the church and glanced around. Despite my nerves and queasy stomach I nearly laughed out loud. Sarah, Doris and Beth were marching in led, of course, by Doris: Sarah sporting plaits, Dorrie a blond wig, and Beth a curly black wig. Oh my god, they knew that would lift my spirits. At school we'd always called ourselves the Four Marys after the comic strip in *Bunty*, and now they'd turned up dressed as them for my mum's funeral. After feeling so long alienated from them, I was touched that they remembered our early bond. I stifled a giggle as Doris winked broadly at me. Trust her to come up with that idea.

'Shh!' Auntie Nora turned and glared at my friends as they rustled their way in at the back.

I turned to face the front once more, having just clocked Charlie sitting alone in one of the back pews. I hadn't been at all sure whether he would come, and though he'd been a tower of strength since I'd turned up semi-hysterical on his doorstep the day after Mum died, his girlfriend, Nadia, clearly hadn't liked it. So I'd not asked him directly to the funeral. It gave me a warm fuzzy feeling to think he'd come anyway.

The organ started to play 'Abide With Me'. I hated it. Such a gloomy, gloomy tune, but it had been one of Mum's favourites. She always did favour the dark side of Catholicism. It was all about hellfire, damnation and suffering for Mum. She didn't appear to have much time for a forgiving kind of Redeemer. No wonder I was fucked up.

I didn't watch the coffin as it made its way down the aisle. I stared instead at the altar, so familiar to me from childhood. The light shining through the stained-glass window of the paschal lamb casting colourful shadows on the huge cross that hung above the altar. That cross had terrified me as a child, the statue of Jesus had seemed so lifelike, the crown of thorns, the nails through his hands and feet, had seemed so real to me, I felt like he was suffering up there for me. For, as Mum was always reminding me, He'd died for my many sins.

Now the moment I'd been dreading all week came to pass, as the undertakers solemnly placed the coffin in front of the altar, bowed their heads and left. How could Mum really be in there? How was it possible that someone so vicious and spiteful and hideously alive, could actually die? I'd been on the receiving end of her bitterness all my life, it had shaped and blighted me, and now it was gone. And there was no way I could ever put it right. An overwhelming sense of loss and rage came over me, a wave of grief so strong I wasn't sure I could withstand it. I wasn't just mourning the mother I'd lost, but the one I'd never had, and the life I surely deserved to have had.

The service passed in a blur, and I barely took notice of what was happening. All too soon it was time for the sermon. Another thing I'd been dreading. What could Father Miserecordie (or Misery Guts as Mum insisted on calling him) say about my mother that could possibly show her in any other light than the vicious harpy she was? He'd asked me and Auntie Nora to fill in bits of her life for him and I'd tried to be positive, but found it almost impossible to do so.

'Dearly Beloved, what can we say about the life of Patricia? She was born Patricia O'Connell, in County Donegal in 1948. She came to England, married and produced a daughter, Caroline. Her sister, Nora speaks of the fun and laughter in the family home . . .'

Father Miserecordie droned on, painting a picture of my mother which I simply didn't recognize. Of her work with charity, of her kindness to strangers, of her sincere faith and knowledge that she was a long way from God. And not once did he touch on her alcoholism, or the monstrous way she'd behaved.

A bubble of anger formed inside me as I listened to this travesty of an account of my mother's life. It seemed dreadful to me that the congregation, which was somewhat larger than I'd been expecting, should be misled in this way.

We'd discussed whether or not I should say something before the funeral. Father Miserecordie had thought it might help me. Originally I'd said no, but now, when he looked in my direction, without even realizing what I was doing,

I found myself moving towards the pulpit and standing up to address the congregation. Who were all these people? Surely none of them could have known my mum? She didn't have any friends. She was the original rock, that woman. That's where I get it from.

'Father Miserecordie has been immensely kind about my mother,' I began. My pulse was racing, and I was coming out in a cold sweat, but my fury impelled me on. 'The truth is, as anyone who knew her well could tell you, my mother was an alcoholic who hated the world, especially me. The only thing keeping her here was her precious God, and it seemed He'd deserted her for most of her life. Maybe things would have been different – my aunt tells me she was great fun as a young girl – if she hadn't had the misfortune of meeting my dad, who duly impregnated her and then left her high and dry. There wasn't a day that went by in my childhood when I wasn't uncomfortably aware of that fact.

'So, Father Miserecordie, I'm sorry, I can't find any forgiveness for her in my heart. Nor for my father. They brought me into this world, and then they failed me. I'm glad she's gone. At last I'm free of her.'

I looked at the coffin resplendent with the wreaths of crocuses, daffodils and freesias I'd insisted on having, despite Mum's typically austere wish for no flowers. It was true. She was gone. Finally I was free. So why did I feel so bereft?

I was suddenly uncomfortably aware that I'd said more than I ought. I looked at the congregation who all seemed to be stunned into silence. One man at the back took it upon himself to leave. I didn't recognize him, but then I didn't know who most of these people were, Mum didn't have any friends. I looked at Father Miserecordie in horror.

He must think *me* the monster. That was my mother in there. Never speak ill of the dead.

'Sorry,' I whispered. 'Sorry, I shouldn't have said that.' Then gathering what little dignity I had left, I went back to my pew. Of all the nasty shitty things I'd done in my life, that surely had to be the worst.

'Neat speech.' Charlie appeared at my elbow, a welcome relief from the hordes of Mum's cronies from the old people's lunch club, and the WI most of whom were unfamiliar to me, having arrived since I'd left home. Apparently Mum had taken to doing a lot of voluntary work. The old guard had stayed away – they knew what Mum was like. The new lot spoke about someone I didn't know: a kind, caring soul who'd listened to their problems. I was having a great deal of difficulty fitting this in with my knowledge of her.

They'd all been far too polite to mention my appalling outburst in the church, and I was so ashamed, I'd been avoiding both Father Miserecordie and Auntie Nora ever since. Auntie Nora had never been able to speak aloud the shame that was my mother's addiction. She'd probably never speak to me again.

'*Not* my finest hour,' I said.

'Well, you could have laid into the dearly departed a bit more,' said Charlie. 'I thought you were rather restrained myself.'

'Stop it,' I groaned. 'I doubt I'll ever be able to show myself back here again.'

Here was the church hall, much beloved of the Irish mafia run by Auntie Nora and her cronies. Not that I'd ever have much cause to come back, not now.

131

'Christ,' I said, 'this is going to take some getting used to. I really can't believe she's gone.'

'Fancy a beer when you've finished doing your duty?'

'What about Nadia?' I said. 'It's not fair on her. And she hates me enough as it is.'

'I've got a late pass,' said Charlie, 'and don't be daft, she doesn't hate you.'

'Well she should,' I said. 'I hate myself right now.'

'And that is totally self-pitying and stupid,' said Charlie.

'Isn't it?' Dorrie came bounding up; irrepressible, puppy-like, wonderful Dorrie.

'Look, Daz has got to go home and relieve his mum from Woody watching, but the girls and I can stay on for a bit if you'd like.'

Would I like? Trust Dorrie to know exactly what I needed right now.

'That would be fantastic,' I said. 'I'll just hang on to say goodbye to all these people, whoever they are.'

The wake was beginning to break up and people were peeling themselves away, reasserting the need for normality in their lives. And who could blame them?

Just as I'd said goodbye to two of Mum's lunchtime club, who seemed for some unfathomable reason to think she was Mother Teresa, Father Miserecordie caught up with me.

'Caroline,' he said.

'Father,' I said, feeling like I'd felt at school when, aged eight, I'd stolen a lollipop from Martyn Fraser's satchel.

'I think your mother was a very troubled soul,' he said, 'and at the end, despite her problems, my belief is that she was very close to God.'

I didn't know what to say. This kind of talk had always embarrassed me.

132

'I'm sorry for what I said. Wrong time. Wrong place. Story of my life,' I said. I liked Father Miserecordie, he'd been nothing but kind to me.

'But maybe you needed to say it.' He patted my arm.

I blinked back sudden tears at his kindness. I didn't share his and Mum's faith, and he knew it, but he offered his tolerance anyway.

'It's just so hard, knowing how much she hated me,' I said.

'What gives you that idea?' he said, genuinely surprised. 'She always talked of you with great pride.'

'So why did she say I ruined everything, when she died?' I asked.

'Are you sure that's what she said?' said Father Miserecordie. 'She told me on several occasions that she felt like she'd ruined *your* life.'

'Oh.' I was stunned. 'Well, maybe I did get that wrong, but I didn't imagine the look in her eye. It was one of pure hatred.'

'Maybe that wasn't directed at you, but at herself,' said Father Miserecordie. 'She was trying to kick the bottle you know. You walking away from her like that did her the power of good. She drank less, and got more involved in the parish. My guess is that she hated herself for having fallen off the wagon.'

'You think?' I said, my heart lifting a bit. I wanted badly to believe him.

'I think,' he said. 'I also think your friends are waiting for you. In the meantime, if you ever need me, you know where I am.'

I mumbled a thank you, and made my excuses. But I wasn't about to escape the wrath of Auntie Nora. She came

133

bustling up to me with a righteous indignation I knew all too well. My heart sank. Now was going to come the tirade to end all tirades. But to my surprise, she flung her arms tearfully around me.

'You poor pet,' she said. 'I had no idea it had been so hard for you.'

Thinking about it, when I was growing up, Auntie Nora hadn't been around so much, as she had been lately. She'd had her own family, and Uncle Paddy to care for. Uncle Paddy who had a tendency to wander, but at least he never left her. No wonder she and Mum had turned out so bitter.

'Your mam wasn't all bad, you know,' she said. 'It's just that life wasn't very good to her.'

'She certainly wasn't good to me,' I said.

'It was the drink,' said Auntie Nora. 'She was very proud of you really.'

'Was she?' I wished I could believe that. But the malevolent look in her eye as she'd died would haunt me forever.

134

Chapter Twelve

Doris

There's nothing like a funeral to concentrate the mind when you're feeling gloomy about your future. I sat in the church throughout most of Caz's mum's funeral in a state of abject terror, imagining how it would be for Daz, for my mum, for Woody, if I weren't around any more.

It also brought back memories of Dad's funeral. I hadn't really known Caz's mum, and hadn't liked what I had seen of her. She'd always been rude and aggressive the few times we'd met. Plus, I had some small idea of how miserable Caz's life had been, just from the way she seemed so starved of affection and lapped up the love in my house. The love I took so much for granted.

So the sight of the coffin had me in a puddle, and the service itself left me feeling incredibly sad. By the time Caz had let rip about the misery of her childhood, I was a blubbering mess. Daz squeezed my hand tightly, instinctively understanding how I felt. Beside me, I also was aware of Sarah sobbing quietly, and I noticed Beth wipe a tear away; it was as if we'd all had a reminder of how hard Caz's life had been and of how much she needed us.

After it was all over, the girls and I went back to the

wake, which was held in the church hall where we'd been to so many chaperoned discos when we were younger, and I managed to persuade Sarah that Steve could cope with the boys for a while longer so we could all go for a drink. Caz was the only one of us who'd moved away from North London, and Sarah and I both still lived in Northfields itself. None of us had too far to go home.

We got to the pub first – the Green Man, much favoured haunt of our teens, where we'd sneak in and see if we could get served. I'd never got away with it, but Caz with all her chutzpah usually managed to wangle a half, which we'd nurse all evening, sharing secretive sips and thinking ourselves daring and grown up. I felt a pang of nostalgia for our innocence.

'There you are,' I said, as Caz made her way into the pub garden – it was a warm evening for early May, so we thought we'd sit outside – followed by a gorgeous-looking bloke, whom I'd clocked her with at the wake. Not that I have eyes for anyone other than Darren you understand, I'm a strictly One Man Woman, but still, he was stunning. Dark hair, dark eyes, strong torso. Caz had certainly kept him quiet.

'Sorry, got pounced on by my ageing aunt,' said Caz. She looked a little shy, which was very unusual.

'Aren't you going to introduce us?' I said.

'Oh, yes, sorry.' Caz looked flustered. 'This is my friend, Charlie. We work together sometimes.'

Charlie. Could this really be Charlie? *The* Charlie whom Caz had married in a drunken spree in Las Vegas all those years ago? I could feel my eyebrows rise, and looking at the others I saw they were equally gobsmacked.

Caz shot me a warning look as if to say don't you dare

say *anything* – which I took to mean that it *was* the same Charlie. I'm well known for my ability to put my foot in it, so I kept schtumm.

'Charlie, how lovely to meet you, I'm Sarah.' Sarah stood up first and shook his hand. Wonders will never cease. Maybe she was beginning to come around to some kind of rapprochement with Caz. Beth and I introduced ourselves and we all sat down for a good old gossip. We kept things light, deliberately – Caz looked in no mood for confidences – laughing at the WI contingent, gently mocking Father Miserecordie's booming voice, generally prattling about the way we used to be back when we were all friends.

'I'd better be off.' Charlie pushed his empty pint glass away, and got to his feet. 'Will you be OK?'

'I'll be fine,' said Caz. 'You know me, tough as old boots.'

'Hmm,' said Charlie. 'Nice to meet you all, ladies. See you again I hope.'

'Is that *the* Charlie?' I hissed, as soon as he'd gone. 'Blimey, he's a bit of all right. Why ever did you divorce him?'

'Oh, that,' said Caz. 'We very young, very stupid and very drunk. Charlie's a mate that's all.'

'So, you don't fancy trying again?' said Sarah.

'No,' said Caz. 'Besides, he's got a girlfriend.'

There was an awkward pause, which Beth and I both leapt in to fill, before Caz stopped us, and said, 'I just want to thank you guys for coming. It really meant a lot to me. You didn't have to.'

'I think we did,' I said. I leant over and touched her arm. 'One four all, all four one, remember?'

Caz blinked back tears. 'I'm not sure I've ever been much good at being for anybody,' she said.

'Maybe that's because you never had anyone looking out

for you,' said Sarah, somewhat unexpectedly. 'We're all so lucky. Our families supported us. I knew you'd had a tough time growing up, but until today I hadn't appreciated how tough. I had no idea. None of us did. I'm sorry if I wasn't more understanding.'

Caz looked as if she was going to burst into tears, so I said hurriedly, 'Did you like our costumes?'

'The Four Marys – or three of them anyway,' Caz grinned. 'I might have known you'd think of that.'

'Actually, it wasn't my idea,' I said, 'it was Beth's.'

Caz turned to Beth, who as usual was sitting quietly in the corner. 'Really?' she said. 'I nearly howled with laughter when I saw you all.'

'I thought it might cheer you up,' said Beth.

'It did,' said Caz. 'Thanks again, you guys. I'm not sure I deserve it, but I really do appreciate you being here. Anyway, enough of my misery, what about the rest of you? How are the wedding plans, Dorrie?'

'Don't,' I said, pulling a face. 'I've got Darren's mum on my back, morning noon and night to ask why I haven't asked Great Auntie Joan that Darren hasn't seen for about a hundred years, while my mum's not with it half the time and acts as if she couldn't care less.'

And me, wondering if it's all going to be worth it, whether the day I've been waiting for my whole life, would turn out to be a day I'd never forget for all the wrong reasons.

'I've got some news,' Beth popped up shyly. 'Well, I hope I have.'

I looked at her and then twigged. She wasn't drinking. In fact, she hadn't had a drink when we'd been out for ages. 'You're not—?'

'Pregnant?' said Beth. 'Not yet, but hoping to be. We've

138

had IVF. Matt didn't want anyone to know, but I can't keep it to myself any longer.'

'Oh Beth, that's fantastic,' I said. 'When will you know?'

'They only implanted the eggs last Friday,' Beth said. 'And it takes at least a fortnight. Already it feels like the longest fortnight of my life. I've read through all the magazines in the house and I'm bored stiff of daytime TV.'

Sarah frowned. 'Should you be out?' she said. 'I thought you were supposed to try and rest as much as possible when you'd had IVF.'

'That's what Matt said,' admitted Beth. 'We had a bit of a row about it actually. But I've been resting for a week, and I was going bonkers at home. And I couldn't have missed this. I'll be fine.'

'Are you sure?' said Caz, looking a bit anxious. 'I'd feel terrible if it didn't work.'

'Absolutely sure,' said Beth. 'We've spent a long time waiting for Foetus, I refuse to accept that anything more will go wrong.'

'Well, here's to Foetus,' I said, and we all raised our glasses and drank to Beth and Matt. I felt an overwhelming sadness. Would I ever get pregnant again? And was Woody even going to remember me as I was now? I looked around at my three friends. Finally I'd got them back together. I thought back to our childhood and the day we'd made the Bridesmaid Pact. I had always imagined my wedding day as being the most perfect day of my life. And now I was dreading it.

A couple of days later, visiting the woman who was going to do the flowers, I felt a bit better. Whatever happened, I was going to do my best to enjoy my wedding day. Sarah had

139

come with me for moral support, since Mum was still showing hardly any interest. I wished I knew how to reach her, but she was locked away in her private, grief-stricken world.

'Oh dear, I'm sensing your aura is rather dark and gloomy today. Normally I'd say you were a turquoise, but oh dear, oh dear, you look rather grey today, not at all what I'd expect from a blushing bride.' The flower lady, a plump blonde, tottering on high heels, with the longest nails I'd ever seen, was full of such psychobabble. I seemed to vaguely remember her mentioning auras when I spoke to her on the phone, but she'd come highly recommended via Darren's Auntie Lottie's third granddaughter, Kylie. Kylie was all into New Age Philosophy, I should have known better than to go with her recommendation.

How did she know how I was feeling inside? I was a scientist, I didn't believe in that kind of crap. My work before having Woody had consisted of looking at cells down microscopes and doing experiments, not feelings, or colours, or auras. She'd only just met me, how could she know anything about me?

'Actually, I'm feeling quite chirpy today,' I said, 'I'm surprised my aura's not orange.'

'No, it's most definitely grey,' she said, patting my arm firmly. 'I have a gift.'

I tried not to eyeball Sarah, who was snorting in the corner.

'We need to cheer you up by showing you some fabulous flowers,' she continued.

'That is why I'm here,' I said sweetly.

'So what is it you're looking for, dear?' she said. Dear? She must have been around my age. I was being patronised by a blonde Barbie.

'Well, I'm going for a Disney theme,' I said, 'so I'd like my bouquet to have delicate, pink roses, and maybe some gypsophila. I'd like my side of the family to have pink carnations in their buttonholes and Darren's to have white. Can you show me some samples?'

Aura Lady condescended to talk me through her books. She appeared to only have heard the word 'Disney' in what I'd said and produced picture after picture of overblown bouquets stuffed full of massive baby pink or tangerine roses, nothing delicate or subtle at all. Not only that, Aura Lady's prices were extortionate. With these OTT flowers, and my gloomy grey aura, the wedding was doomed.

I really wanted a wreath in my hair, but wasn't sure that I could get away with it. I tried one on and Sarah frowned.

'Oh that's very you,' cooed Aura Lady. 'I think tangerine is definitely your colour.'

Sarah frowned and shook her head. 'It's a bit eighties isn't it?'

'I suppose,' I said sighing. 'I've always loved the thought of flowers in my hair, but more kind of woven in. Like something from a Disney movie.'

'You are a crazy woman, Doris Bradley,' said Sarah.

'I know,' I said, grinning and feeling a bit better. It was good to have Sarah with me. I wished the others could have been there too.

'Do you remember doing this for your wedding?' I said.

'Oh god, yes,' said Sarah. 'What a hoot. We kept mucking about and choosing the most awful colours for my brides-maids' dresses. We nearly sent Mum bonkers when we told her we wanted to wear black and carry lilies.'

'Yes, well, Caz was in her *Heathers* phase then, wasn't she?' I said.

'I hadn't quite realized how far she'd take the bitchiness though,' said Sarah dryly.

I glanced across at her. Her face was sad and set. It was a look I knew well. She'd confided in me often enough about Steve's infidelities. I don't know why she put up with him.

'Steve been misbehaving again, has he?'

Sarah pulled a face.

'How did you guess?'

'Just the way you speak about him,' I said. 'Why don't you just leave him? I'd never put up with that from Darren.'

'Well Darren wouldn't cheat on you,' said Sarah.

'True,' I said, 'he knows I'd kill him.'

Sarah sighed. 'Maybe I'm just a coward,' she said. 'I've been thinking about it more and more. Even on my wedding day, I knew it was wrong. I knew *we* were wrong. And I was so stupidly in love with him, I let him persuade me that Caz had come on to him. Steve's been lying to me since the day we were married. What kind of relationship is that?'

'A bad one,' I said. 'You deserve better.'

'But the boys . . .' said Sarah.

'Are an excuse,' I said bluntly. 'How good is it for them to have unhappy parents?'

'Well we're not exactly unhappy,' said Sarah. 'We rub along OK. We just lead very separate lives.'

I raised my eyebrows.

'Don't look at me like that,' said Sarah.

'Like what?'

'All disapproving and like you know best,' she said.

'That's because I do,' I said. 'And I think it's time you faced facts. Steve's not going to change and you shouldn't have to be this unhappy all your life.'

Sarah sighed and stared into space.

'I know,' she said. 'I just wish it were that easy to walk away, but it isn't.'

'How's the wedding co-ordination going then?'

Darren came in and wrapped his arms around me.

'What's wrong?' I laughed. 'Shouldn't you have washed off the zillions of germs you picked up from the tube before hugging me?'

'I washed my hands in the downstairs loo when I came in,' he said solemnly.

He went to kiss Woody, who was sitting in his highchair banging a wooden spoon on the top of his head.

'Honestly, Darren,' I said. 'Did your mother never tell you a little bit of dirt ain't never hurt no one?'

'My mother didn't study microbiology. Do you know how many particles there are in the average sneeze?'

'Enough,' I said. This was a well-worn theme with Darren, whose obsession with cleanliness at times reached Howard Hughes proportions. 'I think I'd rather talk about the wedding.'

'How was it today?'

I groaned. 'How wasn't it? Your mum is still banging on about inviting your Auntie Joan, but I just can't see how we're going to squeeze her in without losing someone else we'll offend equally.'

'I'll talk to her,' promised Darren. 'How was the flower lady?'

'Nuts,' I said. 'Honestly, I don't know how Auntie Lottie can have thought Kylie's flowers were so wonderful, I've never seen anything so tasteless in my life.' Darren raised a sardonic brow as I said this. 'Even by my standards they

143

were gaudy,' I added. 'As well as being waaaay out of our price range.'

'Kylie did get married in not much more than a lacy bra and knickers though,' said Darren.

'What? You never told me that,' I said. 'Anyway, we're not using that woman. She kept talking constantly about my dark aura and pretty much made me feel the wedding was doomed.'

'Well don't use her then,' said Darren.

'But like an idiot I paid the deposit,' I groaned. 'And there isn't time to find anyone else.'

'Well un-pay it,' said Darren. 'Or we'll just swallow the loss. The amount of Freecycling you've been doing, we can afford some cock-ups. And I'm sure we can find someone else.'

Dear dependable Daz. What would I do without him?

I laid myself contentedly against his chest, while Woody gurgled happily in the background. I wished life could always be like this. Me and Daz and Woody, safe, secure. Together. Forever.

Sarah

September 1997

What do I remember?

I was nervous as hell. Fretting that it was a bad omen that the wedding I'd planned for so many months was going to take place on the day of Diana's funeral. And thanks to Caz, the Bridesmaid Pact we'd made all those years ago wasn't now going to happen. Feeling that I was missing something somehow, that things were happening I didn't know about, that people were talking about me behind my back.

Pacing up and down the lounge in my bridal finery wishing I could have a fag, but not daring to escape upstairs and smoke one out of the loo like I used to.

Doris. Barking, crackpot loony Doris, face caked with make-up as ever, spotting how I was feeling and slipping me a G & T.

'Where did you hide that?' I ask when she passes me the hip flask, but I already know the answer.

She hitches up her skirt and pops it back in her garter. The obvious place for it really. What would I do without dear old dotty Doris in my life?

'I feel like a naughty schoolgirl,' I confess.

145

'Every girl should have G & T for Dutch courage on their wedding day,' declares Doris before having another swig herself. Shit. At this rate she'll be pickled going up the aisle.

Beth comes in and says the car's here. Mum bustles over and gives me a hug. I almost can't look at her. Daren't let her see the panic in my eyes. Am I doing the right thing, *am I?*

Then, alone with Dad. Both of us pacing the lounge. Me not wanting him to ask the question that's been hovering on his lips for months now. *Are you sure? I don't think he's the right one for you, pet.* Don't say it, Dad. Then I don't have to think it.

'Wish I didn't have to make a speech,' says Dad, pulling a crumpled-up scrap of paper out of his pocket and peering at it myopically.

'You'll be fine,' I say, suddenly clocking he's as nervous as I am.

'Pet—' he begins and I shush him, the car arriving prevents the need for a heart to heart. If I can just get to the church without having to talk to Dad about the way I feel. Without thinking about why Caz decided to desert me in my hour of need. Without that fatal stab of jealousy when I think of how well she seems to get on with Steve, who was more interested in Caz than me to start with. Without that fear that he's going to leave me. Without all the doubts that have kept me awake at night resurfacing now, at the wrong moment. If I can do all that, and get down the aisle to see him standing there, waiting for me, I know it will be fine. Everything will be fine. This is the best day of my life. It has to be fine.

I keep a bright patter up all the way to the church; it's

only ten minutes in the car. The busy suburban streets of my youth are silent today though, everyone's inside watching Diana's funeral. My chatter is so bright and breezy, Dad's casting me odd looks as if to say, *Calm down, love*. I know I must sound vaguely hysterical. I *feel* vaguely hysterical. We're approaching the church now, I can see the last-minute guests rushing through the wooden doors, and my stomach's in my mouth, my heart is beating erratically, my hands are beginning to sweat. I feel faint.

'Are you all right, pet?' Dad squeezes my hand and looks at me, and suddenly as the car prepares to pull up in front of the church I can't hide it from him any more.

'I can't do it, Dad,' I say. 'I'm sorry, but I can't marry Steve.'

'Right,' says Dad firmly, leaning over to the chauffeur, 'don't pull up, go past the church and once around the block.'

He takes my hand, and holds it firmly.

'Now, pet, what's this all about? Are you sure it's not just wedding nerves?'

I glance out of the window as we pass Mum and the girls staring in surprise as we don't stop. I can't see Steve anywhere. Presumably he and Joe, his younger brother and best man, are already in the church. Oh god. I feel so churned up. All those people. Waiting for me. Waiting for us. I can't cancel now. I know how much this has cost Mum and Dad for starters. They've been determined to push the boat out for me, their only daughter, and I've had the feeling I've been on a rollercoaster I can't get off for months and months.

'I don't know,' I say, beginning to blub. Damn. Now my mascara will run. 'I just don't know if I'm doing the right thing.'

147

'Well,' says Dad slowly, 'your mum and I have wondered that ourselves. Steve isn't the person we'd have chosen for you.'

'I knew it,' I say. 'You've never liked him, have you?'

'It's not a question of whether we like him,' says Dad. 'He's your choice. What do you think? Can you face a life without him? Because if you walk away now, that's it. It will be all over. But if you're having doubts, maybe it's better to get out before it's too late.'

I take a deep breath. I think about a life without Steve and can't imagine it. He is so much part of my life. And I love him. Whatever I imagine has or hasn't happened with Caz, I love him. Looking back, it seems so stupid. But I am young. More, naïve. I still think love is enough.

'I'm not,' I say firmly. 'I was just having a last-minute wobble. It's just such a big commitment.'

'It is that,' says Dad dryly, 'you just ask your mother.'

I laugh.

'Have you ever had doubts about you and Mum?' I ask.

'Never,' says Dad. 'I knew she was mine from the moment I clapped eyes on her. Which isn't to say that everything's always run smoothly, mind. We've had our ups and downs over the years, but nothing serious.'

I think about that. I am sure of my feelings for Steve, but can I be sure of his for me? I shove the insecure nagging doubt which says I should be sure of *that* on my wedding day, and take a deep breath. Better to love and lose and all that, and I do love Steve.

'I'm being stupid,' I say. 'Come on, Dad, get me to the church on time.'

* * *

The wedding itself passed in a blur. I remember walking down the aisle to Clarke's 'Trumpet Voluntary' on Dad's arm, churning with emotion. I'd picked it out of sentimentality, remembering Diana's wedding. It seemed to bode ill today.

The church was packed to the rafters, my family and friends all jammed in on the left side: aunts I saw once a year, cousins I'd barely seen since childhood, friends of my parents, a few of my nursing friends. Somehow since I'd been with Steve there hadn't been so much time for my own mates, though I could see all of Steve's pals crowded together in the middle of the church.

Thanks to my indecision, we were running ten minutes late. Steve looked furious as I approached him.

'I thought you weren't coming,' he hissed as I arrived. 'I was mortified.'

'I nearly didn't,' I felt like hissing back, but I just smiled and apologized, foolishly setting a pattern for a marriage which only was ever going to work in one person's favour.

The sun shone through the stained-glass window, as Father Cormack joined our hands, and we solemnly made our vows, and I promised to love, honour and obey Steve till death did us part. When we'd exchanged rings, Steve lifted my veil and said, 'Congratulations, Mrs Johnson,' before planting a huge kiss on my lips. For the first time all day my nerves calmed down and I began to think everything would be OK.

Walking back down the aisle, my spirits lifted, and we came out of the church as the sun shone, laughing and smiling as our friends and relatives jostled to congratulate us, and take photos, and throw confetti.

Steve held my hand tightly throughout, and kissed me every time someone took our photo. I began to relax and enjoy the moment.

Finally I'd married the man I loved. And I wasn't going to let anything or anyone spoil my day.

Chapter Thirteen

Beth

'I can't believe you told the girls,' said Matt in disgruntlement, as we waited outside the clinic for our appointment to see if the IVF had worked. Matt was still cross with me for going to Caz's mum's funeral, though I'd tried to persuade him it wouldn't make any difference.

'I'm sorry,' I said. 'It just slipped out. I was dying to tell someone.'

'But what if it hasn't worked?' said Matt. 'I'd just rather we'd kept it to ourselves till we know for sure.'

'Don't be so negative,' I said. 'It's going to have worked. It know it's worked.'

I was so determined not to allow myself any negative thoughts I had practically convinced myself I was already pregnant. My period still hadn't come, and I took that as such a good sign I hadn't even taken the pregnancy test the hospital had given us. I had to be pregnant, I just had to be.

It was ridiculous of me to be so positive. And part of me kept saying I was riding for a fall. But I couldn't help myself. The last fortnight had been so incredibly long and tense, I'd had to keep optimistic or I'd have gone mad. And after the months and years of disappointment, I felt we were so close to Foetus becoming a reality I couldn't bear to think it wouldn't happen.

We did have a Plan B, which was to dip into our savings should we need to have a second go at IVF, but we could only afford one attempt like that. And we'd so wanted that money for Foetus. Despite trying to keep positive, I couldn't help it. Now we were here, my heart was hammering in my mouth, what if it hadn't worked? Perhaps I was destined to be one of those women who suffered from phantom pregnancies. I couldn't rid myself of the thought that I was being punished for what I'd done.

'Mr and Mrs Davies?' The nurse ushered us into Mr O'Brian's office.

'Well I won't keep you in suspense,' said Mr O'Brian. Oh god. There was something about his tone, something about the way he wasn't quite looking at us.

'I'm really very sorry,' he said. 'Your blood tests were negative. The IVF hasn't worked this time.'

A wave of cold shock washed over me. The procedure had failed. Despite the doubts and the worry, I had been so sure he was going to tell me that Foetus was finally real. I couldn't take it in.

I was vaguely aware of the doctor talking about our other options, and what we could do next. I even think I heard him saying, 'It's not the end of the road,' but I couldn't focus on anything. I wanted to let out a howl of despair, but I couldn't do it here, not with all these people. I clutched blindly at Matt, as he led me from the room.

'It's all my fault,' I said. 'All my fault. I'm sorry, Matt. I shouldn't have—'

I was going to tell him the truth. I couldn't stand keeping it secret any longer.

Matt sat me down in the hospital café and got me a cup of tea.

'Deep breaths, Beth, deep breaths,' he said. 'Look, this isn't your fault. I know I got cross with you for going out to Caz's mum's funeral, but you heard the doctor, it wouldn't have made a difference. I know you feel terrible right now. So do I. But this is just the beginning. We can try again. It will all come good in the end.'

'But—'

'Shhh,' Matt put a finger to his lips. 'We have to stay positive, remember. It hasn't worked this time, but we've got our savings. We can have another go. It will be fine, you'll see.'

I sipped my tea and tried to focus on staying positive. The moment of confession had passed. Matt still didn't know my guilty secret.

'Well would you ever believe it?' my mother greeted us at the front door. 'It's Matthew and Elizabeth. It's been that long since we've seen you both we were beginning to forget what you looked like.'

'Oh, will you be quiet you silly woman.' Dad came up behind her. 'It's only been a fortnight. These two young things don't want to be spending all their time with awdies like us.'

'Less of the awd, Kevin McCarthy,' said Mum. 'I'm not in my grave yet. Though I might well be before these two get round to producing our grandchild.'

She'd said it. I'd known she would, and I hadn't wanted to come because it was the same every time. Less than subtle hints about who in the parish had become grandparents this week, and wondering why some people (with a heavy emphasis on the *some*) were taking their time about it. I couldn't tell her the truth.

I wished I did have the sort of mother I could confide in about all things gynaecological. Apart from vague pronouncements from time to time about the curse and Eve's punishment being a harsh one, Mum had remained silent about the facts of life, presumably expecting me to absorb that sort of information by osmosis. Had it not been for Dorrie, Sarah and Caz I'd have thought I was bleeding to death the first time I had my period.

'Oh will you leave them alone, woman,' said Dad. 'They'll have babbies when they're good and ready. It's none of your business.'

Matt shot him a grateful look and squeezed my hand.

'I'm sorry about that,' I whispered, 'you know how she will go on.'

Matt still didn't get why I wouldn't come out and talk about it. His mum knew all about the IVF and had commiserated soundly when Matt had rung her to say it had failed.

'I notice your brother never gets this treatment,' murmured Matt as we went down to sit in the lounge with Dad, while Mum clucked off to the kitchen to carry on cooking for the army that she apparently thought she was feeding.

'Shh.' I smacked his hand. It was true that my brother James didn't get asked every five minutes when he was about to produce a grandchild. Maybe even Mum had managed to subliminally get the message he was gay, even if she'd never ever be able to say it out loud. The fact that he and his 'friend' George had been living together for five years, had the neatest house you've ever seen and only had one bedroom, should have been a dead giveaway. But my mother has the greatest capacity of anyone I know to see what she wants to see and ignore the rest. George was a nice young man who was 'helping James out with his mortgage' till James found himself a suitable young woman.

'I'll laugh if James and George come home with a baby one day,' said Matt.

'Yes, that would be hilarious,' I said, deadpan. 'I can think of nothing more hideous.'

'It'd be one way of outing themselves,' he said.

'Shh,' I said again. Dad had come back in the room bearing drinks. I didn't think Dad would have minded so much, but he was a traditionalist too and it was hard for them to understand the choices we made.

I loved my mother warts and all, even with her blind prejudices and her ability to drive me demented. She had a heart of gold, but had been brought up with a narrow puritan set of values which seemed out of kilter in the modern world. I knew from the little I'd seen of Caz's mother how lucky I was.

'Are you OK?' Matt said quietly as they laughed and joked in the kitchen.

'Not really,' I said.

'We shouldn't have come this week,' said Matt. 'I knew your mum would go on about babies.'

'They'd be suspicious if we hadn't,' I said. 'And Mum *always* goes on about babies, so it's never going to be easy.'

'Who's going on about babies?' said Mum, bustling in to say lunch was ready.

'You,' I said, trying to make a joke of it. 'But I promise you, if I ever get pregnant you'll be the first to know. But for now I keep telling you, I'm concentrating on my career.'

'You career girls,' Mum said shaking her head. 'It was all different in my day.'

Not so very different, I longed to say, but instead, I laughed and said with a certainty I didn't feel, 'There's plenty of time for babies, isn't there, Matt?'

'Plenty,' echoed Matt, squeezing my hand as we went to sit down. I wished I could believe it.

'I'm so sorry the IVF didn't work,' Sarah had rung me when I was on the tube going home, a couple of days later. I'd had a tiring day at work, and felt miserable most of the day. Apart from my boss, I hadn't told anyone at work about the IVF. They were all twenty-somethings with plenty of time ahead of them, how could they possibly understand?

'Did Dorrie tell you?' I'd rung Dorrie first. Doris was always the one you turned to in a crisis. She could be relied on to be there, supporting, helping, cheering you on.

'Yes,' said Sarah. 'How are you doing?'

'I'm fine,' I said.

'Really?' Sarah sounded sceptical.

'Sarah, I'm on a crowded commuter train. I don't wish to talk about my private life here,' I hissed.

'Oops, sorry,' said Sarah. 'I forget real people go out to work.'

'Yeah, well it's all right for you, at home with your four-bedroom house and perfect family.'

'Oh Beth,' said Sarah, 'don't be like that, I do understand how tough it is for you.'

'How can you possibly understand what I'm going through?' I said. 'Do you know how long Matt and I have been trying for a baby? For the best part of five years. You have no idea what that feels like.'

It was uncharacteristic of me to let vent to my emotions to my friends. I hate confrontation and normally avoid arguments. But, and Sarah wasn't to know this, a nasty ignominious part of me felt jealous and resentful that she'd had her babies so easily without any trouble, when it seemed so hard for me. It didn't seem fair.

'Right,' Sarah sounded a bit stiff and hurt. 'I'm sorry. I was just trying to help. Clearly this isn't a good time.'

'No. It isn't,' I said savagely and snapped my mobile shut.

I leant against the window of the tube and sighed heavily as the train pulled out of the station and went underground again temporarily. I felt like getting swallowed up in the darkness. I shut my eyes and wished that all my pain would just go away, and I would wake up and find out it had all been a ghastly mistake. Foetus was real and we were going to have a baby. It had to happen. It had to. I couldn't bear the thought of it not.

Chapter Fourteen

Caz

I mooched through Brent Cross trying to get ideas for the next assignment I was working on. It was just over a fortnight since Mum's funeral and I'd ducked out of a few jobs recently. Hattie, a stylist I knew, had sorted out a replacement for me. I knew she was up to her eyes in work at the moment, so to pay her back I promised I'd sort out the accessories on this one – a commercial for a soap company celebrating 'real' women. What the difference between a 'real' woman and an unreal one was, I hadn't worked out, but I was rather looking forward to working with a bunch of normal people who might enjoy themselves for the day, rather than the tantrum-filled divas I often encountered.

I was engrossed in the bracelets in Accessorize, when a familiar voice said, 'Hi, what are you doing here?'

'Sarah,' I said. 'This is a surprise.'

I felt a bit nervous as I said this. Sarah had seemed to thaw towards me at the funeral, but I couldn't be sure she was really ever going to accept me back into the fold.

'What are you up to?' she said.

'Looking for accessories for a bunch of models for next week,' I said.

'Ooh, glamorous,' laughed Sarah.

'Not exactly,' I said. 'My job might seem glamorous from where you're standing, but most of it is dull, mundane stuff, really.'

'It can't be more mundane than being a bored housewife,' said Sarah. 'I'd give anything to have a job again.'

'You should really go back to work,' I said. 'You were a good nurse.'

'Well, funny you should say that,' said Sarah. 'I've been looking at back to work NHS training schemes since we last spoke. It's been great being at home with the kids, but William will be at school before I know it, and I'll be reduced to watching daytime TV and polishing my kitchen floor every day, with Valium to get my kicks.'

I looked at Sarah. She looked so sad. I remembered the joy with which she'd told me she was getting married, and how stupidly jealous I'd been. Now, she seemed like such a downtrodden housewife. She'd always been so together growing up; I'd spent half my life envying her.

'Have you got time for a coffee?' I asked hesitantly. Suddenly I craved a girlie chat like we used to have all those years ago.

Sarah paused.

'Yes, that would be great,' she said. 'I've got about an hour before I have to pick Will up from nursery.'

'This is nice,' I said lightly as we sat drinking our lattes in Starbucks.

'Yes isn't it?' Sarah said. 'It's been a long time.'

'My fault,' I said. 'All my fault. And for what it's worth, I am so sorry for all the grief I caused you. You didn't deserve it. I was just a jealous cow.'

'Ha, you wouldn't be jealous now,' said Sarah sourly.

'Oh?' Something about the way Sarah spoke made me sit up.

'Steve's been seeing someone,' Sarah said, eventually, fiddling with her mat. 'He denies it of course, he always does. But her name's Kirsty and she's taken my boys to the zoo. Can you believe the cheek of him?'

Thinking that it sounded like typical Steve, but feeling it wouldn't be diplomatic to say so, I merely nodded.

Sarah fiddled with her mat some more. 'Can I ask you a direct question?' she said.

'Um – depends what it is . . .' I said, my heart somersaulting.

'With Steve – was it really you that instigated things?'

'Blimey, that is direct,' I said weakly.

'Well?'

I sat feeling a conflict of emotions. I'd lied to Sarah in the past to protect her, to try to make up for the hideous wrong I'd done. I sensed that she needed the truth now. But if I told her the truth, it would mean the whole of her marriage had been a sham. I wasn't sure I could do that to her.

'Yes,' I said. 'I fancied Steve and I was jealous of you. On a couple of occasions I came on to him a bit strongly and he responded. It was my fault, not his. I'm sorry, it was crap of me, and I wish to god I hadn't done it, but I can't turn the clock back and put it right.'

'Oh,' said Sarah. 'Well, thanks for being honest.'

I felt terrible lying to her again, but what else could I do?

Sarah sat in silence for a few minutes.

'Right,' she said. 'Good. Now I know.'

'Sarah,' I said urgently, 'if I could take it back, if I could do it differently, I would. I've never been sorrier about anything in my life, than I have been about the way I hurt you.'

Tears prickled my eyes. All those wasted years without Sarah's friendship. And all my own fault.

'Well, you did,' said Sarah, 'and it's water under the bridge now. You're not the threat to my marriage any more. And the difference is I'm not blindly infatuated with Steve any more.'

Now we were both blubbing.

'Just look at us, this is ridiculous,' said Sarah, wiping her eyes and laughing through her tears.

'I feel about fifteen again,' I said through my sobs.

'Me, too,' said Sarah.

'Do you think . . .' I said uncertainly, 'do you think we could ever make up?'

Sarah looked into the distance, toying with her spoon.

'I don't know, Caz,' she said. 'There's so much between us, I'm not sure things can ever be the same. Maybe, given time.'

I knew that was all I was going to get for now, so I changed the subject and asked, 'What are you going to do now?'

'About what?'

'The shit, and Kirsty of course.'

Sarah looked thoughtful. 'Something I should have done a long, long time ago,' she said.

'You're early,' Charlie greeted me at the soap photo shoot.

'Well, there are so many of them. Hattie and I thought we should get everything ready.'

They arrived one by one, nervous, excited, talking loudly

162

to cover their nerves, all ordinary women about to have an out-of-the-ordinary kind of day. I loved this part of my job. Each new face was like an empty canvas to work on, which I could bring to life. A dash of eyeliner here, some blusher there, pale rose lipstick for a darker complexion, bright red to jazz up the more conservative souls. Soon the women, who were all in their thirties and forties and, from the sounds of it, mostly kidded up with husbands who worked long hours away from home, were giggling and laughing as if they'd known each other for years. It helped that Charlie was working his magic, cracking jokes, getting the shots right, bringing out the best in all of them.

There was one woman there that I'd particularly noticed. She'd come in fussing like an old mother hen, looking dowdy and older than her years. I'd insisted she unpicked her bun, which reminded me unfavourably of Mum, and curled her hair softly which instantly made her look younger and more girlie. I'd also given her the cherry red lipstick, guessing that she'd never in a million years choose a colour like that. Hattie had found her a little black velvet number. Suddenly she looked ravishing. And with Charlie's gentle teasing, it soon became apparent she was the star of the show. She flirted naturally with the camera, and the shots Charlie was getting were fabulous. The people from the soap campaign were clearly pleased and were muttering about making her the face of the campaign.

Good, I thought with satisfaction. It was nice to feel that maybe you'd made a bit of a difference to someone's life. I liked my job and it paid the mortgage, but you couldn't exactly say it was terribly worthwhile, like being a doctor or something. It wasn't even as if it were vital to the economy or anything.

As I watched Charlie tease yet another winning smile from my ugly-duckling-turned-swan, I felt a sudden pang of longing. I knew he just had his professional face on, but I wanted him to smile at me like that, to give me that teasing smile and ready charm. I'd known that he had that talent for years, why did I suddenly want it directed at me?

The session took most of the morning but by 1 p.m. we were done.

'What are you up to later?' Charlie said, as I headed for the door.

'Not a lot,' I said. 'I'm heading over to North London to go through some of my mum's stuff with my aunt, but I'll be back around teatime. Why?'

'Nadia's gone away for a couple of days on business,' he said. 'I was just wondering if you'd be free for a drink.'

'Are you sure she wouldn't mind?' I said, a bit dubiously.

'Why should she mind?' said Charlie. 'She sees male friends, I see female friends. It's part of our deal.'

'Right,' I said, wondering if Nadia really were that sanguine about things. Charlie could be a bit dense sometimes. Just because he didn't have a jealous bone in his body, it didn't occur to him that other people might. He should have known better by now, nearly all his girlfriends had been jealous of our friendship, and he could never see it. Which was infuriating but part of his enduring charm.

I got over to Mum's place in Northfields in less than an hour and Auntie Nora and I sorted out her clothes into piles, things which were too far gone to be saved and ones which were decent enough for the charity shop. It made me feel sad going through Mum's things. There didn't seem to be much to show for a life. I wondered if

164

my life would look like this when someone came to do this for me.

Auntie Nora was evidently finding it as difficult as I was because she was in full-on abrasive no-nonsense mode, and any warmth she'd shown to me at the funeral seemed to have vanished.

Eventually, we'd done with the clothes, so I suggested we go and look in the loft to see what needed clearing out there. Mum had been an inveterate hoarder, and from my previous glimpse up there, I had a feeling it was going to take us months to sort out.

I went up first. There wasn't enough room to swing a cat up there, and with it being a warm day, was unbearably hot, so casting around with the ancient torch Mum kept in the cupboard under the stairs, I grabbed at the first couple of boxes I could find and passed them down to Auntie Nora. They'd been sitting on top of an old, battered suitcase, which I'd never seen before, so I took that down too.

'Well this should keep us going a while,' I said. 'I think I'll just put the kettle on, I have a feeling we're going to need it.'

As I came back into the hall, I noticed that Auntie Nora was rummaging away in the suitcase.

'Anything interesting in there?' I said.

'Nothing of any consequence. A few letters and some old photos,' she said. 'I think most of this is junk. I'll get rid of it if you like.'

'No it's all right,' I said. 'I like looking at old photos. Here, let me see.'

'There really is nothing to see,' said Auntie Nora, who seemed curiously reluctant to show me what she'd been looking at.

'You never know, there might be something of interest,' I said. I went over to the suitcase and started rummaging through the contents. Which is when I found them: bundles of letters, and cards, with postmarks dating back over twenty-five years. All with my name on.

'What—?' I said in confusion. 'What are all these?'

'They're nothing,' she said. 'They mean nothing.'

'Well, they're addressed to me,' I said. 'So I think I should be the judge of that.'

Pursing her lips, Auntie Nora stood up and said, 'Some things are best left alone.'

I picked up the first envelope. The date was from 1977. The year I was four years old. With shaking hands I opened it. I had a feeling I knew what was inside.

To my beautiful princess on her 4th birthday, the card read, *with lots of love from Dad xxx*

'Oh my god,' I said, 'are all these from *him*?'

'Your mum didn't want you to have them,' sniffed Auntie Nora. 'He left her high and dry with you, she said he didn't have the right.'

'But what about my right?' I said. 'How dare she? How dare you?'

I grabbed the bundle of letters, and my coat, and got up and left in a towering rage. How could Mum do this? How *could* she? It was like she was laughing at me from beyond the grave.

'Do you really need another drink?'

I'd gone straight from Mum's house to a pub in Soho that Charlie and I liked to frequent after work. For a London pub, it was small enough to be cosy, but big enough not to get overcrowded. Stuck as it was down a side alley, it

166

wasn't known to all and sundry and was the closest I had to a local. I'd rung Charlie when I was on my third pint.

I squinted into my empty glass of vodka and coke. How had it emptied so quickly? I glanced around the pub we were in. Charlie and I seemed to be the only people left, apart from one stalwart propping up the bar. How had that happened? One minute the place had been buzzing and now it was empty.

'Come on Caz, I think you've had enough,' said Charlie. 'Time to get you home.'

I suddenly felt very tired and Charlie's hectoring tone, which would have irritated me normally, suddenly seemed right and proper. Yes. It was time to go home.

'What time is it?' I slurred.

'Late,' said Charlie as he propelled me to the door. My legs didn't seem to work very well and twice I found myself sitting on the floor. Sensing somehow that my giggling incoherence wasn't helping the situation any, I tried to shut up.

'Sorry,' I said. 'Sorry for being such a drunken lush.'

'It's OK,' said Charlie. 'It's not like I'm not used to it.'

The cold night air hit me as we emerged into the street. Suddenly, I was reeling. Where I'd felt merely drunk before, now I felt wildly out of control. All the way home in the cab that Charlie had commandeered, I babbled away like a mad thing. On and on, till Charlie must have been sick of me.

'How could she?' I kept saying. 'How could she have kept those letters from me?'

'Maybe she didn't want to upset you,' said Charlie as he got me out of the cab and tried to steer me to the front door.

'And what the fuck do you know about it?' Suddenly

I turned all my rage with Mum on Charlie. 'You have no idea what she was like.'

'Yeah, I do,' said Charlie. 'I've spent years listening to you telling me. Caz, I don't need this right now. It's late. And we've both got work in the morning.'

He stood at the front door looking tired and disillusioned. Suddenly I saw with clarity how I must look to him. A crazy drunk whose life was careering out of control. Why on earth was he still friends with me? My anger dissipated as fast as it had come.

'Oh god,' I said. 'I'm turning into her, aren't I? Sorry. Sorry. Sorry. If I don't have you, I don't have anyone.'

I turned away and slumped against the front door, feeling like an idiot. As always I had picked the wrong person to hurt. The trouble was, the right person was dead.

'Caz, don't be daft,' said Charlie. He sat down next to me and put his arm around me. 'You're not your mum. You're you. You're lovely, and funny, and gorgeous. You've just been having a tough time lately. That's all.'

'And I screw everything up.'

'Like what?' he said. 'You have a good career, and look at this place. You've managed to buy this all by your own hard work. You should be proud of yourself.'

I looked at him, so full of tender concern for me. He was always so kind. So thoughtful. I was immensely lucky to have him in my life. My heart lurched, as I felt a sudden rush of heady desire. The thought struck me that I could probably kiss him and he wouldn't mind. I knew he was thinking the same thing, because he looked away, embarrassed. Guiltily, I thought of Nadia. I didn't like her, but after Sarah, I vowed I'd never cheat on anyone again. I hadn't broken that promise and I wasn't about to start now.

'You're right, as always,' I said. 'It's hard to change the feelings of a lifetime.'

I got up and fell down again.

'Come on, let's get you inside,' said Charlie. 'I'll make you a coffee, then I'd better go.'

We sat drinking coffee into the early hours. I had slumped on the sofa, and Charlie sat by my side. It seemed natural to lay my head on his shoulder, and he didn't stop me. My eyes felt heavy, and I kept dozing off.

'I should go,' said Charlie, his voice coming from very far away.

'You should,' I agreed lazily. But neither of us moved, and so we leant against one another till we fell asleep. It felt cosy and right. He wasn't mine to have, but I felt like I'd come home.

Chapter Fifteen

Doris

'Do you think Beth will be all right?' Sarah had joined me for coffee as we were ringing through the list of numbers for recommended flower shops that she'd managed to produce via her vast network of school mum chums.

'Why do you ask?' I said while trying to pour the water out of the kettle carefully. I'd had a major spillage the previous day and nearly burnt my hand.

'I rang her up to see how she was, and I think I made things worse,' said Sarah.

'How so?'

'Well, you know she's always been a bit funny about me having kids?' said Sarah.

'I thought that was just because she was pissed off because you were pregnant at her wedding and kept throwing up,' I said.

'Well, so did I,' said Sarah, 'but honestly, she bit my head off when I asked if I could help. I suppose it must be hard for her. She sees us getting pregnant no problem, and then she can't seem to manage it.'

If only you both knew, I thought. The way I felt right now, I'd have happily swapped their lives and problems with mine. At least they had the chance to put their difficulties right. What chance did I have?

'It must be hard,' I agreed, 'but surely just because it hasn't worked once doesn't mean they have to give up, do they?'

'Oh good lord, no,' said Sarah. 'IVF is difficult though, and I think they'll have to wait a month to try again. There's only a twenty-five per cent chance of getting pregnant, so if it hasn't worked, it does up the ante rather. And the more stressed people get, often the less likely it is to work.'

'Well, with any luck, it will work for them next time,' I said. 'Let's hope so. I feel bad, I hadn't realized how much Beth wanted this. She's always been so private about it.'

'Maybe we weren't the right people to talk to,' said Sarah. 'It can't be easy talking about how you're not getting pregnant to people who clearly find it a doddle. Oh god, I hope I haven't really pissed her off.'

'She was probably just upset,' I said. 'It's not like Beth to hold a grudge.'

'True,' said Sarah.

'And it's not like you to be so sensitive,' I said. 'How are things at home?'

'Not great,' said Sarah, pulling a face. 'I'm trying to pluck up the courage to tell Steve I want a divorce. But it's not that easy.'

I whistled slowly. Sarah had often confided in me about her difficulties at home, but much as I wanted her to make a break from Steve, somehow I never thought she would.

'Steve, I want a divorce,' I said. 'There. Easy.'

'Oh shut up,' said Sarah. 'I have at least enrolled on a back to work course.'

'Well that's a start,' I said.

'Yes, isn't it?' said Sarah. 'Now, enough about me, we need to crack on and find you some flowers.'

After making dozens of phone calls we had a shortlist of three. The one I liked the sound of the most was a lady called Mrs Trim from Rose & Thorns. She sounded about a hundred and was the most positive and enthusiastic person I'd spoken to. I arranged to meet her the next day.

'Sorry I can't help you tomorrow,' said Sarah. 'I've got Sam's assembly to go to, and then some wretched PTA thing. Can you manage alone?'

'I think I can cope,' I said, laughing.

But when she'd left and I went to put the things away in the dishwasher, I dropped both our cups on the floor. Suddenly I wanted to rage at the world. It was so insidious the way this was affecting my life. Not for the first time I wondered if marrying Darren was the right thing to do.

'How lovely to meet you, my dear,' said Mrs Trim, ushering me into the back of her tiny shop, which exploded with flowers of all colours and hues, from tall purple irises, soft violet and yellow freesias, pink and yellow chrysanthemums, roses of every shade, massive daisies and small delicate handmade posies of gypsophila entwined with pinks. The smell was gorgeous. It was like coming into an inside garden, and despite the rainy gloom of the day, it felt like summer had come at last. I was in heaven

I fell instantly in love with Mrs Trim, a tiny little lady of indeterminate age, but I judged around seventy.

'Do call me Ivy,' she said, as she gurgled over Woody, which endeared her to me even more. We'd had a fractious morning. Him with his teeth which had kept us both awake half the night, me with my clumsiness, which today had found me slipping in the kitchen and dropping a pint of milk. It was soothing being in Ivy's presence. She supplied milk for Woody and tea and biscuits for me. She even found a set of toy bricks to keep him occupied.

'So, do you have a theme in mind?' Ivy asked, as we sat down to look through photos.

I laughed.

'You could say that,' I said. 'I love fairytales, you see. My fiancé thinks I'm mad, but I'm going for a Disney theme. I even have a Cinderella dress, white with pink roses. It's a replica of one I had as a child.' Much as I loved the blue, in the end the lure of a traditional white dress had been too much. I'd kept the blue shoes though.

'Ooh, lovely,' Ivy clapped her hands. 'You could have some of these baby pink roses, with some lilies or gypsophila.' She grabbed a few flowers and expertly wound them into a spray.

'Which would you rather, a spray like this, or a drop bouquet?'

She produced pictures of bouquets of various shapes and sizes. I oohed and aahed over them. It was going to be a tough choice.

Eventually I plumped for a drop bouquet with pink and white roses entwined with pink lilies.

'A perfect choice,' said Ivy with satisfaction. 'I shall so enjoy working on it for you. So what about the dashing bridegroom?' said Ivy.

'Ah,' I said, 'the dashing bridegroom is still mad at me for making him wear white . . .' Darren had been furious when I'd suggested it, but I refused to countenance another suggestion from my knight in shining armour.

Darren. It hadn't just been Woody's teeth keeping me

awake. More and more often of late, I'd found myself unable to sleep as I fretted over what was to happen to me, and how Darren would be able to cope, and whether it was something I could really ask him to do.

Suddenly, sitting there in Ivy's little lounge, I was overcome with doubt. Was I doing the right thing by marrying Darren? Wouldn't it be fairer to let him go and find someone else, someone who wasn't likely to get ill and become handicapped, and eventually die a miserable death? Someone who could be a proper mum to his children? Because if he stayed with me, the likelihood was there would be only Woody. But then if Darren left me, who'd look after Woody, when I couldn't any more? I loved Darren with all my heart and soul, and I knew he loved me more than anyone deserved. But was it going to be enough?

'Are you all right, my dear?' Ivy must have caught my sudden change of mood.

'It's just . . . oh. Dammit. I'm not sure I should go ahead with the wedding.' To my consternation, I burst into tears. I never ever cry. Crying is for other people. I'm the happy perky friend who wipes away everyone else's tears.

'There, there, dear,' said Ivy, patting my hand and passing me a tissue. 'You're not the first bride who's sat here crying. It's a stressful time getting married. The important thing is, do you still want to do it?'

'Oh I want to,' I said. 'More than anything in the world I want to marry Darren. It's just I'm wondering whether I *should*.'

'I don't follow,' said Ivy.

'I have MS,' I said. 'No one knows but Darren. In a few years I could be in a wheelchair. It's quite possible I'll die young. I just don't know whether I can put Darren through all that. It's all been so sudden. One minute we were happily planning our wedding and then this hit us between the eyes. I just don't know what to do. My dad had MS and I saw what caring for him did to my mum. I love Darren too much to want to do that to him.'

'Darren isn't your mum,' said Ivy. 'You're also still young and where there's life there's hope, I always say. Besides, isn't it up to your young man to say whether or not he wants to help you through this?'

'I suppose,' I conceded.

'And do you know what his answer would be if you put it to him?' said Ivy.

'I guess,' I said.

'And?'

'I know he'd say yes,' I said.

'Well, there you are then,' said Ivy. 'Marrying Darren won't make you better, but neither will not marrying him. If he's prepared to give it a go, so should you.'

I thought about everything Ivy had said on the way home. When Darren came home I'd already got Woody into bed, lit the candles on the dining room table and prepared a proper meal for us, rather than my normal haphazard chucking-something-from-the-freezer-into-the-oven routine.

'What's all this in aid of?' Darren asked.

'To say I love you.' I went to kiss him.

'Not yet.' Darren held his hands up firmly. 'I need to wash the germs of five million Londoners off me first.'

'Oh get away with you,' I said, 'as if they could give me anything worse than what I've already got.'

'Oh Dorrie.' Darren immediately folded me into his arms. 'If I could make this all better for you, I would.'

'I know,' I said, biting my lip. I didn't want to cry. I tried perky brightness instead. 'So, how was your day then?'

'The usual. Looked at a lot of germs down a microscope. Talked to people about possible endgame scenarios if terrorists ever develop germ warfare. How about you?'

'I saw the flower lady,' I said.

'Any good?'

'Brilliant,' I said. 'I'm really happy with the flowers I've chosen. She was really kind and understanding. I even told her about my MS.'

'Good,' said Darren, 'I think it's healthier for you to tell people.'

He pulled me close to him again.

'So, you've sorted out the flowers, that's one less thing to worry about.'

'I suppose so,' I said. 'I really wish I could sort out the bridesmaid situation as easily.'

'I thought you said the girls seemed to be getting on well,' said Darren.

'Well they are,' I said. 'But I told them all in Paris that I didn't want to have bridesmaids.'

'Tell them you've changed your mind,' said Darren.

'I'd like to,' I said, 'but I'm still not sure it's a good idea. Caz can be so volatile and she's having a hard time right now. And Beth seems a bit scratchy with Sarah at the moment. I just don't want anything to ruin our day.'

'What about your cousin's daughters?' said Darren.

'I did say I didn't want to ruin our day,' I laughed. 'Those kids are wild. If Mum wasn't so spaced out at the moment, she'd never have suggested it.'

'She'll get better,' said Darren without much conviction. He loved Mum nearly as much as I did, but we both despaired of ever pulling her out of the deep depression she'd fallen into since Dad died.

I sighed. 'It's ironic. Most brides to be spend their time fending off their mum's interference. I'd kill to have her show a bit of proper interest.'

'You know the doctor said it would take time,' said Darren.

'I think that's half the problem,' I said. 'She has so much time to think and so little to do since Dad died. If only I could get her interested in the wedding, I'm sure it would help.'

'Maybe you could take her with you next time you have to see the flower lady,' said Darren.

'Maybe,' I said. I paused. Everything I'd talked about with Ivy came flooding back. 'You do still want to get married, don't you? I'd really understand if you changed your mind.'

'Hang on, where's this come from all of a sudden?' said Darren.

'I just can't help thinking about my illness and what a big impact it's going to have on you,' I said. 'I will understand if you don't want to go through with it.'

'We've been through all this,' said Darren firmly. 'I would still want to marry you if you had two heads and a blue bottom. Get that into your head, you silly woman.'

'But—'

'Sshh. But nothing.' Darren held his finger to my lips. 'For better for worse, in sickness and in health, remember? We're in this together. I'll be with you whatever it takes. That's all there is to it.'

Chapter Sixteen

Sarah

Knowing what I should do and actually doing something about it were of course two very different things. Every day Steve came home from work and I geared myself to have The Conversation and then bottled it. I even started practising in the mirror, starting with the incredibly (to my ears anyway) clichéd, 'Steve, we need to talk,' until William came in and said, 'Mummy, why are you talking to Daddy in the mirror, he's downstairs?'

'I'm not,' I said guiltily, though why *I* should feel guilty was beyond me.

It depressed me how little notice Steve even took of me any more. I was beginning to realize that I had finally fallen out of love with him, but to be so ignored was really hard. He never noticed how jumpy I was, how tired I seemed after endless nights lying awake worrying about how I'd cope financially if I left Steve. And as for sex, well that was never on the agenda any more.

I would have confided in Beth about it, but I felt a bit edgy round her after our recent phone call. Although we'd spoken since, she'd been distant, and I knew she was stressing about her failure to get pregnant. I didn't want to add salt to the wound by going on about my problems.

I also didn't feel it was fair to impose on Dorrie, who naturally only wanted to talk about weddings when we met. Although Dorrie knew that I was thinking of leaving Steve, now it had actually come to the crunch point, I couldn't face saying it out loud. It made it seem so final and absolute. So I just carried on with the usual routine: doing the school run, sorting out the house, meeting Dorrie for the occasional coffee and wedding talk. It was easier to pretend everything was normal.

I suppose in a way, I had only myself to blame. Over the years everyone from Caz to my parents had hinted that Steve wouldn't make me happy, and I'd always papered over the cracks and pretended he could and did. Now I was done with pretending, but like the boy who cried wolf, no one was ever going to believe me.

In the end Steve forced my hand. Dorrie and Darren had invited us to dinner over the May bank holiday weekend. Being Doris, she'd insisted it was going to be a games evening. So long as it wasn't a Murder Mystery night, I didn't mind. I'd never quite forgiven her for the Murder Mystery night where Steve ended up playing the murderer who'd killed the lovely young thing he'd been shagging. The lovely young thing in question had been one of Doris's work colleagues and Steve had spent far more time flirting with her than I would have liked.

This time, Doris had assured me that it was merely going to be things like *Pictionary* and *Trivial Pursuit*.

'I promise this isn't a Talk About the Wedding Evening,' she said as we arrived, although I could tell she was dying to tell us all about place settings, flowers and the like. I couldn't blame her. I'd bored for England when it was my turn.

'Oh go on, you know you're dying to,' I said. 'So, you sorted out the flowers then?'

'That flower lady was brilliant.' Doris was off immediately. Steve, in barely disguised disgust, headed for the lounge where there was beer and the promise of male company in the form of Darren.

I heard female laughter coming from the lounge.

'Are Beth and Matt here already?' It was a longstanding joke that Beth was always the last one to arrive anywhere.

'Er, no,' said Doris. 'I didn't think you'd mind.'

Oh my god. My heart started thumping erratically in my chest. Caz was here. And I'd just sent Steve in to her.

'You could have warned me—' I said.

'I was a bit worried you wouldn't come if I did,' said Doris. 'Besides, you have been getting on better, haven't you? Come on, lighten up, she had to meet Steve again sooner or later.'

'I suppose so,' I said, but I didn't feel convinced. I walked into the lounge feeling like a condemned woman. All my battered self-esteem needed now was to have Steve flirting with my ex-best friend as if the past had never happened.

'Such a pleasure to see you after all this time,' Steve was saying smoothly. 'You haven't changed a bit.'

'The pleasure's all mine,' Caz's smile was sweet. 'You haven't changed either.'

What was she doing? She couldn't be flirting with him, could she? Not after everything she'd said.

I had to look away. I was so disappointed. Caz hadn't changed and Steve clearly was revelling in the reunion.

'Caz is looking well, don't you think?' Steve said to me.

He looked at me pointedly. He didn't have to say anything, I knew what he was thinking, I'd heard it so many times before: you've let yourself go, you should lose weight, do something about your hair. Steve was full of unsubtle ways of making me feel less than adequate. I'd put up with it for far too long. I picked up the generous glass of wine that Darren had poured for me and headed for the kitchen where Doris was ladling an orange sauce over the duck she was cooking.

'Do you need any help?' I asked.

'No, I'm fine thanks,' said Doris, 'but you can stay and chat for a minute, if you like.'

'Thanks,' I said. 'I couldn't take any more of Steve's snarky comments about my appearance.'

Doris didn't comment as she was busy concentrating on picking up the dish with the duck, but her hand seemed to shake a little, and the dish flew out of her hands. I leapt to rescue it, and managed to stop it landing on the floor, but not before we both had a generous helping of orange sauce all over us.

'Ouch!' I said. 'That's bloody hot.'

Gingerly I put the dish back on top of the oven.

'Oh, just look at us,' said Doris. 'Here, let me give you a cloth and wipe you down.'

By now we were in fits of hysterics, though mine were slightly on the edge of tears. I really didn't know how I was going to get through the evening.

I was on my knees scrubbing duck fat off the floor when Beth and Matt arrived, for which I was immensely grateful. Beth and I had maintained an uneasy silence since she'd snapped at me about babies and I wasn't feeling strong enough at the moment not to take it personally, even though I well knew she had troubles of her own.

I followed Dorrie back into the lounge where she regaled everyone with the tale of the slippery duck, while I slipped into the corner and took a huge sip of wine.

'Honestly Sarah, you have to cause chaos wherever you go, don't you?' Steve's comment sounded light-hearted to all but my ears, it stung me to the quick.

Over dinner I relaxed a bit. Dorrie had put me between Matt and Darren, and it was a relief to talk comfortably about noncommittal subjects like football, the weather, and global warming without feeling I was going to offend or be offended. Darren was incredibly generous about filling up my glass, so I was soon giggling like an idiot and trying to remember to have a glass of water in a minute. Normally I was the one driving, but we were only ten minutes' walk from Dorrie's so we'd left the car at home. I tried not to look Steve's way. He and Caz still seemed to be flirting with one another. I might as well have not existed. My stomach was in knots as I felt old jealousies reassert themselves.

'Right, time for games.' Dorrie clapped her hands as everyone announced that the expert lemon soufflé she'd produced had stuffed them to the gills. 'Come on Darren, get this lot cleared away.'

I volunteered to help Darren and by the time we'd loaded the dishwasher, Dorrie had *Trivial Pursuit* set up. I hate *Trivial Pursuit*. I am just not geared up for general knowledge at all. Dorrie and Darren of course always do brilliantly on the science, Beth and Caz tend to do well on the arty ones and Steve who is competition personified always does well on sport and geography. Matt tends to be in the dunce's corner with me.

As there were seven of us, Darren decided it would work best if the rest of us were in pairs, and he was on his own. As he is a total brainbox, this made sense to the rest of us. He elected to keep us in our couples apart from Caz who he put with Dorrie. My heart sank. I knew how sarcastic Steve would be if I didn't get the answers right.

To begin with things went well. I knew the answer to the film which starred Laurence Olivier, and even got us our first wedge with a momentary flash of inspiration when Steve's geography deserted him and I worked out that the country which bordered Lebanon, Syria, Jordan and Egypt was Israel.

'Way to go!' Steve slapped me on the back rather more enthusiastically than I'd have liked. At least he'd said something positive for a change. After that, our luck ran out.

Caz and Dorrie flew off into the lead, following Dorrie's ability not only to know what the oldest and most numerous class of animals were (insects), but Caz's encyclopaedic knowledge of films, knowing as she did, who starred in *Gone with the Wind* and *Streetcar Named Desire* (Vivien Leigh) and which 1972 Marlon Brando film was banned (*Last Tango in Paris*).

Soon they were heading for their sixth wedge and victory, while Darren who seemed to know something about absolutely everything, was close on their heels with his fifth, and even Beth and Matt were on three. In the meantime we were still stuck on one. It wasn't just that I'd wrongly stated that vampire bats went for the neck of humans (trick question, it's their toes), or that I didn't know the phone number of the White House, Steve was doing disastrously too. I'd left him all the sports questions, but he'd got a series of obscure questions like *What does a notaphile collect?*

(bank notes) and *What Swiss town has hosted two Winter Olympics?* (St Moritz).

Being Steve, of course he couldn't accept that it was his failings as much as mine that had led to our parlous position. So when I wrongly answered that the sequel to *Little Women* was *Jo's Boys* and not *Good Wives*, an answer he would never have got in a million years, he hissed, 'Can't you get anything right?' I bit back the retort that was on my lips because I didn't want to have a public row, but I was steaming. How dare he be so rude in front of my friends? It wasn't the first time, but in the past I'd always given him an excuse for his behaviour, not seen it for what it was, appallingly obnoxious and self-centred.

I sat back and sipped at my wine, and watched with a smile as Caz and Dorrie cleaned up the game, enjoying Steve's barely suppressed fury when they won.

'I think we should play something different now,' he said before Darren, Beth and Matt could complete our humiliation. '*Trivial Pursuit* gets so boring after a bit.'

'Good idea,' agreed Dorrie. I could tell she was trying to keep the atmosphere jolly, so enthusiastically supported the suggestion of *Pictionary*.

'Let's mix it up,' suggested Steve, 'to make it more interesting. Why don't Caz, Darren and I make a team, and Sarah, Matt, Beth and Dorrie make a team?'

Once again I didn't want to rock the boat and ruin Doris's evening, so I acquiesced. But I was silently seething when Steve planted himself right next to Caz. I gratefully accepted Darren's generous topping up of my glass and started to drink with wild abandon, deliberately ignoring Steve's bitchy asides about my drinking habits. As it happens, I'm quite good at *Pictionary*, but even I couldn't manage to get across to Matt that my drawing of an insect was in fact a termite.

'Never mind,' said Steve smugly as his team went storming ahead, thanks to a brilliant moment by Caz who managed to interpret Steve's rather dubious picture of a stick and a tree as beating around the bush. 'We all know drawing isn't your strong point.'

I glared at him, but said nothing. I could feel Dorrie squirming by my side.

On the next round Steve's team wasn't doing so well. Steve had drawn a heart and someone falling off a cliff, but though the answer was obvious to me, Caz and Darren were stuck.

'I'll give you a clue,' I said cattily, 'it's something Steve does often.'

Time ran out and they still hadn't got it.

'So what was it?' Caz wanted to know.

Steve glared at me. 'Sarah can tell you. It was a stupid one anyway. Falling in love.'

'Oh, I got it wrong then,' I said sweetly. 'I thought it was being a lover.'

The game rolled on. I was beginning to feel rather drunk and wishing I could go home. I could tell everyone else was also starting to flag a little. When it came to my next go, my mind went blank and all I could think to do was draw a picture of Tammy Wynette singing. My teammates remained baffled.

'Singer?' said Darren.

'Music?' said Beth.

'Microphone?' said Matt.

I drew a heart next to it splitting in half.

'Broken heart?' said Beth.

'Yes, go on,' I said, putting a wedding veil on Tammy.
'Marriage?' said Matt.

'No!' I said, frustration mounting. I couldn't think of a clearer way to do it.

'I know,' said Steve when the timer ran out. 'It's "D-I-V-O-R-C-E" isn't it?'

'That's the one,' I said, staring him straight in the eyes. The tension between us was palpable and everyone seemed a bit embarrassed. 'Ironic don't you think?'

Steve looked at me and said, 'Sarah, I really think you've had enough to drink. It's time we were going home.'

Suddenly something snapped. How dare he lecture me as to how I should behave?

'No,' I said. 'I don't think you have the right to tell me to do anything any more.'

'Sarah, you're drunk,' said Steve stepping forward. 'Come on, let's go home.'

'And you're a lying shit,' I said, and threw my glass of wine all over him. My moment of triumph was followed by an overwhelming sense of embarrassment and humiliation. I hated public scenes. What the hell had I done?

'Oh my god, Dorrie, Darren, I'm so sorry,' I said and only stopped to grab my things from the hall as I ran out of the house. I ran down to the end of the road and sat on a garden wall, sobbing hysterically. It was cool for May, but I was so fired up I barely felt the cold.

Two minutes later, Steve came marching up the road behind me.

'What the hell do you think you're doing?' he said. 'How dare you humiliate me like that?'

'Me, humiliate you?' I said bitterly. 'That's a laugh.'

I got up and walked away from him.

187

'And where do you think you're going at this time of night?' said Steve.

'Home,' I said. 'If I can still call it that.'

'Oh, you're impossible,' said Steve. 'I've had enough of your jealous fits.'

I stopped walking and stared at him. Even now he was trying to blame me. Even now.

'It's all right, Steve,' I said. 'Whatever lies you can come up with, I know you're seeing Kirsty. Our marriage is a sham. It's time we got a divorce.'

Sarah

September 1997
The wedding reception was in full flow when I saw her. I had half hoped she was coming, but a bit of me didn't want to see Caz on my wedding day. Ever since she'd said she didn't want to be my bridesmaid, I'd been racked with suspicion and guilt. I'd tried to talk to Steve about Caz, but he'd laughed at me and said that Caz was a sad, mad maneater and he wouldn't touch her with a bargepole. The weeks leading up to the wedding had been tense and anxious, but now I was here, I had started to unwind and enjoy the big day. After his initial irritation with my late arrival, Steve had seemed genuinely thrilled when I came down the aisle, I heard the catch in his voice as he repeated his vows. Surely he couldn't have made that up, or the emotion in his voice when he'd said in his speech how proud he was to be my husband? I had to face it, my best friend was a troubled soul and bad news around men. I'd always known that. Just never expected her to shit on *my* doorstep. I had to trust Steve, I had to. Otherwise this day would be a complete farce.

I was busy doing the rounds of Steve's relations, and he was taking mine, when I saw Caz sneak in. I saw her make for Beth and Dorrie, both of whom were talking to her in animated fashion.

I stood immobilized for a moment, barely noticing that Steve's granny was still commenting on how beautiful the flowers were and what a lovely bride I made. I couldn't breathe. I hadn't seen Caz since the day of our dress fittings, and had assumed as she didn't want to be my bridesmaid, she wouldn't come to the wedding at all. I couldn't ignore her. It was my wedding day, and she was – had been – my best friend from our first day of primary school.

I started moving towards where Caz and the girls were, but was waylaid by Joe, Steve's lovely younger brother.

'The band's about to start up,' he said. 'Come on, nearly time for your first dance as a married woman.'

He dragged Steve away from my Auntie Norma, and then made a huge announcement as we walked onto the dance floor. I felt like a total dummy, as Steve took my hand and held me close, as we smooched to 'I Will Always Love You'. *The Bodyguard* was the first film we went to see together and inevitably Whitney Houston became the theme tune to our relationship, even if I did find her a bit cheesy.

I felt exposed in the middle of the room. I was aware of Caz, somewhere in the shadows, her eyes boring into my back. I'd become uncomfortably aware in the last month of how intensely jealous she could be. Was she watching me dance with Steve, enviously wishing it could be her? That was Steve's take on things.

'Happy?' said Steve, pulling me close and kissing me on the lips, which elicited a roar of approval from the crowd.

The answer he was waiting for was yes, but Caz's arrival had put me off guard. I tried to smile, conscious it wasn't reaching my eyes.

'Ecstatic,' I said with an enthusiasm I didn't feel. I longed for the dance to end, for the feeling of exposure to go away. I didn't want to be here any more. This couldn't be right. Not on my wedding day. I shouldn't be feeling so churned up and nervous. This was meant to be the happiest day of my life.

Eventually the torment was over, and Steve's dad cut in demanding a dance with his 'beautiful daughter-in-law'. I have to confess to a little thrill at those words. I had longed to be married to Steve for so long, and now here I was, the new Mrs Johnson. Steve dutifully went off to dance first with my mum, then Beth and Dorrie, but by the time Joe had turned up to take his turn to whisk me round the dance floor, I noticed Steve sneaking off to the bar. Typical. He hated dancing.

'Having a good time?' said Joe, as he pulled me firmly around the dance floor. It was different dancing with Joe, he seemed to lead me, so my steps felt fluid, whereas Steve just pushed me about and I felt like an enormous klutz.

'Yes,' I said, but my eyes kept darting to the door.

'Sometimes my brother is a big, dumb prat,' said Joe as the dance came to an end. 'If I'd just married you, I wouldn't leave your side all evening.' He pecked me softly on the cheek. 'Congratulations, Mrs Johnson, you look lovely.'

I stood there a bit stunned, as Joe walked away, wondering what on earth he meant.

There was a natural pause as the DJ started to ramp it up a gear to get more people on the dance floor. I stood in a daze, as people all around me came out to party on down. I'd never felt less like partying in my life, so I gave my excuses and made my way to the bar. I was feeling thirsty and wanted to catch up with Steve.

There was no one much in the bar apart from two elderly chaps from Steve's side of the family. Odd. I frowned; where had he gone? I wandered back down the corridor to the dance floor, feeling a little bit like a ghost at my own funeral. Everyone else seemed to be having such a good time. How come I wasn't? I couldn't face either dancing or small talk, so I made my way out to the front of the hotel, to get some fresh air.

It was then that I saw them. Standing, huddled together quietly in the shadows, murmuring urgently to one another. He had her hands in his, she went to stroke his cheek. Oh god, no. Not on our wedding day. How could she? How could *he*?

I stood rooted to the spot. The flowers from my bouquet wilting in the summer heat, along with my dreams. I didn't know what to do or say, but then Caz pulled away and said something I couldn't catch in a choking sound of voice.

'Don't be like that,' I heard Steve say, as Caz ran towards the light.

Seeing me there, she stopped in horror, the look of anguish on her face almost comical, if it hadn't been so bloody tragic.

'It's not . . . this isn't what you think,' she said.

'No?' A month's worth of bitterness and suspicion trickled off my tongue. 'What is it then? Do you both think I'm completely stupid? For fuck's sake. This is my wedding day. Why do you have to spoil everything?'

Caz didn't say anything. She didn't even try to deny it. She just looked awkwardly down at her feet, and mumbled an apology.

'I should go,' she said. 'I was leaving anyway.'

'Yes, you should,' I said acidly.

Caz looked at me, and then back at Steve, as if trying to make a decision.

'It's not his fault,' she said eventually. 'I put him in an awkward position. I'm sorry. I should never have come.'

Throughout this exchange, Steve had said nothing. I wasn't sure I wanted him to.

'Well?' I said.

'Well, what?' Steve looked at me belligerently. 'I can't help it if your friend is a tart who can't stop throwing herself at me.'

I so wanted to believe that was true. But I'd seen the way he looked at her. I'd seen the way he held her.

'Why aren't I enough?' I said dully. 'You're enough for me, why aren't I enough for you?'

'Don't be like that, baby,' he said, seeing I was crying. 'Come on, this is our wedding day. Look, maybe I've had a bit of a silly infatuation with Caz. But it's over. Honestly. I was telling her that when you came along. I married you, didn't I? Can we forget this ever happened? Today's the first day of the rest of our lives. Let's forget all about her.'

I stood, uncertain, churned up, feeling I was being taken for a mug, but wanting to believe him. We'd made vows to one another. How could I say my marriage was over before it had even begun? How could I face all those people knowing what a mistake I'd made?

As if sensing my uncertainty, Steve moved towards me, and took my hands in his. 'I'm sorry,' he said. 'I am so sorry. I've always been a terrible flirt, you know that. And things got a bit out of hand with Caz. I should never have gone there, would never have gone there if she hadn't thrown herself at me.'

'You didn't have to respond,' I said, feeling myself weaken.

'I didn't, not really,' he said. 'Nothing happened. And I promise you I'll never do anything to hurt you again. It's you I love, and I always will.'

He looked so sincere. He seemed so sorry. I loved him so much. I was hurt. I was distrustful, but maybe this was the first hurdle of our marriage. I couldn't trip over it. I took a deep breath and said, 'OK, I forgive you, but please Steve, never do that to me again.'

'I promise, I won't,' he said. Then, sweeping me into his arms, he marched me back down the corridor. 'Now let's make this the best night of our whole lives.'

I wanted things to be right. I wanted them to be perfect. So I shut my eyes and pretended that they were.

Part Three

In Sickness and in Health

Beth

April 2005

I hadn't wanted a hen night. I hated the idea that you should have a night to mourn the passing of your freedom. I couldn't wait to be married to Matt. After so many years in the wilderness, watching Sarah and her growing family, and Dorrie being so happy with Darren, it was my turn. Why would I want to do anything other than celebrate that? Plus, I hate being centre of attention, and I dreaded some well-meaning and misguided attempt to make me wear a learner's plate and force a stripogram on me. My pleas were in vain though.

'You *have* to have a hen night, and that's that,' said Dorrie. 'We won't hear otherwise.'

'Will Sarah be able to cope if Caz is there though?' I fretted. Sarah and Caz barely saw each other these days. Dorrie and I had still kept in touch with her, and I had put my foot down and told Sarah and Caz they were both going to be my bridesmaids, reasoning that so long as they could manage to be civil for the ceremony and the photographs they needn't talk to each other for the rest of the day. But a whole evening of them together? With alcohol involved? I wasn't sure it was a good idea. At least Sarah was in the early stages of pregnancy and wouldn't be drinking, but Caz could be unpredictable at the best of times. I hoped she didn't cause any trouble.

But I couldn't have a hen night without Caz being there. After all, even though Dorrie and I had been angry with her for the way she'd treated Sarah, Caz had always been a good friend to me when I needed her. She was still the only person who knew my secret. Not even Matt knew about it. I still felt I owed her.

The evening didn't get off to the best of starts. I was so knackered from weeks of negotiating my way through the minefield of dealing with Mum's increasing neuroticism of all things wedding related, all I really wanted to do was have an early night and a soak in the bath. I've never been much of a party animal, but Dorrie was determined I was going to be one tonight. She'd come round to the house Matt and I had just bought (though to please Mum we weren't officially living in yet) to pour a few drinks down my neck and get me going, as she put it. Despite my protestations, she insisted that I wore a veil, and had arrived with a bunch of pink balloons saying *Hen's Night.*

Before long she'd packed me in a taxi and we'd arrived at a restaurant, where a sundry group of my friends (though thankfully none of my relatives) were waiting. Sarah was already there, drinking sparkling water of course, with more balloons at the table, and an L Plate that she insisted on me wearing. Caz turned up late and already the worse for wear.

'Here, you've got to wear this,' she said, producing a blue garter.

'No, I don't,' I said.

'Yup, you need something blue, and it can be your

something borrowed as well,' she insisted, and to my mortification made me put it on.

'Caz, have you been drinking?' I said. It wasn't that I didn't like a drink myself, but the night was still young, there was plenty of time to get hammered.

'And what if I have?' Caz's tone took on an aggressive belligerence I recognized. Bugger, if she was like this early on in the evening, it didn't bode well.

'Caz, it's my hen night,' I pleaded. 'Please be nice.'

She looked crestfallen for a moment. 'Sorry, Beth, I didn't mean to.' She ran her hand through her sleek, short gamine haircut. 'It's been a bad week.'

'Your mum?' Caz never said much, but I knew she was often called upon to deal with results of her mum's drunken rampages.

'Got it in one, but I don't want to talk about it.' Caz took a swig of her bottle of Beck's. 'Come on, Beth, this is your night, we're here to have fun.'

I can't say I didn't have a laugh that night. The early part of the evening was great. We were all getting on really well, and Caz and Sarah were dutifully being polite to one another for my sake. My friends from work mixed well with my friends from uni and Dorrie cooed and charmed her way round the crowd, making up for my shyness and ensuring everyone was having a good time.

Just as it was time to pay the bill, there was a commotion and in strolled a copper.

'Oh god, no,' I groaned. 'Doris, I'm going to kill you.'

'It wasn't me,' said Doris.

'It was me,' said Caz. 'I thought you could do with lightening up.'

'Well, I don't,' I hissed. But it was too late. The guy was

already going into his routine, and showing off his bronzed and impossibly toned body, rather closer to my face than I would have liked. The rest of the girls went wild, shouting, 'Get 'em off, get 'em off!' as he removed each item of clothing. I have never blushed so much in my life, particularly when invited to rub him all over with cream. I was mortified, but felt obliged to go along with it, hating every minute, wanting to kill Caz for putting me through this humiliation.

When it got to his g-string, I politely declined any suggestion that I might like to remove that for him and have some *extra* fun as he put it. And no amount of teasing from the girls would change my mind. Caz looked as if she wouldn't mind taking over where I left off – by now I realized she was very drunk – but the guy fortunately had other jobs to get to, and to my relief left with his bits still all in the right places, and my dignity intact.

'Don't ever do that to me again,' I said. 'That was hideous.'

'Oh come on, Beth, you really need to learn to relax, you know,' said Caz, slurring her words a little. 'I reckon that Andy the bastard has a lot to answer for. I hope Matt's managed to heat you up a bit.'

Andy the bastard. Why was Caz mentioning Andy the bastard at my hen night?

'Shut up, Caz,' I said. 'That's all in the past.'

'That's funny, Andy the bastard nearly had his own little bastard,' said Caz, as if struck by a sudden revelation. 'He's probably got heaps of little bastards by now.'

'Will you be quiet,' I hissed. 'I'm getting married to Matt. I never want to think about Andy again.'

'Right, who's for a club?' Caz suddenly changed tack, and led the charge as we sorted out the bill and started heading for the door.

All I wanted was to go home and curl up with a cup of hot chocolate, but I realized my chances of that happening were about zero. So I allowed myself to be dragged along by the rest of them, as we piled into cabs which took us up the road to nearby Hadley, where apparently there was a new nightclub called Dreams.

'What was that all about?' said Sarah, looking tired and a bit wan, her normally sleek fair bob lank and lifeless. Nobody would compare her to Meg Ryan now. The pregnancy was clearly taking its toll.

'All what?' I said shortly. I'd deliberately avoided getting in a cab with Caz, who'd gone off with Dorrie and a couple of my livelier uni friends.

'About Andy's bastard,' said Sarah.

'Nothing,' I said. 'Caz just mouthing off as usual. I don't know why she had to bring him up tonight of all nights.'

Sarah didn't look convinced, but the cab was drawing up in front of Dreams and before long we found ourselves in a nightclub with pounding music and flashing lights. I had a headache and wanted to go home.

Caz wouldn't hear of it though, she had us all up on the dance floor, even me. It was clearly her idea of a great night out, particularly as she'd found a couple of good-looking guys to smooch with. Part of me admired her self-possession and confidence, another part of me was slightly horrified. I could hear Mum's voice in my head saying, 'Will you look at her making such a show of herself?' And I couldn't help but agree.

Eventually the place started to slow down, and things were getting on the quiet side. Time, I thought with relief, to go home. Everyone was beginning to flop on the comfortable sofas in the corner of the club, away from the dance floor. At least we could hear ourselves think here.

'We should play *Truth or Dare*,' said Caz suddenly. 'Come on, it's a hen night. We should be having fun.'

Everyone woke up a bit then. I must admit even I started off thinking it might be a laugh. Most of the early questions were quite innocuous, *What was your most embarrassing moment of the week? When was your first kiss?* That kind of thing.

Caz, of course, had to up the ante.

'This is way too tame,' she said. 'I think we should have a few more dares.'

'OK then,' said Sarah. 'I dare you to go and snog the barman.'

Caz marched over bold as brass, walked behind the bar, and to our joint hysteria did just that.

'See, it's easy if you know how,' she said. 'Right, Beth, I dare you to do the same.'

'Not on your nellie,' I said. 'I'm nearly a married woman.'

'OK then, let's have the truth,' Caz continued. 'What's your guiltiest secret?'

'I don't have one,' I said.

'You must have done *something* bad, once in your life,' said Dorrie teasingly. 'Even Goody Two-Shoes Beth must have stolen sweets or something in her childhood? Go on.'

'Yes, tell, tell,' the others chanted.

'I stole sweets when I was six years old. There. Satisfied?'

'What about with Matt?' said Caz. 'Don't you get up to anything naughty with him?'

'No,' I said, turning puce again. God, would this evening's humiliation never end?

'What, you've never been a little bit naughty?' Dorrie was teasing I know, but I just wanted her to shut up. 'Not even with Andy the bastard? He always seemed like a right dirty sod to me.'

'I reckon Andy the bastard left her frigid,' said Caz. 'That's where the problem lies.'

'Caz, will you just shut up,' I said. 'I do not want to talk about Andy now or ever again.'

'I'm not surprised after what he put you through,' said Caz.

'Caz, just leave it,' I screamed. I got up and ran to the bathroom, shaking with anger. How could she do this to me? Why did she have to keep on and on?

Dorrie came running after me. 'I'm sorry, Beth, I was messing about. I didn't mean to upset you.'

'It wasn't your fault, it was Caz's,' I said. 'She's a liability.'

'What did Caz mean?' said Dorrie. 'What did he put you through?'

'Nothing,' I said. 'He was just a rotten bastard who broke my heart, Caz is pissed and doesn't know what she's on about.'

I went back to the bar, where Caz had seemingly forgotten what she'd said and was smooching with one of the guys from earlier. It was quite clear where she was going to end up tonight.

I thought about her behaviour tonight, and on so many other nights like it. She'd never betrayed my secret but tonight she'd come very close. In the morning I was going to ring her and tell her I didn't want her as my bridesmaid any more. Everything she touched turned to dust, and I wasn't going to risk her ruining my wedding.

Chapter Seventeen

Beth

I was in a cold and impersonal hospital bed. The walls were dark and I was surrounded by shadowy figures. I knew I was about to do a very wicked thing and my heart was beating wildly. I felt sick and dizzy. Should I tell them to stop? Or should I face the music and go ahead with it?

The doctor came towards me, holding a ghastly-looking instrument which looked as if it had come out of a nineteenth-century torture chamber. Oh my god. Was that what he was going to use on me?

I screamed out loud, and then the doctor took his mask off and it wasn't a he, it was a she. My mother stood before me saying, 'You'll be punished for this, don't you worry.'

I sat bolt upright in bed, sweating profusely in the sticky June night, my heart hammering, and my breath coming in short sharp bursts. I knew it was a god-awful dream, the real thing hadn't been anything like that. The doctors and nurses involved had been nothing but kind, but I had always felt a nagging doubt of worry that somehow I would be punished for what I'd done. And now I felt like I was.

We didn't appear to be able to have children, and I couldn't help feeling it was all my fault. I wished I could get over it. What's done is done. But the sound of Mum's voice rang in my ears as if she were actually in the room with me. And as for Matt . . . I sighed, and rolled over looking at him sleeping. He'd been far more upset about the failure of the IVF than I thought he would be. I wished I could talk through all my worries about getting pregnant properly, but that was impossible. He'd told me early on in our marriage how strongly he felt about having children, and not willing to lose the only man who'd ever cared for me, I had kept silent about my past. And now it was too late.

Matt stirred and woke up.

'Hallo beautiful,' he said, his unfailing way of greeting me in the morning. 'Can't sleep?'

'No,' I said, blinking back tears, which Matt misinterpreted.

'It'll be all right,' he said. 'We'll get our baby. We just need to be patient.'

I snuggled up into the warmth of his arms, wishing he was right with all my heart. But what if he wasn't? What would we do then?

'Fancy a girlie night on Friday?' Dorrie rang me at work. 'Sarah needs cheering up, and so do you.'

'I don't know . . .' I felt incredibly guilty about the way I'd spoken to Sarah the last time she'd rung me. I'd been so embarrassed about it I had barely spoken to Sarah at all during Dorrie's disastrous games evening. I couldn't help myself. I was so jealous of the ease with which she'd had children. And even now, when it was clear from her dramatic outburst that her marriage was in big trouble, I couldn't help envying her her boys. Even if she lost Steve, she'd still have them.

Despite having my second IVF booked, I was beginning to fear it might never happen for me. And I didn't know what I'd do if I couldn't have children. My visions of the future had always contained the husband, the country cottage, the happy, smiley children. I was frightened that without that dream coming true, Matt might not want to stay with me. And I'd be left with nothing.

But Dorrie being Dorrie, had managed to persuade me that a girlie night with Sarah was just the thing I needed, and Matt was encouraging too, telling me it would be good for me to go out with my friends.

Which is how I found myself on Friday evening knocking on Sarah's door with Dorrie.

'We come bearing gifts,' said Dorrie, producing chocolates, a bottle of wine and a DVD of the *First Wives Club*.

Sarah smiled wanly as she greeted us. She looked pale, and had bags under her eyes.

'How are you doing?' Doris hugged her and I followed suit.

'I've had better weeks,' said Sarah. 'I don't know what I'd have done without you though, and I am still really sorry for ruining your evening.'

'Don't be daft,' Dorrie laughed it off. 'Darren said he hadn't had so much fun in years. Mind you, he did fumigate the place afterwards in case the wine Steve wiped off himself was full of germs.'

'He didn't—' Sarah looked horror struck.

'No, of course he didn't.' Dorrie fell about laughing. 'I know Darren's obsessive, but he's not *that* bad.'

Sarah gave us a weak grin and we followed her into the lounge.

'So, what are you going to do?' I said.

'I don't know yet,' said Sarah. 'Steve's barely been home all week. It's weird, Joe often helps out with the kids in the week; I've just realized we probably see more of him than we do of Steve. I'm not sure if he's got wind of what's going on, but he's always popping in. I don't know what I'd do without him.'

'You sure picked the wrong brother!' said Dorrie mischievously. 'You know, you could always do something about that.'

'I think that might feel a bit like incest,' said Sarah. 'Besides I've sworn off men for the time being.'

We sat and chatted for several hours, dissecting Sarah's marriage, finding suitable punishments for Steve, trying to work out what Sarah should do next. Though Dorrie had bought wine, none of us drank very much. I was still trying to be sensible, and our next IVF was planned for the third week in June. I didn't want anything to go wrong this time.

'You're not trying again are you?' I asked Dorrie. She didn't seem to be drinking very much either.

'Me, no chance,' said Dorrie, although she looked a bit shifty when she said this, so I wondered perhaps if she was hiding something. 'I'm aiming to be slim for my wedding you know.' Then she put her hand over her mouth. 'I'm so sorry, Sarah, I didn't mean to mention the "W" word tonight.'

'No worries,' said Sarah. 'It's not like anyone died. Just because I'm getting divorced, doesn't mean you can't talk about your wedding. You know how pleased I am for you.'

'You know that's a dangerous thing to say,' said Dorrie. 'You have been warned that there may be no other topic of conversation for the rest of this evening.'

'So how much have you got left to do?' I said.

'Loads,' said Dorrie. 'I keep having arguments with the hotel about exactly what I want. They don't seem keen for me to have a Disney-style castle in the hotel foyer for some reason.'

'Can't think why not,' said Sarah with a grin.

'I've sorted the flowers out now though, and we've finally agreed to get married at St Philomena's. Father Miserecordie is going to marry us. I had a job persuading Darren, he wasn't at all keen on a church wedding. We've still not ordered our rings yet, and we're undecided about the honeymoon. But the thing that's bothering me most is every time I look at my wedding dress, I wish I did have bridesmaids after all.'

'But I thought you didn't want any?' said Sarah.

'I didn't say I didn't want bridesmaids,' said Dorrie. 'I do. But I want all three of you – One four all and all four one, remember? – and that's never going to happen, is it?'

Dorrie looked so sad when she said this, my heart went out to her. The Bridesmaid Pact had been her idea, and one by one we'd let her down.

'Never say never,' said Sarah unexpectedly. 'I am still cross with Caz. I can't believe she could flirt with Steve like that, and I'm quite hurt she hasn't rung me since it happened. But if it means so much to you, I'll put my feelings aside. It's only one day.'

'To be fair to her,' I said, 'she didn't seem like she was enjoying Steve's attentions all that much.'

'Well, maybe I could give her a second chance,' said Sarah grudgingly.

'Would you? Would you really?' said Dorrie. 'It would mean the world to me. Especially now.'

She looked wistful and rather sad when she said this.

'What do you mean, especially now?' I asked.

'Nothing,' said Dorrie. 'Nothing. I'm feeling a bit melancholy is all.'

It didn't seem like nothing. Something was clearly troubling her. But she clearly wasn't prepared to tell.

'Well, just for you,' said Sarah, 'I might be prepared to share bridesmaiding duties with Caz. But only if you promise not to dress me like a meringue.'

'You know I can't promise *that*,' said Doris, smiling. 'Thanks guys, it means a lot to me.'

'Then consider it settled,' said Sarah. 'If Caz is up for it, so am I.'

A few weeks later I was back in hospital with Matt. It didn't really matter how kind or nice people were, the room felt cold and unwelcoming. It made me feel gloomy. I was trying to fight it, but I couldn't help feeling we were doomed for failure. It hadn't worked last time, why should it work now? I tried to banish such negative thoughts from my head. I knew Dorrie would tell me to think good karma otherwise I'd screw it up, but I couldn't help feeling I'd screwed it up anyway.

'It'll be fine.' Matt squeezed my hand. 'Remember, lots of people don't succeed first time, they told us that before.'

'I know,' I said, trying to give a wan smile, 'but what if it fails again?'

Matt squeezed my hand. 'Let's cross that bridge when we come to it, eh?' he said. 'Let's be positive. And maybe Foetus will want to hang around this time.'

The procedure was the same as before: uncomfortable, humiliating, a little bit terrifying. Last time I'd left on a high, so sure that I would be pregnant. But this time I was racked with doubt. I lay on the bed, my heart pounding, feeling faintly sick. We couldn't afford to go through this again, either financially, or, I suspected, emotionally. Yet the lack of a baby was causing me a pain so intense that I wasn't sure I was going to be able to survive without it.

So this time I wasn't leaving anything to chance. Although he wouldn't come right out and say so, Matt was still sure that my going to the funeral had caused the IVF to fail. I couldn't tell whether it had been a factor or not, but just in case, I'd taken two weeks off work, and was going to lie around and do absolutely nothing. I had to give Foetus every bit of help I could. And maybe this time our dream would finally come true.

Chapter Eighteen

Caz

'Caroline.' Auntie Nora stood at Mum's front door, stiff and awkward.

'Auntie Nora,' I said. I felt equally uncomfortable. It was several weeks since I'd walked out on her, and I'd rather have carried on clearing Mum's stuff out without her being there, but there was so much to do. Besides, Auntie Nora was the executor to Mum's will and there was still paperwork to sort out. Unfortunately we both needed to be there.

'Well, let's get on with it then,' I said. We went into the lounge where the boxes I'd taken from the loft still remained from the last time I'd been there. I'd taken the letters away with me, but left everything else. I sat down and started sorting through things. It was a welcome distraction to be honest. I had spent the last few weeks mulling over the fact that Mum had lied to me my whole life. And churned up in my misery was the memory of that strange night with Charlie. Nothing had happened, but I now felt odd around him. He was my mate, the person I always turned to when I was in trouble. I hadn't thought about him *that* way in years. And yet, spending such a close and tender night with him, even though nothing had happened, had reawakened feelings I'd forgotten I had. Bloody hell. I couldn't be falling for him. I *shouldn't* be falling for him. Much as I might want him to, Charlie didn't belong to me.

And seeing Steve again had reawakened all those guilty feelings and knowledge of how destructive I could be. I hadn't intended to flirt with him, but unconsciously I'd fallen into my old patterns of behaviour, it was so instinctive to me to seek out male approval. Then I'd seen Sarah's stricken face and kicked myself. Just when we'd got back on an even keel it looked like I'd blown it again. I couldn't do to Charlie and Nadia what I'd done to Sarah and Steve. Even though I had never really liked Nadia, I respected Charlie too much to cause him any grief.

So after giving it a lot of thought, I'd organized my time so I could take some more time off work, ostensibly to sort out Mum's things, and ensured that for my next few jobs, I'd be working with photographers other than Charlie.

'Sure and your mam was always such a hoarder,' Auntie Nora cut into my thoughts. It was the first time she'd really spoken since she'd arrived. She had a dreamy smile on her face as she said, 'She kept everything under her bed when we were children: her diaries, her old dolls – everything. It used to drive our mam mad. She always got a hiding for it.'

'Did she? I never knew.' My memories of Nana Riley were hazy, but she'd always seemed a benign presence. As I talked to Auntie Nora, I realized there was a lot I didn't know about Mum's early life. She rarely talked about either Ireland or her parents. But from the hints Auntie Nora had dropped, it seemed they hadn't had the happiest of families. Nana Riley didn't sound like much of a role model. It was no wonder Mum made such a hash of it with me. I picked up an old photo album. The spine was cracking and the pictures looked faded and grey. Some were pictures of Mum and her siblings in Ireland – little waifs in hand-me-down clothing – a fair few of me as a gurgling smiling baby, and then one of Mum with a man I didn't recognize. She looked so happy – pretty, light. A version of Mum I'd never known.

'Who's that?' I said, passing the photo to Auntie Nora.

'You really don't know?' she said. 'That's your da. He was a handsome fella. I was that jealous of your mam at first.'

'Oh,' I said. I'd never seen a picture of Dad before. Mum had no record of him in the house to my knowledge, and any enquiry about him had been met with a smart, 'You don't want to talk about him, he's bad news that one.'

But I did. I did want to know about him. Despite what I'd said at the funeral. I'd always made out I didn't care about my dad, afraid of being rejected again. But deep down I'd always been curious. Who was he? Where was he? And why had he and Mum gone from being so happy to him leaving us – leaving me?

'What was he like?' I said.

'Charming, handsome,' said Auntie Nora, 'but no staying power. Couldn't stick around after your mam had you. It was all too much for him. So he upped sticks and left her literally holding the baby. She never recovered.'

'Is that why she never let me see his letters?' I asked.

Auntie Nora sniffed, 'Well he didn't want you both, so what was he doing sending you cards?'

I could think of plenty of reasons. He'd left Mum. That meant leaving me, but maybe he hadn't wanted to.

'Do you know where he is now?' I said.

'What do you want to know that for?' said Auntie Nora.

'Because I want to find him,' I said. 'I've lost my mum, but there's still time to meet my dad. If he still wants to be found.'

'So your dad's been writing to you all this time?' Dorrie said. I hadn't got round to telling any of the girls about my discovery. I was at a loose end after we'd finished sorting through the photos, and was feeling restless like I needed to talk to someone. Dorrie's house was nearest, it only took me five minutes to get there. Being Dorrie, she'd immediately dropped everything and dragged me into the kitchen to have a cup of tea, though I could see that the dining room table was set up like a military operation with lists and brochures, all things wedding related.

'My whole life, she kept it from me. Can you believe that? How can anyone be so wicked?' I said.

'People do all sorts of things when they're hurt and angry,' said Dorrie. 'I guess we never know what goes on in someone else's head.'

'Do you know what the worst is?' I said. 'I can never ask her now. I can't even get cross with her. I've got all this rage and nowhere for it to go.'

Dorrie leant across and squeezed my hand. 'I wish I could do something,' she said.

'You already have,' I said. 'By being here. I'm sorry I've been so crap over the years.'

'Oh don't go all martyred on me,' said Dorrie briskly. 'It really doesn't become you. Now let's have another cup of tea, and then I'll co-opt you into ticking off acceptances with me.'

She got up to put the kettle on, and suddenly she was on the floor.

'Dorrie, are you OK?' I leapt up to help her. She was shaking and a large bruise was forming on her leg, while her nose was spouting blood.

'God, I hate the sight of blood, especially my own,' Doris joked. I got her to put her head back and made her hold her nose while I fetched a tissue.

Eventually we stemmed the flow and I sat her down while I made the tea.

'You're obviously doing too much,' I said. 'Did you get up too quickly? It was like you fainted or something. You must take it easy.'

Suddenly I was aware of Dorrie sobbing. Dorrie *never* cries. She's always the one to pull things together.

'Doris, whatever's the matter?'

'It's nothing,' she said. 'Just wedding stress. I just want it all to go well, and for you to be my bridesmaids, and for Mum to be happy.'

'So you still want us as bridesmaids then?' I said.

'The others said they'd do it,' said Dorrie. 'I was just waiting for you.'

'I'd love to,' I said. 'And Dorrie, I'm so sorry. We all do this to you. We burden you with our stuff and never think about your problems.'

'Problems? I don't do problems,' said Dorrie. She wiped her tears away, gave me a typically Dorrie grin and said, 'Come on, I need some help with my seating plan.'

I followed her into the dining room, but couldn't help thinking that there was something she wasn't telling me.

When I got back home I decided it was time I had a proper look at all the cards Dad had sent me. There were dozens of them. He'd remembered every birthday and Christmas.

217

Every one. All the cards were the same. *To my beautiful princess. Always thinking of you. Love, Dad.*

The letters were varied. Some were short, telling me what he'd got up to – going home to Ireland, or getting a new job. Some were longer, detailing travelling he'd done and promising to take me to places if he ever got a chance.

There was a gap of a few years when he didn't appear to have sent any, but they resumed again around the time I was thirteen. He'd dropped the princess bit by then.

My darling Caroline, he wrote,

I'm sorry you haven't heard from me for such a long time. I've been moving around and only just found out your mother's been sending my letters back. I suppose that's her right, but I didn't want you to think I'd forgotten you. I'd never do that.

But this is just to let you know I have some exciting news. I've got married again and my new wife, Lindy, is having a baby. I hope that we can all meet up really soon.

With much love, your Dad xxx

That was it. There were no more. A scrap of paper fluttered down. Another letter from Dad to Mum this time. *I think you're being unreasonable. I only want to see Caroline. Please don't send my letters back. I shall keep writing them.* But there were no more. The last address I had for him was over twenty years old. How on earth was I going to track him down?

Chapter Nineteen

Sarah

Oh god. Every day I woke up and the pain was still there. A dull ache lying across my stomach. I knew in my head that divorcing Steve was the only sensible way forward. I'd known it for months, but now it was happening a kind of paralysis had set in. I got myself through the days like an automaton and dreaded Steve's return at night. We hadn't spoken properly since my outburst at Dorrie's. But every day he grew colder towards me. He'd taken to sleeping in the spare room, rather than in our bed. In fact I was sure he must be spending most of his time in hers, as there were several nights when he didn't come home at all.

The day of reckoning was drawing near and I knew I had to face it. But now it was so imminent I couldn't bear the thought of my marriage being over.

'Get it over with,' Dorrie urged me on a near daily basis. The only refuge I had from my misery was coffee and biscuits and wedding plans at Doris's – somehow the thought of her tying the knot with Darren was immensely comforting in my misery. At least one of us was happy.

'I know, I know,' I said. 'But how do you begin to have that conversation? Where do you start?'

Dorrie didn't have an answer to that. Why should she? Sympathetic and fabulous as she was, she couldn't really understand. She and Darren were so loved up, I couldn't imagine them ever splitting up, or Darren being unfaithful to her. She was so lucky. Not for the first time in my life, I felt a tad jealous. Dorrie had always had it all: looks, brains, money, a fabulous home, a great life. She had always seemed so blessed to me. It was unworthy I knew, but I couldn't help myself.

In the end, I got sick of the sound of my own voice, so insisted I help Dorrie source some more stuff on Freecycle. We'd already got napkins and name places all with a Disney theme, but Dorrie had set her heart on having Mickey Mouse disposable cameras on the tables, and Mickey and Minnie Mouse ears for everyone to wear (insisting that the grown ups wore them as well as the kids). I said I'd do that for her. She seemed so tired all the time, it was the least I could do.

'You haven't forgotten we're going to lunch for Mum's birthday on Sunday,' said Steve without any preamble as he came in through the front door towards the end of June. It was the most he'd said to me in the tense weeks since Dorrie's games evening.

'What, you still think we should go?' I said. I couldn't think of anything I'd like to do less than spend a birthday lunch with my soon-to-be-ex mother-in-law. I got on with Maggie all right, but spending a day playing happy families would be excruciating.

'Yes,' said Steve, casually pulling off his tie. 'Of course I do. We can't miss her birthday. She'd be devastated.'

'Like you'd care,' I said. It had been my job all these years to remind Steve when his mum's birthday was. 'When was the last time you bought your mum a present?'

'You don't need to worry about that,' he said. 'Kirsty's already sorted it.'

'So let me get this straight. You want us to go to lunch with your mother, pretending everything is fine between us, and you will be giving your mother a present from us, supplied by your mistress. That is so bloody ridiculous it's almost funny. You *are* planning to tell her we're splitting up, aren't you?'

'When the time's right,' said Steve. 'But I can't ruin her birthday.'

'Well, I'm sorry you feel like that,' I said stiffly. 'You can take the kids, but I won't be coming.'

'And what do you want me to tell them then?' Steve nodded in the direction of the lounge, where luckily the kids were obliviously watching *The Simpsons*. The unfairness of that infuriated me.

'Don't you think you should have thought about that before you found yourself a mistress?'

'There's no talking to you,' said Steve. 'I knew you'd be unreasonable.'

'*Me* unreasonable?' I felt like picking a knife up and stabbing it through his heart so he'd really know what unreasonable was. 'You chose to end this marriage by having an affair and *I'm* the unreasonable one? You are so full of shit, Steve. I wish I'd divorced you years ago.'

'I wish you had,' said Steve. 'It would have saved us both a lot of grief.'

He took himself upstairs to get changed, then went in to say goodnight to the boys. He then came back into the kitchen. 'I'm going out,' he said.

'Where?' I asked.

'It's no longer any concern of yours what I do,' he said, and walked out of the house.

If he'd punched me in the stomach, he couldn't have hurt me any more.

'More pudding, dear?' Steve's mum proffered some raspberry cheesecake.

I didn't think I could eat another thing. I'd barely touched my food since I'd been in her house. What on earth had possessed me to come? I should have left Steve to go alone, but the kids had been so excited about seeing their granny on her birthday, and I felt churlish ruining the day for her, so I'd come, albeit reluctantly. We'd been pretending for so long that we were a happy couple, one more day wasn't going to make any difference.

For Better, for Worse. In Sickness and in Health. Those vows had meant something to me. They clearly hadn't meant anything to Steve. In Love and in Divorce – no one had yet written a vow to cover that one. And I didn't even have any happy memories of the wedding day itself. My whole marriage had been a complete disaster.

To make matters worse, Joe was there too. His steady unflinching sympathy had been both a source of comfort and embarrassment to me through the long, farcical years Steve and I had played out this charade. I liked and respected him – amazing how different two brothers could be – but I couldn't face him at the moment. I'm sure Steve had filled him in on what was happening. Joe was never backward with coming forward when he thought Steve was in the wrong, but they were close, and for all I knew had known about Kirsty all along. He was loyal to his brother, even if he hated the way Steve behaved.

'You look a little peaky, dear,' said Maggie. 'Steve, you

need to look after Sarah better. She looks peaky, doesn't she, Joe?'

'I'm fine,' I said, with embarrassment.

'You're too thin,' Maggie continued oblivious. 'You silly girls will insist on dieting.'

'I'm not dieting,' I protested, as Steve snorted into his glass of wine. God he could be cruel sometimes. All my married life I'd heard him going on about how fat I was and yet, I'd never gone above a size twelve, except in the months after my pregnancies. I had, I realized, let him brainwash me into thinking I was overweight.

'I think Sarah looks lovely,' said Joe, glaring at Steve warningly, who ignored him and said nothing.

Even Maggie couldn't fail to notice Steve's glaring omission. 'Steve?' she asked in a good-natured kind of way.

'What?' said Steve savagely. 'Will you all get off my case? There's nothing wrong with Sarah. She's not dieting, she looks fine. Boys, why don't you come for a kick about in the garden with your Uncle Joe?'

'Yay!' Sam and Will jumped to their feet, luckily unaware of what was going on, and never passing up the opportunity to play football with their dad and uncle.

I shot a glance at Steve. He seemed quite anxious. I almost felt sorry for him. *Almost.*

'Maggie, let me help you with the dishes,' I said, both her sons being absolutely hopeless on that score.

'Oh, thank you, dear,' she said. She appeared completely unaware of anything untoward. As far as she was aware this was just another birthday lunch with her family.

I went into the kitchen and started to pile things up in the dishwasher while I watched the boys playing in the sunshine outside. They were all having such fun and I was

223

no part of it. I felt a sudden stab of loneliness as I felt keenly for the first time how great the distance between Steve and I actually was.

Eventually Joe came back in, panting heavily. 'Sorry,' he said, pouring himself a glass of water. 'I didn't mean to lumber you with the washing up. Phew, it's hot out there.'

'It doesn't matter,' I said. 'I'm used to it. I managed to persuade your mum to sit down with a cup of tea and read the paper for five minutes. I needed some head space.'

'Sarah,' Joe looked at me hesitantly, 'what's going on?'

'Can't you guess?' I glanced out of the window at Steve who was chasing the boys around the garden pretending to be a monster. Why could he be so loving with them and not with me? 'We're splitting up.'

Joe thumped his hand down on the work surface. 'God, my brother is a prize idiot. He's never deserved you.'

We both had our back to the door, and were slow to hear Maggie's strangled gasp of 'Oh no'. We turned round to see her drop the cup she was holding (her best bone china), her jaw falling open. In the midst of my unhappiness, it was a wild comedy moment, and I had to stifle the impulse to giggle hysterically. She stood frozen there for a long while before shutting her mouth.

'Oh,' was all she could manage, before she sank against the work surface, completely oblivious to the china smashed at her feet. 'Well, I realized you two had some problems . . .'

I bit my lip and refrained from saying, *Problems caused by your son's inability to keep it in his pants*. Maggie had always been kind to me. She didn't deserve my bitterness.

Joe took his mum gently by the arm and steered her back into the dining room.

'I'll go and get Steve,' he said, 'and keep the boys outside. You need to talk.'

'This wasn't my idea,' I said. 'I'm sorry.'

'What do you have to be sorry for?' said Joe. 'It's Steve who should be apologizing.'

Steve looked in no mood to apologize, when he came storming into the dining room. 'What the hell do you think you're playing at? I told you not to tell Mum today.'

'I didn't tell her,' I said wearily, bored of having to justify myself to him. 'She overheard Joe and I talking.'

'Oh Steve, I knew things weren't right between you . . .'

'Mum, it's quite simple,' said Steve. 'I don't love Sarah any more. And I've met someone else.'

To hear it said so baldly, so coldly, was too much for me. Particularly as Maggie's reaction was to wail loudly and hysterically.

'Oh this is just like your father all over again. Steve, how could you do this to me?' It didn't seem to occur to her that he'd actually done it to his *wife*.

I got up and went back to finish putting the dishes away. I was not about to be lumbered with looking after Maggie, so I buried myself in the kitchen cleaning – anything was better than sitting in the dining room with my mother-in-law and husband and that atmosphere – and stared out of the window at Joe playing football with the boys. That's the life I should have had.

Eventually they came piling in, and I pulled myself together to joke about Uncle Joe and how many goals they'd scored before sending them into the lounge to watch TV. I didn't want them wandering into the dining room where Steve and Maggie were still in deep conversation.

'You OK?' Joe touched my arm awkwardly.

225

'I'll survive,' I said.

'I'm so sorry,' said Joe. 'I wish there was something I could do.'

'You're already doing it,' I said, snivelling a bit. 'But it's OK, Joe, I'll manage.'

'For what it's worth,' said Joe, 'I think my brother's bloody stupid.'

'Please don't be so nice,' I said, 'otherwise I'm really going to lose it.'

'OK, I'll start being a bastard then,' said Joe.

I flicked him with a tea towel, but he'd done enough for me to pull myself together, gather the children, and say goodbye to Maggie, who'd managed to compose herself too. We couldn't put off telling the kids any longer, but I wanted to do it my way.

Joe hugged me tightly as we left. 'Look after yourself, kid,' he said. 'You know if you need anything, you only have to ask.'

I sat in the car all the way home with Steve, who barely spoke. Not for the first time I wished Steve was more like his brother.

Chapter Twenty

Doris

'Are you sure that you don't want to make an appointment with Mr Mason?' Darren said as he got ready for work. Woody was happily sitting in his highchair dropping bits of bread on the floor. Dear god, for a small person he made a helluva mess. I was busy sorting the washing and Darren watched me for a moment as I struggled to transfer it to the tumble dryer before saying, 'Here, let me help you.'

'I can manage!' I snapped at him. 'I'm not an invalid yet,' even though the task felt ridiculously hard. I had good days and bad days, and this was most definitely a bad day.

'I never said you were,' said Darren, looking hurt, and I immediately felt a pang of guilt. Is this how it was going to be between us now? This bloody disease eating away at our happiness? I'd seen what it had done to Mum and Dad. Could I bear that happening to us?

'I'm sorry,' I said, burying my head in his broad shoulders. 'It's not your fault.'

'It's nobody's fault,' said Darren. 'And I still think you should see Mr Mason.'

'What can he do, really?' I said. 'I've got MS, it's going to get worse, end of story.'

'You have to be more positive than that,' said Darren. 'There's always hope.'

Ah yes, hope. I remember I had that when Dad was first diagnosed. But the years of watching his progression with the disease had eroded the hope to nothing. And now I was so terrified of the same happening to me, I could barely bear to think about it. I knew it was foolish, but I was burying my head in the sand, hoping it would all go away. In my own way, I was as paralysed as Mum by Dad's death, which is why Darren was the only person who knew about my illness.

'I nearly told Caz about it the other day,' I said.

'Perhaps you should have,' said Darren. 'You've got good friends. It might help to talk it over with them.'

'I don't want to upset them though,' I said. 'And, after all, what can they do?'

'Be there,' said Darren firmly, kissing me on the head. 'But if you don't want to do that, you could think about a support group.'

'What's the point of that?' I said.

'It might help talking to other people in the same situation,' said Darren. 'However hard I try, I'm not going to understand the way someone with the disease would.'

'I suppose,' I said.

'Think about it,' he said. 'Look, I've got to get to work, will you be OK?'

'I'll be fine,' I said. 'I'm just having a wobble. I've got plenty to keep me occupied today. I'm researching bridesmaids' shoes on the Internet.'

'Now, that's something to be cheerful about, isn't it?' said Darren. 'At least you'll have your bridesmaids at the wedding.'

If I get that far, I thought, but didn't say it.

'Yup,' I said, giving him my brightest, cheeriest smile, and kissing him full on the lips. 'Say goodbye to Daddy, Woody.'

'Dadda, Dadda,' Woody gurgled, banging his spoon.

After Darren left, I finished feeding Woody and gingerly lifted him out of the highchair. I hadn't yet fallen when I was carrying him, but I lived in dread of it. Luckily he was now crawling, so I popped him on the floor and guided him to the lounge, where I folded laundry and watched *GMTV* while Woody played with bricks beside me.

I couldn't stop thinking about Dad. I wanted so badly to remember him as he'd been when I was little: tall and strong, and always there for me. But my early memories were crowded out by the misery of his last years, of seeing him retreat into grumpy despair as his world wore away to nothing, and he became totally dependent on Mum. In the end, he couldn't even speak, but his eyes said it all. I've never seen such unhappiness as I saw in his eyes. He was trapped in a body he hated, and I know he longed for release.

I don't think I could bear to put Darren through what Mum had gone through. I shut my eyes and tried to make my darkest thoughts go away. But they crowded me, making me feel faint and breathless. There had to be another way, another solution. Surely I didn't just have to sit here and accept my fate?

I felt so drained and exhausted. What kind of future did Darren and I have together? Maybe I should call the whole thing off, and let him find someone else. Someone fit and healthy, who could live a life with him.

No. I knew Darren wouldn't buy that one. He's a stubborn cuss and when he asked me to marry him *again*, just

229

after I'd been diagnosed, he had refused to take no for an answer.

The first time Darren asked me to marry him, I thought it was a joke. We'd only been together a few weeks and though I knew without doubt that beyond the dizzying feelings of early love lurked a deeper, stronger feeling, I also wanted to be sure. I'd been planning my wedding down to the last detail since childhood; I wasn't going to make the mistake of marrying the first man who asked me.

Of course, having given him the knockback, it took years for Darren to pluck up courage to ask me again. But when he did, he did it in style. We had combined a trip to see my Aunt Sophie in Switzerland, with a European tour. Discovering we were in the environs of Neuschwanstein, the fairytale castle featured in *Chitty Chitty Bang Bang*, I'd badgered Darren to take me there. Darren, though, was one step ahead of me. On the battlements of the throne hall, overlooking the lake, he got down on one knee and produced the biggest diamond ring I've ever seen in my life. I'd never been so blissfully happy, and couldn't wait to get the wedding plans started.

But things didn't quite work out as we planned. Dad's MS was diagnosed shortly after our return, and somehow after that the time had never been right to fix a date. And when he died, and Woody came along in short succession, I was so at sea, the last thing on my mind was my wedding. I was just coming out of all of that when I found out I had MS. But Darren insisted that didn't matter. I wished I could believe him.

This was no good. I tried to concentrate on the TV to take my mind off things. I nearly turned it off when I realized they were doing a piece about terminal illness. Then I heard the doctor they were interviewing say, 'I believe I give people hope, and the ability to choose. Knowledge is power. I don't tell them what to do with that knowledge.'

I'd heard about this guy. He was on a lecture tour of the UK, telling people with terminal illnesses how they could commit suicide. There'd been a lot of controversy about it. People called him Dr Death. I leant forward to listen some more.

I didn't tell Darren about Dr Death, but like a secret addict, I began to read more and more about him and his theories. I avidly followed all the stories in the papers about people trying to change the laws on euthanasia or travelling with relatives to Switzerland to assist them in dying. Before I was ill, I'd never have thought about myself in such a position, but reading the stories, all of them personal, all of them tragic, I realized it was different for everyone. And it was different for me now. Could I contemplate a future with Darren caring for me 24/7? I shivered at the thought. But could I ask him to help me die? That didn't seem right either. I spent far too much time on the Internet looking at my symptoms and wondering if I was already showing signs of the progressive form of the disease. Every time I lay awake at night because a muscle had twitched, or I got up and felt my vision go, I convinced myself that the disease was worsening, even though I knew from my Internet trawls that it was by no means certain that my MS would get worse that quickly.

I thought constantly about what I would do when the time came for me to be permanently cared for. I am by nature a sunny, cheery kind of person. I'd never harboured suicidal thoughts before, and I wasn't harbouring them now.

Part of me kept hoping ludicrously, ridiculously, that maybe someone would find a cure, or at least a means of halting this wretched disease. How stupid it would be to end it all when maybe there could be a cure around the corner. But did I have the courage to carry on if there wasn't?

The more I thought about it the more terrified I became, but I couldn't tell Daz what was going on in my head, because I had a feeling I knew what he'd say about it. I was in so much turmoil I didn't know where to turn. Until Sarah took the bull by the horns during one of our usual coffee mornings, towards the end of June. We were going through her Internet trawls – she'd sourced the Mickey Mouse cameras and was close to finding a job lot of Minnie and Mickey Mouse ears – but I was feeling lethargic from lack of sleep and my head was pounding. I couldn't concentrate on what she was saying, and found my left hand was starting to twitch – a nervous tic that had recently appeared, which might be psychosomatic or could be a sign of the disease, I wasn't quite sure.

'So when are you going to tell me what's wrong then?'

'What do you mean?'

'Come on, Dorrie, I wasn't born yesterday,' Sarah said. 'And I'm a nurse remember? Something's wrong. You never used to be this clumsy. And you fall down such a lot. I'd say some kind of motor neurone thing myself.'

I stared into space. Could I tell her? It would be nice to confide in someone about what I was going through.

'It's, oh god, this is so hard to say,' I said. 'Darren's the only one who knows. I've had odd symptoms for a while now, but six months ago I found out I've got MS.'

It was a relief to finally talk about it. Once I started, I couldn't stop. I told her about my fears of ending up like

Dad, my worries for Darren and Woody, and how I'd feel if I ended up in a wheelchair.

'One thing at a time, eh?' Sarah said, giving me a hug. 'It's still early days. It may not progress that fast. And it's not a given that you'll end up in a wheelchair. You're probably still in a state of shock. Are you going to a support group?'

I grimaced.

'That's what Darren said I should do,' I said.

'Well, he's right,' said Sarah. 'Talking to other people in your situation can help, you know.'

'Don't you think that's a case of pots and kettles?' I said.

Sarah had told me about her disastrous family lunch, but very little else, and I knew she was bottling stuff up. She looked completely washed out and far too thin.

'Touché,' said Sarah. 'Actually, I'm thinking of going to counselling. I feel so bonkers at the moment.'

'Excellent idea,' I said. 'Now all you need is to get together with Joe and your life will be sorted.'

'I haven't divorced his brother yet,' said Sarah, laughing. 'Anyway, we're talking about you not me.'

'Suppose I don't want to talk about me?' I said, blinking back tears.

'Oh Dorrie, I wish you'd told me before,' said Sarah, 'I feel terrible you've been going through this alone.'

'I haven't been alone, I've had Darren,' I said.

'You know what I mean,' said Sarah, hugging me. 'Look if there's anything I can do, you will let me help, won't you?'

'Of course,' I said. 'But you *have* to promise me you'll think about Joe.'

'Don't change the subject,' Sarah said, sternly. 'Promise me you'll go to a group?'

'I promise,' I said.

'I think that's a brilliant idea,' said Darren when I told him. 'I'm sure it will help. It might make you feel not so isolated.'

'True,' I said. 'But what if they're all awful? Or being with them makes me more depressed? It could be even worse than going to antenatal classes. After all, the only thing we've got in common is this bloody awful disease.'

'But that's the point,' said Darren. 'You will have that in common. You won't know until you try, will you?'

'Why do you always have to be so bloody reasonable?' I said. 'Have you any idea how annoying that is?'

'Yup,' said Darren, gathering me into his arms and kissing me. 'But it's good to see you smile. You haven't done enough of that lately.'

'Well, I haven't felt much like it lately,' I admitted. 'I feel lousy a lot of the time, and I haven't been sleeping.'

'You should have said,' said Darren.

'So what? To make sure you couldn't sleep too? I have to feel this way, no point moaning on to you about it.'

'That's what I'm here for,' said Darren.

'Oh, don't be so bloody nice,' I said. 'I want to sit here and feel properly sorry for myself, can't you let me?'

'Nope,' said Darren, 'because you know that's not going to get you anywhere.'

'It's really hard to be positive though,' I said. 'I keep thinking about the future and how you'll manage when I can't look after myself any longer.'

'Dorrie, it may never come to that,' said Darren. 'I refuse

to hear such defeatist talk. So come on, let's go and put Woody to bed, and then sit and cuddle up on the sofa, watching a good film.'

Sitting on the bathroom floor, watching Darren splash water on Woody's face, and sing him nursery rhymes, I felt more content than I had in months. Somehow we would get through this. Darren was right. We had to because we had no other choice. Unless I took Dr Death's route. I shivered. I wasn't sure I wanted to think about that.

'Welcome, welcome,' a friendly lady greeted me at the door of the community centre where the MS support group was held.

Tuesday mornings, 9.45-11.30. Drop in for a coffee and a chat, the flyer I'd picked up from the local library said. I'd left Woody with Darren's mum, making some pretext up about wedding shopping. Darren's mum wasn't to know that I'd got most of my stuff off eBay. Darren was keen for me to tell his parents the truth about my illness. I knew we should, but I kept putting it off. I was worried Darren's mum might persuade him not to marry me. Jenny was great, but she was a very clear-sighted, black and white kind of person. I could just see her thinking her son was heading for disaster. I wouldn't blame her if that were her attitude. I'd probably think the same if Woody was planning to marry someone with a terminal illness.

'Hi everyone, this is Dorrie. She's new, so do make her welcome,' a warm woman called Jean, who seemed to be in charge, introduced me to the group.

There were half a dozen or so people there. Not all of them, I was relieved to see, were in wheelchairs. There were a couple using sticks, and one like me still able to walk unaided. Holding court in the middle of the room was a jolly woman in a wheelchair whose name I learnt was Flo. She had a tube coming out of her nose, and a loud booming voice which she used to crack any number of un-PC jokes. She was so cheerful. I didn't get it. How could she be that happy in her condition?

I felt shy and foolish. I was the youngest here by miles. But everyone made me feel very at home and I quickly learnt that black humour was the order of the day, and it seemed to be what pulled them all through.

'I was a right misery guts before I came here,' confided Flo. 'Now I'm fed through a tube and my guts can go stuff themselves.'

'You want to watch it though,' said an older man called Tony. 'I used to be able to do cartwheels before I met this lot.'

'I'm sure they put something in the tea to keep us all quiet,' said Carol, another quieter woman who walked with a stick.

Despite my initial reservations, it was a relief to talk to people who understood what I was going through. They were full of practical advice on everything from how to deal with the pins and needles which afflicted me regularly, to how to adapt my house should I need to.

'I don't want to think about that yet,' I said. 'It's too soon.'

'Ah, still finding it hard to accept, are we?' said Tony.

'You could say that,' I said. 'But really, I was only diagnosed six months ago, after my baby was born. And so far, apart from falling down a bit – well, a lot – and having pins and needles in my arms and legs, I don't have that many symptoms.'

'We've all been there, love,' said Carol with sympathy. 'You're only at the start of this, it's bound to be scary. But look at us, we're all here and surviving.'

'Have they told you what type of MS you have?' Flo said.

'Um – no,' I said. 'I've only seen the consultant once.'

'What?' everyone chorused.

'You must go back,' said Tony. 'There are things they can do.'

'Like what?' I said. 'I can take all the drugs in the world, but I'm still going to end up in a wheelchair.'

'You mustn't think like that. Not everyone ends up in a wheelchair,' said Carol. 'You have to live in the now. Think about the positives in your life. What have you got to look forward to?'

They were saying all the things that Darren had been saying to me for months. And the optimistic, positive side of me was beginning to resurface.

'Well, I'm getting married in September,' I said.

'That's great,' said Flo encouragingly. 'You've got a lovely baby and a new life to plan. Focus on that rather than your symptoms.'

Slowly, gradually, I started to feel better, as I talked to these disparate lovely folk.

'You know most of us have been living with this for a long time,' said Tony. 'I've had it for fifteen years. It doesn't have to be a life sentence, even if it seems like that now.'

'I'll try and bear that in mind,' I said.

'And look at me,' said Carol. 'I've currently been in remission for two years. It's not the life I imagined I'd lead, but I do have a life that I enjoy and live to the full.'

'What about you?' I turned to Flo, who was nodding wisely through all of this. 'How long have you had it?'

I imagined she'd say at least five years – Dad's condition had taken that long to take hold.

'Ah, well I've not been quite so lucky as the others,' said Flo simply. 'Two years ago I was as fit as you. Now look at me. Pretty much fit for nothing.'

'You're still fit for one thing,' Tony winked at her lasciviously.

'You are awful,' said Flo.

'But you like me,' said Tony and they were both off, roaring with laughter.

Two years. *Two years*. What if that happened to me? I looked around at the group. They'd done their best to make me feel positive, but right now, I'd never felt less cheerful in my life.

Beth

April 2005

'Is the car here yet?' Mum must have asked the same question a thousand times. 'Oh what's the matter with him? We're going to be late.'

'Will you hush, woman,' said Dad, ever calm and pragmatic. 'The car's booked to come at 1.30, it's only 1.15 now and your photographer man's after taking that many pictures he'll probably make us all late anyway.'

'I can't believe the timing of this,' said Mum, flapping some more. 'What with the Holy Father dying, maybe we should have cancelled the wedding.'

'Don't be daft,' Dad and I said automatically, and then we laughed out loud. This was, after all, the woman who'd made us drive around Wimbledon late at night when John Paul II had come to England on the strength of a rumour that he was staying in the area.

'I'm sure His Holiness won't be turning in his grave because our Beth is getting married today,' said Dad.

'Well Prince Charles changed his wedding plans to Camilla, and he's not even a Catholic,' sniffed Mum. 'Not that I approve of him getting married again. Doesn't seem right to that poor girl.'

'And he got to go to the funeral and we didn't,' I said, although I'm sure Mum would have gone to Rome if she could have wangled it. The day before, I'd been forced to watch the whole Papal funeral while writing out table settings.

'And wouldn't that have been a fine thing to do,' sighed Mum.

'But it's a finer thing that we're finally marrying our Beth off,' said Dad, with a twinkle in his eye.

'I suppose so,' said Mum. 'But Elizabeth, can't you pull that veil straight.' She turned her attention to me and I patiently submitted to having my veil, which was perfectly all right, rearranged for the thousandth time.

I loved my wedding dress, which, daringly for me, was strapless ('You can't flaunt yourself like that in God's church!' had been Mum's initial horrified response, but I'd won her round), with a flared-in waist and a wide skirt that flowed out behind me. The bodice was decorated in delicate lace patterns. With my dark hair coiled in curls on top of my head, the gorgeous ivory satin shoes Dorrie had managed to find me, and the train that went down my back, I felt like a million dollars. Thanks to my falling out with Caz at the hen night, she clearly could no longer be expected to do my make-up, so I'd had to make do with the hairdresser down the road. She'd done an OK job but I knew Caz would have done better. For the longest time I hadn't cared about my appearance and Caz was always nagging me to let her make me over. The night I was finally persuaded to was the night I met Matt at a work colleagues' birthday. Another reason I had to feel grateful to her.

Guiltily, part of me had wanted to ask her to come along again. Caz had been a good friend to me on more than one occasion, but she knew too much about me, and was so unpredictable, I daren't let her. What if she got drunk and blurted out my secret to Matt?

Mum had been horrified when I told her that Caz wasn't going to be my bridesmaid after all.

'But what about the dress?' she kept saying. 'We spent a fortune on it.'

She was so busy bewailing that she didn't really quiz me too much on why Caz was no longer coming, so I fudged some story about Caz having to go on a last-minute assignment that she couldn't get out of, and promised I'd resell the dress on eBay.

'Well, at least you've still got two bridesmaids,' she'd sniffed.

'Yes,' I said brightly, determined not to show how upset I was at the loss of my third.

'I'm so sorry, Beth.' Sarah appeared, looking ashen, the pale blue strappy dress that I'd chosen turning out not to be a good look for someone who was newly pregnant and looking rather green. You could see the faint swelling of her tummy and I wished I'd chosen a dress with a looser fit. Too late now of course. 'Can I use your loo again?'

'Of course,' I said. It was the third time Sarah had been sick. She'd had a terrible time with morning sickness first time around but this seemed to be interminable. I hoped she wasn't going to throw up in the bridal car.

'Car's here!' Mum screeched. 'Where are the bridesmaids?'

Dorrie, who of course looked fabulous in the blue, was comforting Sarah in the loo, and I was trying to be supportive, but I couldn't help feeling a bit miffed. This was my day, and the fact that my friend was pregnant seemed to be taking over.

Finally, Sarah was recovered enough to leave the house, and she went off palely with Dorrie and Mum and my youngest cousin Niall, who Mum had assured me would make an adorable pageboy. I had my doubts, having already found him trying to stuff the cat in the washing machine.

'So, just you and me then, Dad,' I said. I felt sick and dizzy. 'I hope nothing else is going to go wrong.'

'And what could possibly go wrong with you looking like such a princess?' said my dad, my hero, the first love of my life. 'It's your big day, sweetheart, you go and enjoy it.'

He was right, this was my big day. I tried to remember it as we pulled up outside the church and I had to avoid the neat pile of sick left by Sarah as she'd arrived.

Enjoying my day might take some doing . . .

Chapter Twenty-One

Sarah

'Right, so what kind of ridiculous dresses do you want us to wear?' I said. We'd all convened at Beth's house. She was meant to be resting after her second IVF treatment, and after Dorrie's revelation, I felt it was more important than ever that we fulfil her dearest wish. I didn't know whether I was breaking a confidence, but I'd told the others what Dorrie had told me. I figured it would iron out any lingering doubts we had about the four of us being together again, and despite not feeling one hundred per cent happy to be in Caz's presence – as far as I was concerned, she was still on probation – it was time we put our differences aside and thought about the one person who'd always, always thought about all of us.

I was glad I'd done it. I'd told Dorrie I was going to let the others know about her condition and I could see she was pretty choked when she arrived and saw all three of us waiting for her. But being Dorrie, she pulled herself together and put on her cheery face to say, 'Well, I rather thought you could all be Disney princesses, of course.'

'You *are* joking?' said Caz, groaning.

'You know I'd never joke about a matter as serious as

that,' said Dorrie, a glint of her old self returning, but I could see this was an effort for her.

'I'm going to be Cinderella, naturally,' Dorrie continued. 'But Sarah, I thought you could be Snow White, Beth, Sleeping Beauty and Caz can be Belle.'

'No way am I wearing a Snow White costume,' I said flatly. 'I'm sorry, Dorrie, but I'll look ridiculous.'

'Oh, you don't have to,' Doris reassured me. 'You can wear the dress she wears at her wedding instead; Caz can have the yellow dress that Belle wears when she's dancing with the Beast—'

'How appropriate,' muttered Caz, 'I seem to have had my fair share of beasts.'

'—and Beth, I've got a lovely pink Sleeping Beauty dress for you.'

'What do you mean, you've got a dress for me already?' said Beth, puzzled. 'How did you organize that so fast?'

'Oh ye of little faith,' said Dorrie. 'eBay is a wonderful thing. Actually, I bought all the dresses months ago, hoping that I'd get my bridesmaids in the end.'

'Dorrie, you're priceless,' I laughed. 'But what if we hadn't agreed to do this?'

'I'd have been devastated,' admitted Dorrie. 'I had everything crossed that you would eventually come round.'

I knew this was directed at me. I'd had no idea that Dorrie had been so determined, though I should have guessed, I suppose.

'What would you have done with the dresses if we hadn't?' said Caz.

'Oh, I'd have kept them,' said Dorrie airily. 'For the next time we had to go to a Disney-themed fancy dress party.'

'When on earth will that be?' I said. 'I don't know anyone

who has Disney fancy dress parties who isn't five years old.'

'Well, I'd have one,' said Dorrie. 'But I'm really glad I'm not going to have to do that.'

She looked around at us all, beaming, and we tried to smile back, but I know we were all thinking the same thing. There was a slightly awkward pause, which Caz broke in her direct way. 'So, are we going to talk about the elephant in the room, or what?'

'What elephant? What room?' said Doris. 'I can't see any elephants.'

'Don't be obtuse,' said Caz. 'If no one else is going to say it, I will. How bad is it, Dorrie?'

Dorrie didn't answer straight away. She looked away from us all, as if trying to compose herself.

'It's bad,' she said simply. 'That's all you need to know. I really don't want to talk about it.'

'You should have told us,' said Beth. 'You're the one who always looks after us. You must know that we want to look after you.'

'I do,' said Dorrie. 'I just don't want people to feel sorry for me. I'm not sorry for me. I've got Daz and Woody, and we'll get through it somehow.'

'But is it – do you think – I mean – is it terminal?' blurted out Beth, her dark eyes anxious and worried. 'It doesn't have to be, right? Sarah?'

I paused. 'I don't know much about it,' I said. 'But MS is a really difficult disease to predict with accuracy. Some people have long periods of remission when they're quite well, and some have the progressive form which moves really fast.'

'And what form do you have?' Caz asked.

'I don't know,' said Doris. 'I was only diagnosed six months ago. It's too early to tell. But if it's anything like the version Dad had, I could be in a wheelchair in a few years' time.'

'Oh Dorrie!' said Beth, tears in her eyes. 'That's terrible.'

'Oh Beth, don't take it to heart so,' said Dorrie, giving her a hug. 'Let's look on the bright side, eh? Just because Dad had it like that, doesn't mean it has to be that way for me. My Auntie Sophie's got it too and has had it for years. I'll be fine, I'm sure. And right now we're concentrating on my wedding day. It's taken years for me to drag Darren down the aisle, I'm not about to give up on it now. And I refuse to have bad thoughts. Not when I've got to find ways to humiliate you all.'

'How's Darren coping with it?' Beth wanted to know.

'Fine. He's brilliant. Supportive. Lovely. Everything you'd expect,' said Doris. 'That's why I'm marrying him.'

She wouldn't be drawn beyond that. So we all tried to be cheerful for her. But from time to time I caught a look in her eye that was so sad and lost, it made my heart ache. No one deserved what Dorrie had. Least of all someone as lovely as her.

'So how are *you* doing?' Joe had taken to pitching up unexpectedly after work to check on how I was. I didn't know whether he'd spoken to Steve, who was barely ever here any more. Sometimes he came home at the weekends to take the boys out – we'd at least managed to break the bad news to them together, and so far they were coping with the new state of affairs – but mainly he seemed to be spending time with Kirsty. At least, that's where I presumed he was. Every time he left again, some more of his stuff disappeared. It was like he was leaving me by degrees. I presumed they were shacked up in his flat in town. Maybe he'd had Kirsty installed in it years ago. I didn't really want to know. The thought of it made me feel sick, as did the thought of starting divorce proceedings. I knew I was going to have to do it eventually, but I couldn't bring myself to start just yet.

'Oh, so so,' I said. 'You know. Good days and bad days.'

'And today?'

'Today's a really bad day,' I said. 'The drains have blocked, Sam's had a temperature half the night and been throwing up all day, I've had your mum on the phone telling me I should give Steve another chance. It's all been a bit crap really. But you don't want to listen to me going on.'

'I think I can cope,' said Joe. 'What have you eaten today?'

'Um, a doughnut at lunchtime and the kids' leftovers at tea,' I said.

'Not good enough,' said Joe. 'I thought you were looking thin. You finish getting the kids to bed, I'll sort your drains out, and then I'll cook you dinner.'

'But I've got nothing in,' I protested.

'Lucky I came prepared then,' said Joe, holding up two bags of shopping.

By the time I got back downstairs, Joe had cleared the drains. 'I just needed to give it a bit of a poke with the rodding iron, and it cleared through quickly,' he said. 'I'll get you some stuff for cleaning them out next time I come.'

'Oh, thanks,' I said. 'That's such a relief. Steve always deals – dealt – with that kind of thing. Thank god he's still paying the bills, I don't know how I'd manage if he didn't.'

'Yeah, well he'll have to answer to me if he starts mucking you about,' said Joe. 'Now sit yourself down, drink this glass of wine, while I set about cooking.' He'd already cleared up the kids' tea and set the table.

'But—' I started to protest.

'But nothing,' said Joe firmly. 'You're to do nothing, you understand?'

'Did Steve send you out of guilt?' I asked, sipping at my wine. It was lovely to be bossed about and have someone doing all the work for a change.

'No,' said Joe. 'I came because I worry about you. My big bro has some great qualities, but he's an utter pillock when it comes to women. If you were mine, I'd never have let you go.'

My heart gave a little lift at that and I felt a warm glow descend on me. I knew Joe was just being nice, but it was an age since I'd felt so pampered and cared for. It was a nice feeling to think that Joe, at least, thought a lot of me.

'Have you thought about what you're going to do?' said Joe.

'I'm job hunting right now,' I said. 'It's difficult though. I can't really do it until Will goes to school in September, and I really need term-time hours. The people on my back to work course are being very helpful though. I've seen a part-time position at our local GP's surgery. But that wouldn't be enough to live on. I expect we'll have to sell up, and move into something smaller. I couldn't manage the mortgage on my own.'

'That seems a shame,' said Joe. 'This place is so lovely.'

'Do you think?' I pulled a face. 'I loved it when we moved in, but now it just seems like an empty shell. I don't want to live here any more. Anyway, let's change the subject. How are things in the furniture business?'

Joe made and sold his own furniture, which had always

fascinated me. We had a few of his pieces in the house, though I suspect Steve had only bought them out of a sense of duty. He preferred modern, shiny – to my mind, sterile – furniture, whereas Joe's more traditional creations seemed altogether cosier and nicer to me.

'Business is a bit tough at the moment,' said Joe, 'but we seem to be weathering the recession OK.'

'Still no woman on the horizon?' The wine had loosened my tongue and I was teasing Joe in a way I was used to doing. Despite the odd fling here and there, Joe had stayed resolutely single all the time I'd known him. Steve and I joked with him about it a lot. Although suddenly, without Steve, teasing Joe didn't feel so much like a joke.

'Well, there's only ever been one woman for me,' he said lightly.

I became uncomfortably aware of his gorgeous blue eyes boring into mine. It felt he was penetrating my soul. I thought back to our wedding day, when Joe had been annoyed with Steve. I'd been too preoccupied to pay attention at the time, and since then he'd only ever shown me brotherly concern. Oh my god . . .

'I can't think who that could be,' I joked back lightly. Change the subject, you idiot. Change it now.

His eyes locked onto mine. They really were the most startling shade of blue. How come I'd never noticed that before?

'Can't you?'

I swallowed and started to clear the dishes away.

'I don't mean to be rude,' I said. 'I've had a lovely evening and I'm so grateful for all your help, but I've got an early start in the morning—' I gave an exaggerated yawn.

'Yes, it probably is time I was off.' Joe took his cue from

249

me, helped me get the things in the dishwasher, and then saw himself to the front door.

He enveloped me in a huge bear hug in the doorway. It felt so good to be held. So good. I allowed him to hold me a fraction longer than was necessary.

'Thanks,' I said. 'Thanks for everything. I don't know what I'd do without you.'

He let me go and pecked me on the cheek.

'Bye then,' he said, turning to go.

I felt a mild surge of disappointment, until he suddenly pulled me to him and kissed me passionately on the mouth.

'Oh shit,' he said. 'Sorry. I'm so sorry.' And disappeared into the night.

Chapter Twenty-Two

Caz

My phone rang while I was in the middle of making up a notoriously fussy soap star. She had just signed a major deal with the BBC and appeared to be starring in every show in the autumn schedule. My job was to make her up for her publicity shots. So far she'd arrived late, bitched about the clothes we'd chosen for her, moaned that Charlie (with whom she'd flirted outrageously last time I'd worked with her) wasn't there, and despite apparently having asked for my services, grumbled at my every suggestion.

She had dry skin so I was using a cream foundation. I had to work quickly so it didn't dry too soon, and suggested a powder to stop her skin looking too shiny, but she wasn't having any of it.

'Old ladies wear powder,' she growled.

'But your skin will look greasy in the photos,' I said, which she completely ignored.

She also overruled me on colour – I'd gone for something light and discreet, but she preferred a colour which I knew would look orange in the shots. When she saw the first takes, she hit the roof and accused me of, as she put it, 'tangoing' her.

So I had to start again from scratch; the morning's schedule was shot, and the photographer sat around kicking his heels. If Charlie had been there we'd have joked about it, but Gavin, his replacement, was a taciturn sort of chap and nearly bit my head off when I tried to make light of the situation. It had not been a good morning.

I ignored my phone and carried on touching up her lips. But whoever was on the other end was very persistent.

'I'm really sorry,' I said, putting down my lip liner. 'Would you mind if I answered this?'

Throwing a great sigh, the actress said, 'If you must. Anything to stop the sound of the *Dr Who* theme tune.'

Charlie, knowing my penchant for SF, had programmed the tune onto my phone the last time we'd been out together, when he ended up back at mine. I hadn't been able to turn it off since. Belatedly, I remembered that despite wild Internet rumours about the actress having a major part in the new series of *Dr Who*, she'd been passed over. Oops.

I picked up the phone. Sarah. What did she want? We'd agreed to put our differences aside because of Dorrie's condition, but I wasn't really sure that she'd stopped blaming me for the way Steve had behaved at Dorrie's dinner party. Maybe she thought I still fancied him. Admittedly, I had had a frisson at the thought of seeing him again, but it was quickly followed up not only by the realization Steve had put on weight and had a bald spot, but that he was a total and utter git. I was so cross with myself for even letting myself think for a minute about him in that way, when I was tentatively trying to reassert my relationship with Sarah. I felt terrible – but I wasn't sure that Sarah actually believed that.

'Hi Sarah,' I said. 'I'm sorry, I'm at work. I can't talk for long.'

'It's just I keep thinking about Dorrie and ways we can help her. She's got such a lot on her plate at the moment, and I was wondering if we could take on more of the wedding stuff for her. Now we're all going to be her bridesmaids.'

'Great idea,' I said. 'When and where?'

'Beth's, tomorrow evening,' said Sarah.

'See you there,' I said, snapping my phone shut.

'When you've finished making your social arrangements, I've got a shoot to finish,' snapped the actress.

Making soothing noises, I went back to touching up her eyes. The taciturn photographer was looking grumpier than ever. I sighed. I wished Charlie were here.

'Sarah not here yet?' I said when Beth answered the door.

'Not yet,' Beth said. 'Sorry to drag you out here again, but I'm still taking it easy.'

'So when will you know?' I asked.

'Actually, I took a test yesterday,' said Beth, shyly. 'And it was positive.'

'That's fantastic,' I said, then looked at Beth, who seemed rather down. 'Isn't it?'

'Well it is . . .' said Beth, 'it's just after last time, I'm not counting my chickens till they tell me for certain.'

'And when will that be?'

'I've got a blood test next week at the hospital, and a scan three weeks after that,' said Beth. 'And in the meantime I'm meant to be resting. I'm really glad you could come. I'm going demented with boredom. I thought the two-week wait was bad enough last time. This time it went on forever.'

Guiltily I thought about Beth coming to Mum's funeral.

I really hoped that hadn't contributed to her not getting pregnant last time.

'Maybe you're through the worst,' I said.

'I hope so,' said Beth, 'but I don't want to take any chances.'

'Well you go back to the sofa, and I'll make the tea,' I said. Typical of Sarah to organize us all and then be late. When we were growing up she was always the one to boss us about, but often ruined it by not being where she said she'd be at the right time.

'Thanks for the tea,' said Beth, when I came back. 'Sorry I'm being such a lame duck, it's just so scary, not knowing if this pregnancy will last.'

I squeezed her hand. 'It will be OK,' I said awkwardly. The world I inhabited didn't include any of this kind of stuff. Most of the girls I worked with were younger than me, or single, like me. And while my clients were occasionally pregnant, they always seemed to manage those off the shelf, designer, trouble-free pregnancies, gave birth ridiculously easily and were back at work in two months looking impossibly trim.

'You just have to be positive.' Sarah breezed in, dealing with the situation in a much better way than I could have done. Or so I thought. 'Worrying about it won't help.'

'Well that's easy for you to say,' Beth snapped. 'You never had any of this trouble.'

'But I did have to stay in hospital for a few weeks before Will was born with high blood pressure, worrying that I was suffering from pre-eclampsia. Not the same I know, but I do understand the worry.'

'You're right,' said Beth. 'It's not the same. At least you could *get* pregnant. You have no idea what it's like.'

Woah. Where had that come from? I'd always assumed

I was the one to cause trouble within the Fab Four. It was quite refreshing in a way to discover Beth and Sarah also had their tensions. I wondered if Beth was jealous of Sarah's children. She'd made no secret before her marriage of wanting children, and five years on, none had appeared, while Sarah seemed to get pregnant at the drop of a hat. It must have been rather galling for Beth.

'Enough,' I said. 'Beth, Sarah's only trying to help. Come on, we're here to talk about ways to help Dorrie.'

'Sorry,' said Beth grudgingly. 'It's just so stressful, this whole baby thing.'

'I know,' said Sarah. 'I didn't meant to be insensitive.'

'So how do you think we can help?' I said.

'Well I know that Dorrie is getting wound up about the venue,' said Sarah. 'She wants to theme the room like a scene from *Cinderella* and they've been a bit arsy about it. No one's returning her calls at the moment. I thought we could offer to deal with it for her.'

'It must be awful having to do it on her own,' said Beth. 'I know I was really stressy with Mum when I was getting married, but at least she was interested.'

I thought about my ill-fated wedding day. My mum hadn't even known I'd been married, and probably wouldn't have cared. I couldn't imagine Dorrie's lively, bouncy mother not being intimately involved in every aspect of her big day.

'Is Dorrie's mum really not bothered?' I said. 'I just don't get it. It seems so unlike her.'

'From what Dorrie says, she's withdrawn completely since Dorrie's dad died,' said Sarah. 'It's really sad, but I gather it was pretty hideous towards the end and Dorrie's mum just hasn't got over it.'

'And now Dorrie's ill too,' said Beth. 'It doesn't seem fair.'

It wasn't fair. Lovely, gorgeous, funny Dorrie having to go through so much pain, maybe even ending up in a wheelchair, being fed through a tube. It was too hideous to contemplate.

'It isn't,' said Sarah. 'But at least we can all try and be there for her.'

'And at least we're fulfilling the Bridesmaid Pact at last,' said Beth.

'All four one and one four all,' I said.

Sarah gave me a brief flicker of a smile. Maybe once she'd got over losing Steve she could accept me back. At least one thing was starting to go right in my life. Even if I was going to have to dress up as a Disney princess.

Cormack Riley. Who'd have thought there were so many of them? I sat on the Internet trawling through all the C Rileys in the phonebook. I'd started in the Manchester area, which was the last address I had for him, but the sheer number of C Rileys in the book was filling me with despair. Even if I had the courage to ring one of them up, how could I possibly know which was the right one? And what was I going to say if I did find him? 'Hi, I'm your long-lost daughter – remember me?' Maybe he'd given up on me by now. Maybe he thought that because I hadn't contacted him as an adult, it meant I didn't care. He couldn't possibly know that I'd been brought up to believe my dad would reject me. It hadn't meant that I hadn't bothered; I just couldn't risk the hurt. Besides, another thought occurred to me, I didn't even know if he lived there any more. He could be dead for all I knew.

All my life Mum had prevented me from finding Dad.

A familiar surge of anger swept over me. But this time it was touched with a tinge of sadness. Mum must have been so very bitter. Right to the end.

This was getting me nowhere. I wondered if my errant father was Internet savvy enough to be on Facebook, but a quick search revealed so many Cormack Rileys, I didn't know where to start. In the end I decided to bite the bullet and see if Auntie Nora knew anything.

'And why are you suddenly so interested in meeting your da, now?' said Auntie Nora. 'You've never wanted to know before.'

I sensed she was stalling. Hadn't it occurred to her the letters and cards were a sure-fire way of whetting my appetite for information about my long-lost father?

'That's because I didn't know he wanted to keep in touch with me before,' I said. 'Mum should have told me. It wasn't fair that she didn't. And now she's gone I need to find him. Please, Auntie Nora. If you know anything, tell me.'

There was a long pause at the other end of the phone, before Auntie Nora said, 'Well, your mam said he'd stopped writing, so I assumed he'd lost interest. So I let sleeping dogs lie. I thought you were both better off without him.'

'It wasn't your call to make,' I said bitterly. 'I've spent my whole life thinking my dad didn't care about me. And now it turns out he did, and I've lost all those years.'

There was a pause on the other end of the phone.

'I had no idea you felt like that,' said Auntie Nora.

'You never asked though, did you?' I said. 'You and Mum just assumed because you hated Dad I should too. All my life I've felt there's been something missing. I just want to find him.'

'Is that right?' Auntie Nora said. I could almost hear the

cogs of her brain working as she seemed to be coming to a decision. Finally she said, 'Caroline, I believe I owe you an apology,' which was unexpected. I couldn't recall her apologizing for anything in her life.

'Oh?' I said, my fury abating somewhat.

'I've always been that angry with him for what he did to your mam – using that Riley charm and blarney till he got her in the family way and then leaving her alone in a foreign country with you a wee babby. It wasn't right, I tell you. That's why I told your mam to have nothing to do with him. I thought I was doing the right thing. And I'm sorry. I've been talking it over with Father Miserecordie and he thinks you should know the truth.'

'Which is?'

'That I've known your father's whereabouts for the last thirty years. I'll give you his address and phone number. If you want to see him, it's your choice, not mine.'

Chapter Twenty-Three

Doris

'So now that you've finally got your bridesmaids sorted, do you think you can calm down about the wedding a bit?' said Darren, as he expertly spoon fed Woody. He managed to do it without making any mess, which was quite miraculous. 'It will all be all right on the night, you know.'

'It is a great relief to know the girls can do it,' I said. 'And things do seem to be slotting into place. Flowers are sorted, Caz has taken over dealing with those wretched people at the Claygate, so I don't have to worry about that any more. I've got all the dresses, the table decorations are all sitting in boxes in the spare room, Sarah's tracked down some Mickey Mouse cameras, the DVD man and photographer are both booked, my family are all happy, even *your* relatives seem happy. I do feel much better about the wedding at least.'

'Good,' said Darren, imitating an aeroplane as he spooned food into Woody's mouth. Then he looked at me. 'What do you mean "at least"? You're not having any more stupid thoughts about the wedding not going ahead, are you? Just because that woman at your support group is in a bad way, it doesn't have to follow that everything will go downhill as fast.'

I'd told Darren all about Flo. I couldn't stop thinking about her, and how awful it must be for her.

'You're right,' I said. 'If Flo can cope with what she has to deal with, I'm sure I can manage. I mean, so far my symptoms aren't so bad, and I may even go into remission, if I'm lucky.'

'That's my girl,' said Darren. He put down Woody's spoon and came over to me and stroked my hair. 'You know I'm going to be so proud to marry you, don't you?'

'I know,' I said, blinking away the tears. 'And it's OK, I'm. not planning to leave you standing at the altar.'

'Glad to hear it,' said Darren dryly.

To be honest, I still wasn't sure I was doing the right thing marrying Darren, but I didn't want to upset him. Besides, I felt like I was riding an unstoppable juggernaut. Everything was booked, all the guests had confirmed. If I pulled out now it wasn't just Darren I'd be letting down, but all of our friends and family.

And then I thought back to my childhood. Sarah, Beth and Caz had been so important to me growing up and the breakdown of our little group had caused me such a lot of pain over the last few years. If one good thing had come from my illness, it was that my friends all seemed to be together again. I had to try and think things would all work out for the best. And then maybe they would.

I had taken to going to my support group every week. They'd become a necessary part of my life. And slowly I realized that there was life and hope after a diagnosis of MS. Tony was forever reminding me that he'd had it for fifteen years, and while he occasionally needed a wheelchair for outdoor trips, in the main he walked pretty well with a stick. Carol clearly relished her life and didn't appear to let her MS affect her at all. I found her resilience and strength quite remarkable. But the one I loved and admired the most was Flo. She was always so upbeat, always had a smile on her face. Yet you could see sometimes that she was in pain and that the feeding tube was a source of constant frustration to her. But she never complained, not once. Just smiled and put a brave face on it. Every week, I came away feeling more heartened than I had on the first occasion. After all, with Darren and Woody in my life, I had a lot to be thankful for.

Darren's mum couldn't always look after Woody, so I'd started asking Mum to do it. I told her I was doing a yoga class. To my delight, she was relishing the responsibility of having Woody – she'd always had a way with babies, one of the sadnesses in her life had been that she'd only had me, which is why she'd always been so welcoming to my friends. And for the first time since Dad died, she seemed to be emerging from her shell. She was even beginning to show a bit of interest in the wedding.

'Is there anything you want me to do?' she asked one day when I came round to drop Woody off. The first time she'd volunteered to do anything in months.

'Would you . . . could you make the cake?' I asked. Mum was brilliant at cake making. I'd been the envy of all my friends every birthday when Mum would bring out yet another amazing creation – normally Disney based, it had to be said.

'I'd love it if you could make a Cinderella cake,' I said. 'You know, just like the one you made for my sixth birthday, only it has to be a fruit cake and have proper icing.'

'Doris, how old are you? I can't make you a Cinderella cake,' Mum protested.

'Oh yes you can,' I said. 'Please, Mum. Just for me.'

'I'll think about it,' said Mum. 'Now you'd better get off, or you'll be late.'

I got up a bit too quickly and stumbled. Damn. I'd been careful to control my symptoms in front of Mum up until now.

'Are you OK?' she said as I righted myself.

'Yes, fine,' I said. 'Why wouldn't I be?'

'No reason,' said Mum. 'But if there was something wrong, you would tell me, wouldn't you?'

'I'll trip over my own feet next,' I tried to laugh it off. 'There's nothing to tell, honestly.' But I caught her eye and saw a glimmer of worry there. I'd counted on the combination of Mum being wrapped up in her grief, and my ability to cover up ensuring that she wouldn't notice anything wrong with me. But maybe she'd been more aware than I thought. I probably couldn't keep it from her much longer.

The support group seemed less busy this week. I wondered at first, this being the middle of July, if people were already on holiday, but a sombre mood pervaded the air. I looked around for Flo, usually the life and soul of the party, but there was no sign of her. I had missed the previous week as Woody was ill, I wondered if Flo had been there then.

'What's the matter with everyone?' I said to my neighbour, a middle-aged man in a wheelchair, to whom I'd never spoken before. 'It seems very quiet today.'

'Oh, hadn't you heard?' he said. 'Poor Flo passed away yesterday.'

'Oh no!' I put my hand to my mouth. I knew from Dad how rapidly the disease could take hold, but Flo had seemed fine a fortnight ago. 'But . . . she was OK two weeks ago. Was it very sudden?'

The man looked at me pityingly. 'Oh, no,' he said. 'She'd planned it down to the last detail. Came in here last week to say goodbye.'

'What?' I said, but a creeping feeling of dread was spreading over me.

'Her death,' he said. 'She planned it. She knew she was getting to the end of the road, so she flew with her family to Switzerland and yesterday she finally found peace. It was all over the news this morning.'

'I didn't have the radio on today,' I said dully. I couldn't believe what I was hearing. Flo, jolly, happy Flo, committing suicide? I just couldn't credit it.

'It'll be in all the papers,' said my new friend. 'They're saying the family shouldn't be prosecuted, but it must be immensely stressful for them, don't you think?'

'Yes,' I said.

'I wouldn't like to think of my poor wife going to prison because of me,' he continued.

'No,' I said automatically, shivering – what would happen to Darren if I asked him to help me die? Could I do that to him or Mum? My thoughts were reeling. It must get really, really bad for someone as vital and alive as Flo to take the drastic steps she had. I had thought she was so positive. She was the last person I could imagine taking her own life. If she couldn't hack it, what chance did I have?

I got up and walked out of the centre, completely numb with shock. I didn't really know where I was walking, and it was a surprise to find myself outside St Philomena's church. It was years since I'd practised Catholicism properly. I'd had

Woody christened to please Mum and Father Miserecordie, and I had my own version of spiritualism. But the truth was, since Dad became ill, I'd been pretty angry with God and my mood hadn't improved much since my diagnosis.

I stood on the porch, thinking about going in. At least it would be a quiet place to marshal my thoughts, if nothing else.

'Going in?' Father Miserecordie was by my side, appearing out of nowhere.

'Sorry, you startled me,' I said. 'I'm thinking about it.'

'Come and join me,' said Father Miserecordie. 'You don't have to pray if you don't want to, but I sense a soul in trouble.'

I followed him down the aisle, the same aisle down which I was hoping to walk in a couple of short months.

'So, do you want to talk about anything in particular?' asked Father Miserecordie, as we settled ourselves down in a front pew.

'I was just wondering what you thought about assisted suicide,' I said.

'What *I* think, or what the Church teaches?' he said.

'Well, I can guess what the Church teaches,' I said. 'And I'm sure you'll say the same, and until recently I'd have agreed with you. But now I'm not so sure.'

'So what's changed your mind?'

I poured out the story of my illness and my worries for Darren and Woody.

'And now with Flo having gone ahead and done it, well I just can't think straight,' I said. 'She seemed so full of life; I can't believe she's gone like that. And if she couldn't find the strength to carry on, how can I? I'm not nearly as brave as her.'

'Courage comes in many forms,' Father Miserecordie

said. 'You know I'm not going to tell you that I think she was right to take the path she chose, because I don't. But I can understand why she did it. It was a courageous decision, even if I cannot approve the outcome. Do you really think you could do the same?'

'I don't know,' I said. 'I just saw how hard it was for Mum and Dad and I don't want Darren to have to go through it too.'

'But your dad would never have taken a decision like that,' said Father Miserecordie.

'I know, far too Catholic,' I said with a wry smile.

'I'd say it was more than that actually,' said Father Miserecordie. 'He loved life so much that he clung on even when it seemed at its most dark and difficult. I think that's brave too.'

'I suppose so,' I said. 'I'd never looked at it like that before.'

'I believe your father was very close to God,' said Father Miserecordie.

'Maybe,' I said. 'But I'm still not convinced that I can be so long-suffering, and I don't have his faith to sustain me. I really don't know what I should do.'

'You'll find the right path I'm sure,' said Father Miserecordie. 'Time will tell.'

I was touched by his faith, even though I couldn't feel it. But despite all the positive signs to the contrary, I couldn't escape the feeling that time might be running out on me.

Chapter Twenty-Four

Beth

We were both feeling nervous as we were ushered into the waiting room. We'd had the results of our blood tests, and they too were positive, but although we'd greeted the news with a cautious optimism, neither of us could quite believe it. Waiting a further three weeks for the scan had felt interminable, and now we were here, we were so tense we could barely even look at one another.

So here we were, back in St Mary's hospital having a scan, which could prove definitely that Foetus existed. I was sick of the sight of hospitals and I felt faintly nauseous. Matt clearly felt the same, as he looked really pale. He gave me a weak smile and squeezed my hand. This was hard on him too. I had to remember that.

Eventually our names were called and we went through to a tiny room where a radiographer was waiting with an ultrasound machine. I lay flat on the bed and stared up at the ceiling, while she put some gel on my tummy. I marvelled at how underneath that flat stomach, there might be a baby growing. After the long wait, it still didn't seem possible.

The atmosphere was tense as she passed the scanner over my stomach. She didn't say anything, but stared fixedly at the screen. I tried to squint at it. I didn't even know what I was looking for. I could see the shape of my womb, but no blob-like creature attached to it.

The radiographer continued in silence. It made me want to scream. I didn't know if it was better or worse than her saying something, but I was going mad from not knowing. Matt gripped my hand tightly and gave it an encouraging squeeze, but I could feel the hope leaching out of me. Maybe the test was wrong? They were supposed to be super accurate, but suppose we got the duff test? It would be just our luck.

'Now let's try and find baby,' she said eventually.

My tummy wasn't even slightly distended. It didn't seem possible that I could be pregnant.

'There, got you,' she said triumphantly.

Matt and I looked in awe, as the monitor filled with the cavity of my womb, attached to which by a tiny thread, was a tiny little tadpole. A tadpole with buds for arms and legs, and a steady, beating heart.

I felt a combination of relief and ecstasy. I didn't know it was possible to be this happy. Matt squeezed my hand and gave me a great big grin.

'We did it,' he said, giving me a kiss. 'We finally did it!'

I lay back on the bed, staring at the screen, in a state of semi-shock. After all the waiting, Foetus was real.

'Hello Foetus,' I said. 'Welcome to the world.'

'Jesus, Mary and Joseph, and I thought you must be barren,' was Mum's greeting as we arrived straight from the hospital, bursting with our good news. Matt had wanted to wait for the full twelve weeks, but I was too excited. I had to tell someone.

'So you're making me a grandda at last,' said Dad with a twinkle in his eye. 'Your mam will be having the knitting patterns out before you know it. And the phone line between here and Galway will be buzzing, I tell you. Can't you make sure it's two to make it worth the trouble?'

'Actually,' said Matt, but I shushed him. There was a fair chance we *were* having two babies – two eggs had been implanted – but I didn't want to let on we'd gone for IVF.

Luckily Mum was clucking away about how wonderful it was to be a grandma at last, as if we'd deliberately kept her waiting.

'Now I can hold my head up high in the parish,' she said. 'And next time Mary O'Donnell boasts about her gazillionth grandchild, I can let her know I've got one of my very own.'

Poor Mum. Mary O'Donnell had been producing grandchildren at the rate of one or two a year for the last decade. Mum was never going to match that, but at least I'd given her something to boast about. I felt a wave of warmth come over me. Not only had Foetus made our day, I suddenly realized how much joy this baby was going to bring to my parents.

'Will you wisht going on, woman,' said Dad, teasing Mum as usual. 'Sure and they're not after having a baby to keep *you* happy. Although, you have made your old da very happy today. Let's crack open a bottle of bubbly and have a toast.'

'None for me,' I said. 'I'm not taking any chances.'

Dad went to the kitchen and came back with a bottle of champagne.

'It's left over from Christmas,' he said. 'Sorry, if I'd known we were having a celebration I'd have put it in the fridge hours ago.'

He popped the cork expertly then poured out three glasses, and a glass of lemonade for me.

'To the new member of the family,' he said, raising his glass.

'We've waited long enough,' said Mum, but Dad glared at her. 'Sorry,' she said, 'I'm going on again. I'm just so thrilled for you both.'

'Us too,' I said, giving her a hug. 'Us too.'

The next couple of weeks flew by. Already it was August. Normally Matt and I would be planning to hole up on a beach somewhere, but this year with Foetus a reality, we were saving our pennies. Each day I awoke with a buzz and a feeling of great excitement, coupled with nervousness. I felt strange and odd, my taste buds were awry, but I wasn't feeling sick yet. I had tender boobs and occasional pain in my groin, which worried me till Sarah told me it was perfectly normal. The girls were thrilled for me when I told them, though Dorrie said, 'Oh no, I hope you're not going to be too far gone to wear your bridesmaid's dress.'

'I should be all right,' I said. 'And if not you can always let the dress out.'

We'd found out so early, it seemed an impossibly long time to wait for the magic twelve weeks, when I'd discover if everything was all right or not. Although I was excited, there was a little residue of anxiety too. I hoped that nothing would go wrong now, but though it had seemed like a big hurdle just to get pregnant, I now realized there were a great many more hurdles to jump till Foetus was born.

I was back at work, but trying to take it easy. I hadn't confided in anyone other than my boss about what was happening, and she'd been very understanding, letting me go early when she could. So this evening I was heading home at 4.30, sitting on a less crowded tube than normal, thinking about whether Matt would already be in. He'd been so attentive of late, cooking me dinner, buying me flowers and generally making a fuss of me. Which was wonderful, as I was so tired all the time I hardly had any energy to do anything.

I got home to find that Matt wasn't in. As I walked through the door, I felt a familiar cramping sensation. No, it couldn't be. I wouldn't let it be. I tried to stem the rising tide of panic, as I went to the loo. There was blood. Not a lot. But some. I felt cold all over. I was pregnant. I was bleeding. No. No. No. This couldn't be happening to me. Not now. Not ever.

Matt found me half an hour later, curled up on the floor. 'What's the matter?' he asked.

'Oh Matt, I'm bleeding,' I said and burst into tears.

'How much?' said Matt. 'Try not to panic. Remember, you could be spotting. The doctor did say that can happen. Look, go and lie down and I'll ring the hospital.'

After a long conversation with a midwife, the gist of which seemed to be that we should try not to panic, it might be nothing to worry about, Matt and I lay on the sofa for the evening. We watched television but I wasn't taking it in, and I doubt Matt was either. The knot of worry in my stomach was eating away at me. It might be all right if I rested, but suppose it wasn't? All the fears I'd had about this baby came rising to the surface once more. Maybe I didn't deserve a baby. Maybe I'd never be able to carry full-term. Perhaps I was going to lose Foetus before he or she had even got going.

Throughout the night I took regular trips to the loo, and

271

by morning things had settled down again. To be on the safe side I took the day off work, though I made Matt go in. By lunchtime I was beginning to think my fears were unfounded. My panic from the previous evening had subsided and I was starting to calm down. But then the cramps started again, the pain coming in stronger and stronger waves, and even before I went to the loo, I knew what was happening. There was so much blood. I was losing the baby.

I called Matt hysterically and he flew back home. I was in a daze as we went to the hospital, where we had hoped our baby would be born. I allowed myself to be subjected to scans, examinations and other humiliations. It didn't matter. Nothing mattered now.

Eventually a young doctor came in, he looked ill at ease, and despite my pain I felt sorry for him. I knew what he was going to say. What a rotten bloody job for anyone to do.

'I'm sorry,' he said. 'It seems you've lost the baby.'

Matt let out a howl of despair, which was almost the worst moment of a terrible day. Almost. The worst moment was still to come.

'How?' he said brokenly. 'Why?'

'It appears that the damage Beth incurred from her previous abortion has led to some scarring, which is one of the reasons she's had difficulty getting pregnant and may have led to this miscarriage. It's quite possible she may never carry a baby full-term.'

I felt as though the sands under my feet had shifted and my world had just collapsed. Oh my god, why did this have to come out now?

Matt let go of my hand and looked at me in bewilderment.

'I don't understand,' he said. 'Beth hasn't had an abortion.'

'Oh,' the doctor looked disconcerted. 'I'm sorry, it's in her notes. I assumed you knew.'

'I didn't,' said Matt. His expression was unreadable. 'Beth, what's going on?'

'Matt, I'm sorry,' I said. 'I never meant to keep it from you, but I know how strongly you feel about abortion. I didn't know how to tell you . . .'

Matt got up without a word and walked out of the room.

'Matt, don't go—' I said.

But he'd gone, leaving me alone with a pain in my heart and a Foetus-shaped hole that could never be filled.

I'd finally got the punishment I deserved.

Beth

'Do you, Matthew Charles Davies, take this woman, Elizabeth Margaret McCarthy, to be your lawful wedded wife?'

'I do,' said Matt giving me a broad smile. The sun shone through the stained-glass window above the altar casting reds, blues and yellows across us. Matt looked gorgeous in a traditional morning suit with a white cravat, but thankfully no top hat.

'Do you, Elizabeth Margaret McCarthy, take this man, Matthew Charles Davies, to be your lawful wedded husband?'

'I do,' I said, shyly and with some amazement that I could actually be here, in this church saying these words. For so many years I was always the wallflower, the one left on her own, I still couldn't believe I'd finally met the man of my dreams.

I repeated my vows almost in a dreamlike state because I knew, without doubt, that I was never ever going to break them. Standing at the altar next to Matt, as he shyly came to kiss me, was the most perfect moment of my life. It didn't matter that Sarah kept swaying in the background and was being propped up by Dorrie, or that Niall spent most of

275

the service either lying in front of the altar on his stomach or untying the ribbons from the flowers decorating the church. From the moment we committed ourselves to each other it didn't matter that I only had two of my bridesmaids with me on my special day. Matt and I had promised to love, honour and cherish each other, for better for worse, in sickness and in health, till death did us part. At last I was Mrs Davies. That was all I cared about.

I floated out of the church, leaning on Matt's arm, in a kind of quiet but happy daze. We didn't take many photos outside the church (just as well as Sarah was puking up in the loos again), but headed for the West Lodge hotel a few miles to the north of Northfields, in the white Rolls Royce that Dad's mate Archie from down the club had lent us for the day.

Matt and I were photographed in the substantial grounds, underneath trees, in front of the lake, with peacocks trailing behind us, sitting on a heart-shaped bench put there for occasions such as this, kissing underneath the rose arch. It was a perfect, perfect afternoon. A warm spring sun shone down on us and we drank champagne on the terrace over-looking the lake, before Matt and I stood in the line-up to greet our guests. Sarah had to abstain from the line-up on the grounds that she was feeling too unwell. I felt sorry for her, but didn't have time to think about anything else as I shook people by the hand and slowly got used to my new relatives.

Then it was time for our wedding breakfast, most of which I barely touched. I was so happy drinking in the occasion, leaning against Matt, feeling like the luckiest woman alive. I found Matt and Dad bonding in the bar before the speeches, both of them hating the whole thing.

'You are so lucky you don't have to do this,' groaned Matt. 'I can't wait for it all to be over.'

'At least you don't have to go first, Matthew,' said Dad with a groan. 'I wish I could be anywhere but here right now.'

'I don't care what you say,' I declared, delighted that my two favourite men were getting on so well, 'I'm just happy to have you both. You can just give a toast if you like.'

In the end that's pretty much what Dad did, leaping up looking distinctly awkward in his morning suit, to say very briefly, 'Well, there's not much I can say on a day like today, but I'm sure these two will be as lucky in love as Elizabeth's mother and I have been. We wish them every joy in their new life together and so may I ask you all to charge your glasses for the bride and groom!' before sitting down with relief and taking a large swig of champagne.

Matt lasted a little longer, managing to remember to compliment the radiance of the bridesmaids (even if Sarah didn't get to hear it because she was out puking again), thank everyone necessary and managing to get the words, 'My wife' in before collapsing next to me, gibbering like an idiot.

'Thank god I never have to do that again,' he said.

'Well you might at our daughter's wedding,' I said.

'You're not . . .?'

'No, of course not, now sssh,' I said, while we settled to listen to Matt's best friend Henry who made up for their totally inadequate speeches with a witty and amusing effort that just bordered on the right side of decent. We then gave bouquets to our respective mothers-in-law, bracelets to our bridesmaids, and a toy engine for Niall, who'd spent most of the proceedings rolling around under the table. Everything had gone swimmingly well.

By the time we came to have our first dance, I was floating on a sea of happiness and champagne. This had been the best day of my life.

'Happy, Mrs Davies?' said Matt holding me close.

'Ecstatic,' I said, as he whirled me round the dance floor.

'You know, I wouldn't mind if you were having our daughter,' he said.

'Really?' I said. 'You don't want to wait a bit?'

'No time like the present,' said Matt. 'You know, I'd love to be a dad, and Mum can't wait to be a granny. I think we should go for it straight away.'

'Well that's sudden,' I said, suddenly feeling a bit panicky. I wanted children, I really did, but I thought back to my abortion, and wondered if it would make a difference. I'd never told Matt about it, maybe I should get things perfectly straight before we started down this road.

'You don't have a problem with that, do you?' said Matt.

'No,' I said. 'I'm not sure I'm ready.'

'Well, no one's ever ready,' said Matt, 'but look at my mum, look how she coped against all the odds. We'll be doing it together.'

Matt's mum could have had an abortion and chose not to, as he had frequently told me, he was proud of the fact that she'd brought him up alone, despite her struggles. Maybe now wasn't the time to come clean. I should enjoy the moment and let the future take care of itself. I let myself drift away in Matt's arms, thinking how much I belonged there, and tried not to think about the third bracelet, which lay unwrapped on my dressing table, and making me wonder if I'd ever see Caz again.

Part Four

Till Death do Us Part

Doris

Back Then

For my wedding, I will have a white carriage like Cinderella and six white horses. And I will wear a big dress just like Princess Diana. And my husband will be very handsome. And my best friends in the whole universe will be my bridesmaids.

Caz, Sarah, Beth and Dorrie. Best friends forever. All four one and one four all.
Doris, July 1981

For my wedding I will have the biggest, whitest, pouffiest dress I can imagine. Fergie's would do. My husband will be very handsome. He will wear a white suit and kneel down and kiss my hand. I will have three bridesmaids. They will be Sarah and Beth and Caz.

Best friends forever. All four one and one four all.
Doris, July 1986

For my wedding, I'd still really like that big Cinderella dress, even though the others laugh at me about it. And I'd like my husband to lead me on a pony, like Sting did

for Trudy Styler. That would be really romantic. And my best friends, Sarah and Beth and Caz will be my bridesmaids. All four one and one four all.
Doris, August 1994

For my wedding I'd always dreamed of romance, of the beautiful white dress, of being a fairy princess. Dad was meant to walk me down the aisle. Mum was meant to organize the day. And the groom wasn't supposed to be wondering if his bride would ever be well enough to be a proper wife. At least my best friends are going to be my bridesmaids. That part of the dream is intact. All four one and one four all.

For my wedding, I'd just settle on being well.
Doris, now

I should have married Darren straight away, when he first asked me. I knew pretty much immediately I'd found the man of my dreams. But I figured we had plenty of time. And then Dad got ill, and everything was too difficult. He deteriorated so quickly, and knowing how much he hated that bloody wheelchair, I couldn't bear to put him through the humiliation of being wheeled into church. Maybe that was wrong. Because it turns out we didn't have much time after all . . .

I first met Darren at work, but we never said much to one another, just talked test tubes when we encountered each other in the lift. I thought he was cute and his obsession with germs rather sweet. I didn't ever think about how he viewed me. I know I scared off most of the science boffins I tended to encounter at work. I wasn't like anyone they'd met before. Somehow they couldn't get their heads round the fact that just because I liked wearing bright red nail varnish, didn't mean I couldn't show interest in the cells I was experimenting on.

But it was one night before Christmas, when I was out with the girls celebrating Sarah's engagement, that sealed our fate. I'd like to say it was love at first sight, except, much as I want to, sappy romantic idiot that I am, even I don't believe in a real *coup de foudre*. A great word that, for the sudden rush you get when you fall in love. *Coup de foudre*. It literally means lightning strike, which always puzzled me. Why does Cupid, a Greek god, get muddled up with Thor, a Norse one?

Anyway, I digress. There I was, with the girls in the champagne bar in Kettner's, and in walks Darren. I remember clocking him and thinking, *Oh it's the cute guy from work*, but no one could have been more surprised than me when he asked me out. That was the last thing I was expecting. I endured days of teasing from the others about Yakult Man, as Caz had instantly christened him, before we eventually made it on our first date in the New Year.

If I did have a *coup de foudre*, it was probably the moment we met at the restaurant and Darren held the door open for me and took my coat. Old-fashioned as it might sound, I love a guy to show courtesy, and Darren had me hooked from that moment, and no amount of teasing from the others about his microbe obsessions were ever going to change that . . .

From that moment on, I knew Darren was the one for me. He'd always made me so happy. He still made me so happy. I just hoped I was going to have time to bring him the joy he'd always brought me.

Chapter Twenty-Five

Doris

Matt rang us just as I was clearing away Woody's tea. As usual, more food seemed to have gone on the floor than in his mouth, but I guess that's what plastic mats are for.

'Are you OK?' I said. He sounded really strained.

'Not really,' he said. 'Beth's had a miscarriage.'

'Oh no,' I said, my hand flying to my mouth. 'That's terrible. How is she?'

'Not good,' he said. 'But I was wondering, could you come round? I think she needs a girl to chat to.'

'Damn,' I said. 'Darren and I are booked up for our first meeting with the priest and we have to leave in about ten minutes. I'm really sorry but we can't get out of it. I'll ring Sarah to see if she can come though, and I can definitely call in tomorrow. Are you sure she'll want to see one of us now though? Don't you need time to yourselves tonight?'

'Believe you me, that's the last thing we need,' Matt laughed hollowly. There was a bitterness to his tone which surprised me. He was the epitome of the supportive, understanding husband. I couldn't possibly think why he didn't want to be alone with Beth tonight. Maybe he felt hopeless. I know Darren had felt utterly useless when I was giving birth and had hated me being in pain. Yes, that must be it. Matt was in shock and felt he couldn't help Beth, but realized she needed some TLC from her friends.

I rang Sarah, but there was no answer. Then I remembered she was probably at the pool. Sam had swimming lessons on a Thursday. I sent her a text, but didn't get a reply, so I rang Caz. I was running out of time as Darren and I needed to be out by 7 p.m.

'Caz?' I said. 'Where are you?'

'Over at Mum's sorting through stuff,' she said. 'I finished work early. Why?'

'Beth's had a miscarriage and Matt's just rung me asking if I'd go over. I'm on my way out and I can't get hold of Sarah. So I was wondering if you could?'

'Of course I can,' said Caz. 'Oh the poor thing, what a rotten piece of luck.'

'I know,' I said, shivering as I thought how I would have felt if I lost Woody. I looked at him gurgling in the corner and felt a sudden rush of fierce protective love. 'Can you send her my love and say I'll see her tomorrow?'

'Of course,' said Caz. 'I'll ring you later.'

'What was all that about?' Darren had just come in from work.

'Beth's lost the baby,' I said.

'Oh, that's dreadful,' said Darren. 'They must be distraught.'

'I know,' I said, 'and I feel awful because I can't get over there now.'

'Don't feel bad,' said Darren. 'You always look out for your friends; Beth knows that you're there for her. Come on, we'd better get on or we'll be late.'

Mum arrived then to babysit and coo over her grandson and he clapped his hands in delight, saying 'Na-na. Na-na.'

'See, he knows me already?' said Mum rubbing her nose in his face and coochy-cooing all over him. Privately I didn't like to say that 'na-na' was Woody's default position in the word department. I was just so pleased to see her acting a bit more normally at last.

'I remember going for marriage lessons with your dad,' Mum said wistfully. 'It was different in those days of course. We had to be attending church regularly, and the priest scared me half to death with telling me what a serious obligation marriage was. I nearly bottled out of it.'

'Seriously?' I said.

'Seriously,' Mum said. 'Up until the day I wasn't sure I was doing the right thing. Then, when I saw your dad, standing there at the altar, looking so handsome, I knew I'd made the right choice. And I never regretted it.'

'What, never?' I said. 'Not even at the end?'

'Never,' said Mum firmly. 'I wish more than anything that he hadn't had to suffer the way he did, but I'm glad I was with him till the end, and I shall miss him every day till the day I die.'

Tears prickled my eyes, as I gave Mum a hug.

'I miss him too,' I said.

'I know,' said Mum, wiping her own tears away. 'Now go on, get along with you both or you'll be late.'

'Welcome, welcome,' said Father Miserecordie, as he ushered us into the lounge of the presbytery which I'd last visited in 1987, when I'd giggled my way through Father Cormack's confirmation classes with Beth and Sarah. Caz, typically, had refused to come.

The room was much cosier than I remembered it. The huge crucifix that had dominated the fireplace in my youth

287

had been replaced by a more modest one. The dark wooden skirting and dado rails that I remembered making the room so gloomy had been brightened with a flock wallpaper. Even the seats were much cosier than the hard-backed chairs of old.

It had taken a while for me to persuade Darren to come to marriage classes. He hadn't been brought up in a religious family and didn't see the point. Nor did he understand my sudden longing for a link with my childhood. I'd wavered for ages about having a church wedding, and I thought it would be too late to book St Philomena's. But Mum had a word with Father Miserecordie who had suggested we got married on a Friday and miraculously a Friday slot had come up at the hotel we were after. So, here we were, me nervously wondering if we were going to get some kind of Catholic indoctrination of the sort I remembered from childhood, and Darren looking like he wanted to be anywhere else but here. Another indication of how much he loved me, I realized with a jolt.

I needn't have worried.

'Would you like a cup of tea, or something stronger?' Father Miserecordie asked. That was the first surprise.

'Erm . . .' Darren looked at me in bemusement. 'I wouldn't mind a beer if you have one.'

I pulled a face.

'What?' he whispered. 'I gave up the pub for this, remember?'

'Doris, how about you?'

'It's all right,' I said dryly. 'I appear to be driving.'

Father Miserecordie helped himself and Darren to a beer and poured me an orange juice, then said, 'How are you both feeling? Is the pressure getting to you yet?'

He gave no hint of our earlier conversation. I was grateful

for his discretion. I wasn't sure Darren would have understood.

Darren raised his eyes to the ceiling. 'Well, if I could get Dorrie off the computer long enough to discuss anything more sensible than the colour of her shoes, I'd be lucky.'

How we laughed. Would that our stresses were as minor as that.

'And you, Doris, are you feeling the strain yet?'

'Only a little,' I admitted. 'It would be nice if my mum could help a bit more, but she hasn't been too well.'

'And is that a problem?'

'Not really,' I said. 'My friends are all being great, and anyway, I love organizing stuff, don't I Daz?'

'Yup,' said Darren, 'that's my girl.'

We carried on in this vein for several minutes, light-hearted banter covering the way we were both really feeling. The seriousness of what we were about to do had never been more evident to me. Or the sacrifices I was asking Darren to make.

'So have you given any thoughts to your vows?' said Father Miserecordie.

'Don't we just have to do the usual stuff about for better for worse, in sickness and in health?' Darren asked.

'Well yes, that's the traditional version,' said Father Miserecordie, 'but I always think it's nice if couples make the vows a little bit personal.'

'Right, so I could pledge my life to Yakult Man and promise to keep you bacteria free forever,' I said jokingly.

'And I could promise to always take you on holiday to Disneyland,' responded Darren.

'Not *quite* what I had in mind,' said Father Miserecordie. 'I was thinking of something particularly special to the both of you. Darren, is there something you'd like to say to Doris?'

Darren looked embarrassed, but then said, 'I'd just like Dorrie to know that I'll love her always, whatever it takes, and I *mean* whatever.'

He didn't look at me when he said this, but I knew what he meant and I felt silently choked. How could I put him through this? How could I?

'And you, Doris?' Father Miserecordie prompted me.

I looked at Darren and my eyes filled with tears.

'We don't know what it will take though, do we?' I whispered. 'I can't ask you to do this for me.'

We sat in silence for a minute and then Father Miserecordie said, 'I know we talked about this before, Doris—' Darren shot me a look of surprise '—but I think you're wrong. I think you can ask Darren to do this.'

'How can you say that?' I said. 'I've got a potentially debilitating disease, and I may die a horribly early death. I just don't think it's fair to the man I love to ask him to sacrifice himself for me.'

'Dorrie, you don't mean that,' Darren said. 'Come on, we've been over all of this. I will stay with you through this. You know I will.'

I fell silent then. I couldn't bear to voice the thought in my head, which said, *Suppose I don't want you to?*

'What was all that about?' said Darren as we left. 'Since when were you talking to Father Miserecordie about your MS?'

'It was the day after Flo died,' I said. 'I was upset and went to church and met him there. For what it's worth, he's on your side.'

We didn't speak again till we got home. Mum left while I went upstairs to look at Woody, who was sleeping peacefully on his side, his thumb in his mouth and a chubby fist stuffed in his ear, an endearing habit he'd inherited from his dad. I gently stroked his forehead. He was so very, very precious to me, and I couldn't bear the thought that I might not be there to see him grow up.

I came back downstairs again to find Darren watching football on TV.

'Woody OK?' he said.

'Yes, sleeping peacefully,' I said.

'You OK?' he asked.

'No,' I said.

'Didn't think so,' he said. 'I thought you'd got over all that nonsense about not marrying me.'

'I have . . . I had,' I said. 'Darren, there's nothing I want more than to marry you. It would make me the proudest woman on the planet to call myself your wife. But it feels so selfish.'

'Hey, hey.' Darren took me in his arms and held me close. 'I know how hard you're finding this, but you have to stay positive. You might be well for years. We don't know what the future brings.'

'But what if it takes you to places you don't want to go?' I said.

'What do you mean?' Darren said.

'Oh, nothing,' I said.

But later, when we sat watching the news and Flo's face flashed up with a news item about how her family weren't going to be prosecuted after all, Darren said, 'Is that what you meant? About places I don't want to go?'

He knows me so well. It wasn't hard for him to see the way my mind was working.

291

'Yes,' I said. 'You should have seen Flo. She was so vibrant and full of life. She just couldn't take any more. And the thing is, I can really understand why she did what she did. If MS affected me the way it affected her, I think I'd consider going to Switzerland.'

Darren looked at me, appalled.

'How can you even begin to think that?' he said. 'You're young, your MS may not progress fast – remember as a woman you have a better prognosis. Hell, they might find a cure.'

'But they might not,' I argued. 'And what if I do go rapidly downhill? Have you really thought what it would be like feeding me through a tube, or changing my catheter for me? I couldn't stand you having to do all that. I'd rather die.'

'You don't mean that,' said Darren.

'I do,' I said. I was suddenly furious. How could he be so obtuse? Why didn't he understand?

'You must promise me that you won't think of doing that,' said Darren. 'I will be there for you always, but I couldn't help you to kill yourself. I just couldn't.'

'Darren.' I sat up slowly and looked at him, feeling a sharp pain of regret in my stomach. If I didn't have him with me on this, I didn't know what I was going to do. 'I'm so frightened of what the future holds for us both. I know you say it won't happen, but I just don't want to be a burden to you. I'll promise you anything, but I can't promise you that.'

Chapter Twenty-Six

Beth

Matt came back eventually. He had to. Someone needed to get me home. We didn't speak all the way back. I guess we were both too wrung out. When we got in, Matt did at least settle me on the sofa and try to make me comfortable, but his manner was so cold and he appeared so distant from me, I'd rather he hadn't been there. The only thing he did say was, 'How did you do it without your parents finding out? I take it they don't know.'

'Of course they don't know,' I said. 'They'd never have understood. Caz helped me. I couldn't have done it without her.'

'Great, so everyone knew apart from me.' I couldn't work out what was angering Matt the most, the fact that I'd had an abortion, or the fact that I hadn't told him.

'It was just Caz,' I said. 'I've never told anyone else. I wanted to tell you . . .' My voice trailed off when I saw the cold look on his face, there was no point talking to him in this mood, none at all.

Matt disappeared into the kitchen and banged pots about angrily while I lay looking up at the ceiling, silent tears pouring down my cheeks. Finally my sins had come back to haunt me. I deserved this. And I deserved Matt's opprobrium. I had ruined everything.

I must have fallen asleep because I was woken by the doorbell. Groggily, I looked at the clock; it was nearly 9 p.m. Who could be visiting at this time of the evening? I could hear Matt talking to someone, then I heard him say, 'I'm not sure that's a good idea—' before someone came rushing through the door. It was Caz. The last person I wanted to see.

'Oh Beth,' she said. 'I'm so sorry.' She proffered a rather wilted bunch of flowers. 'These were all I could find. I came over the minute Dorrie rang me. She sends her love and will come and see you tomorrow.'

I felt an overwhelming sense of rage. How dare she come here offering apologies and flowers? If it hadn't been for Caz, I wouldn't have had the abortion. And I'd have had at least one child. A tiny part of me knew I was being unfair, but I felt gripped by the blackest mood I'd ever experienced.

'*You're* sorry?' I said bitterly. 'Not as sorry as I am. Matt, why did you let her in? I don't want to see Caz ever again.'

Caz looked as if I'd punched her in the stomach.

'This clearly isn't a good time,' she said. 'I'd better go.'

'Yes, you do that,' I said. 'It's partly your fault I might never have a baby. I really wish you'd never interfered in my life. You're poison. You destroy everything you touch.'

'I don't know what you mean,' stammered Caz.

I looked away, but Matt filled in the gaps.

'We've just found out that the abortion you persuaded Beth to have all those years ago may have caused her miscarriage. It also might mean she never carries full-term. I think you'd better go.'

'I thought I was helping you,' said Caz. 'I only meant it for the best.'

She got up and walked out. I turned over and faced the wall. I'd lost my baby, my husband and my friend all in the same day. Things couldn't get any worse.

'Sure, and you'll never get on if you sit around moping all day.' Mum descended on me like a ton of bricks. She'd been really patient with me for the first week, but I could tell her patience was wearing thin.

'Will you look at this place? It could do with a good spring clean. You've been letting things go. And you in your dressing gown at this time of the afternoon.'

It was true, the place was in a mess. Normally I'd have been horrified by the state it was in, I loved to keep the house pristine, but I had no energy or inclination to do anything other than look at the TV. My whole life was in a shambles, why should I care about the state of the house?

Weakly I tried to protest, but Mum was having none of it.

'Will you get upstairs and have yourself a bath and a hair wash. Then you can get yourself dressed. You'll never be enticing Matthew again if you look like that.'

I didn't mention that Matt had been sleeping on the sofa ever since I came out of the hospital and there was a fair chance that even if we got through this – and it was a big, big if – we might never conceive a child together. Mum was unstoppable in this mood, and it felt soothing to have someone else take control.

By the time I got downstairs, she'd been through the house like a whirlwind, tidying up dirty cups, plumping up cushions, dusting, restoring my little dream house to its normal state of domestic perfection.

'Right, now let's have a nice cup of tea,' she declared. 'Everything feels better after a cup of tea.'

She plonked a steaming cup of very hot sugared tea in front of me. I didn't like to tell her I normally drank herbal.

'Strong enough to stand a spoon in,' she said with satisfaction. 'Just the way Nana O'Rourke used to like it.'

I smiled at the memory. Nana O'Rourke's capacity to drink gallons of nearly black tea was part of the family mythology.

'You know, it seems like the end of the world right now,' said Mum thoughtfully, 'and believe you me, the pain never quite leaves you, but there will be another baby, you'll see.'

'What would you know about that?' I said savagely, gearing myself up for some lecture full of platitudes about Jesus sending us only the troubles we could deal with.

'Have you never wondered why there was such a big gap between you and your brother?' Mum said.

I must confess I'd never given much thought to why there were five years between James and me.

'Not really,' I said.

'The Good Lord saw fit to take three little ones away before he blessed me with you,' said Mum, a shadow passing over her face. 'They were five painful years, Elizabeth but your dad and I got through them, and then we were given you, and though I've never forgotten the loss and pray for those babies every night, your arrival healed some of that pain.'

I was stunned. 'I had no idea.'

'You had no need to,' said Mum. She took my hand. 'And pet, you must stop your fretting and look to the future. Because once you hold that baby in your arms, this will become a thing of the past. You'll see.'

I couldn't tell her I might have blown my one chance of

getting pregnant. So I squeezed her hand and said, 'Thanks Mum.' Only time would tell if she was right.

I couldn't stop thinking about what Mum had said. Maybe there was hope for the future after all. Doris and Sarah came to see me a couple of times and I thought about the problems they had in their lives, particularly Doris, and it made me realize I wasn't alone with my troubles. At least I still had my health, unlike poor Dorrie. And if Matt could only find a way of forgiving me, maybe we could still have a happy life together. Perhaps we could even adopt.

I was feeling better enough to venture out of the house, so I took a bus over to Mum's. One good thing about the miscarriage was that I recently felt closer to her. It was nice to know someone understood what I was going through.

On the way to Mum's I couldn't help thinking about my childhood and one thing in particular kept coming back. The thought that I could seek forgiveness for what I'd done.

Which is how I found myself getting off the bus two stops early and walking down the High Street to St Philomena's. As I stepped into the back of the church I felt myself relax. It was so familiar, safe, comforting. Unlike the other girls, I'd never quite been able to let go of my Catholicism. It was in my blood and I badly wanted to believe in it. But I'd also spent too many years thinking I didn't deserve to. It was time I put that right.

'Can I help you?' Father Miserecordie, who I remembered from the funeral, came striding up the aisle.

'Would you . . . could you hear my confession, Father?' I said.

'Well normally we hold the sacrament of reconciliation

on Saturday evening, but I am getting the feeling you can't wait that long.'

'You could say that,' I said.

'We could sit right here if you like,' he said. 'Or if you prefer, I can go and hide my face from you.'

'Well you've seen what I look like now,' I said. I felt remarkably at ease, considering I barely knew him, but Father Miserecordie was so kind and easy to talk to.

Father Miserecordie blessed his stole and put it round his neck, and then said, 'Would you like to begin?'

'Oh gosh, this is awkward,' I began. 'It's so long ago, I've forgotten the words.'

'Never mind the right words,' he said. 'Use the words that come naturally to you.'

I sat silently for a few minutes before stumbling, 'Bless me, Father, for I have sinned. It's fifteen years since my last confession.'

I'd tried to talk to the university chaplain about my abortion but he'd been so unsympathetic, I'd never been back since. I swallowed hard. What would this lovely man think of me?

'Father, I've done something terribly wrong,' I said. 'When I was twenty-one I got pregnant. The boy concerned said it wasn't his and refused to support me. I was lost and confused and didn't know where to turn.'

'You must have felt very alone,' prompted Father Miserecordie. 'Couldn't you have talked to your mother?'

'You've met my mother,' I said. 'No, I couldn't have talked to her.'

'So what happened?'

'Oh god, I'm so ashamed,' I whispered. 'I had an abortion.' There was a pause.

'You must think me very wicked,' I said.

'Not at all,' said Father Miserecordie. 'I'm not here to judge you. I'm here to help you find your way back to God. You did something that the Church teaches us is wrong, all life is sacred. But you were very young and vulnerable, and I sense that you have been punished for this ever since.'

'Yes,' I said. I was sobbing now. 'I've never stopped regretting it but I couldn't have had a baby, not then. And now I've lost a baby and it's my fault. I think God is punishing me for what I've done.'

'No,' he said. 'God is a loving, forgiving God. He hates the sin, not the sinner. So long as you truly repent, He will forgive you. Do you truly repent?'

'Yes,' I said.

'Can you remember your act of contrition?' said Father Miserecordie.

I stumbled through a half-remembered formula from my school days and Father Miserecordie lifted his hand above my head and said, 'Then by the power invested in me by the Almighty, I absolve you of your sins, go in peace and sin no more.'

I felt a great weight lift from my shoulders.

'What should my penance be, Father?' I said.

'I think you've been doing your penance for the last fifteen years,' he said. 'Go in peace and accept God's blessing.'

I thanked him and got up and left. I felt so much better. Now I'd finally forgiven myself, maybe I could get Matt to forgive me too.

Chapter Twenty-Seven

Sarah

'How are you doing?' I asked Beth as she, Dorrie and I walked into Caffè Nero on Northfield High Street. It being the school holidays, Maggie had kindly offered to take the boys off my hands, and I was relishing the unfamiliar freedom. When we'd been younger, a downmarket Wimpy had stood on this site. How things changed. Where once there'd been a drab seventies precinct, now stood a new range of shops offering exotic goods our teenage selves could only have dreamed of. I was glad I lived near enough to come mooching about when the kids were at school. It gave me something to do on days when I felt I couldn't cope.

Dorrie and I frequented Caffè Nero most weeks. We'd been getting worried that Beth was becoming apathetic while on leave from work, so had persuaded her to join us. Both of us were still reeling from the shock of hearing about her abortion. I wish she'd told us earlier, I felt like we'd let her down.

'I'm getting there,' said Beth. 'Don't laugh, both of you, but I went to confession.'

'Well, frankly I've always thought that was cheaper than seeing a therapist,' said Dorrie, who'd thoughtfully left Woody with her mum for the morning. 'Did it help?'

301

'Yes,' said Beth. 'At least I don't feel guilty any more about the abortion. And I think I'm beginning to accept that it's not my fault we can't have babies.'

'How are things with Matt?' I said.

'He's still sleeping on the sofa,' said Beth. 'He won't talk to me at all. It's like he's shut me out. I can't blame him really, but I wish he'd at least be angry with me. This not showing any emotion at all is so hard to deal with.'

'He'll come round in time,' I said. 'You'll see.'

'I hope so,' said Beth giving me a sad smile. Then in an effort to cheer herself up, she said, 'Sorry I'm wittering on about my crap. How are you both?'

'Getting there,' I said. 'Steve's pretty much moved out now and I've got a job interview at the local GP's surgery. Steve's mum's offered to help with childcare. I think she feels a bit guilty that her son's behaved so badly.'

'Don't knock it,' said Dorrie. 'When I went back to work for those three months after Woody was born, it would have been a nightmare if Mum and Darren's mum hadn't helped out.'

'I'm really glad things are picking up for you,' said Beth.

'Now all we need is to get you hitched up with Joe,' said Dorrie briskly.

'I think that's a really bad idea,' I said blushing. 'It would be seriously weird.'

'Nonsense,' said Dorrie. 'It says in the Bible that a man may marry his brother's wife.'

'I think you'll find that the brother has to be dead first,' I said.

'I still bet you want to,' said Dorrie.

I blushed again, thinking about Joe's kiss.

'You little hussy,' said Dorrie. 'Something's happened, hasn't it? Go on, give us all the goss.'

'It was nothing,' I said.

'Right, so something *has* happened. But it was nothing,' said Dorrie, raising a knowing eyebrow.

'All right, it might have been something,' I said. 'Last time I saw him, Joe kissed me.'

'Fantastic,' said Dorrie. 'So now what?'

'Nothing,' I said. 'It was a mistake. He's my brother-in-law. It stops there.'

'Shame,' said Beth. 'I always thought Joe was really cute.'

'And I always knew you'd married the wrong brother,' said Dorrie.

'One Day My Prince Will Come' suddenly trilled out from a mobile.

'Yours, I take it?' I said to Dorrie.

'Yup,' she said grinning.

'Oh, hi Caz, what's up?' I felt Beth stiffen beside me. She hadn't said much about what had happened, but I'd heard from Caz she'd been pretty upset and didn't want to see Caz again. I was racking my brains to work out how to effect a reconciliation before the wedding, because Dorrie had been distraught when she found out. But being Dorrie, she hadn't wanted to upset Beth by bringing it up.

'You're joking,' Dorrie said. 'And there's really no way we can use the place? Did they say anything about our deposit? Right. Thanks for letting me know. It's OK, it's not your fault.'

She snapped her phone shut.

'Damn, damn and double damn,' she said. 'That was Caz. The hotel has only gone and double booked. We're getting married in a month, and we've got nowhere to hold our wedding.'

She put her head in her hands, and started to cry.

'Oh sod it,' she said. 'Everything's going wrong. Why does everything have to go so awfully wrong?'

I'd never seen her so despairing. We tried to comfort her. Suddenly our troubles seemed like nothing compared to Dorrie's.

'Something will turn up, Dorrie,' I said. 'Come on, it's not like you to give up.'

'I've not got a venue and thanks to Beth and Caz's row—' Beth looked a little guilty at this, '—I won't have bridesmaids. Darren's putting his head in the sand about my condition. I just feel like giving up.'

'Don't say that,' I said. 'You never give up. It's not in your nature.'

'Isn't it?' Dorrie raised bleak eyes to mine. 'I'm really beginning to wonder.'

Later, Beth left us to go and visit her mum.

'I may as well, now I'm out,' she said. 'And it beats sitting at home looking at four walls.'

Not having to get back for the boys just yet, I offered to fetch Woody with Doris and go back to her house to help her ring round to find a new venue. It was an impossible task so close to the wedding day. And it wasn't being helped by Dorrie's loss of interest in the whole thing.

'What's the point?' she kept saying. 'I don't even know why Darren still wants to marry me. I'll be a cripple before long and he'll soon tire of me.'

'Dorrie, you have to stop this,' I said. 'I know you're going through a difficult time, but you have to think of Darren and Woody.'

'Believe me,' said Dorrie, 'I think of nothing else. They'd both be better off without me.'

'That's a ridiculous thing to say,' I said.

'Is it?' I said. 'How can I be a proper wife to Darren if I end up in a wheelchair? And how will Woody feel in five years' time, when his mum is the one at the school gates on sticks? I just look at them both and it rips my heart out. I can't do this to them.'

'Don't say that,' I said. 'This just isn't you talking.'

'Maybe it's the new me,' said Dorrie. 'I hate what I'm becoming. Not just physically, but mentally. I saw what MS did to Mum and Dad. I can't bear the thought of that happening to me and Daz, and I resent it. Why me? It's not fair.'

'No,' I said, pausing for a moment. 'It's bloody well not fair. In fact, it's so bloody unfair, I feel like screaming along with you.'

That elicited a small smile, so I continued, 'Do you fancy a doughnut to take your mind off things for five minutes? I bought them specially. Seems a shame to waste them.'

'Oh Sarah,' Doris burst out laughing, 'I do sound like a right old misery bag, don't I? I'll be amazed if Darren doesn't divorce me after a week at this rate.'

'Now you *know* that will never happen,' I said. 'But that's better. Come on, Dorrie. You're the bravest and the best of us. I wish to God this wasn't happening to you, but it is. So you have to find a way through.'

'You're right,' said Dorrie. 'I know you're right. I just keep thinking that maybe there's an alternative.'

'Like what?' I said.

'Oh, nothing,' said Dorrie.

She got up to see to Woody, and as she did so knocked

305

some papers on the floor. I went to pick them up. *Die the dignified way. Your right to die.* Leaflet after leaflet proposing euthanasia. Surely Doris couldn't be thinking of this as a viable option? I didn't know what to say.

'Doris, you can't be serious?' I was trying to remain calm, but inside I was screaming. I'd had no idea that Dorrie felt so bad about what was happening to her. Surely she couldn't be contemplating this?

'Oh those. I just picked them up somewhere.' Doris seemed vague. She shoved the leaflets under some other paper. 'I'm just looking at all options. Nothing's certain.'

She seemed distracted and I wanted to press her further, but I sensed her closing up on me. Maybe now wasn't the right time. But then I looked at the leaflets again. Dorrie seemed uncharacteristically low.

'You aren't really thinking about this, are you?' I said.

'Well, put it like this, I haven't ruled it out,' said Dorrie. 'I just don't want to be a burden to Darren.'

'Oh Dorrie, you mustn't be like that,' I said.

'I'll be how I please,' snapped Dorrie. 'I'm the one with the incurable disease. I knew you wouldn't understand. So I don't want to discuss it any more.'

There didn't seem to be any proper response to that, so I did as she said and changed the subject.

'Right, let's see about getting some more phone numbers,' I said brightly. 'I'll go online and see if I can find something suitable.'

I tried to be cheerful, but inside I was deeply disturbed. What if she really was planning to end it all?

I was so worried I rang Caz and invited her over the following evening. I had never invited her to mine before, but I thought the situation warranted it. She came over after I'd put the kids to bed.

'Can you have a drink?' I said. 'Or are you driving?'

'No, I'm still staying at Mum's,' said Caz.

'Aren't you going to put the house on the market?' I said curiously. I knew how Caz had hated her home growing up, and yet she seemed to be spending an inordinate amount of time there.

'I'm still sifting through piles of stuff,' said Caz. 'In a weird kind of way, I don't want to let go. Once it's gone, then she's gone too. I can't really explain. It's complicated the way I feel about Mum. It just seems as if I'm finally getting to know her at last. I'm still really angry with her, especially for holding back all those letters from Dad from me. But I don't know, I've been chatting to Father Miserecordie about it, and I'm beginning to feel sorry for her. He says she was a lost soul, and I think maybe he's right. Apparently she did an awful lot of good in the parish. And she talked about me all the time. I wish we'd had the opportunity to make up.'

Caz looked very wistful as she said this. She had never said so much about her mum before. I knew things had been bad for her growing up, but when you're a kid you can't imagine anyone else's life. It must have been so hard for her seeing us all with our happy families. No wonder she was so bitter and resentful.

'I'm sorry,' I said. 'I don't think I've ever really understood how difficult it was for you back then.'

'It's not your fault is it?' said Caz. 'It's just bad luck that I got the pisshead mum, while you lot got the normal variety.'

'But I could have been more understanding,' I said.

'And I could have been less of a bitch,' said Caz. 'I'm really

307

sorry for what I did to you with Steve. I was so jealous of what you had. It was unforgivable of me.'

'It does take two,' I said. 'And it was pretty naïve of me to believe that it was all your fault.'

'Well, I wanted you to believe that,' said Caz. 'That's why I never denied it. I felt so guilty about what happened, I thought if I took all the blame, your marriage at least had a chance of working.'

'But when I asked you, you told me that you'd instigated things,' I said.

'I know,' said Caz, with a sigh. 'I still thought if there was a chance that you and Steve could make it, I shouldn't put a spanner in the works.'

'And what about at Dorrie's games night?' I said. 'You looked like you were enjoying his company that evening.'

'Oh Sarah,' said Caz. 'For a brief moment he flirted with me and I thought, *I remember this* and was flattered. But then I realized I was doing it again.'

'What?'

'My usual thing of being flattered by male attention, and responding to it without thinking about it. I looked up and saw your face and wanted to kick myself,' she said. 'I am so sorry, it was really stupid of me, particularly when I looked at him and do you know what I saw?'

'No,' I said.

'A balding, middle-aged sleazeball, who hasn't grown up and still thinks he's God's gift to women,' she said. 'Honestly Sairs, I can't think what either of us ever saw in him.'

I burst out laughing. God, I'd forgotten just how much Caz could make me laugh.

'Oh Caz, it's as much my fault as yours. I shouldn't have believed him so readily,' I said. 'I knew deep down you weren't such a cow that you'd have betrayed me without at least *some* encouragement. And I punished you because I couldn't face the truth.'

'Well truth is sometimes overrated I find,' said Caz. 'But on this occasion, I think you deserve to hear it. I was the lousiest of friends to you, and when I was very drunk (which is no excuse, mind) I allowed myself to be seduced by your fiancé. It was very, very wrong of me, and I'm not proud of myself, but it was a two-way street. I'm sorry I didn't tell you that before.'

I should have felt bereft at hearing Caz confirm what I'd always known, but suddenly I realized Steve had lost the power to hurt me any more.

'God, what idiots we are,' I said, 'letting a man come between us for so long.'

'So does that mean we're OK again?' Caz looked at me tentatively.

'I should coco,' I said. 'Now, enough of our troubles. What are we going to do to help Dorrie?'

'Do you think she's serious about this euthanasia thing?' said Caz. I'd filled her in about what I'd seen at Dorrie's when I'd rung her the previous day.

'I don't know,' I said, 'but I know how badly affected she was by her dad's illness. She once said to me she'd rather someone shoot her than end up like that. I think the problem is she's seen first hand what it could be like and it's frightening her.'

'Will it really be that bad?' said Caz.

'I don't know a great deal about MS,' I said, 'but when I was working on the wards I saw one or two patients with it, and it can be horrific. It doesn't have to be like that for Dorrie of course, but I can understand why she's frightened, and why she might think ending it all when the time comes is a viable option. There've been lots of cases of people going out to Switzerland. I just can't see Doris wanting to put Darren through that.'

'I hope you're right,' said Caz. 'But I think we should keep an eye on her. You know how determined she is once she's put her mind on something.'

Just then the doorbell rang.

Joe was at the front door, looking embarrassed and proffering a bunch of red roses. I had neither seen nor heard from him since our last encounter. Dozens of things had gone through my mind since then, namely that he might turn out to be the same lying cheating bastard his brother was, but it was tinged with heady excitement too. It felt odd, certainly, to have kissed my husband's brother, and a part of me felt guilty, but a bigger part of me felt that it had seemed right and natural.

'Er, hi,' he said, and thrust the flowers in my face.

'Thanks,' I said nervously. 'They are lovely, but I don't think I need to smell them at quite such close range.'

'About the other night—'

'Shouldn't have happened,' I said. 'Sorry if I led you on.'

'Oh god, no,' he said. 'It was my fault. I took advantage of you and I'm sorry. It won't happen again.'

'Oh, right,' I said, slightly bemused.

'Well that's that then,' said Joe, and just as I was about to ask him in, he practically fled down the road.

He was right, this couldn't go any further. It would make things way too complicated. But I felt a twinge of disappointment nonetheless.

'What was all that about?' said Caz when I came back into the lounge, holding the roses.

'Do you know what?' I said. 'I really have no idea.'

Chapter Twenty-Eight

Caz

'Hallo stranger.' Charlie hugged me, a couple of days later, as I made my way into the old factory turned photographic studio for a fledgling popstar's photo shoot.

I felt ridiculously awkward. It had been weeks since we'd seen each other and while I hadn't *exactly* been trying to avoid him, I hadn't been answering his calls either.

'A paranoid type of person might think you were avoiding me,' said Charlie. 'Lucky I'm not a paranoid type of person, eh?'

'Sorry, been busy,' I mumbled. 'I've been at Mum's sorting stuff out and not been home much.'

'I know,' said Charlie. 'I've probably worn out your answering machine leaving you that many messages.'

'Sorry,' I said again. I edged away from him. I didn't really want to be having this conversation or I might be forced to admit that yes, I had been avoiding him, and then have the awkwardness of coming up with a convincing lie as to why.

'Sorry Charlie, got to go. I think I'm needed. Catch you later,' I mumbled and then fled.

I busied myself discussing the kind of foundation the

lead singer of the boy band favoured. Turned out he was as clued up on the latest skin products as any diva.

'I still think you're avoiding me,' Charlie breathed in my ear while we took a short break from shooting. The band couldn't quite decide on the look they were going for and there were several heated arguments going on.

'I give them till Christmas,' said Charlie. 'So are you going to tell me why you won't see me, or do I have to guess?'

'I'm not avoiding you,' I said weakly. 'It's just been a funny time.' I paused for a moment. 'I didn't tell you, did I? I've found my dad. Well, I've got his address and written him a letter. But I haven't heard anything back yet.'

'That's fantastic,' said Charlie, looking really pleased for me.

'I hope so,' I said, 'but I'm really nervous. Suppose he doesn't want to have anything to do with me?'

'What makes you think that, you daft mare?' said Charlie. 'Your dad wrote you all those letters, didn't he?'

'So why hasn't he written back?' I said.

'I don't know, maybe he's been away, maybe the post office has burnt down. There could be all sorts of reasons,' said Charlie. 'Never give up. That's my motto.'

He gave me a wink.

'Now to prove you're *not* avoiding me, you'll be free to come out for a drink tomorrow night, won't you?'

'What about Nadia?' I said.

'Ah—' began Charlie, before he was called away to set up a shot.

I sat mulling it over while I watched Charlie at work. I really, really liked Charlie, both as a friend, and perhaps something more. Clearly my avoidance tactic hadn't worked, so I was going to have to take the bull by the horns and tell him we couldn't see each other any more with Nadia on the scene. It was the only decent thing to do.

I'd just come in from work and my back was killing me. It had been a productive day, but my nerves were jangling from the contact with Charlie. Dammit, I'd forgotten just how necessary he was to my existence. Jeez, at this rate I was going to turn into Julia Roberts in *My Best Friend's Wedding*.

I came into my tiny minimalist flat, dropped my bag on the black leather sofa, trying not to remember Charlie's head leaning against mine the last time he'd been here, poured myself a glass of wine and headed for the bathroom. I deserved a long luxurious soak.

I hadn't been there very long and was drifting off into a dangerously tempting daydream which involved me, Charlie and thoughts I really shouldn't be having, when the doorbell rang. That was odd. I wasn't expecting anyone and didn't lead the kind of life where people just dropped in. I envied Sarah, Beth and Dorrie. They all lived so close to one another, they were frequent visitors in each other's houses. It must be nice to have that sense of community. Yet another thing I'd screwed up.

I shut my eyes; it couldn't be anyone important. They'd probably just go away if I left them.

The doorbell rang again, this time more persistently. Dammit, I couldn't ignore it any longer. I leapt out of the bath, threw on my cosy bathrobe and shouted 'Just coming,' as my unseen visitor rang impatiently once again.

I flung open the door and there was a tallish, thin man with greying hair, an uncertain smile on his face, standing there, looking nervous as hell.

'Who are you?' I said, slightly more belligerently than I intended, but I felt slightly caught on the hop, standing there dripping wet.

'Caroline, may I come in?' he said shyly, with a strong Irish lilt.

Caroline? He called me *Caroline*? Could it possibly be—?

'Who are you?' I said again. My voice sounded far away and reedy. My heart was thumping in my chest, as I tried to rein in the hope that was flaring up inside me.

'I got your letter,' he said, the same uncertain smile playing on his lips, as if he wasn't quite sure of my response.

'Did you?' I said. I was feeling slightly giddy with expectation, nerves jangling, mouth dry, feeling faintly sick. 'You're not—?'

'I wasn't sure after the way you spoke at the funeral whether you'd want to see me,' he continued— What? *Dad* had been at Mum's funeral? 'So I was thrilled to get it. I'd have come before but your stepmother and I were on a cruise.'

I leant back against the door, pulling my dressing gown tightly around me, unable to take this in.

'Dad?' I croaked. 'Is it really you?'

'One and the same,' he said huskily. 'And how proud I am to finally meet my beautiful daughter.'

'Do you want to come in?' I stuttered, suddenly aware that I was semi-naked and dripping wet.

'If you'd like me to,' said Dad.

How weird it was to say that name. He looked nervous and vulnerable, and I instinctively knew I was going to like him. I dressed in double quick time and returned to the lounge to find Dad pacing up and down.

'Be careful, you'll wear the carpet out,' I quipped.

'Sorry,' he said. 'Only I'm that nervous about seeing you.'

'Me too,' I admitted, still feeling shaky, 'but in a good way.'

'You're sure?' Dad said. 'I could understand if you didn't want to see me. In fact, all these years, I thought you wouldn't. Your mam always sent my letters back.'

'I only just found out about the letters,' I said. 'I've wanted to find you my whole life, but never had the nerve. And now you're here.'

'I'm sorry,' said Dad. 'I was too young when I met your mam, not ready for the responsibility. I should have tried harder to stay in touch.'

'It wasn't all your fault,' I said, touching his sleeve. 'Mum was so bitter and angry she sent everyone away, but in a way I think she thought she was protecting me.'

There was a pause, then Dad looked at me with tears in his eyes and held his arms out. 'It's grand to see you at last, Caroline, and see what a beautiful woman you've grown into,' he said, with a flash of the charm that Auntie Nora had mentioned.

'Oh Dad, I'm so glad you came,' I said, my tears flowing too. I flung my arms around him and hugged him like I wouldn't let him go. And as he held me tight, for the first time in my life, I felt like I wasn't alone in the world.

'So he turned up just like that?' Charlie whistled over his pint of beer, the next evening.

'Yup,' I said. 'I was gobsmacked, I can tell you.'

'And how was it?' said Charlie. 'What you expected?'

'Strange,' I said. 'Nice. Brilliant, actually. He seems lovely.'

'Are you going to see him again?'

'Yes, but not just yet,' I said. 'He's gone down to Cornwall to see his wife's family for a few days. He said he'd call me when he was back.'

'Oh Caz, I'm thrilled for you.' Charlie squeezed my arm. 'You deserve a break.'

I was slightly taken aback, Charlie wasn't usually this touchy feely.

'The weird thing was, he was actually at the funeral,' I said.

'So why didn't he say hello?' Charlie asked.

'Um, he heard my speech and thought I didn't want to know.' I was mortified when I realized Dad was the person I'd seen leaving the church and had apologized to him profusely. He kept telling me not to worry and that he was the one who was sorry.

'Now, why doesn't that surprise me, Caroline Riley sends away yet another person who's on her side?'

I blushed. 'Yeah, well, you know that's my major sport.'

'At which I'd say you were champion.' Charlie's dark, thoughtful eyes held mine for a moment, and I turned away embarrassed. I didn't have to be reminded how often I'd done that to him.

'Did he say why he hadn't kept in contact?' Charlie wanted to know.

'He did try, hence all those letters I found,' I said. 'But Mum returned them all and then didn't let him know where we'd moved to. It was only when she died and Auntie Nora got in touch, he found out where I was. Dad said he didn't blame Mum, he feels terrible about the way he left her in the lurch. I guess he just wasn't ready for the responsibility at the time.'

'So how did he know about the funeral?' Charlie said.

'Get this: Mum told Father Miserecordie to contact him in the event of her death. I guess he would have told me if I hadn't sounded off so much, he must have thought I didn't want to know my dad either. Bloody hell, I've made a mess of things.'

'No you haven't,' said Charlie. 'We're still friends, aren't we?'

'I suppose,' I said. 'But you've got Nadia. You don't need me.'

'You can be incredibly dumb sometimes, Caz,' Charlie said. 'You're talented, successful, funny and utterly gorgeous. There's always going to be room in my life for you.'

He held my gaze for a few seconds and I blushed before looking away. Could he be – was he – flirting with me?

'I bet you say that to all the girls,' I said lightly, trying to deflect him.

'Yes, but I mean it with you,' said Charlie as he went up to the bar to get another round in.

Bloody hell. He *was* flirting with me. This had to stop.

'Look Charlie,' I said when he came back. 'I think maybe we may have got things a bit wrong lately.'

'You do?' said Charlie. 'I rather think we've got them right.'

'I do,' I said. 'I've changed. I like you, really I do. But I'm not about to go jumping into bed with someone who's in a relationship anytime soon. I just thought you should know that.'

'Well, firstly, it's highly presumptuous of you to assume I want you to jump in my bed—' Oh god, mortification, he *doesn't* fancy me, '—and secondly there's something you need to know about Nadia—'

Just then my phone rang. It was a number I didn't recognize.

'Hi,' I said.

'Oh Caz, thank god, I can't get hold of anyone else.' It was Darren.

317

'Darren, are you OK?' I said. I was trying to concentrate on what Darren was saying, but part of me was distracted with wondering what Charlie meant.

'Not really,' he said. 'Doris has disappeared taking her passport with her. She wrote me a note telling me not to follow her, and she's not answering her phone.'

'Wha-at?' All thoughts of Charlie fled from my mind. 'Where do you think she's gone?'

'I looked at what she's been doing online and she appears to have bought a plane ticket to Zurich. I've got a horrible feeling she's gone to that clinic in Switzerland. She's been so down about her condition lately. I think she's going to try and kill herself.'

'Oh my god. I'll be over right away,' I said, and hung up. I looked at Charlie. 'I have to go, Dorrie's in trouble. What was it you were saying?'

'Oh, just that Nadia's ditched me and I was wondering when you were going to swallow your stupid pride and come out with me.'

I was stunned, this was more than I could bear.

'Don't tease me,' I said. 'It's not kind.'

'I'm not teasing,' he said. 'You know I'd never do that. So? What do you say?'

I looked at him, lovely Charlie, who'd always been there for me all these long and lonely years. How could I have been so dense as not to see it?

'Um – wait for me?' I said.

'Caz, I've been waiting for you for fifteen years,' said Charlie. 'I think I can wait a bit longer.'

Interlude

Doris

I was feeling so low after I heard that we'd lost the venue for the wedding. It seemed like a sign. And my symptoms, which had subsided a little of late, seemed to be coming back big time. I had a pounding headache and my left leg was constantly painful. I was certain the MS was getting worse. I ignored the logical solution which was to go to the consultant and find out what, if anything, he could do for me, and I couldn't face the support group, because all I could think about was how dark and black my future was going to be. I had to do something to sort it out now.

So one day, at the end of August, while Darren was at work, I sat online and looked up everything I could about the Right to Die clinic in Zurich. I had to go and find out for myself what it was like. Auntie Sophie lived on the outskirts of Zurich. I'd tell Mum I was going to stay with her and use it as a base for my research.

Mum was delighted to see me when I came round with Woody. Every time I saw her, she was more and more like her old self. But of course that meant she was waking up to the fact that I was hiding something from her.

319

'Dorrie, I want you to tell me the truth,' she said. 'I know something's wrong, will you please tell me what it is.'

I'd been dreading this moment for months, and when it came to it, I just burst into tears. 'Oh Mum,' I said, 'I didn't know how to tell you.'

'Tell me what, love?' Mum said. 'You and Darren aren't splitting up, are you?'

'No,' I said. 'It's much worse than that. I'm sorry.'

'What for?' said Mum. 'It can't be as bad as all that.'

As I looked at her, I felt my heart might break in two. I was going to cause her so much pain, but I knew I couldn't keep it a secret any longer.

'Oh Mum,' I said, 'I've got MS too.'

Mum put her hand over her mouth and uttered a little moan. 'Oh Dorrie, my poor, poor love. I've been that wrapped up in myself, I haven't been thinking about you. I'm the one who should be sorry.'

'I didn't know how to tell you,' I said, between hiccupping sobs. 'I can't bear it that I'm putting you through this again.'

'Now don't be so ridiculous,' said Mum. 'I will not hear that defeatist talk, do you hear? Come on, there are plenty of things they can do.'

'Like they did for Dad?' I said bitterly.

'Yes, but it may be different for you,' said Mum. 'You're still young. Dad wasn't. What does your consultant say?'

'Not a lot,' I mumbled.

Mum looked at me shrewdly. 'You *have* seen a consultant haven't you?'

'Yes, of course I have,' I said. 'I've just been so busy with wedding stuff I haven't had time to book myself another appointment.'

'You'd better,' said Mum. 'Or you'll have me to answer to. How's Darren taken it?'

'He's been brilliant,' I said, my lower lip wobbling. I nearly cracked and told her how I was feeling when she hugged me fiercely and I wept some more. I just couldn't bring myself to do it though, and despite my pain, I felt a stab of joy. I had my mum back.

'So why do you want to visit Auntie Sophie?' said Mum, when we'd both done crying.

'I just need to get away for a bit,' I said. 'Clear my head. Mum, I know this is a big ask, but could you look after Woody for me? And promise me you won't tell Darren where I've gone?'

'Why don't you want Darren to know?' said Mum suspiciously.

'Just . . . it's complicated, Mum. Daz and I have had a difficult few months, I just need some time on my own.'

'Well, all right,' Mum said reluctantly. 'But promise me you won't do anything stupid?'

How could she know what I was thinking? Only Darren knew the true extent of my dark thoughts.

'I promise,' I said. 'I just want to spend time with Auntie Sophie and chill a bit.' But I crossed my fingers behind my back as I said it. It wasn't a lie exactly. I had no idea what I was planning to do.

Chapter Twenty-Nine

Sarah

As soon as Darren got hold of me, ignoring the potential awkwardness of the situation, I got Joe to come and sit with the kids and flew round to Dorrie's house.

'Did you know she's been looking at all this death with dignity stuff?' I said. 'I found some leaflets last time I was here.'

'I didn't,' Darren said, 'but I'm not surprised.' He looked utterly wretched. 'She keeps talking about how it's not fair on me if we get married. I never envisaged she would do something like this.'

'Um, you are sure that she's gone to Switzerland, aren't you?' I said. 'I mean, maybe she's just taken herself off somewhere to clear her head.'

'Yes,' said Darren. 'She left Woody with her mum and told her she was flying to Switzerland and to tell me not to worry.'

'Did she say anything about when she was coming back?' I said.

'No. She told her mum she needed time to think and left me a note,' said Darren, looking bewildered. 'I don't understand it. She said she doesn't want me to follow her.'

'She was very upset the last time I saw her,' I said. 'Maybe she's just gone on a fact-finding trip.'

'Maybe,' said Darren.

'Bugger,' I said. 'I knew how upset she was about your venue falling through and I've sorted something out. It was meant to be a surprise. I wish I'd told her now.'

'It's not your fault,' said Darren. 'It's nobody's fault. It's this bloody disease. If only she had something you could treat with antibiotics. I feel so helpless.'

'We all do,' I said. 'But Dorrie knows how lucky she is to have you and Woody.'

'If it's anyone's fault she's gone, it's mine,' said Darren. 'I should have listened to her worries more. I should have listened to what she wanted and not thought about what I wanted.'

Darren looked so desolate I gave him a hug.

'You can't blame yourself,' I said. 'You two have been through such a lot in the last few months. It's bound to take its toll.'

We sat in silence for a few minutes, then I said, 'There's no point sitting around moping. We should go after her.'

'But she doesn't want me to follow her,' said Darren. 'And I don't know where to start.'

'Well she didn't say anything about us, so we'll go after her,' I said. 'I think we should start with that clinic. I'm betting she's gone there.'

'Actually,' said Darren slowly, 'thinking about it, she might not have. She does have an aunt who lives in Zurich.'

'Well, we could try there then, couldn't we?' I said. 'Do you have an address?'

'No, but I'm sure her mum does.'

Caz arrived then, breathless and frantic.

'Sorry it's taken me so long to get here,' she said. 'I was in town and the underground took ages. You don't really think Doris would have gone to that place in Switzerland, do you?'

'I don't know,' I said, 'but it looks as if she might have. She won't be expecting us to follow her though, and she can't keep her phone switched off forever. Darren, can I borrow your computer? I'll start looking up flights now.'

'What about the kids, aren't they due back at school?' said Caz.

'Not till next week,' I said. 'I'll ring Steve. This is an emergency. It's about time he did some childcare.'

Having sourced a few flights I dashed back home to relieve Joe and ring Steve, who was, predictably, completely unhelpful.

'No chance,' he said. 'You can't just drop them on me like that. I've got back-to-back meetings for the next three days. Maybe I could fit them in next week. Ring my mother.'

'Oh bloody hell, now what are we going to do?' I said. 'I've found us a flight for lunchtime tomorrow, but I won't be able to go if I can't get anyone to look after the kids.'

'Steve said no, I take it?' Joe had been quietly sympathetic about Doris, but I didn't feel I could ask for his help. 'God, he makes me furious. What was his excuse this time?'

'Too much work,' I said. I felt flat and let down. Bugger Steve. I hated the fact that he could still impact on my life in this way. I banged my hand on the table in frustration. 'That's it then, I can't go.'

'Well I'm not doing anything for the next couple of days,' Joe said.

'But what about your work?' I said.

'There are advantages to being your own boss, you know,'

he said. 'Besides, I'd like to spend time with my nephews and I'm happy to do anything to help you out, you know that.'

'Are you sure? It seems like a hell of an imposition.'

'Haven't you worked it out yet, you idiot woman?' said Joe. 'Nothing you could ask of me would ever be an imposition.'

'Oh,' I said.

'You know, I've been thinking,' Joe continued, smiling at me with his lovely lazy smile. 'I think we acted hastily. Because, by an accident of birth, I just happen to be your brother-in-law, doesn't mean that we can't have a relationship. It might be a little awkward—'

'A little?' I snorted. 'Can you think how difficult Christmas is going to be?'

'—but you know,' said Joe, completely ignoring me, 'life's too short. I've been in love with you for the best part of fifteen years. I've stood by and watched my prat of a brother cock up your life and make you unhappy. I don't want to let anyone else ever do that to you again.'

'Oh,' I said again. I suddenly was aware my jaw was hanging wide open and shut it quickly. Despite my worries about Dorrie, my heart was singing. Joe, lovely, gorgeous Joe, who'd always been there, quietly in the background, these long barren years of my marriage, was telling me he had feelings for me. Whatever else life threw at me, I knew I could handle it with him at my side.

Joe pulled me into his arms and kissed me so passionately and tenderly I never wanted it to end.

'Good,' he said with satisfaction. 'I've been wanting to do that again to see if it matched up to last time.'

'And did it?' I said.

'More than,' he said, and kissed me again. I could have stayed there all night in his arms, but reluctantly I pulled away. Dorrie's problems weren't going away just because mine had got sorted.

'So, what do you say?' Joe said. 'Shall we give it a go?'

'I – er, yes,' I squeaked. 'But first I really have to book these flights to Zurich.'

'Still no word?' Caz rang me later that evening.

'None,' I said. 'The earliest flight I could get was 2 p.m. from Heathrow. Where are you staying tonight? Do you want to hook up with us, or shall we meet there?'

'I'm at home,' she said. I heard a muffled giggle in the background. 'I'll meet you at the airport.'

'Are you on your own?' Caz sounded slightly odd, as if she was trying to keep her composure.

'Um – tell you tomorrow,' she said. Another time I would have been intrigued, but right now I couldn't think of anything but Dorrie. 'Look, don't mind about me, let's concentrate on getting to Switzerland. What terminal do we need?'

'Terminal One. If we meet at the information desk around eleven that should give us plenty of time.'

'Will do,' said Caz. 'Who's looking after the kids?'

It was my turn to be slightly disconcerted. 'Um, Joe,' I said.

'Joe, as in "sexy brother Joe"?' Caz whistled. 'Tell me more.'

'Tomorrow,' I said. 'By the way, I hope you don't mind, but Beth's coming too. I spoke to her after I got home. I think this is more important than any of us, don't you?'

'Sarah, Dorrie needs us, simple as,' said Caz. 'If Beth

doesn't want to talk to me, that's fine by me, but nothing on earth is going to stop me from getting on that plane tomorrow.'

'What about Darren?'

'He's still working out what to do,' said Caz. 'Poor thing, he's so gutted that Dorrie didn't want him to follow her, he's going demented.'

'And Dorrie's mum?'

'Doesn't know,' said Caz. 'Darren thought with everything she's been through, the last thing she needs to worry about is Dorrie trying to—' Her voice trailed off; we both knew what she meant.

'Oh god,' I paused, the reality of it sinking in. I'd been on an adrenaline rush all evening and not given myself time to think about it. 'What if she's already at the Right to Die clinic?'

'Don't even go there,' said Caz. 'We can't afford to think like that.'

'No, you're right,' I said. 'Best get packing then.'

'Yes,' Caz said. 'I'll meet you at Heathrow tomorrow.'

I put the phone down with a heavy heart. I just hoped we weren't too late.

Chapter Thirty

Beth

Matt came home late as usual, and went straight to the computer. He barely acknowledged me when I told him supper was ready and ate his meal in complete silence.

'Aren't you even going to ask where I've been?' I said.

But his response was to get up and return to the computer. Something snapped inside me. This was ridiculous.

'How long are you planning to keep this up?' I said.

'Keep what up?'

'Giving me the silent treatment, acting like a spoilt child,' I said. 'We have to talk about this sooner or later.'

'What's there to talk about?' Matt said. 'You lied to me. There. I've been thinking all this baby business is my fault somehow. Feeling like I wasn't a real man – when all along the problem was you. If you hadn't put it about when you were young, we might have a baby by now.'

'Matt, that's bloody unfair,' I said. 'I know I lied. And I'm really sorry I can't undo that. But can you put yourself in my shoes for one minute and spare me an ounce of compassion? I met this guy when I was twenty. He was charming and clever and funny.'

'Spare me the details, please,' said Matt.

'I had never had anyone like that pay me any attention. And what's more he told me he loved me. Which, like a fool, I believed. As soon as he found out I was pregnant, he was off. He left me to deal with it alone. Can you imagine what it was like? I couldn't tell my mum or dad. I didn't know anyone at uni well enough to confide in them. And the slimy sod was spreading rumours that I'd been sleeping around and everyone believed him—'

'Bastard,' said Matt. That was better. At least Matt sounded like he was more on my side.

'The only person who I knew would understand was Caz. She was more experienced than me, and less judgemental than Sarah or Dorrie would have been at the time. And she knew what to do. I couldn't have had a baby back then. I was too young and my mum would have died of shame. I didn't want an abortion, but I didn't have a choice. Can't you see? I had no idea that it might affect me like this later.'

'Why didn't you tell me?' Matt looked desolate. 'That's what hurts the most, that you couldn't trust me.'

'It wasn't that.' I knelt down next to him and grabbed his hands. 'I couldn't. You'd always made it so clear to me how much you disapproved of abortion. You've always gone on about how your mum chose to have you rather than abort you. I just couldn't. Besides, I felt too ashamed. I felt like I deserved to be punished. And now I have been.'

'Now that's being really stupid,' said Matt, lacing his hands over mine.

'Catholic guilt,' I said. 'It has a lot to answer for.'

Matt paused and took a deep breath and then said, 'I can't pretend I'll get over this quickly. It was a huge shock. But I will try. I promise.'

He kissed the top of my head and went back to his computer.

The phone rang and I picked it up.

'Darren?' I said. 'What's wrong?'

'Are you sure you're fit enough to go?' said Matt as I frantically packed a bag the next morning. 'You've been through such a lot recently.'

Sarah had rung straight after Darren to say that she'd found flights for us the next day, and would I be able to come? I didn't give it a second thought.

'I'm fine,' I said. 'Doris has always been there for me – for us. And now she needs us. We have to help her. It's the only thing we can do.'

'You look peaky,' he said.

'I feel a bit peaky,' I said. 'And to be honest, I feel really queasy and a bit achy. I expect it's nerves.'

'Ring me when you get there,' he said.

'Do you want me to?' I said. 'Or are you just saying that?'

'No, I'm not just saying that,' he said. 'I didn't sleep very well last night. I thought a lot about what you said. It must have been really hard for you. I'm sorry I've made it harder.'

'I'm sorry too,' I said. 'I should have been straight with you from the beginning.'

He pulled me to him gently and stroked my hair. It felt like an age since I'd been in his arms. It was wonderful to be held again.

We stayed there a long time. Eventually Matt kissed me on the top of my head.

'I'd better go to work,' he said. 'Ring me, won't you?'

'I will,' I said.

He kissed me goodbye.

'It will be all right,' he said. 'We'll work things out. Maybe try again.'

'Or adopt,' I said.

'So long as we're together, nothing else matters, does it?'

Watching him walk down the garden path, I felt a lightening of my heart. At least I'd got that sorted. Then I thought about Doris and Zurich, and I retched, my nerves getting the best of me. I hoped we weren't going to be too late.

Sarah and I took a cab to Heathrow and met Caz at Terminal One. I was nervous seeing her again, we hadn't spoken properly since Matt had chucked her out of our house. I knew I should be the first to apologize, but I didn't know how.

'So Dorrie's phone is still switched off?' Caz said, not looking at me directly.

'Seems to be,' said Sarah.

'How's Daz?' I asked.

'In a terrible state,' said Sarah. 'I wouldn't be surprised if he ignored Dorrie and came anyway.'

'This is daft. We don't even know where we're going,' I said. 'How are we going to find her in Zurich?'

'Oh, but we do,' said Sarah. 'Darren reminded me that Dorrie has an aunt who lives outside Zurich. I bet she's gone there. I got the address off her mum.'

'You didn't tell her what was going on, did you?'

'Not in so many words,' said Sarah. 'I pretended I needed to get hold of Dorrie to talk wedding stuff.'

'Since when were you so pally with Dorrie's mum?' I said. 'I thought she didn't talk to anyone any more.'

'She seems a bit better recently,' said Sarah, 'and she's been helping me sort out the wedding venue.'

We checked our baggage in and went through to the departures lounge.

'Coffee anyone?' said Caz.

'Good idea,' I said, addressing her directly for the first time, though actually the thought of coffee was making me feel a bit queasy. I hated flying at the best of times, but it was even more nerve-racking not knowing what we were going to find at the other end.

We managed to squeeze ourselves round a small table in a crowded coffee shop. The place buzzed with business travellers, who probably made up most of the people on our plane. I hoped we weren't going on a fool's errand.

'So, tell me what's going on with you and sexy Joe then,' Caz said, digging Sarah in the ribs.

'What's all this?' I said, it was good to have something to distract me from my anxiety.

'Joe is looking after the kids for me while I'm away,' said Sarah, but she turned deep crimson as she said it.

'And?' said Caz.

'And, well, I think we might have just got together,' said Sarah looking slightly embarrassed.

'That's classic,' said Caz. 'Keep it in the family, why don't you?'

'Oh my god, how are you going to cope at Christmas?' I said. 'It's bad enough having in-laws without having your ex as one of them.'

'I did point that out to Joe, but he refuses to acknowledge the problem, he says life's too short,' Sarah said.

We all thought about Dorrie.

'Amen to that,' I said.

333

'And what about you?' said Sarah, turning to Caz. 'You had someone at your flat last night, don't pretend you didn't. I heard him giggling.'

Now it was Caz's turn to look embarrassed.

'Ah, well, yes, um, the thing is, it's been a weird couple of days,' she said. 'First of all, my dad turned up on my doorstep.'

'Your dad?' Sarah and I chorused. 'How? When?'

'Well, it was thanks to Auntie Nora in the end. Turned out she knew where he'd been all the time.'

'Why didn't she tell you?' Sarah said.

'I think she was still protecting Mum, and she genuinely thought I didn't want to know.'

'So what's he like?'

'He seems really lovely,' Caz said. 'I know, he left Mum and me all those years ago, and that was wrong, but from the way he told it, Mum practically threw him out. He did try to keep in touch, but Mum started sending his letters back. Then when he came to the funeral, he heard what I had to say and thought I wouldn't want to meet him.'

'He was at your mum's funeral?' I said

'I know, bonkers isn't it?' said Caz. 'But I've met him now, and it does feel fantastic.'

Caz explained what had happened. 'And you know the best of it?' she said. 'I've got a family. A proper family. Step mother, step brother and sister. I just can't believe it.'

'I'm really happy for you,' said Sarah. 'But you don't get out of it that easily, who's the mystery man?'

Caz blushed again. 'You'll never believe it,' she said, 'but it's Charlie.'

'What, Charlie as in "I got married in Vegas in a drunken

moment Charlie"?' I said, and whistled loudly. 'What's going on there then?'

'I dunno,' said Caz. 'I think we both suddenly realized that we'd been in love with each other all this time without knowing it.'

'What about you?' Sarah turned to me. 'Are things any better with you and Matt?'

'I think so,' I said cautiously. 'He's finally come round to understanding why I didn't tell him about the abortion and we're thinking that maybe we'll adopt.'

'That's one way forward,' said Sarah. 'But you never know, you still might be able to get pregnant.'

'Maybe,' I said. 'It was weird this morning, I was feeling so wound up and nervous I was nearly sick and for a moment there, I thought I was still pregnant. Stupid isn't it? How the mind plays tricks on you.'

'Not at all,' said Sarah. 'It's been a tough time. But it will get better, you'll see.'

We sat saying nothing for a while and then Sarah said, 'Isn't it weird, how everything's suddenly come right for us all when it's going so badly wrong for Dorrie? I wonder where she is. I hope she's all right.'

'I bet she'll still be reading her texts,' said Caz suddenly. 'I just can't see Dorrie not wanting to be in communication with *anyone*. We should send her one. Tell her we're coming.'

'Great idea,' I said.

Caz had been standing quietly in the background, trying to keep out of my way, I'm sure. She looked at me uncertainly and said, 'Beth, I'm so sorry about the baby. And for my part in causing you problems with Matt. I never meant to.'

'I know,' I said. 'I was in a state of shock and overreacted. I'm sorry too.'

We hugged slightly awkwardly. And then gave each other a proper hug. We were both really choked up.

'I'm the one that should be sorry,' I said. 'You were there for me, when I really, really needed you. I couldn't have coped without your help, and I shouldn't have let you go away thinking I didn't know what you'd done for me. I just lashed out because I was hurt and angry. Can *you* forgive *me*?'

'Nothing to forgive,' Caz said gruffly. 'Really. You were upset, and with good reason. My coming in just then must have rubbed salt right in the wound.'

I wiped away my tears and hugged her again. 'The most important thing right now is Dorrie. We need to let her know that we all really care about her.'

'What shall we say?' Sarah said, mobile at the ready.

'There is only one thing to say,' said Caz. '*One four all and all four one. You don't get rid of us that easily.*'

Chapter Thirty-One

Caz

The plane touched down at Zurich airport at 1 p.m., local time. We all looked at each other in mutual anxiety.

'You don't suppose,' said Beth, 'she's already done it?'

'Don't even think about it,' I said.

'You know, I don't think it is that likely,' said Sarah. 'All the cases I've ever read about euthanasia seem to imply that it's not rushed. People take their time about it. And she's not that ill yet, is she? Besides, why is she going to see her aunt if she means to top herself?'

'So where does this aunt live?' said Beth.

'It's about an hour away I think,' said Sarah, peering at her *Rough Guide to Switzerland*. 'In the mountains by the looks of it.'

It seemed to take an age to get through passport control and we were all getting seriously grumpy with one another. Eventually we were through and greeted by signs welcoming us to Switzerland in German, Italian, French and English. The airport was bright and modern and not too frantic, in stark contrast to the shambolic busyness we'd left behind at Heathrow.

337

'I've never been to Switzerland before,' said Beth. 'Isn't it clean and shiny?'

'I have,' I said, 'but it's mainly been on boring photo shoots in Berne. Though I did once do a rather spectacular job looking across Lake Constance.'

I looked at Beth, she was looking very pale.

'Are you feeling OK?' I said.

'I'm not actually,' said Beth. 'Oh god, I think I'm going to be sick, do you mind looking after my things?'

She raced off to the loo, and returned about ten minutes later looking somewhat better.

'Do you feel any better?' I said.

'I think so,' said Beth. 'It's probably just the food on the plane.'

Sarah gave me a knowing look.

'What?' I mouthed.

'Nothing,' she mouthed back.

We queued up for a taxi to take us to the hotel Sarah had booked.

'What should we do?' I said. 'Look for Dorrie straight away?'

'I think it's a bit late now,' said Sarah. 'From what Dorrie's mum said, this aunt is rather frail, and I don't think we should just turn up.'

'I'll text Dorrie again,' I said. 'You never know, she might have turned her phone on.'

I'd just sent the text when the phone rang. To my disappointment, it wasn't her.

'Is that Caroline?' A welcome Irish voice was on the other end.

'Dad, yeah, hi,' I said. 'How was Cornwall?'

'Grand,' he said. 'Only I'm on my way back to London and thought we could meet up again if you'd like.'

'I'd love to, really I would,' I said, 'but actually I'm not in the country right now, and I'm not quite sure when I'm going to get back.'

'Well I'll be in town for a week, and your step mam and your brother and sister are with me. What do you say to a nice quiet meal, the five of us when you get back?'

'I'd say that would be lovely, Dad,' I said, treasuring the novelty of saying Dad out loud. 'And I'll introduce you to my new boyfriend.'

'So are you going to meet them all?' said Beth as we lay on our hotel beds.

'Yes,' I said slowly. 'I can't believe that after all these years of being on my own, it turns out I actually have a family. It's going to take some getting used to.'

I stared up at the ceiling. It seemed so odd and unnatural for the three of us to be here without Doris.

'Isn't it weird without Dorrie?' Beth said.

'That's just what I was thinking,' I said.

'Me too,' said Sarah. 'Do you know that character Sid in *Ice Age*? Dorrie's like him – she's the sticky stuff that binds us all together. We're lost without her.'

'You know, guys, I've been really crap to you both in the past,' I said. 'And I am really sorry. I was just so wound up in my own misery I couldn't see how selfish and destructive I was being.'

'I could have handled things a bit differently,' said Sarah. 'Not marrying Steve would have been a great start. I shouldn't have put him above our friendship.'

'And I shouldn't have tried to take him from you,' I said. 'And Beth, I truly thought I was doing the right thing by you all those years ago. I'm sorry for the way I behaved

339

on your hen night, and all the grief I've caused you with Matt.'

'It was my choice,' said Beth. 'And I thought I was doing the right thing at the time too and, despite everything, I still do. I couldn't have known where it was going to end. And as for my hen night, I'm sorry too. I think I was probably a bit harsh on you. And Sarah, I know I've been a cow to you, this whole baby thing has been so stressful.'

'Oh stop it,' said Sarah. 'Or I'm never going to stop crying.'

We were all sitting up by now, and enveloped ourselves in a communal hug.

'I do hope Dorrie is OK,' said Sarah. 'What will we do if she's not?'

Just then my mobile bleeped.

It was a text from Doris. *Don't worry. Am fine. Want to be alone. Tell Darren I love him.*

In your dreams, pal, I texted back. *And tell him yourself.*

We rose early in the morning. I don't think any of us had slept much. Beth looked particularly washed out.

'My nerves are up the spout,' she said. 'I keep throwing up.'

'Really?' said Sarah. She looked at me and then at Beth. 'Have you actually had a period since the miscarriage?'

'No,' said Beth. 'I keep waiting for it to happen.'

'Beth,' said Sarah gently, 'you had IVF. It is quite likely there were *two* babies.'

'They did warn us that there could be,' said Beth. 'But they only saw one on the scan.'

'Which was when?'

'At eight weeks,' said Beth. 'And then I lost it.'

'And that was what, a couple of weeks ago?' said Sarah.

'I don't want to get your hopes up, but I reckon you could still be pregnant.'

'No, no, don't say that,' said Beth. 'I don't think I could stand the stress.'

'Well there's one way of finding out,' said Sarah. 'I spotted a chemist's on the way in last night. Anyone know the German for "How do I buy a pregnancy test"?'

Half an hour later, armed with said test despite Beth's protestations, we marched her into the hotel lobby where Sarah insisted she did a test before we went on our way. I swear she'd have sat over Beth and watched her do it if Beth hadn't made a fuss about going into the loo alone.

Sarah and I waited anxiously for ten minutes for Beth to come out. It seemed an age before she emerged white faced and slightly stunned from the loo. Damn.

'Oh Beth, I'm sorry,' I said and I really was. Though I'd never felt the need for children myself, I could understand the pain of losing something you longed for.

'Caz, Sarah,' Beth said in a dazed kind of way, 'you don't understand. There *were* two babies. I *am* pregnant.' She sat down on one of the hotel chairs. 'I can't believe it,' she said, tears rolling down her cheeks. 'I'm going to have a baby.'

Half an hour later, having phoned Matt with the happy news, we were on our way to see Dorrie's aunt. We eventually found ourselves being driven down a sweeping drive, with fantastic views overlooking Lake Zurich, and the taxi driver deposited us in front of a magnificent house.

'What is this place?' said Beth. 'I know Doris's family is wealthy, but this looks like it belongs to a millionaire.'

'This isn't her house,' said Sarah suddenly. 'It's some kind of care home.'

There was a sign saying something incomprehensible in German, but suddenly we realized that the majority of people going in and out of the impressively large building were either elderly or in wheelchairs. There was a café to one side of the building, which gave the place the air of a holiday home, but as we approached the front door we could see a reception desk.

'Right, now what?' I said. 'I thought we were coming to Dorrie's aunt's house.'

'We go to the desk and ask to see Frau Wiesen, I suppose,' said Sarah. 'I hope they speak English.'

We came into a clean, shiny interior. Staff in smart white uniforms glided serenely about. There was an atmosphere of peace and tranquillity.

'You don't suppose this is the clinic, do you?' I said. 'Doris and her aunt might have made a suicide pact.'

'I don't think it can be,' said Sarah. 'I know Switzerland has progressive attitudes, but even here, I'm sure they don't gather old people in large groups and allow them to be bumped off and turned into Soylent Green.'

We approached the desk nervously.

A bit of schoolgirl German floated into my head, 'Entschuldigung, bitte. Sprechen Sie Englisch?'

'Naturally,' the receptionist said, smiling. Of course she did. The whole world speaks English. 'May I help you?'

'We were wondering if it would be possible to speak to Frau Wiesen. We're friends of her niece.'

'Oh yes, her niece is with her now. They're having breakfast in the lounge, through there.'

We walked into the lounge to find Doris sitting pouring coffee for an elderly lady in a wheelchair.

'You've led us on a merry dance,' I said.

'Caz, Sarah, Beth,' Doris looked white with shock. 'What the hell are you doing here?'

Chapter Thirty-Two

Doris

It had been restful staying with Auntie Sophie. The home she was in provided rooms to rent for visiting relatives and I'd found the atmosphere very calming.

'How are you?' I had asked her.

'Well, I'll not be running any marathons this year,' she said.

'There's always the wheelchair event,' I laughed.

That was the great thing about Auntie Sophie. She always made light of her condition. But then, she'd lived with it a long time. Even so, she was slightly worse than the last time I'd seen her.

'How are you really?' I said. 'Doesn't this ever get you down?'

'Of course it does,' she said. 'It's not what I'd have chosen, and I'm glad that Uncle Fritz died before I got to this state. But you know this isn't a bad place to end my days. And there's always someone worse off than me.'

'So you've not thought of ending it all?' I said.

'Good heavens, no,' Auntie Sophie said. 'I've still got all my faculties, just. I can read, the nurses push me round these lovely gardens. I know all about their families and their lives.

For someone as nosy as me, living here is a dream. Besides, I was getting lonely at home.'

'But what about the end?' I said hesitantly. 'What happens then? You know how bad it was for Dad. How can you bear it?'

'I'm not sure that I will be able to bear it,' she said. 'But for me, this gift of life we have is so precious, I will fight to my last breath to keep it.' She looked at me shrewdly. 'Why all the questions? What's going on, Doris?'

'I'm ill,' I said. 'I've got MS too and I can't bear the thought of Darren having to look after me. I saw what it did to Mum and Dad. I keep thinking the only rational thing to do is to go to that Right to Die clinic. I just don't want to live half a life.'

'That is your choice,' Auntie Sophie said. 'It's not something I could ever do, but I can understand why you feel that way. But you're young – you still have so much time ahead of you. Who knows how long you've got? Are you *really* sure this is what you want?'

'No,' I admitted. 'I just don't know what to do.'

'Have you talked it over with Darren?'

'He doesn't want to talk about it,' I said. 'I don't think it's fair to burden him with my illness, but he's insistent he wants to care for me.'

'Well then maybe you should let him,' said Auntie Sophie. 'Not every man would react like that. You're lucky to have him.'

'I know,' I said, 'which is why I don't want to put him through all this.'

'But do you think by pushing him away you'll stop him suffering? Whatever happens, he's in this with you already. If you still feel the same when things get tougher, well then

346

you'll have to think again. But *together*. So go home, marry Darren and be happy for as long as you've got. Look at me. You might have years before this happens.'

'I might,' I said.

Just then there was a commotion, and I saw three familiar faces bearing down on me.

'Caz, Sarah, Beth,' I said faintly. 'What the hell are you doing here?'

'Well, *that's* a nice greeting,' said Sarah tartly, when I'd recovered from the shock. 'You wouldn't *believe* the effort we went to to find you.'

'Glad to see you've not topped yourself,' said Caz, her dark eyes mischievously bright.

'You wouldn't, would you?' said Beth anxiously. She looked pale and wan. I hoped that wasn't my fault.

Looking at their worried faces, I felt a pang of guilt. In my determination to seek out answers, I'd been really selfish.

'Why on earth did you think I was going to top myself?' I said.

'Those leaflets I found,' said Sarah.

'The fact that Darren said you'd been looking at that Right to Die clinic online was a bit of a worry,' said Caz.

'And you *did* come to Switzerland,' said Beth.

'To visit my *aunt*,' I said, 'and to get some auntly advice from someone in my situation. I don't even know where the Right to Die clinic is.'

'Oh,' they said sheepishly.

'Aren't you going to introduce me to your friends, Doris?' said Auntie Sophie, looking slightly bemused.

'Sorry. Auntie, this is Caz, Sarah and Beth. For some reason they've got it into their heads I was going to that clinic.

347

They're completely mad, but they're my best friends in the whole world. And I've really really missed them.'

'With friends like them, I think you should be grateful, and not give up on yourself just yet.'

'I won't,' I promised.

'Now, I'm a bit tired,' said Auntie Sophie. 'Why don't you take your friends on a sightseeing tour? I'm sure you've got a lot of catching up to do.'

'So you weren't thinking about going to that Right to Die place?' said Caz.

'I did think about visiting it,' I said. 'But then I bottled it when I got here. It's just that with everything that's been going on, I freaked out a bit.'

'A bit?' said Sarah.

'OK, a lot,' I said. 'I'm so sorry, guys. You must have been really worried.'

'Not as worried as Darren,' Beth pointed out. 'You should phone him.'

'I know,' I sighed. I had a lot of explaining to do.

'Now, if no one minds, I need to sit down,' said Beth. 'I am not going to lose *this* baby.'

'You what—?' I said.

'It's been a busy few days,' said Sarah. 'You'll be pleased to know you've got your wish and I will be seeing a lot more of Joe.'

'And I've found my dad and seem to be going out with Charlie.'

'Blimey, I leave you lot alone for five minutes and look what happens,' I said. 'Can't be trusted, the lot of you. I should never have left you to your own devices. I'm glad I didn't go to that clinic – I clearly need to sort you all out.'

We sat waiting in reception while Sarah called a taxi.

'Doris Bradley, you had better not try and end it all now,' Beth said. 'I want you to be godmother.'

'Bloody hell, this is a day of surprises,' I said.

'And there's another one,' Caz dug me in the ribs and I looked out of the window to see a taxi drawing up outside. Out leapt Darren holding Woody in his arms. I had never been so pleased to see them in my whole life. My heart felt like it was going to explode. I ran out and flung my arms around Darren, and hugged Woody close to me, feeling his lovely soft baby features and smelling his baby smell. Had it only been two days? I had missed them so much.

'I couldn't wait,' he said. 'I had to find out if you were OK. I know you asked me not to follow you, and I told the girls I wouldn't, but I just couldn't do it. I'm so sorry, Dorrie. I had no idea how terrible you were feeling. I don't want you to take this step, but if you do, I'll be there, every bit of the way.'

'I'm the one who should be sorry,' I said. 'I love you, Daz, more then anything in the whole world. And whatever the future holds, I know it will be all right so long as you're by my side.'

'I love you too,' said Darren.

'I know,' I said. 'Come on, let's go home.'

'Don't you want to visit that clinic before we go?' he asked.

'Nope,' I said, though I was thrilled that he was being so understanding about it. 'We've got a wedding to plan.'

Epilogue

Dorrie

When I grow up, I am going to marry the man of my dreams and arrive at my wedding in a horse-drawn carriage with my three best friends. We will all wear Disney princess dresses and walk down the aisle to 'One Day My Prince Will Come'. I will dance back up the aisle with Darren to 'Congratulations'. Darren will wear white and Woody will be dressed in a miniature costume the same as his dad's. The sun will shine all day long and the birds will chirrup in the trees, and any minute now a Disney chorus line will burst into song.
Doris, aged thirty-six

Well even I couldn't manage to find a Disney choir on eBay, but my wedding day in September dawned fair and bright. The girls had all stayed the night at mine, Darren, Matt, Charlie and Joe were consigned to Sarah's house on baby-sitting duties. I felt guilty thinking Darren might want a last drink with his mates, as he hadn't managed a proper stag do, but he said he had no regrets about losing his bachelor status – and besides, going to nightclubs was the best way he could think of to pick up all manner of unseemly germs. Bless him. Only Yakult Man could worry about a thing like that on his stag night.

We woke early in the morning, just as I'd always planned I would on my wedding day. I was up first, watching the sun rise over the back garden, as I brewed a cup of tea in the kitchen. As I stood looking out on the dew-dropped lawn, a startled deer, that must have escaped from the nearby common, jumped over my fence. It paused and we stared at each other for one long minute, before it leapt away and fled off in the rosy pink dawn. It was a tiny moment of Disney magic to mark my special day.

Caz had provided buck's fizz and croissants for breakfast and the four of us sipped it lying in bed, well Beth didn't of course, but she raised a glass of orange with us, as we toasted the Fab Four.

'All four one, and one four all,' we cried.

I went to the box I'd treasured since childhood.

'Look what I found when I was clearing up,' I said. I opened it up, and took out a piece of faded paper.

'Oh my god, you haven't still got it have you?' said Sarah.

'Of course,' I said, and read it aloud

'We solemnly declare, that we four will be friends forever. And we promise that when we get married we will only have our three friends as bridesmaids. And we promise that we will be bridesmaids for our friends. From this day forth, forever and ever, shall this vow be binding.'

'Here's to the Bridesmaid Pact,' I added. 'It's only taken us twenty-eight years to get it right.'

'You don't still have our mouldy old hair, do you?' said Caz. 'That's gross.'

'No it's not,' said Beth, picking up the pieces of entwined

hair I'd kept safe all these years in a locket my dad had given me. 'I think it's rather lovely. Don't you remember that day? And how we all wanted to be Diana?'

'I didn't,' snorted Caz.

'Well the rest of us did,' retorted Beth. 'But I think Dorrie looks much more beautiful than Di ever did.'

'I'll second that,' said Caz.

'It's a shame Prince William hasn't had the decency to propose to Kate Middleton yet,' said Sarah thoughtfully. 'Wouldn't it have been neat if you'd married the year they did?'

'I don't care,' I said. 'I don't believe in fairytale endings any more.'

'Dorrie, you can't say that!' said Caz scandalized. 'I'm the one who doesn't believe in fairytales.'

'I said I don't believe in fairytale *endings*,' I said. 'Because the wedding day isn't the end of the fairytale. It's just the beginning.'

Caz threw a cushion at me. 'You are such a soppy sap, Doris Bradley.'

'Always was, always will be,' said Sarah.

'Oh do stop making me laugh,' said Beth. 'My bladder isn't what it was.'

We got ready listening to Billy Idol's 'White Wedding', singing the chorus loudly while Caz vainly attempted to do our make-up.

'Will you all *please* keep still!' she kept saying. 'Honestly, you're worse than most of the prima donna models I deal with.' Which of course made us laugh even more.

I ached with laughter. The world seemed such a joyous place. The darkness that had afflicted me all those long months leading up to the wedding was miraculously gone. With Darren at my side, I knew I could get through anything.

By one thirty we were all ready. The girls just as I'd imagined them, Sarah looking pretty in a pale cream Snow White dress – her fair hair curling in a soft flowing style. She looked much better now she wasn't trying to look like a film star to please Steve. Caz had reluctantly donned the yellow Belle dress, and despite clearly feeling awkward, she looked stunning. 'I am so going to get you for this,' she said. 'If Charlie ever dares to ask me to marry him again, I shall wear black and you'll all have to come as goths.' Beth, meanwhile, looked soft and feminine in her pink Sleeping Beauty dress, the only indication of her pregnancy a slight bump under the full skirt, and a beautiful glow that really suited her.

And as for me, I'd amended my Cinderella dress so it looked like the one Amy Adams wore in *Enchanted*. It had the fullest of skirts, and a long train – perhaps not quite as long as Diana's but as near to what I'd envisaged for myself aged eight as I could get. My hair was piled up in curls above my head and I wore a beautiful headpiece woven with small pink and white roses created by Ivy, with a very simple veil.

'Oh my god, you are gorgeous,' said Caz as I walked into the room.

Mum came smiling to meet me. In the absence of Dad I'd asked her to give me away.

'Your carriage awaits,' she said laughing. 'I can't believe you're really going through with this.'

We came out of the front door, to be met by various neighbours, scratching their heads at the sight of a Cinderella pumpkin carriage drawn by six white horses. It was the one luxury I'd allowed myself. All that scrimping and saving on eBay was just so I could have this.

The photographer took dozens of photos, and then we were off.

'I hope the horses don't turn back into mice before we get there,' Caz joked.

'You are not going to ruin my day, whatever you say, Caz Riley,' I said.

'Wouldn't dream of it, Doris Bradley, wouldn't dream of it,' she laughed and stuck out her tongue.

I walked down the aisle to 'One Day my Prince will Come' in a haze of happiness, with Mum beside me and the girls following behind. And when I saw Darren standing there looking so handsome, holding Woody in his arms, my heart nearly burst with pride. He truly was my handsome prince. How could I have been so foolish as to think I couldn't marry him?

'You look fabulous,' he said, as I came up to his side.

'You too,' I said, as he passed Woody to my mum and we walked up together to the front of the church, where Father Miserecordie called us to make our handwritten vows in front of the whole congregation.

'I promise to love and honour and cherish you all the days of our wedded life,' said Darren. 'And vow to always be at your side through the good times and the bad. And wherever the path of our lives takes us, I will walk it with you.'

'I promise to love and cherish you all the days of our wedded life,' I responded. 'And vow to never shut you out from my thoughts, and take you with me on the journey life takes us on, however dark and difficult the path.'

Then Darren leant over and kissed me on the lips, and the congregation erupted.

We literally danced down the aisle to 'Congratulations'

while everyone roared and clapped. Afterwards we stood outside laughing and chatting while we had our pictures taken, and before we knew it, we were whisked away in our pumpkin carriage.

I still had no idea what was going on with the venue. Sarah and Mum had been extremely cagey about the whole thing. So it was a total surprise when the horses and carriage led us down Mum's road and up her driveway.

'Why are we here?' I said. 'What's going on?'

'Just you wait and see,' said Darren, before leading me down from the carriage and carrying me over the threshold of Mum's front door. We walked through the house into the back garden, which had been transformed.

'Oh my goodness, that's beautiful,' I said, taking on board the magical fairy garden that Sarah had somehow created. Strings of fairy lights crisscrossed the garden and a beautiful marquee stood in the middle, from where I could hear the faint strains of a string quartet. In front of the marquee was a Disney-style bouncy castle.

'Couldn't quite get you the real thing,' said Sarah, arriving moments behind us. 'It was the best we could do.'

I laughed and laughed all day long. I was surrounded by people whom I loved and who loved me, and I'd married the man of my dreams. And as to what happened next, I was going to take the advice of the counsellor I had started to see, and take each day as it came.

The afternoon raced by in a bubble of happiness. I had never been so proud as when Darren stood up beside me, during his speech, his voice slightly cracking as he held my hand, and promised to be by my side whatever happened. 'For,' he said in conclusion, 'as Gaff says in my favourite film, we none of us know what our future holds. All I know is, my future is tied to Dorrie's now and forever.' He bent over to kiss me, and I saw tears in his eyes. 'Now and forever, babe,' he whispered. 'And don't you forget it.'

Then it was time to cut our four-tiered cake with its Cinderella and Prince Charming mannequins, before Darren led me onto the dance floor. The girls roared with laughter when the band struck up 'You've Got a Friend in Me'. A few months ago I couldn't have imagined dancing at my wedding, but thanks to finally having gone to see Mr Mason who'd sorted out my medication, and assured me I was going into remission, I felt better than I had for months, and for the first time in a long while, hopeful about the future.

At the end of the evening, we left to go on our way. The fairy lights lit our path as the long chain of guests all lined up to wish us well.

Everyone crowded round us as we got into the car that was taking us away to the secret location Darren had booked for the night. I threw my gorgeous bouquet of pink roses entwined with gypsophila and lilies up high in the air, watched it tumble and fall – straight into Caz's hands. I saw her look at Charlie and blush, and he grinned at me and gave me the thumbs up. Joe and Sarah meanwhile were smooching next to the bushes like a pair of teenagers, and Matt was protectively patting Beth's bump. My friends were all happy. And all was right in my world.

'Happy, Mrs Maitland?' said Darren as we drove away.

'Blissfully,' I said.

'We've got the rest of our lives together,' said Daz.

'We should make the most of it then,' I said.

'I'll drink to that,' said Darren, as we chinked glasses and drove off into the warm September evening.

357

Things To Avoid On Your Wedding

1. Don't behave like a Bridezilla – treating your friends poorly or asking too much of them can ruin friendships and weddings.
2. Avoid celebrating the night before. You being hung over won't be fun for anyone involved.
3. Don't think about ex's – yours or his. Such thoughts can only end badly.
4. Buy your wedding dress in the size you are – not the size you hope to be.
5. Cash bars are tacky. Very tacky.
6. If you are having an outdoor wedding make sure to have a back-up plan for poor weather.
7. Choose flattering dresses for your bridal party. They will never let you forget if you don't.
8. Avoid drinking too much before or during your wedding. You want to fully remember the day, not just have fuzzy recollections.
9. Don't seat divorced parents together, regardless of how amiable their relationships are.
10. While walking up the aisle don't even consider the possibility that you might trip.

11. If you've never used spray on tan before, don't experiment just before the wedding. You could be orange, red, flaky or streaky. Embrace your natural paleness.

12. Don't forget to eat throughout the day. Lack of food will increase your stress levels and make the many toasts go right to your head.

13. Avoid getting a haircut for three to five weeks before your wedding. Hair disasters happen and you don't want to grimace every time you look at your wedding photos.

14. Be sure to listen to your friends. They aren't being spiteful witches when they tactfully explain that your make-up is smearing – they are being helpful and loving friends.

15. Don't even think about divorce – it simply doesn't exist in your wedding world.

16. Avoid stressing out over small details. It is your wedding day, a day you put a lot of time, money and effort into, so relax and have some fun!